SOUTH OF MAYA

Robert Veres

Inside Information
San Diego, California

South of Maya

Copyright 2017 Robert Veres

Inside Information books may be ordered by contacting:

Inside Information
1804 Garnet Avenue
San Diego, CA 92109

This is a work of fiction. All of the characters, names, incidents, organizations and dialogue in this novel are the products of the author's imagination and used fictitiously.

ISBN 10: 0999830708
ISBN 13: 9780999830703 (e-book)
ISBN 13: 9780999830710 (paperback)

Printed in the United States of America

Cover art by Audrey McGimsey

This book is for the boys:
Jesse, Malakai, Jaden, Gabriel, Asa, Tyson and Atlas

and a special shout-out
to any physicist or mathematician who has the courage to take
the physics in this book seriously.

"The whole world is under the delusion of Maya."

Bhagavad Gita

"There is an extensive literature which explores various aspects of our universe as a simulation, from philosophical discussions, to considerations of the limits of computation within our own universe, to the inclusion of gravity and the standard model of particle physics into a quantum computation, and to the notion of our universe as a cellular automaton."

Silas R. Beane, Zohreh Davoudi and Martin J. Savage;
Constraints on the Universe as a Numerical Simulation

"Neither the elemental particles nor the entire universe exists."

Avadhuta Gita

"We are almost certainly living in a computer simulation."

Oxford University philosopher and
author Nick Bostrom

1

"All things in the world are like a dream, or like an image miraculously projected."

Lankavantara Sutra

Marcus Mann extended his hand toward the sea of bare rock that reached out to the rim of the planet and beyond. Somewhere on the far edge of the horizon the air quivered, trembled, gathered strength and blew hard across the face of the world.

The sky darkened, then exploded in lightning as rains poured down, gathering in rivulets, then rivers, then mighty cascades across the landscape, until the lowlands were filled, stranding mountains that became islands, and uplands that became continents.

Another gesture, and sunlight smiled upon the chastened world. Small, warm puddles, natural petri dishes, nurtured a thin gruel of fragile carbon gossamer which congealed and reformed into myriad tiny forms that clustered at the sun-warmed base of the rocks along the shore.

Mann gestured again, and a mossy growth along the naked soil exploded upward into a thick cluster of cycads that spread their furry branches across the sky.

Driving snow and warm rains alternately froze and thawed the earth. New growth literally flew off the branches, scattering leaves as thick as snowflakes in a blizzard, followed by new growth and another leaf shower, faster than the one before, again and again, covering the earth with a blanket of decomposing mulch that became soil.

Insects, some as large as birds, sprang out of the fetid muck and blurred the air with a muted buzzing that hovered along the lower edge of perceptibility. Tentative sprouts of undergrowth climbed like snakes up thirty-foot trunks toward the great shimmering canopy overhead. Others spread across the ground until the trees seemed to be standing ankle-deep in exotic shrubbery, which crowded against itself and each other in silent, murderous competition for life-giving sunlight.

After a moment, flowers appeared in full bloom along the edges of the forest.

In the dizzying blur of daylight following darkness, lungfish pushed and squirmed between shallow puddles, stretched out their fins and scuttled across the open ground, rapidly multiplying in number and form as they scattered across the face of the warm, moist earth.

After a few moments, feathered creatures flitted across the sky. Mann cast a few clouds into the sky, and with a gesture of both hands, drove continents into ponderous collision, raising mountains across the horizon, covering them with grass that provided food and bedding for new kinds of creatures whose blood was warmed by controlled internal fires.

Finally, the hands of time slowed down, the restless wind faded away, and everywhere the planet was silent.

Mann tasted the air. He reached down to caress the loamy ground, and consider the peaceful orchestra of life here in the center of an endless pine and cycad forest that moments before had been antediluvian rock as bare and craggy as the surface of the Moon.

It was good.

Before he could finish congratulating himself, the world shuddered deep in its core, then again and again. Frowning, Mann extended his hand in a forbidding gesture, but the shudder grew stronger, and the energy of the vibrations began to spread out across the world, opening up cracks in the rock, spewing volcanos, raising earthquakes that lifted the sea high up over the land and back again.

Through the chaos, Mann saw his delicate creatures morphing, adapting to the mayhem, some of them changing into predators of their peers in the ecosystem and adding a certain mayhem of their own.

Mann's hands moved quickly as he tried to unwind the damage that was spreading faster than he could track it. Instinctively, he began to speed up his awareness, so that it seemed as if the world stopped moving altogether, the insects frozen in the air, the breezes halted, the tremor of the leaves arrested.

In this state of hyper-speed, he was finally able to recognize the rumblings under his feet as a kind of speech, rising up from places so deep underground that his awareness was helpless to identify the source.

"WHATEVER YOU CREATE, I WILL DESTROY," the voice rumbled, and the sound echoed off the mountains and rolled up into the clouds.

"I AM THE MASTER HERE," Mann shouted back.

"TAKE THIS REALITY IF YOU CAN."

"WHO ARE YOU? *WHY* ARE YOU?"

In that instant, the sky darkened, and a hurricane the size of a continent threw torrents of rain and hail in Mann's face. The sky gathered itself, and then erupted with a blinding flash of light, blasting a jolt of power deep into every atom of Mann's body, vaporizing the structure that held him together.

He felt himself dissolving into a cloud of agony, a mist of awareness spreading out across the landscape and becoming fainter as it became more tenuous.

Somewhere, a part of the expanding cloud realized that if it wanted to survive, the thing that was rapidly becoming no longer Mann would have to reassemble itself before its component parts drifted too far apart.

And at the same time it realized that every movement back toward density would also reassemble the pain that was easing as it diffused.

With an immense effort, the expanding cloud willed itself, atom by atom, molecule by molecule, structure by structure, to halt the expansion. Like the moving picture of an explosion run backwards, the infinitude of particles began to coalesce into an increasingly dense cloud, the meta-awareness gritting against the mortal agony that its immortal body was suffering, more with each moment of reassembly.

More...

More, pain beyond comprehension.

Finally, after a million years of effort, the cloud collapsed back into the god of this world. Mann flexed his hands and straightened, triumphant in the pain he had achieved.

Then he turned his full, focused attention upward, and felt, for a moment, the thing above him tremble, whether in anticipation or fear he would never know.

"SEE IF I WON'T TAKE IT BACK," he spoke quietly, though the words rolled out across the landscape with the power to create continents. "EVERYTHING YOU DESTROY," he whispered, "I'LL CREATE ANEW."

Mann extended his hands, gritted his awareness and adjusted breeding capacities, raised the efficiency of ecological adaptation and ultimately the conservation of sunlight energy across the varied ecosystems from the depths of the sea to the lichen at the top of mountains, across deserts, plains, jungles and tundra. Where the other sought to kill individual creatures, he sought to preserve the continuity of life.

For age after age, eon after eon, the struggle between adaptation and extinction, life and death continued until, at last, Mann and his adversary had achieved a rough equilibrium.

Mann dropped his hands and allowed himself a tired sense of triumph.

Deep below the ground he stood on, there emanated a tired sense of frustration.

The pain was gone.

The world moved on, and Mann stopped again to consider the creation. The balance was precarious, and he had the sense that his adversary had sown seeds that would tip the global ecology back toward extinction somewhere down the line.

He was deciding where to carve out a trout stream when a woman's face—a new god in this world that seemed to have too many of them already—appeared in the sky, covering half the horizon. A thousand woodland creatures evolved, stared up in terror at the animated sky, and vanished into burrows.

Mann looked up in annoyance. This new god seemed curiously peevish, with tension concentrated around the mouth, muscles clamping the lips strangely, unpleasantly rigid in perpetual disapproval.

Mann resisted the temptation to cover the intruding presence with a sky-blackening swarm of locusts. This must be their way of summoning him back to reality. He felt a hint of regret at his impending demotion from godhood.

"Can it wait?" he asked hopefully.

"You've already wasted too much of my time," the female god's voice rumbled out of the sky, scattering the clouds. "And my time is infinitely more valuable than you realize," she added.

With a sigh, Mann extended his arms to the horizon. With a mental leap, he shifted his body into, through and beyond the sky. In an instant, he was sitting upright in a chair in the basement of the laboratory, surrounded by white-coated engineers who were fussing at dials and computer screens. One of them walked over to disconnect the headset.

"How did I do?" Mann asked.

"For a first try? Not terrible," the technician said, holding the headset and examining it as if he were afraid it was now infested with fleas. "We store all of them. Dr. Washington says that these creations, when we learn how to transfer stories and characters into them, are destined to become the primary art form, replacing novels and movies. Instead of watching the story, the audience will live in it."

Mann hesitated. "There was something else down there," he said. "Can you tell me what it was?"

The technician looked at him curiously. "You don't know?" he said.

"Would I have asked if I did?"

"Could we *possibly* waste more time?" the peevish god's voice called out from the far side of the room. The face in the sky emerged from another helmet in the row of simulation-immersion chairs that faced the bank of computers. The woman stood up and shifted impatiently on her feet.

"I'm Emmaline Witch," she said brusquely. "For the next few days, you answer to me on everything. Understood?"

Mann looked her up and down, swallowed a comment about her name, and nodded.

"Now that you've had a taste of the simulation, we can discuss your assignment. *If* it's convenient for your godship," she added acidly.

2

Look around you. See how many highly-intelligent people have never managed to succeed.

Wonder how that is possible.

Think of the countless hard-working people who have been so diligent that they gave up their lives to do their job well. And yet they, too, have never thrived.

Why?

To Mann, and a handful of specially-gifted people like him, the reason was obvious.

It was the box.

The box, of course, is different for everybody. Its walls are your core assumptions about the world, simplifications of reality expressed in mysterious phrases which, despite their obvious flaws, people accept as if they've been chiseled by the hand of god directly into their brains:

The rich get richer.
It takes money to make money.
The only way to get ahead is to work hard.
The world is against me.
I only deserve to be paid what I've worked for.
I'm not very good at (fill in many blanks).
I just can't (fill in many blanks).

And if you added up all these and at least a million other self-imposed cliches, spoken and unspoken, plus hard-wired restrictions buried so deeply in the human psyche that our species still hasn't discovered words for them, you have roughly defined "the box," as in: "think outside the box."

Yet for a few peculiar individuals, the box isn't there. For such a person, the existence of all these assumptions is mildly perplexing, a puzzle about life and the universe that there is no particular reason to waste your time trying to solve.

These people are born without hard-wired limits on what they can accomplish. Life coaches learn to spot them early. *You have to be careful what you say to that fellow, because you could send him in a direction and he'd be gone before you had your next call...*

A person like that would bring a problem to a psychologist, talk it through, and walk out minus whatever problem brought him there. *In an hour.*

You couldn't test for who's missing this box thing. Missing boxes don't show up on IQ measurements, personality assessments or the interpretations of inkblots on a page.

Certain leaders of certain government agencies discovered long ago that the only way to find this elusive, highly-desirable personality trait is by the crudest form of trial and error.

You hire a thousand intelligent people at extravagant salaries, bring them to Washington and give them situations to rectify. A dozen, more or less, will be killed by various Other Sides in the course of bungling their missions in ways that could not be foreseen.

Eight hundred others, more or less, will simply fail to find solutions. The talented survivors will succeed once, perhaps twice, before failing the tougher assignments due to obstacles of their own creation. The smartest of these will become coveted analysts at Langley.

If the government is lucky, the thousand it hired will produce one individual who can, for reasons unknown to the psychologists, be reliably counted on to walk into a strange and dangerous situation and see what teams of analysts did not. This person will fix the situation in the most straightforward, effective way, without making the kind of splash that attracts the attention of the local spooks, foreign authorities, and most importantly, the press and your elected representatives.

You will hardly notice he was there at all.

This individual will be fast-tracked to the highest circles of his craft, into a very small network that is given deep access to how the world really works behind the dense, multi-layered facade of political posturing and the daily lies spoon-fed to the news outlets.

A person like this is able to know people at a very deep level after a few glances. Periodically, he will be put through days of testing, until yet again the psychologists in the Maryland laboratory have definitively ruled out the ability to read minds.

"You're unusually capable of experiencing the world through the eyes and mind of others," the psychologist told him, in the windowless office, facing the bookshelf filled with titles that he knows, because of their placement, were designed to impress. The psychologist never quite made eye contact, which communicated as loudly as a shout that his interviewer feared this inexplicable skill.

Why?

The subject remembers a young female assistant who came in earlier to hand the doctor a sheaf of papers. He remembers now that, in his presence, the psychologist had avoided eye contact with her, and that, because of this, her face had registered fleeting anxiety. Looking at the psychologist now, the subject realizes that the two are engaged in a clandestine affair.

"You would have been a hell of an actor in Hollywood," the psychologist said, a bit woodenly, making eye contact with the papers on his desk.

"I would have made a lot more money," the subject replied. "And I would have had an easier time believing in my work."

The psychologist did not write this down, which told the subject something important: that the psychologist, too, harbored reservations about the various nudges, meddling and occasional quiet disappearances of people all over the world. He filed it away.

When, long before his time, the subject shocked his superiors with his premature retirement announcement, he knew that the psychologist would be among the few who would experience no surprise. He knew that there would be serious discussion about taking him (now no longer clearly white or black) off the chessboard, but the psychologist's report would tip the scales in favor of his survival.

He'd tell them that Mann's mental makeup is not inclined to treachery. After all, hadn't Mann kept the secret about his relationship with the receptionist?

3

"The world illusion, maya, is individually called avidya, literally 'not-knowledge,' ignorance, delusion. Maya or avidya can never be destroyed through intellectual conviction or analysis, but solely through attaining the interior state of nirbikalpa samadhi."

Paramhansa Yogananda

The assignment started right after Mann pulled himself out of the creamy ocean waves off the coast of Madagascar, wrapped himself in a towel and sat on the rocks. Catching his breath, he watching the shimmering reflection of the newly-risen sun like a broad shimmering pathway of pure light from the horizon, ending, improbably, magically, at exactly the shoreline below his feet. A dolphin had followed him for the last mile of his swim, and now it swam back and forth as if confused by the strange creature's disappearance from the water into some new dimension. *Where had it gone?*

Mann reached down to his backpack and sipped a brew of local herbs with strong stimulants that the Antambahoaka holy man had created especially for his metabolism. A two-hour swim before breakfast had, sadly, become his only exercise routine these past few months.

Behind him, in the house, three extraordinary women would be stirring in the common bed. Soon they would fix breakfast, and find him missing, with no explanation. This had happened before, and they would not worry.

As he contemplated the sunrise, Mann's phone rang.

"Yes?"

"Let's cut the small talk crap already," a woman's harsh voice interjected. "I need to know if you're the right person for a job we have to get done in a hurry."

"Job?"

"This is you, isn't it? Retired intelligence service, many internal accolades—which, of course, meant nothing to you. Served in central Asia and the Middle East, a year in Kashmir, a highly-classified mission to Syria—"

"How could you possibly know that?" Mann blurted out. Looking back, he would realize that this was one of the few times in his life where he'd lost his composure. He looked at the phone. "Who the hell *are* you?"

"If that were important, I would have already told you," the woman's voice said. "It's a remarkable record. But what I want to know is: why did you leave the service?"

Mann sipped his brew.

"It was time to retire," he said. "They offered a very generous pension."

"Strike one," the voice on the other end of the line said in a voice so cold that the phone felt frosty in his hand. "Care to tell me the real reason, or are we both wasting our time?"

"I was bored. You cannot imagine how boring field work really is."

"That is your second strike. I dislike being lied to."

"Maybe if you told me who you are—?"

"Someone who is increasingly less likely to be your next employer, unless you provide me with a plausible answer."

"Did I mention that I'm not looking for work? If you're with the Chindian alliance—"

"We're a privately held corporation located in San Diego. And we're on the trail of something that could save the world from itself."

"And, of course, you expect me to believe that."

But something in the woman's voice *did* make him believe it. And somehow she knew it. She let the silence linger, and suddenly Mann felt a chill run through his body, as if he were passing through a ghost.

He looked out at the ocean, over the horizon, and his eyes glazed over.

"I made the mistake of looking at the bigger picture, and suddenly I no longer believed in my work," Mann said evenly. "I realized that I was helping the world move inexorably toward a global confrontation that had—has, I should say—the potential to send humanity back to the caves. I care about this idiotic planet," he said softly. "I care about it even though I have no rational reason to do so. And I don't believe you or anybody else is going to stop our insane march over a very steep cliff and prevent the senseless annihilation of billions of innocents who deserve far better than what their leaders are even now planning to give them them. I doubt you can imagine how sad that makes me feel."

"That's all I needed to know," the other voice had said promptly. "Turn on your computer. We're sending over a contract. By the time you've finished reading it, a plane will be waiting for you."

As the private jet arched into the sky over Antananarivo and eased through the sound barrier, Mann told his mobile device to call up the contract once again.

"*Would you like me to read you the entire 116 pages?*" the computer asked pleasantly.

"No. Scan pages 73 to 107 for interpretation."

"*Done,*" the pleasant voice said promptly.

"And?"

"*The company requires your complete discretion in all things that you—*"

"A briefer interpretation."

"*If you reveal, to any outside party, anything whatsoever about the existence of this contract, or the work you do for the company or even the fact that you visited the company headquarters, your assets and your life are voluntarily forfeit.*"

"My life?"

"*Under certain provisions in Article 14, Section 7 of the International Legal Code, it is possible to renounce your right to life via legal contract, subject to interpretation—*"

"Okay. All right. And it's offering me twice as much money as I've made in my entire career for—read and interpret again for me."

"*For two days of your time.*"

"Two days."

"*Yes.*" The device in his hand, naturally, betrayed no emotion.

"Is that a misprint?"

"*Unlikely. The time period of the contract is mentioned on pages 2, 7, 23, twice on page 46, and again—*"

"And it doesn't say what I'll be doing over that two-day period."

"*No.*"

"Fine. Take me to the discussion/information trove C11XY38592."

"*I'm sorry. That Internet location does not exist.*"

"Scan my palm print."

"*The host computer is telling me that you are no longer allowed access to that information.*"

"Activate host computer destruction sequence Phi, 9, Xi, Gamma, 39, W, 118, Mu—"

"*I have the site available now. The computer is asking me not to recall any aspect of our interaction during access.*"

"Comply in the strictest possible interpretation with the request. Make the host computer aware of this command. And tell it to stop whining."

"*Done.*"

"What is it telling you?"

"There are messages regarding this company which are classified at a very deep level, mostly dealing with the extreme necessity to protect the secrecy of the company's most recent project. Other messages refer to funding in a general sense, with the admonition that money be very carefully diverted from various military budget line items in order to ensure that Congress and its various oversight committees are not aware of the company or its manner of financial support."

"What does the company do, exactly?"

"Basic research into computer technology."

"Does the Chindian Alliance know about it?"

"There are no messages to that effect. Would you like me to scan Chindian intercepts?"

"Yes."

"There is some indication that Chindian agents have searched for a project that bears the same general description."

"And?"

"They are no longer alive."

Mann leaned back and thought for a long second.

"Can you find a list of employees at the company?"

"I have the list now."

"Anybody I would know?"

"Are you familiar with the Stanford University faculty?"

"Not really."

"William Procter Prize award winners? There are three of them."

"No."

"Pulitzer Prize for literature?"

"What?"

"Dr. Michael Westerly, SRI International president, winner of the Robert H. Goddard Alumni Award, first book of poetry entitled Quantum Verses *published six years ago at age 50, and he has published two volumes every year since then. Pulitzer Prize winner for* Conversations with a Strange Quark. From the Fuzzy Bottom of the Black Hole *has been nominated for the Nobel Prize."*

"Find the latter book."

"Done."
"Read me some passages. At random."
"As you wish."

> *We approach the end*
> *of all confusion*
> *the end*
> *of reflection on our purpose*
> *the end*
> *of love's gentle mysteries*
> *the end*
> *of our experiment in time.*
> *Farewell to self-delusion and*
> *our long journey in the hall of mirrors*
> *To butterflies fluttering over the asphalt*
> *Farewell to lullabies and hope*
> *To every promise made*
> *Let us read a bedtime story*
> *And bleed destiny*
> *Into the deepest corner*
> *Of our graves...*

"Something more recent," Mann requested.

"*Certainly. This was posted less than a week ago on the Internet. It will be part of the next collection.*"

> *You who pass by this vaporous, expanding cloud*
> *Evidencing the crowning achievement of our species*
> *who proudly engineered our loving planet's demise.*
> *Stop a while, read in our world's molecular debris*
> *The terrible epitaph of our mortal enterprise.*
> *The engraved summation of all we used to be*
> *That we were so, so much smarter*
> > *Than we were wise...*

At the airport, Mann engaged an enclosed autocycle with reclining seats, programmed his destination and lay back, allowing the screen to provide the day's news while the cycle circled the waterfront toward Harbor Island. The media blogs, as always, were filled with stories of international tension with the Chindian Alliance. A military analyst soberly concluded that Chindia held a dangerous edge not only in firepower, but also weapons technology. An editorial talked about the catastrophic implications of a global war using the next generation of fusion drones—and, as usual, the reporter had no idea that newer weapons existed which made these armed mechanical insects look like sparklers on the 4th of July.

Another op-ed piece warned of a sneak attack by agents posing as tourists, carrying individual bombs the size of a suitcase that were capable of remarkable damage. Mann knew that both sides were now capable of fitting something into a suitcase capable of vaporizing a city and its most densely populated suburbs.

There was footage of pro-war rallies across the United States.

The stalemate continued. Mann knew that this two-day engagement had something to do with it.

4

"The life of this world is but comfort of illusion."

Qur'an 3.185

Witch waved Mann into a windowless conference room that glowed with harsh fluorescent lighting. She was surprisingly attractive at first glance, blonde hair falling down over her shoulders, body tapered by a daily jogging regimen, Nordic blue eyes... But the more your eyes were drawn to the tense mouth, the more you heard her voice, the more she resembled, to Mann's eye, a Medusa.

Witch deferred to him at the doorway, as three older men instantly halted their conversation at the far side of a long mahogany table. Mann took the limp hand of Dr. Westerly, and found himself looking deeply into a face so pale you wondered if his skin had ever come in contact with sunlight. His body looked as shapeless as bread dough under the loose laboratory robe, and the mouth turned downward, making him appear at once habitually amazed and disconcerted.

For a brief moment, Westerly's eyes met Mann's and turned away again, as if eye contact were somehow painful.

"So, what do you think of the simulation?" Westerly inquired, his eyes on the reflection of the window on the glossy table top.

"Quite a remarkable experience. I've never been a god before."

Westerly nodded as if he already knew the words before they came out of Mann's mouth, and Mann raised his already high estimate of the man's intelligence. Westerly seemed genuinely grateful for the polite response. In the tentative expression on his face, Mann saw a childhood of endless humiliations from older, stronger, cruder boys whose brutal treatment imposed on Westerly a self-image he would carry for the rest of his life—which gave him a genuine modesty that automatically, habitually self-referred to his weaknesses rather than his strengths.

Like an abused animal, Westerly was grateful for any non-hostile interactions. Mann found himself regarding those timid eyes, wondering how such a person could have succeeded so well at two jobs, particularly when the lesser of them involved a Pulitzer Prize in literature.

"Call me Pudge," Westerly said with a hopeful smile as he raised his eyes once again.

Hari Gandhi, the table in front of him littered with candy wrappers, waved at Mann vaguely without rising from his chair. He regarded Mann with a formidable intelligence blazing out of heavily-lidded eyes. He wore his box on his sleeve: a conviction that laziness was a virtue, that it was wasteful and therefore unintelligent to exert any more energy than you had to. His aversion to work had undoubtedly been a major asset in his career, because it motivated him to constantly search for more efficient ways of getting his work done.

Mann kept his gaze on the other man, which eventually forced a reluctant verbal response out of him.

"I am looking forward to being extremely honored to meet you," Gandhi said. "Once I am told why you are here."

The other member of the team, Aldus Washington, regarded Mann solemnly and with frank disapproval. His long sepulchral face showed the bone pressing up against the sallow skin with no intermediary fat, like treeless hills where the underlying terrain was nakedly visible. His head was crowned with a high hairless forehead that bulged slightly forward, as if the brains inside were applying so much pressure that they had managed to press the bone outward into deformity.

Looking into his face, Mann saw himself reflected back not as a fellow human, but as a source of future errors and complications not yet known which would inevitably have to be cleaned up. Inside Washington's box, he was in the habit of blaming himself for whatever problem he was here to fix, irrespective of whether or not it had been out of his control from the beginning. The habit of self-blame dragged his self-esteem down notch after notch, until, over thousands of turns of this particular screw, he could now measure it in negative numbers.

Yet the fact that he was in the room suggested that Witch trusted his competence, and probably also enjoyed his subservience.

Washington took Mann's hand limply, with no visible enthusiasm. "Welcome to the team," he said, and immediately turned his attention back to Witch. "I want to go on record as saying that the situation in the simulation has already moved beyond the critical point," he said. "Even if we got in there this instant, it would take a miracle to prevent the blowup."

"Blowup?" Mann said.

"Suppose I told you that I know what I'm doing," Witch said with a look of smug annoyance—a combination that Mann found different and interesting.

"I am thinking that I would have a very hard time believing you this particular time," Gandhi said with a light Indian accent. "As promising as this iteration has been so far, I really am thinking to myself that we need to move on."

Witch pulled her mouth tighter. She touched the tablet on the table in front of her. "Remember when Russia finally pulled out of Crimea?" she said.

Mann looked up, startled. He glanced over at the tablet. *Who was he dealing with?*

"What would you have done if you were the U.S. policymakers, and you wanted to bring about that outcome?" Witch continued.

"I would have waited until exactly what happened, happened," Washington answered promptly. "A popular uprising, suicide bombers costing the Russian military billions of dollars, too expensive to continue the occupation." He shrugged his shoulders.

"Remember how suddenly it happened?" Witch said. "Suppose, hypothetically speaking, of course," she said, pointedly avoiding even a glance at Mann, "that the agency sent a single operative, who swam ashore near Krasnoperekopsk eight weeks before the first suicide attack, who, recruiting a local hypnotist, planned and executed every one of the 59 suicide attacks on military bases, and that every one of those was actually carried out by trusted Russian soldiers."

Washington looked sideways at Mann. "This is purely hypothetical, right?"

"You better believe it is," said Mann, pulling out his device. "If it were true, that kind of information can get you killed by either side."

Witch scrolled across her screen. "Suppose he arrived in Latvia four days before the uprising there—"

Suddenly she bolted upright, as the words on the screen scrambled and then vanished. She touched the screen, called up another program, scrolled around with a frown, and finally looked over, not quite meeting Mann's level eyes.

"The virus has already found and eliminated anything related to certain files you have no business having access to," Mann told her in a low voice. "It's possible I just saved your life."

Witch stared at the tablet for a second, and then attempted a ghastly smile.

"Those files only existed for recruiting purposes," she said, pushing the tablet aside. "I'm beginning," she said, her voice sounding intrigued, "to think we chose well."

"I'm looking forward to learning why."

Mann found that Gandhi was still staring in his direction. There was something in the eyes... Arrogance? Contempt? A sense of superiority that made Mann feel like a virus under a microscope. Gandhi smiled encouragingly, but the smile never touched his eyes. Mann's whole body went tense.

"Perhaps we *should* explain why we asked you here," Witch continued. She nodded toward the chief engineer, and seemed irritated that he didn't speak up at once.

"We're in the business of harvesting technology," Washington broke into the awkward silence, "from simulated civilizations that we create in the lab, which—we hope—will become more advanced than ours."

"A simulated—"

Westerly found his voice. "It was really an accident," he said with a dry chuckle. "At Stanford, I was working on simulations of planet formation, and of course the goal was to get ever-more-exact estimates of the dynamics in the molecular cloud that formed the proto-solar system, and so after maybe two years of simulating the aftermath of supernova explosions using a series of Bettman-Clomering regressions that—"

"Pudge," Witch said with a withering stare.

The engineer glanced up sheepishly. "What I mean is, after maybe a hundred thousand incremental iterations, I managed to get some really accurate simulations going, 'accurate' meaning that I was producing planetary formations very close to what we actually see in our own and, so far as we have been able to observe, other solar systems. One of them I kind of forgot to shut down when I was finished. It was really amusing when you think about it," he added.

Westerly looked around hopefully, and ultimately fruitlessly, for signs of amusement around the table. He gave a slight shrug of his shoulders.

"The simulation was still running when I got back from vacation," he continued, "which corresponded to something over two point four zero six one billion years, with I would say a margin of error of no more than point zero zero zero zero four percent, because I'm not sure whether or not I looked at it before or after I had my morning coffee—"

"*Pudge.*"

"Yes, well, anyway, before I erased it," Westerly continued hastily, "I decided to check and see what the planets looked like a couple of billion years after they had coalesced and found their proper places in the gravitational matrix. When I looked more closely at the second planet, thinking that maybe I could do some analyses of continental drift, erosion patterns, that sort of thing, lo and behold, what do you think I found?"

Mann waited expectantly. And waited, as Westerly looked at him expectantly.

"*Pudge!*"

"Oxygen," Westerly said.

"Oxygen?" Mann repeated.

"The atmosphere had an oxygen ratio that was outside of my expected tolerances by eight hundred and ninety four point—that is," he said, glancing in Witch's direction—"that is, I could see that something else was going on there that I hadn't factored in. That's when I saw it."

Westerly looked at Mann expectantly.

"Saw what?" he said finally.

"Life."

Mann looked around at the others. "Like the simulation I was just involved with?"

"Oh, what we have now is more sophisticated than your training simulation," Westerly assured him. "But inside that original simulation, I had recreated the conditions, including all the physics and the physical interactions and all the individual material components that you would find in our own reality, and the computer simply took them all to their logical conclusion. The very primitive chemoautotrophs living—if you can call it that—in the shallow pools of water had evolved into photosynthesizing cyanobacteria spitting out oxygen as a metabolic waste product at an approximate rate of—that is," he said, glancing up at Witch, "at a rate fast enough to have depleted the iron in the oceans and allowed a buildup of oxygen in the atmosphere."

"Are you saying that those creatures were alive?" Mann persisted.

"Oh mercy no. What I'm saying is the electronic representations of the individual molecules that made up the electronic representations of those cyanobacteria inside the system were experiencing the electronic representations of changes in temperature and light from day to night, from season to season. They were experiencing the electronic representation of the salinity of the water and the iron precipitating out—and, quite interestingly, 1,000 foot tides due to the proximity of the electronic representation of a moon much closer to the planet than our Moon is today."

"Even so," Washington interrupted impatiently, "if you had entered the simulation, you would have felt the wind on your face, and your toes would have felt wet if they happened to splash in the shallow puddles, and the proto-creatures would have died if you happened to step on them.

"The bottom line," Washington added, "is that Pudge saw an interesting possibility in this, and started our little company to explore them. He reasoned that if the evolution were allowed to continue for a few more years—"

"A few BILLION more years," Westerly interjected. "At least two point four six—"

"A few billion more years," Washington corrected himself with a meaningful look at Westerly, "then the evolutionary process would, sooner or later, produce intelligent life forms. And since the internal time within the simulation can be adjusted so that seconds are eons, we could let them evolve their civilization to a point beyond our current timeline, see what new technological innovations they invent, and then reproduce them here in our own world."

Gandhi was watching Mann closely with heavy-lidded eyes. "Try to imagine that you are one of those venture capitalist fellows," he said, "and you have access to new innovations that nobody has ever thought of before, that have not only been tested, and vetted, but have already become commercially viable in a society much like ours. Imagine knowing the final specifications and design right from the start, and also the impact on society."

"Our little universe in a box would become," Washington interrupted, "the greatest innovation factory in history."

Mann stopped to consider the implications. They extended out of sight and over the horizon.

"What have you gotten so far?" he asked.

"Remember when you could suddenly buy holographic movies?" said Westerly. "Or the new explosive devices that the army is experimenting with?"

"You created those?"

"We found those technologies in prior simulations," said Westerly. "We copied them, and lo and behold, with a few adjustments, they worked in this reality just like they did in the box."

Mann sat back. He looked up at Witch, and caught something in her eyes, a mesmerizing contempt, an assumption of superiority.

What magical trump card was she holding that gave her such confidence? It was an interesting puzzle that he put aside for now.

"So what do you need *me* for?" Mann asked with genuine curiosity. "It looks to me like you have the keys to the kingdom."

The engineers looked at each other. None of them seemed to want to be the first to speak.

"There is just one small, minor insignificant problem," Gandhi said quietly. "It unfortunately seems that we can only get so far with these simulations, and then"—he made a gesture with his hands—"the experiment is over and done completely."

"Over?"

"We've created 89 universes so far," Westerly put in. "All of them were functioning perfectly as far as anybody could tell.

Eighteen of them never produced a truly intelligent life form; the planet's ecology was dominated in the end by creatures whose most significant survival trait was either strength, ferocity or reproductive efficiency, including one where the plants eventually ate all the animals."

"Must have been interesting to watch."

"Nine of our worlds-in-a-box produced highly-intelligent species which eventually settled into an agrarian lifestyle, and sought nothing more than peace and contentment and contemplation," Washington added. "After the equivalent of tens of thousands of years, we terminated those experiments as ultimately worthless."

"That leaves 62," Mann said. "Are you telling me that out of 62 universes, you've only managed to get two significant innovations?"

"Oh, we've gotten a lot more than that," Westerly hurried to interject. "New ceramics, advances in lattice metallurgy, incalculable advances in understanding the potential for evolutionary development, an improvement here and there in our transportation technologies. In fact, I believe you rode in one of our vehicles on the way here. We've given our country's defense department at least two dozen weapons innovations, which is why they've taken over as our primary funding source," he added with a nod toward Witch.

"Crumbs off the table," Witch interjected. "Over and over again, just as we think we're about to get a look at the technologies that the human species will stumble onto a hundred or a thousand years in the future, the same thing happens. Over and over again."

"What?"

"The intelligent civilizations, which seem outwardly to be very different from each other, have all, every one, fallen into increasingly destructive bouts of armed conflict," Witch replied with visible distaste, "which eventually leads to a war that wipes out the experiment. In one case, thanks to a breakthrough in technology that I dearly wish we could have captured, the simulated battle, conducted entirely by creatures composed entirely of electrical impulses on an array of computer chips, somehow melted the computer and a good piece of the flooring under it."

"It was actually quite surprising and rather messy," Westerly added with a dry chuckle. "We're still trying to figure that one out."

Mann considered the implications. "Every time?" he said finally.

The others all nodded in unison.

Witch leaned forward on her elbows with visible impatience, her mouth so tight it looked as if it might rip her face apart.

"You," she said, "are going to enter a simulated world and live in a time and place that we estimate to be roughly 150 years more advanced than the world you see around you, at least in terms of their technology. It's our most promising simulation yet, and our models tell us that it will be blasted back to their stone age in another decade, perhaps sooner. At no time will you be in real danger, because if you were to die down… *there*, you would instantly return to your physical body here, and we would send you back immediately so that you could continue your work. Do you understand what I've said so far?"

Mann nodded.

"Our two scientists are going to be in there with you and do what they've always done: try to delay the inevitable as long as possible, in this case until what we believe are some very promising innovations can be… harvested."

"Are they human—the people living inside the box?" Mann asked.

"Oh yes," Westerly said.

"Do you have a plan in mind for accomplishing this thing?"

"*We* indeed do have a very interesting unworkable plan," said Gandhi. "My brother Washington and I are going to do exactly what we always do, which I think is doomed to failure in this particular case. But we have no idea what your role is going to be," he added. "That will be totally up to you, to invent some creative strategies to succeed where failure seems to be a completely certain thing to happen."

"If I decide to do this," said Mann.

"I believe you signed the contract," said Witch. "And in any case, isn't saving the world what you're up to these days? *That* world and, ultimately, if we harvest what we think we will, this one as well?"

Mann looked around the table from one to the other.

"How soon do I start?" he said.

5

"Everything, from the intellect down to the gross physical body, is the effect of Maya. Understand that all these and Maya itself are not the [absolute] Self, and are therefore unreal, like a mirage in the desert."

Shankara

Mann felt the technicians tightening and adjusting the device around his head. He watched two young men in blue jeans and white coats hover, with a disturbingly agitated movement of their hands, over a bank of dials and switches. The room was suffused with a low hum, barely audible. He couldn't determine if the sound was coming from the headset or the room itself.

"Ready?" somebody asked behind him.

He started to nod, but a hand held his head steady.

"You've done this before, so you realize that there's no pain involved. But there IS some disorientation at first," Westerly warned him. "And I probably should have added that you have one small advantage down there that nobody else realizes they have. Whenever you really need something, think your request into the interface with the computer."

"Think?"

"Let your awareness find the interface. Then make your request as clearly as possible."

"And what happens?"

"Yes, well, we're actually not altogether sure how this adaptation is going to work," Westerly admitted, "since the computer has to interpret whatever simulated electronic impulses pass for thoughts in your simulated host. The computer is very good at these simulations, but it is no genius when it comes to figuring out how best to help you," he added with another dry chuckle. "Call it a *small* advantage, and use it as little as possible. Your natural resourcefulness should be your primary ally."

"You really think I can do this," Mann said, more to the ceiling than anybody in particular. It was a strange feeling, this sudden wave of doubt and uncertainty.

"All we're asking for is a nudge here and there. Prolong the simulation long enough for us to get what we want out of it, and then come home," Westerly was telling him as two technicians made some final adjustments to the complicated skullcap, pulling it down low over his forehead. "And meanwhile, bring back the specifications of their technologies as they emerge."

"That's all?"

From the side of the room, Witch favored him with a long appraising look. Mann had the impression that she was truly seeing him for the first time, and didn't like what she saw.

He took a long look at the computer sitting against the wall.

"I'm going inside that?" he said.

"Not literally," Westerly said with what Mann determined to be a patronizing smile. The engineer sat down at the console, examining a screen with a frown. "Your brain will interface with the program, and your awareness will be projected into the simulated reality, actually inside of a simulated individual in that simulated reality who will suddenly discover that he is no longer in control of his little simulated life, and who will experience a far more interesting simulated existence. It's really quite a feeling."

"You've been down there?" Mann said.

"Many times." Westerly gestured to a row of reclining seats, with headgear resting on the backs. "You'll lie there in a deep coma for no more than four hours, and when you come back, 20 years will have passed inside the box."

"20 *years*?"

"And you'll come back with exactly what we want," Witch interjected impatiently. "Why aren't his boots already on the ground? Do we have to explain everything?"

Gandhi and Washington sat down on the chairs on either side of him.

"Remember that you're not going in alone," Washington said. "We'll be coming too."

"Think of us as your very helpful backup," Gandhi added.

"Once we're in, there will be plenty of time for us to brief you on anything else you need to know."

Witch looked up at the clock. "Let's get moving," she said evenly. "With any luck, we'll all be out of here by midnight."

Mann lay back and kept his eyes open, wanting to fully experience the transition.

"How are you with heights?" an engineer asked, his eyes focused on the console.

"I'm not afraid of heights," Mann answered.

"That's good," the engineer said. "That's very good," he repeated softly, as his fingers made a definitive move across the control board.

Like a techno-savvy Inanna teleporting past the seven gates directly into the netherworld, Mann watched his perceptual framework explode into fragments, and he plunged down unfathomable depths, into the uncharted wilderness south of Maya.

Then, just as suddenly, the universe reassembled itself into a terrifying confusion of sensory impulses. Mann was somehow looking through thousands of eyes at once, hearing through thousands of ears, feeling the sensations, thoughts and emotions of what seemed like all people everywhere.

With an enormous effort of will, he managed to figure out which eyes out of the multitude were *his* eyes, and he looked through them, down—

An involuntary yelp escaped his lips, a violent electrical rush of fear at the incomprehensible distance between his frail body and the ground, where tiny figures were lost in a haze as if he were staring from the top of a mountain at the far horizon.

Mann simultaneously tottered on the edge of a thick railing and on the ragged frontier of sanity.

A command from the brain he occupied but did not yet control tensed his leg muscles, and he sensed the intention to spring out in a long swan dive toward a ground that would take him minutes to collide with so violently that the people below would have trouble recognizing the spattered protoplasm as once-living tissue.

Thousands of voices, thousands of awarenesses watched through the eyes of his host and applauded this existential act of nihilistic courage. Mann felt endless variations of their support as he experienced them experiencing his last seconds of life in a roaring sensory tsunami that overloaded his interloping awareness and sent him reeling.

The mind that controlled this body gave the sensory command to leap. With a fantastic effort, Mann pushed through the confusion and countermanded the order.

The leap became a spasm that disrupted the body's precarious balance. As the startled host's mind wrestled with Mann, Mann sent a firm command to his new body, which arched backwards away from the edge of death.

The fight for control ended abruptly. Somehow, in a desperate lurch, as his feet slipped out from under him, Mann managed to twist in the air and grasp the railing with both hands.

The hands of this body were weak, but with the rush of adrenaline they were sufficient to hold him in place as the storm in his mind turned to an icy calm, as thousands of observers who shared this mind halted in breathless anticipation.

Mann closed his eyes for a long second and pushed away, one by one, the other awarenesses, *move along, nothing to see here, move away, the show's over,* shutting them off with a monumental effort until only one was left. He tried to push it away, too, and it favored him with the mental equivalent of a sardonic grin.

Cool.

"Pardon?" Mann actually said the word aloud.

I intended to visit the afterlife. Instead, the afterlife came to me. Who knew?

"I'm not—" Mann started to say, and then he closed his eyes and took a deep breath, realizing that he was speaking an unfamiliar language as fluently as if he had been born to it. "Look," he said after a moment; "I'm going to pull myself up. I'm going to live. This body is mine now."

You're welcome to it. Nothing but a hassle, it was.

"I'm glad you understand."

Slowly, still testing his control, Mann pulled himself up until he could throw a foot over the side of the ledge, and raise a young, blade-thin body to a shaky stand on the back side of the railing.

Well, so long.

"Where are you going?"

The Synchronicity is my home now.

Mann pulled one leg, then the other, over the railing, and kneeled down, closing his eyes in an attempt to regain his mental bearings.

"Synchronicity?"

But the awareness was already gone, into the cacophony of other awarenesses that felt like a riot tugging at the periphery of his attention.

Still kneeling, his eyes still closed, Mann followed him in.

A thousand chaotic fragments of awareness...

—He was inside what appeared to be a transportation vehicle...

—He lay in a dark room lit with candles, embracing another body in sexual urgency...

—He was drinking an unfamiliar beverage in an eatery...

—He was walking along an unfamiliar street with the sunset to the left...

—He was dreaming many dreams at once, seeing through many eyes, overhearing thoughts, experiencing emotions, and they all blended together into a composite chaos where he saw the sky and the ground and distant buildings and felt grass under his feet as he ran and the bitter chill of an arctic wind blowing through his coat. He felt angry and calm, despairing and triumphant, and most of all comfortable in the not-aloneness of this discordant yet intimate connection.

In the confusion, he somehow also managed to perceive what most of them were looking at: the ex-occupant of this body reunited with an unhappy teenage girlfriend who had committed her own suicide less than four hours ago.

The Synchronicity. Somehow, his host and thousands of others had connected their sensory mechanisms through... what?

The Synchonicity.

The what?

His mind conjured an ill-formed image of a communications/ computer chip surgically implanted in his brain against his parents' vehement wishes, a combination of what in his own world would have been called the Internet and Skype and every kind of social media, all wrapped into a single implanted communication mechanism, shared by thousands of young people who had voluntarily joined their brains and enfolded their personalities into each other so they could share every experience with uncounted others, losing themselves and gaining everyone...

Mann, eyes still closed, watched the joyful reunion of the mind that once inhabited this body with his young love, two disembodied personalities held together by the group awareness, swirling together in a freedom that neither could have known in their crude flesh-and-blood existence... *True love! Pure love!*

Pushing the image aside, Mann stood up and removed elaborate high-tech sunglasses that completely concealed his eyes—and took his first real look at the world inside the box.

He was standing at the edge of a crush of pedestrians dressed in colorful tunics and flowing robes. People were walking in every direction at once through a massive glass atrium so large that in his reality it might have had its own zip code.

Waterfalls cascaded down from various corners of the atrium into pools the size of lakes, which were surrounded by green vegetation studded with colorful flowers.

Beyond the glass walls, extending out to the horizon, he regarded a fantasy landscape of spidery towers surrounded by spiral ramps, projecting, in various directions high above the streets below, gleaming glass atria like the one he now occupied.

His eyes were distracted by a speedy soap bubble that darted past the near edge of the outer glass wall, and he realized that the air was full of these transportation vehicles.

Mann searched the disorderly files of his host mind for the name of his new home.

Aurora. Capitol city of the Western empire.

As he tentatively pushed his way into the flow of pedestrian traffic, Mann tasted the air and allowed himself to fully experience a light breeze across his face. The... *reality* of it was a surprise. Somehow, as he walked, the computer's synaptic electricity was creating and updating, instant by instant, the tight coordination of neural signals between his simulated mind and the simulated muscles in his legs, remembering, instant by instant, to have his simulated feet encounter a solid surface every time they touched the simulated flooring of this atrium, and to transmit the feeling of solid ground through the bottom of his feet back to his brain, all the while keeping track of his balance.

His ears caught the noise of the crowd faintly echoing against the glass dome, sounds that, in his real existence, would have been nothing remarkable. But here, knowing the miracle of the computer tracking each and every vibration in the air, he found it intoxicating.

Where were Gandhi and Washington? If they occupied any of the entities in this crowd of pedestrians, they were making no visible effort to catch his attention.

Or were they? His eyes came to rest on a person in a dark robe at the edge of the crowd, who was watching him intently with eyes that seemed to glow with a kind of fever that could have been anger or blissfull happiness. Taking Mann's returned gaze as permission, the stranger approached.

"How are you, sir? Are you having a blessed day?"

"I was... just... looking for somebody," Mann replied carefully. "Are you, by chance—"

"Brother, I can relate," the other said before he could finish, a light of enthusiasm adding to the glow in his eyes. "You can be sure that every single one of us is searching, with our empty hearts and unfulfilled minds, for that thing that we crave so mightily. Brother, you won't find it in this world. This world is nothing but a shadow, an illusion, a pale imitation of the true reality beyond."

Mann's eyes narrowed. "Is that commonly known here?" he said in a low voice.

"Only a few of us know the Truth, but we try to share it with all who will listen," the other continued with growing enthusiasm. "Brother, I can show you how to get to what's real. I can guide you up out of the mists, to the place that IS real."

"I just arrived," Mann said, lowering his voice, hoping the other would do the same. "But I need to know, what did I do that gave it away that I'm not—"

"The Lord God knows every secret, and He welcomes everyone," the stranger assured Mann, putting a hand on his arm and drawing him closer. His eyes burned into Mann's. "All you have to do is turn your heart over to the Almighty Creator, and experience the love that fills you up to overflowing in that place where the craving has been eating away at your soul. He loves you more than your own mother ever did. Have you ever stopped to consider that right now, the One who created this entire universe is watching you, right this very minute?"

Mann regarded the other for a moment. He pushed a rising tide of perspectives, views, synchronicity visions out of his mind with an impatient shake of his head.

"Yes," he said. "As a matter of fact, I do know that."

Gently disengaging himself, Mann lost himself in the crowd, the strangest creature imaginable: a god with no special powers.

6

"Only after we are awake do we know we have dreamed.
Finally there comes a great awakening, and then we know
life is a great dream."

Tchuang Tzu, co-founder of Taoism

A long chain of pods, select your destination on a touchscreen map,
lights in the floor direct you to your seat toward the front of the
chain.
*Pull down an adjustable screen and scan the weather report (*Weather
service has scheduled a light rain tonight, ending promptly at 8:45
AM tomorrow morning*) as the modular train whirls away into a long*
tube whose walls flash past for long minutes before the centipede splits apart,
your group of pods entering a tunnel to the left, another detaching from
the back and flashing off to the right. After many of these branches, your
individual pod detaches from a diminished chain and emerges up out of the
ground into...

The area surrounding the western edge of the city resembled,
to the unfamiliar eye, a tangled cluster of vines built to the scale
of giants. Sinuous transparent "trunks" became micro-arteries of
the tube network, so this pod and others streamed up and down
like quicksilver sap. Above, the trunk environment unfolded into

thousands of silvery "leaves," each an individual residence, each catching sunlight to power its internal electronics.

The ground below and between these trunks sorted into a myriad of brilliant gardens interspersed with fountains and ponds and recreational fields marked off in triangles and rectangles and circles, with small groups of people engaging in confusing competitions that were familiar to Mann's host brain.

As the pod entered the trunk and became an elevator to his residence, Mann wondered with amusement if the overlords "above" might want to harvest the ideas for new competitive sports. Then, abruptly, a round door unfolded in the side of his pod, and he found himself standing on a carpet facing a room that stretched out forever, across a wide meadow toward a spectacular mountain scene, with a waterfall cascading off the upper slopes into a river which appeared to flow across his feet and through the wall behind him. It took him long moments to realize that the far wall and floor were a video screen.

Searching his host's mind for guidance, Mann raised his hand and the screen instantly became a news report, which consisted of dire warnings of imminent global conflict, the latest diplomatic reports and military movements, a report on weapons research whose advancements might frighten the Other Side into submission. His host mind seemed to be programmed to dismiss the warning with weary cynicism, so it was an effort for Mann's tired awareness to force his ears to focus on the words, and ponder their implications.

He raised his hand again, and the wall became a path deep into a dense tropical forest. Another gesture, and the floor opened up and swallowed a reclining couch and several chairs, while other parts of the floor delivered an unfolding table with chairs around it, and several couches facing a large coffee table. Another gesture, and luxurious sleeping cots folded out of the walls.

Mann let his feet guide him to a bathroom dominated by a hot waterfall cascading into a steaming pond large enough to accommodate a bull elephant, then to an exercise room with mirrored walls, filled with mysterious isotonic gadgetry that he intended to explore later. Through a door, he entered a library cum cinema cum sound chamber with streaming access to holographic movies, musical performances and a direct connection to the literary resources of the planet.

Mann, hungry, began searching for the kitchen, which turned out to be a small nook that was strangely missing anything resembling a stove or refrigerator. The memories of his host mind led him, instead, to what appeared to be a soda fountain dispenser built into the wall, next to a small shelf of glasses. A screen displayed a bewildering list of what appeared to be ingredients that he could include in his drink. Mann tentatively touched a few buttons and filled a glass with a blended mixture of the nutrients that a human body requires, whose recipe and flavoring were fully subject to adjustment.

The "meal" tasted like a thick beer, which Mann downed quickly, alleviating his hunger but not his appetite.

Then, more curious this time, he touched the screen experimentally, making adjustments, following instincts. This time, the fountain produced a mixture not unlike a red wine which compared favorably with some of the better wines Mann enjoyed on his German and Japanese postings, with a smooth finish.

He carried the glass out to the retractable balcony, gazed down at the sporting activities below, and considered the possibility that the next 40 years might be bearable after all.

7

*"The Implicate Order of the universe has been recorded
in the complex movement of electromagnetic fields... and
in principle enfolds the entire universe of space and time
in each region... The totality of the movement of enfold-
ment and unfoldment may go immensely beyond what has
revealed itself to our observations. We call this totality by
the name holomovement."*

Nobel Laureate David Bohm

Mann had no idea what he was looking for. And he was becoming impatient with himself.

As he pushed and jostled his way into the city crowd at the base of the towers, Mann experimented with his mental muscles. He reached out with his mind and touched what he thought might be the interface, feeling its slippery surface carefully, trying to determine how best to send a message into (through?) it.

Holding the mental contact, he tried to leap up twenty feet in the air to touch the bottom of a bubble transportation vehicle as it whizzed by. But the simulation applied the force of gravity to his simulated body with the same impartial rigor as everyone else's.

He willed a sandwich in his hand, but nothing appeared. He and everything around him were forced to obey the internally consistent laws of physics that had been built into this reality by the gods above, who copied the handiwork of their own inscrutable deity.

He was irrevocably here, in this world in a box.

And no contact from Gandhi and Washington, wherever they were.

The cityscape beyond the edge of the ramp seemingly extended as high as it did far, out to the mists in both directions, with an undergrowth of smaller, older buildings concealed below the towers. It reminded him more and more of Dubai in its pretension to be the first city of the future, yet there was something of Mumbai, or perhaps Calcutta, in the visible disparity between the gleaming towers and the older blocky structures huddling at their feet. At every street corner, a breeze blew across Mann's face, focused by the tunnel that was the street between buildings. Where the sky was visible, it was a clear day, as the weather report had promised.

Mann leaned harder on the interface, mentally framing his request, remembering Westerly's warning. Where could he find a connection with whoever was living below the surface in this large city? Where could he find the outcasts who would give him an unfiltered view of what was really going on?

He felt almost as if he was getting his request through when his concentration was interrupted, annoyingly, by a voice.

"Hey, fella. You look lost," the voice said. Mann looked around sharply, but nobody in the crowd seemed to be giving him their attention. He took a step down the ramp.

"I'm talking to you. You have a name, don't you?"

Mann whirled around, peering suspiciously into the faces of the people around him. An emaciated dog with white-gold fur stood near his feet, looking up at him with its tail twitching. Mann bent down and patted the dog's head and then turned away.

"That's it? Touch and go, as they say? Come on; I thought we had a connection here."

Mann turned back around. The dog was still there.

The dog opened its mouth.

"You seem like a nice guy," the dog said to him. "You have a good smell. I could see the two of us together."

Mann stared at the animal for a long second.

"You can talk?" he said finally.

"That's not a problem for you, is it? I could be quiet, if you wanted. I'm pretty good at being quiet. In fact, just yesterday, I think it was, I—"

"How are you doing that?"

The dog wagged its tail.

None of the people walking by seemed to notice this astonishing conversation. After a moment, the dog motioned with its head that they move closer to the railing.

"Okay, I'm a little bit confused," Mann said, stepping off the rampway. "Can all dogs talk here?"

The dog sat down and stared at Mann's face curiously with its head turned first to one side, then the other. The body language was eloquent: *What planet were you born on?*

"You've been genetically modified," Mann said, more to himself than the dog, rummaging through the unfamiliar and poorly-organized memories in this brain he had inherited. "Pet owners of the future will desperately want to communicate with their pets," he added. "A huge market; the first real commercial use of genetic modification. I should probably collect how this is done."

He looked back at the dog speculatively, his mind still troubled by the... by the apparent *realness* of this universe in a box.

"Can you remember yesterday?" Mann asked the dog.

"Yes," the dog answered promptly.

"What do you remember?"

"I remember that I was hungry."

Shaking his head, Mann stepped back on the walkway, which carried him toward and finally into a broad glass-enclosed hallway with floor-to-ceiling screens on either wall. Whenever someone passed, a large panel on the wall would light up with a hopeful computerized image of an attractive woman who would ask what the pedestrian wanted to purchase. Somewhere ahead, his host mind recognized a transportation hub.

"So what's your name?"

Mann looked around, startled, and saw that the dog was matching his step.

"You don't give up, do you?"

"That's a very strange name. Ha, did you think that was funny? I can be amazingly entertaining whenever you need cheering up. Aren't you going to ask me *my* name?" the dog asked after a moment.

As he looked down at the dog, an unfamiliar emotion intruded on Mann's thoughts. He wondered where the dog slept at night, and then pushed the thought away impatiently. What could be less relevant?

"Okay," Mann said, turning right and following a downslope. "Tell me your name, and then I have to go. I'm—kind of busy right now."

"What would you like my name to be? It could be anything you want. I can answer to anything that pleases you."

"How about Bowser?"

"That would be unnecessarily cruel."

"Jack?"

The dog fell silent. "Kind of exotic," it said after a moment. "But I could work with that."

"Maybe you should tell me your real name. And then—"

"I know. And then you have to go." The dog lowered its head. "Haven't you even *thought* of taking me home with you? Am I that awful?"

Mann stopped. The feeling rising up in his chest was so strong that it felt like his thoughts were drowning in it. He took a long breath and allowed himself to experience the sensation more fully, familiarizing himself with the enemy before he crushed it back down into his breast.

There was a word for it. It was called empathy. A strong emotion that sat heavily in his chest. He had no time for it now.

He looked down at the dog again.

"Let me guess; you've been homeless and wandering the streets since you were born." Mann said, his voice more gentle than he intended.

The dog swallowed, swallowed again and looked up hopefully. "I could be yours," it said earnestly, making eye contact and holding Mann's gaze with its brown eyes. "Just say the word. Excuse me for saying so, but you look to me like the loneliest person I ever saw. I could be just what you need. Plus I know my way around. You look to me like you haven't a clue where you're going."

Mann reached down and touched the place behind dog's ears, and the dog moved into the touch, turning it into a caress. Mann kept his hand on the dog's head, scratching behind the ear, and the dog closed its eyes appreciatively.

The feeling was stronger, and Mann realized that the interface was contributing to it somehow. It was telling him something. What? This was exactly the opposite of what Mann intended. What was happening to him?

"Hey, what about us?" a rough voice called out from behind them.

Mann whirled, already chastising himself for being so unaware of his surroundings. A dozen dogs had materialized along the edge of the ramp, representing every possible shape, size and color combination—thin faces and thick jowly ones, tiny and huge, dark, mottled, spotted—the pack faced him with visible hostility in every body posture, the smallest ones looking the most ferocious and ready to attack.

"Hey, come on; give a dog a break," the dog called out in a whiny voice from Mann's side. "He's mine. I saw him first."

"Yeah?" one of the dogs—bulky as a St. Bernard, with the face of a wolf and a curly tail—answered with a visible sneer. It slowly stepped forward with surprising grace, and the dog at Mann's side cowered. "What if I decide he's mine? Or maybe he's nothing but food."

"You can't have him. Please don't screw this up. Please—I like him. I think we could be good together."

"I think maybe, for the first time in your punk life, you should shut the hell up. You're in enough trouble already."

"For doing what? Finding a home? Isn't that what we all want?"

The lead dog snarled. Its teeth glittered in the sunlight through the glass roof. It took a step forward. "Right now, the only thing I want to do—"

"He's right," Mann interrupted. "I'm his."

"You stay out of this," the lead pack dog said without looking up.

It took another step forward, and looked up with evident surprise when Mann moved over to block its path. Instantly, the pack of dogs stiffened.

"Well, aren't *we* the brave one," the dog said, regarding Mann languidly with visible contempt. "Or are you saying you'd rather die than take this stupid mongrel home with you?"

"I'm saying," Mann said calmly, "that you should go away and leave the two of us alone. Both of us," he emphasized.

The dog snarled again, and their eyes locked for a long second as Mann's simulated brain ran quickly through a rainbow spectrum of emotions, from delicious, unfamiliar, giddy levels of fear that he filed away for future analysis, to a nervous uncertainty about the capabilities of this poorly toned body he inhabited, to a rush of physical knowledge that seemed to flow into his muscles and veins through the interface, a rapid download of decades of the most advanced martial arts training his home world had to offer, settling with growing certainty into a body that was hardly more than a skeleton.

The last emotion in the long sequential journey, the place where his mind ultimately rested, was total confidence and a clear mind.

The other dogs would attack as a distraction, while the lead dog, the only truly dangerous one, would go for the kill. Therefore, Mann needed to kill the lead dog immediately, before the others had a chance to join the attack. There would be a bit of damage to his body, but his mind had already discounted the physical price he would pay before the other dogs ran off. At a glance, Mann recognized a dozen ways that this dog could be killed with his bare hands. Then his mind moved on to the rest of the mob, which of the animals he would disable first and which he would dispatch at his leisure if they persisted in the attack.

But—and here again, this unfamiliar emotion that had no place in the cold calculus of the situation at hand—he felt a gentle regret at the idea that he would have to be the one to end this unhappy creature's life.

He shook it off and stepped forward, close enough that his next step would be an attack.

Suddenly the dog behind him called out: "Don't kill him!"

Mann and the lead dog both stopped.

"Which one of us are you talking to?" the lead dog asked after a moment.

"My new master, you idiot. Listen, he's not really a bad dog; he doesn't deserve to die like this. Yeah, if you're starving and he's merely hungry, he'll take your last bit of food without any thought or concern, and if you're cold and you find a warm place, and he finds you, he'll kick you out, and if you—"

"Can't you shut up already?" the lead dog demanded, sitting back with a visible shrug of indignation.

"He's not as much of a monster as everybody thinks he is, most of the time, anyway, or at least I—"

"Maybe you really ought to stop talking," Mann added. The confrontation had passed. The other dogs relaxed.

"I'm his," Mann said again, his voice more gentle than he intended. "You all can go now."

The lead dog continued to stare into Mann's eyes. A dog's survival depended on its ability to accurately evaluate the capabilities of any potential opponent. Size and strength could always be misleading, so the dominant instinct, evolved over evolutionary millennia, was to assess the potential opponent's confidence level. What did IT know about this prospective confrontation that the dog did not?

The dog opened its mouth to say something, but Mann shook his head imperceptibly, holding the other's eyes with his own.

Abruptly, the dog turned away. "You can keep this loser," he called over his shoulder. "What?" he said as the other dogs stared at him. "Come on. We're wasting our time here."

As Mann watched them walk down the ramp, he was aware of applause rippling through the circuits of the Synchronicity. He watched the dogs vanish into an opening he suspected a human would have trouble fitting through, and with an effort, he cleared his mind, stilling the babble of many minds so he could consciously direct the rest of the download. He would need every one of his skills in this new place.

"Whoah," the dog was saying at his side. "You owe me big-time for that perfect bluff. I mean, I just saved your life there, and I'm still amazed that he bought it. Seriously; you could have been eaten alive."

"It's pretty tough out here on the street, isn't it?" Mann said, reaching down to touch the dog's head. He felt that same deep twinge almost exactly at his center of gravity.

The dog looked up and met his eyes for a long searching moment.

"You have no idea," the dog said.

"So when do you think we should eat dinner?" the dog asked.

"You've eaten four times already, and we've been together less than two hours."

"Those were snacks. I'm talking about a real meal."

Mann looked around. He was trying to identify street level among all the different layers of the different buildings. Finally he realized that there WAS no street level, per se, in this place called Aurora, and let his feet guide him, walking like a tourist.

"We'll go to my place in a while," Mann said. "I want to explore a little first."

"What do you want to see? I know this town inside out. You want a nice alley to pee in, where there's a thick sediment of garbage? You want to know where the tastiest rats live? I probably know every garbage bin in town; I could give you a tour."

Mann stopped at the open entrance of what appeared to be an art gallery. The walls were covered with strange, disturbing pictures of geometric designs shattering spontaneously into chaos. Inside, he saw smooth stone sculptures of bodies half melted and screaming in silent agony. Above him, on the giant cyberscreen overlooking the street, news commentators talked unemotionally about the threat of war, but none of the pedestrians seemed to notice.

Always before he had started with a briefing, a basic understanding of the people and culture. Here, he would have to build all that himself, and he didn't have a clear idea where to start.

"Tell me about the people in this city," he said.

"What about them? As far as I can tell, they just walk around giving off the scent of fear. They pretend not to notice me. They throw away a lot of good stuff just because it has a few maggots crawling around on it. I think—"

"Tell me about the fear," Mann said.

"We dogs have a lot of names for what you call by one word," the dog said. "There's the fear where you pee all over the sidewalk and you think you're about to die. There's fear that comes when you think that something you really want or need is being taken away from you. You can smell a different fear when you walk up to a stranger and she thinks you're going to bite her. There's fear of the unknown, like when you stand at the doorway of a very dark building and you hear something scuttling around and your imagination starts to play tricks on you. And then there's a vague dread that lives in the back of your soul. That's what we smell on the humans wherever we go."

"For how long?"

The dog dropped its head, the equivalent of a shrug. "As long as I've been alive. It's just a background smell to the city, so familiar that nobody talks about it."

The screen overhead showed a hand-laser weapon that was being tested by the military. Mann watched it thoughtfully. It was an example of the technology he was expected to bring back to his world. At the same instant, his mind wondered how he might penetrate whatever wall of secrecy the military had thrown up around its various inventions, and whether it would be a good idea to introduce such a thing to his world's catalogue of brilliant ways to exterminate other people.

"I need to get to a place where strangers talk to each other," he said to the dog. "Where do people go to have fun?"

"You mean like sporting events where they smash into each other like idiots? Or the quieter kind of fun where they drink until they're too stupid to notice how unhappy they are?"

"Music," Mann said after a moment. "When they open the door, and you hear music come out."

"There's too many of those to count."

"Someplace where there are a lot of them. Within walking distance."

The dog immediately led him onto the walkway, and after a few minutes, they were moving back down again. "I'm not sure what goes on in this place," he warned his master. "They never let me inside."

"I think I'll know it when I see it."

As the dog led him off the ramp into a wide space between buildings, Mann allowed his mind to reach once again into the interface, testing it like an unfamiliar muscle. Then, slowly, gaining strength, he exerted his will, tried to formulate what he needed even if he wasn't sure himself what it was.

Nothing. Nothing again. Then, suddenly, he felt something give, painfully, deep in his psyche, a pulled muscle in his mind.

His eyes swam, and then he realized that he was looking up at a garish hologram extending into the sky above a low, squat building so nondescript that in his world it could have been a bowling alley. The hologram, the equivalent of a neon sign in his world, was a shimmering silvery image of a man and a woman dancing in a way that would make a grandmother blush, with glittery images of drinks and bottles bouncing around like the little balls in a sing-a-long.

A dance club? A bar?

A place where conversation was expected, where strangers met on equal terms.

Perfect.

Silently projecting his gratitude to the interface, he stepped toward the entrance.

"Wait here," he told the dog.

"How long?"

"I have no idea."

"Good enough for me," the dog said quickly. "I'll check out those guys who are waving at you."

"Who?"

"Hey."

"What?" Mann turned, squinted, and finally turned his face toward the darkness of a crevasse between buildings, where a hand gestured toward him. He shook his head and took a step toward the club.

"Hey, I'm trying to help you here."

In spite of himself, Mann stopped. "Help me how?"

"You'll never in a million years get into the Misanthropolis looking like you do now."

"Why not?"

"Yeah, why not?" the dog echoed.

"If you don't believe me, try. But you won't get a second chance."

Mann stopped and assessed the scene at the doorway. Two crude-looking muscular guards were turning away two-thirds of the people who approached the door, seemingly at random, not unkindly. The others were nodded inside with hardly a glance.

Once, in what the locals still called Ossi even though it had been 40 years since the unification, he had been trailing a young man who sold very sophisticated explosives on the black market. The young man had walked into a converted industrial plant-turned-nightclub known as Berghain, but when Mann tried to follow, the people at the door had denied him entrance. He never found out why.

He looked back at the alley.

"Is it safe for me to go in there and talk to these two?"

"If I'm with you," the dog said. "I can smell fear on them."

"What would you do if they tried to kill me?"

"Bite their testicles off," the dog replied readily.

"What can you do for me?" Mann said to the alley.

"We understand the code. We can get you inside."

"How much?"

"Fifty."

"Fifty??"

"Trust me, once you get inside, you'll realize it's worth it. There's people who've been trying for years."

Mann tested the interface. He felt drawn to the club, although there was no clear revelation telling him why. Warily, he approached the dark space between buildings. Two indistinct shadows looked him up and down.

"What do you think?" one of them said.

"Those eyes," the other said. "They talk to me. They say: police official, guardian of the public order. The way he stands: paramilitary. The clothes say he's a voyeur sent by the Synchronicity for their vicarious pleasure. And then there's the dog."

"What about the dog?" the dog demanded indignantly.

"Maybe you should stay out of this," Mann said warningly.

"I could stay out of it, sure. See? Not a word out of me. Until you say the word, I'll just shut up and—"

"I think we can help him."

"I disagree."

"What the hell are you talking about?" Mann blurted out in exasperation.

"We guarantee success; otherwise you get your money back," one of the shadows explained. "We're trying to decide if there's any hope for you."

"First thing you do is take off that robe," the other shadow said. He pulled off his own shirt. "Put this on. No, don't tuck it in—for god's sake. Are you sure about him?"

"What about his pants?"

"That's not the problem. Here—"

The first shadow stepped forward, and suddenly Mann felt a terrific explosion across the side of his face. The next instant, he was holding both shadows by their necks, examining them coldly as they gasped for air. His face stung, and he could feel the bruise forming along his cheekbone. A trickle of blood ran down the side of his mouth.

The dog growled.

"It's—the—only thing—" the first shadow, who Mann could see clearly for the first time, was gasping. He released his grip a bit, disturbed by the weakness of his hands.

"He was helping you," the other one, shorter, with stringy blond hair nearly to his waist, was forcing out through his constricted throat.

"How is hitting me in the face going to help me?"

"Yeah. How is—"

"I'll handle this, if you don't mind."

"He's going to handle this. Answer my master, or I'll have your testicles for dessert."

"I just took that—straight shine—off of you—is all. It was all I could think of."

Mann released them and turned away.

"Wait—"

"What? You want to hit me again?"

"I want you to rub some of the blood on your sleeve. When you walk up to the door, whatever you do, don't make eye contact with the guards. Whatever they ask you, tell them it doesn't matter to you, because you're going to die tomorrow anyway."

"I'm going to what?"

"He's going to what?"

"I told you to stay out of this."

"If you're going to die, I want to know about it."

"It's just what he's going to say. He isn't going to actually do it. Why am I talking to this dog?"

"Say it like you believe it," the shorter one said. "Tell them this is the last day of your life. If you can say it like you believe it, then you've got half a chance."

Mann gave them both a long appraising look, and turned to go.

"Didn't you forget something?"

Without turning, Mann pulled most of the money out of his pocket and dropped it on the ground.

"Stay here," he said to the dog. "Don't bite anybody," he added as an afterthought. He walked up to the guards at the doorway, who were politely, even kindly, telling a young couple that it didn't look like they were going to get inside tonight. They said the same thing to a group of men who were next in line. Mann walked around the line, but the doormen turned away, ignoring Mann completely.

"What about me?" Mann said after a moment.

Both of the guards turned. They looked him up and down like dueling X-ray scanners. Their eyes lingered on the expanding dark bruise on his face.

"Beat it," one of them said.

Mann shrugged. "I'm going to die tomorrow anyway," he said. He turned back toward the street.

"Hold on."

"For what." Mann said flatly.

"This is your lucky day." With a slight bow, one of the guards stepped aside. "Your last day should be a lucky one. Right?"

Mann shrugged.

"It's customary to say thank you."

Mann shrugged again, and pushed his way through several layers of hanging strips of dark fabric, like Arjuna entering the Khandava Vana.

He had no idea what to expect, and therefore had no expectations, but even so he was shocked by the mind-shattering chaos that surrounded him the instant he cleared the fabric door. The roar of the music, a pulsing beat that found its way directly into your muscles, driving the urge to dance, a purely utilitarian dance beat without melody or—

It took a long moment before Mann's eyes adjusted to the darkness and swirling chaos, but finally he was able to make out the fact that he was in the middle of a crowd of barely-dressed men and women writhing in what seemed like a parallel dimension made up of flash and glitter as music pounded the air from everywhere at once. He realized that all the light in the room was coming from the clothing of the women, which glittered over their breasts and loins and covered little else.

He pushed timidly out to the edge as couples of all genders performed simulated sexual activities imperfectly visible in the intermittent pulsing. With an effort and a test of his balance, Mann was able to seat himself at an empty table with partially-emptied glasses all over it.

His face throbbed. He touched the expanding bruise lightly with his finger, realizing that it was nothing more than a figment created by the internal logic of the simulation. But the insistent pain felt real, solid, strong on his face, and it grounded him in this immaterial place and time. With the pain came a heightened awareness of his surroundings that helped convince his mind of his physical self in a way that somehow felt deeply satisfying—and, on balance, when the net impact of the pain was subtracted from the satisfying sense of being, the result was more positive than negative.

Was this the recipe for masochism? When a certain degree of physical pain was linked in one's mind with a greater degree of emotional pleasure?

The music throbbed and pulsed, pure rhythm. It was, Mann decided, a more insistent relative to the techno music he had heard in clubs in his own reality. Purely functional, every instrument functioning like a drum, pounding out a rhythm that somehow passed directly through and beyond his higher consciousness, tapping into and awakening rhythms in the musculature in the most direct possible way, like a drug injected into his body, bypassing his digestive system.

A tall woman with a voluptuous physique, wearing what appeared to be a flashing G-string and a series of feathers across her enormous breasts, danced over and touched her lips with her finger. He stared at her blankly. After a moment, she danced off with a disapproving backward glance.

As Mann watched the dance floor, his eyes began to sort out the chaos. The scene also told him where the long evolution of civilized music was going, back all the way around the bend to its pre-civilized origins. Music was always fundamentally an accessory to dance, and dance was always fundamentally an accessory to the libido. Whenever music—or, he supposed, also dance—strayed too far from facilitating the libido, and tried to assert its independence, it lost its fundamental relevance and much of its power, a dissociation of musical sensibilities...

Mann closed his eyes and quieted the aimless babble, not for the first time cursing this undisciplined mind he had inherited as the pulse and rhythm came to a climax. The lighting in the room shuddered with simulated orgasm, and he felt a small answering shudder in his own body.

When Mann opened his eyes, a couple was disengaging themselves from the crowd. With an empty mind, he watched them tumble with visible weariness into chairs at his table.

The man, raven black hair cascading around his shoulders, topped with a hat like a fez adorned with feathers, gave Mann an appraising look, his mouth contorted as if all the muscles in his face were fighting to conceal an enormous smile. The effect was to project a smug superiority that somehow invited intimacy. The old talent clicked in: Mann was looking at a man whose life was devoted to making women happy in the short-term, and ultimately, inevitably, perhaps unknowingly inflicting a great deal of pain in the longer run.

Why do I take an instant dislike to him? Mann asked himself. *Because it saves time.*

The other's cynical eyes met and held his own, and Mann realized that the other thought he was establishing a knowing male bond between them. He felt instantly protective toward the woman this man had been dancing with.

"Oh my god, what happened to you?" the woman was saying, her eyes staring at Mann's face. "Forbes, look at this!" She touched the darkening spot on his cheek, and Mann instantly, at the first contact with the finger, experienced a sharp lurch in his belly and a tug along the interface. He looked up into dark eyes that seemed incapable of deception, crinkled now in concern, and then expanded the view to a face whose mouth might have been a touch too wide, the cheekbones a touch too high and prominent, a forehead a bit too high, framed by a cascade of thick hair that bordered between silver and yellow, showering down her bare shoulders. Somehow it all came together and made her beautiful, right down to the mouth, which naturally fell into a wry expression that suggested irony.

His animus was aware of the small flashing beads that appeared to be painted over her breasts and loins, but his gaze returned involuntarily to her eyes. They seemed to be out of focus, as if they were looking through instead of at everything including—

Forbes glanced over and shrugged. "He'll be all right," he said.

"Should we do something?"

"Absolutely. We should continue drinking."

Mann abruptly realized that he and the woman had been staring at each other. Before he looked away, he noticed an expression of surprise that the woman instantly tried to conceal. "It doesn't hurt very much," Mann said lamely, his tongue suddenly feeling thick and uncoordinated in his mouth. "I mean, if that's what you're asking."

"There's nothing quite like a threesome," the man called Forbes commented, lifting one of the many drinks at the table. "Unless it's a foursome. Or a fivesome, now that I think of it. Or a—"

"We get the point," the woman said.

"Is there a point? I was wondering if there were any limits. Certainly not on my end."

Mann started to get up out of his chair, but the woman touched his arm with a forbidding gesture.

"It's all right; you don't have to leave," she said. "This party is just getting started."

The next song swelled up and made the air tremble, and the bodies, seen more clearly now that his eyes were adjusted to the gloom that seemed to close hard on the sparks of light, began writhing in ways that were far more than suggestive. Mann glanced back at the woman and then looked down. In addition to the throbbing on his face, he felt a peculiar twinge at his center of gravity, different from what he experienced with the dog. He made a mental note to check out the medical facilities in this reality.

"Yes, thank you for not asking, I really DID look in the mirror on my way out the door," the woman said, her low voice somehow foregrounded over the music. "And I really DID think with a sense of dismay bordering on self-loathing that I was doing nothing more than packaging myself up for display, and I really WAS tagging my-self at fire sale prices." She took a long drink from one of the glass-es, seemingly selected at random. "Which," she added, "is another way of saying that I fit right into this place."

"You look great," Mann said.

"I mean, what is a dance club anyway, but a place where the wom-en adorn themselves in the most eye-grabbing package they can put on without blushing, and they spend most of their life searching for exactly the very edge of that fine line, so that they can market themselves effectively and find out what the men will buy. It's funda-mentally more honest that we do away with all the pretense and just get right down to it, don't you agree?"

"It strips the whole scene of needless hypocrisy." Forbes raised his drink in agreement. "Why pretend that anything romantic is going on here?"

"I wasn't talking to you."

"Then I certainly wasn't answering you."

"It's this damned war," she said, sitting back. "When everybody's time frame is shortened down below some invisible tipping point, suddenly the women are forced to start thinking like men. I think that's fundamentally the definition of decadence, when the women think like men, and the checks and balances aren't there anymore. Don't you agree?" she said suddenly, turning to Mann.

"It's the absence of hope," Forbes interrupted before Mann could say anything. "There's a red line, and when the needle indi-cating the average level of hope for the future—the temperature of hope in the human stew, so to speak—crosses below that red line, then it's all downhill and decadence."

He raised his glass. "Thank god for it. Or our politicians, who seem to think they're the same thing."

"I want to hear what *he* thinks," the woman insisted.

Mann realized abruptly that he had been looking back and forth at the two of them with his mouth open, and shut it abruptly. "I think I need a drink," he said.

"Excellent idea," the woman said, finishing one glass and picking up another. "The drinks are a big part of it. They reduce your better judgment just enough that you're more likely to risk entering into a bad transaction, and they dull the buyer's and seller's remorse and at the same time provide a convenient excuse when all your friends ask you what the hell you were thinking. That's a lot of accomplishment in one little glass. Or two, or three, or a dozen."

She held up the second glass in front of Mann's face. "Here's to the long, slow erosion of common sense and judgment and hope on the way to mass oblivion."

"Extremely well said." Forbes held up his glass, and they both finished their drinks in a gulp. When they looked back at each other, the woman laughed while the man's face contorted even more in the effort of seeming superior to the idea of laughing.

Then Forbes stood up and adjusted his hat carefully. "And now, my dear, I will say good night," he said, kissing her gently on the forehead. "You seem to be in good company here." His eyes took on a predatory gleam as he surveyed the dance floor, and then, quite suddenly, he was in the middle of it.

The woman watched him for a long second, and then shook her head as if to clear it.

"I didn't mean to—" Mann said.

She waved his words away. "It has nothing to do with you. I talked him into taking me here, and he was beginning to realize that I might not be the sure thing he was expecting."

"For what it's worth, it looked to me like you're worth a thousand of him."

"I think you might have been hit too hard in the head," she responded. "Inside of an hour, he'll walk into one of the dark rooms with the hottest trixie at the top of this little food chain, and that will lead to a domino effect all over the floor, as whoever he dislodges dislodges somebody else and claims the next attractive partner, and so on down the line."

"Is it really that fluid out there?"

"At the end of the world, there is nothing left but opportunism and the moment," she said, regarding the empty bottom of her glass with visible regret.

"And decadence."

"Let's not forget that."

"And hope?"

"*That* we can forget. Everybody has given up."

"Not you." Mann made it a statement rather than a question.

The woman's head whipped around. "What do you know about me?" Her tone was not as harsh as the words. They sounded like a genuine question, rather than a challenge.

"I know that you came here against your better judgment, and you hope against your better judgment that the world is going to survive, and you're realizing the more you drink that it isn't wise to question your better judgment, and you're wondering why the drinks are making you more sensible instead of less," Mann said absently, looking around. "You strike me," he said, his eyes on the dance floor, "as a person with extremely good instincts and judgment who is trying to obliterate all of them in the space of a couple of hours, and you're finding it to be much harder than you expected. You strike me as a person who doesn't belong in this place, but you're not going to admit it to yourself, much less to me or anybody else."

When there was no reply, he looked back, and their eyes locked again. "And you've always relied on your better judgment, so this is all a new experience for you," Mann concluded, talking directly to her. "That," he said, turning away, "is what I know about you."

"Oh..." The woman had been staring at him throughout his assessment, her dark eyes expanding until now it looked like they were about to explode. Then, with a visible effort she turned away and rummaged around the table, looking for a glass with the remnants of something in the bottom.

"Is that what you do for a living?" she asked over her shoulder.

"What."

"Read minds."

"They've actually tested me for that. Apparently I don't have the skill."

"Then what if I told you that everything you said was completely shit."

Mann shrugged. "People lie to me all the time. Why shouldn't you?"

"I—that is, I just want somebody to give me a reason to feel the hope that I can't help feeling. Is that too much to ask?"

Mann shrugged again. "You feel what you feel. Why should anybody else have anything to do with it?"

"So why can't I be like everybody else?" she said, shifting her chair so that their shoulders touched. She looked up into his face petulantly, but still with the irony touching her lips. "What's *wrong* with me?"

"You're too smart to believe what everybody else believes, and somehow too dumb to know that," Mann said. "It's an interesting combination."

At that, she smiled and relaxed her head into his shoulder.

"I'm starting to like you," she said. "I like you enough to trust you enough to let you buy me a drink."

"Which way is the bar?"

The woman raised her hand, and a silver box on wheels scooted across the floor, threading through the dancers with surprising agility. After a moment's hesitation, Mann put his hand on the screen, and in a second, the screen flashed approval. The woman touched the screen once, and then again. Instantly, a round container dropped down onto a small internal platform, and filled itself with a greenish drink that Mann's host's mind told him was highly alcoholic and sweet, with a strong narcotic mixed into it.

"That's pretty aggressive," he commented as she put the drink to her lips.

"It's perfect for—how did you say it? Obliterating my better instincts."

Mann punched a milder drink for himself, put it to his lips and took a slow sip.

"So what about you?" the woman said, turning her attention to the drink, then back to him. "Who are you? What do you do?"

"Until a few hours ago, I was a Synch."

"Really. What's it like?"

"Very distracting. But there's an odd sense of belonging."

"What made you leave?"

"I'm not sure you CAN leave. Let's just say I had a transformative experience."

"So how do you know so much about me?" she said in a quiet voice. "That's really what I want to know."

"In my old job, I had to know about people pretty quickly. It was kind of a life or death thing, although I never really thought about it that way."

"And you quit that job?"

"Yes."

"Why?"

Mann sighed. "I didn't like the people I was working for, and I didn't like the people I was working against," he said. "I didn't see how what I was doing was making things any better."

"What about your new job?"

"I'm not altogether sure what I'm going to do with myself now," Mann admitted. "I thought maybe coming in here would make things clearer."

The woman finished her drink in a long gulp, put the glass definitively on the table and held out her hand. "I'm Gloria," she said. "As in: Glorious Gloria, which is what I'm calling myself this evening. Who are you?"

Mann decided to keep his name from up top. "Marcus Mann," he said.

"Well, Marcus Mann, it's customary for a gentleman to buy a lady a drink in this place."

"I just bought you one."

"It looks like the glass is empty to me."

"Let me ask you a question first. I'm new to this city."

"Fire away. As long as it gets me closer to that next drink."

"What I'm trying to figure out how to ask," he said, watching the lithe bodies of the dancers flashing in the darkness, "is, does all this seem real to you?"

"In what way?"

"Are we really alive, or is everybody here just going through the motions played out by some kind of cosmic script?"

"This is pretty deep for small talk," Gloria said. "But I'll play along. Sure, sometimes I feel like I'm dreamwalking and can't wake up. Haven't you ever felt that way?"

He thought about it, about the events in his own life in the reality outside the computer. "I guess I have," Mann admitted.

"When you get down to it, who do you know who is really alive, and what is the dream and what is the reality?" she persisted.

"I'm trying to figure out how real it feels to be here, in this place, in this time," Mann said. "That's actually closer to the reason why I walked inside."

"I have to say, you came to an awfully strange place to find reality," Gloria commented, watching the flashing lights and swirling colors reflect off of bare flesh. "In fact, I'm guessing that this is your first time here."

He nodded.

"Me too. I figured I might as well have sex while I can," she said. "It would be a terrible thing for the world to end, and me having been celibate in the last days, don't you think?"

"I don't think there's a good answer to that," Mann said.

"So after months of listening to my friends telling me to loosen up and live a little bit before I died, I figured, what the hell? I finally made myself walk out the door and—you know, you seem to be almost as uncomfortable as I feel."

"It's just that—you sound so real. You sound like you have real feelings, real memories, a real personality. I guess I wasn't prepared for that."

Gloria looked back up over her shoulder and gave Mann that appraising unfocused stare. She seemed to be looking through his skin at his internal organs.

"I always thought there was some kind of unwritten rule that men are never supposed to say things like that," she said finally. "It's all a woman wants, is to be recognized as somebody real."

"I'm not sure that's exactly what I meant."

"Don't blow it; it makes you very attractive. Do you want to dance?"

Gloria tossed back her hair and took his hand, already moving her body in time to the music before they reached the crowded floor. He found that his body understood the dance, and they swirled in simulated imaginative sexual embrace, adjusting and avoiding collisions like a couple of oversexed scatbacks in the open field. He mixed in some salsa moves he had learned on assignment in Barcelona, some swing dancing he had picked up during the many hours in Prague nightclubs. They moved closer to the band, who, he saw, created the music by running their fingers over flashing, exotic instruments that seemed to be little more than grids with a thousand multicolored buttons.

Gloria's supple belly gyrated, never moving more than an inch away from his own as they shifted and swirled back away again. One of the musicians stepped forward and added words to the song, a kind of tribal chant behind the relentless beating pulse from the instruments.

These are the days of human ants commuting
Their daily pilgrimage, worshipping
The god machines which fail to live and cannot die
As toxic winds above slow-roast our sky.
Somehow, too slow to see, daily routines
Became bonded servitude to our machines
The holy name of profit on our tongues
As holy industry blows death into our lungs.

Piss and shit your poisons—it's all a game,
And up ahead: nothing but more of the same...

Lift your eyes above the scene
Where words carved in the fabric
Of our darkening reality, seem
In the space behind the here and now
To scream out the question
Nobody dares to say out loud:
        What's the point of it all...?

"Are you happy?" Mann asked over the music.

"It doesn't matter if I am or not," Gloria answered with a shrug as he pulled her close. "Nothing matters anymore. We have to take our pleasure while we exist—that's what passes for wisdom these days."

"I was just trying to get a sense of how you experience reality. How does it feel, at this moment, right now?"

"It feels like, just for once, I want to stop thinking and just merge with the rest of everybody else. Hold me," she said. "I feel better when you hold me."

These are the days of political clones
Selling their souls for campaign loans
In perpetual auction, vote no, vote yes
As the world free-falls into darkness...
So slowly, we gave up political control
Receiving nothing from the sale of our government's soul
Believe their lies, it's all a game,
And ahead there's nothing but more of the same...

Lift your eyes above the scene
Where words carved in the fabric
Of our darkening reality, seem
In the space behind the here and now

To scream out the question
Nobody dares to say out loud:
 What's the point of it all...?

"Where do you work?" Mann asked.

"Why do you care about something like that?"

"Why does it bother you that I'm trying to find out what I can about you?"

Gloria looked up at him, her eyes flashing impatience. "All right. Okay," she said, flowing into the unexpected spin that he coaxed with his hand. "I'm an engineer with four degrees that I earned in three and a half years of higher education before I successfully challenged the doctoral program, and I work in a laboratory, right now doing the worst kind of shit work imaginable, which is creating customized RNA by reducing disulfide bonds using the stinkiest chemical imaginable, beta mercaptoethanol, which seems to adhere to my skin somewhere under the surface where the soap won't penetrate. More importantly, my intelligence level is probably ten times yours, so there is almost certainly no chance you and I will ever be able to relate to each other on anything more than a tawdry sexual level that might last an entire evening until our mutual interest dies down and you start to seem boring to me and I start to intimidate your fragile masculine ego.

"How about you?" she asked brightly as Mann continued to stare at her with a blank expression.

"I'm just trying to get the hang of the place. And you know what? I'll bet you aren't more than five times as smart as I am."

Gloria laughed, and seemed surprised that she had laughed, and embraced him as they swirled near the front door. He noticed the hat with the feather passing nearby, and saw the ironic smile cross Gloria's face for an instant as she sized up Forbes' partner.

These are the days of gathering atomic storm
On the near horizon, death's triumphant form

Darkens in shadow our daily where and how
And there's nothing we can do to stop it now.
As the drums rise up on both sides of the divide
Only traitors, we are told, would turn it aside.
Soon the flaming legions of hell will be hurled
To walk unshod across the face of the world
        and they'll call it war...
Our history told entire in self-extermination
By our own deadly fire
        of light without illumination...

Lift your eyes above the scene
Where words carved in the fabric
Of our darkening reality, seem
In the space behind the here and now
To scream out the question
Nobody dares to say out loud:
        What's the point of it all...?

"So I have to ask, why doesn't a smart girl like you find another job?" Mann said finally.

Gloria sighed. "You think I haven't tried? Our whole operation is working day and night looking for new technologies that will give our military an advantage. But our government contract is about to run out."

"Why?"

"They're putting all their money into this new engineering consortium, called Innovation Insights," she sighed. "And I don't blame them. All the new cool stuff is coming out of there, almost faster than you can keep track of it. I wish I understood how they did it."

Mann stopped. "What do you mean, all the cool stuff?"

"I mean, literally every new interesting invention and breakthrough is coming from the same laboratory, with as near as we can tell no more than fifty or sixty engineers and technicians. They must be beyond geniuses. Why would the government fund any-body else, when they have such a reliable fountain of what they're looking for?"

Mann thought a moment. And then another moment. His eyes misted over and he offered a prayer of thanks to the interface.

"Where can I find them?" he said, carefully keeping the urgen-cy out of his voice.

"Who?"

"These Innovation Insights people."

Gloria favored him with a look that suggested she was reevalu-ating his intelligence downward. "You might try looking up their address on the Locator System," she said. "But good luck getting an interview. I tried."

The song ended with another shimmer of glittering simulat-ed orgasms everywhere around them. Gloria pulled Mann back over to the table, where others were finishing their drinks. She dragged two chairs apart from the others and sat back, catching her breath.

"Was that fun for you? Dancing, I mean?"

"God help me, there must be an exhibitionist somewhere in-side," she said. "All of a sudden, I'm having a ball."

Gloria reached over to the table and held up an empty glass meaningfully. Mann raised his hand and the drink machine darted back to their bench and accepted his palm print. This time Gloria punched the code for an alcoholic beverage that also contained extract from the pituitary of a tropical lizard, and settled back with a purr of contentment. Mann watched the dancers, trying to get his head around something. Finally he realized that the interface was still tugging insistently at his mind. That point at his center of gravity twinged insistently at the threshold of pain, and it felt like he was out of breath, even though he was breathing normally. Was he feeling sympathy toward this strange woman?

"I guess I should have mentioned that for some reason that my rational mind does not quite understand, I find you terribly sexy,"

Gloria was saying. "It's like there's this glow about you that I've nev-er seen in anybody before."

"I'd tell you that you're beautiful, but you know that already," he replied.

"I don't think any woman in this room is capable of believing that on her own," Gloria said. "Our self-image is largely composed of feedback. So give me what you've got, every bit of it, as objectively as possible, as long as you feel it, ignoring the fact that if what you say is charming enough, and I have maybe two more drinks, I might find myself offering you every orifice in my body."

Mann winced. "The way you look is only a small piece of it," he said, trying to find the most objective words he could. "For some reason, when I look in your eyes, the interface—I mean, I feel like whatever it is that controls this entire reality blots out everything else and suddenly you have my full attention, so that it seems like nothing else in the room is entirely real. It's very strange," he muttered.

Gloria closed her eyes for a long second.

"What's the matter?"

"Shut up. I'm savoring what you just said. That was exactly, right down to the letter, precisely what every woman hopes someday she'll hear, and I may be the only one who has ever heard it expressed so perfectly."

"I also think you're a little bit weird," Mann said, taking another sip of his drink.

"Call me unusual and I'll take it as a compliment."

"That's actually a better word."

The next song started up.

"Do you want to dance again?"

"I think I'm going to have to sit this next one out," Gloria said.

"Why?"

"You'll see."

The music seemed to gather itself in the air, as if recovering its breath from the frenetic pace, a slow moan rising up over the floor, a whisper of a beat behind it growing louder, and the flashing on hundreds of breasts and loins began to synchronize into a strobe. Partners held each other more intimately, then cushions and pillows dropped from the ceiling, and dancers, two or three at a time, melted languidly to the floor.

"My god," Mann said. "They're—"

"Shhhhh. Listen to the music. You don't have to watch if you don't want to."

> *Thunder shatters the horizon*
> *nowhere to hide from it now*
> *No time to think, no time to stop*
> *breathe in the final tick of the clock*
> *and give up with no hint of sorrow*
> *The cruel illusion that was tomorrow.*
>
> *Make me laugh, make me bleed,*
> *Hurt me, love me, fill my need,*
> *make me feel to overcome my fear*
> *make me forget that the end is near...*
> *I need to laugh and shed a tear,*
> *And squeeze a lifetime into a year...*

Flesh, oddly hidden by the flashes of discarded clothing and the semi-darkness around them, rolled over flesh on the crowded floor, partners were exchanged at random, the music built toward a slow climax and then retreated, teasingly, as the voice crooned softly, floating somehow above the howling of the instruments.

> *Here on the bitter edge of death,*
> *grabbing at random one last thrill*
> *We plunge into each other's desperate bliss*
> *and momentarily lose sight of the abyss*
> *At the culmination of all time,*

All risk is finally stripped away
Consequence is burned alive
by the fire next door to today...

Make me laugh, make me bleed,
Hurt me, love me, fill my need,
make me feel to overcome my fear
make me forget that the end is near...
Come to me now, it's time to play
And squeeze a lifetime into a day...

Mann touched his face where the darkness of the bruise had finally stopped spreading. It felt numb. A powerful wave of sadness washed across the clinical part of his mind, and he realized all over again how alone he was in this strange place that was not really a place, and this time that was not really a time.

He felt an enormous sympathy for the souls all around him, and without realizing it, he reached his hand out to Gloria.

She took his hand and held it with both of hers, and the next wave of emotion was unfamiliar, strange, oddly at war with itself. Mann felt at once weak in his body and strong, nearly invincible, inside where his center had been mysteriously aching.

Their hands, together, felt more intimate than any of the increasingly urgent activities going on below them. Mann felt as if the music was penetrating the bodies on the floor as much or more than they were each other; they still moved in rhythm to it, still dancing, still exchanging partners at random.

Mann closed his eyes for a moment and held Gloria's hand more tightly. When he opened his eyes, she was smiling faintly, her attention still fixed on the dance that had become an orgy.

When hope has died, pleasure rules
living for the moment
is too long-term for fools

freed at last of expectation,
Where there is no salvation
beyond the instincts of our bodies
and the mass extinction of our rules...

Give what I crave the most
And I'll do the same for you.
We touch our lives like glasses in a toast
so pleasure is our wine
and detonation is the orgasm
that will take us long before our time.

Make me laugh, make me bleed,
Hurt me, love me, fill my need,
make me feel to overcome my fear
make me forget that the end is near...
We'll lose the why and embrace the how
and squeeze a lifetime into the now
> *Toward the dawn of explosive pleasure we run*
> *plunging ourselves into the dark side of the sun...*

There was a general shudder across the floor, and then an odd stillness. Finally, one or two at a time, with dazed, shiny expressions, the dancers stood up, and clothing was kicked aside. After a moment, the next song began, and the dancing continued, awkwardly, this time with the sparkling lights rising up from patches scattered randomly around the floor.

Mann started to withdraw his hand, but Gloria held it tightly, and she looked at him with what could only have been surprise. Then she released him and reached for her drink.

"Any regrets?" she asked.

"No."

"Me neither. I think it was a mistake to come here."

"Will you give me your address?"

Gloria laughed. "Marcus Mann, whoever you are, I know how these things end, and for some unknown reason I very much don't want to go through all of that with you. As soon as I sober up, I'll recover the use of my brain cells, and as soon as you sober up, you'll start asking yourself if you really want to go through a second date without understanding half the things I say."

"Shouldn't I get a chance to find that out?"

"No," Gloria said, standing up. "Aurora is a very large city. The chances are about forty five point zero eight million to one that you and I will ever see each other again."

Mann touched the bruise on his face as he watched Gloria pick her way past the bodies on the dance floor toward the general gloom at the door. He found himself admiring the way she moved, the way her hair reflected the flash of clothing, the way she round- ed the corner and was out the door without a look back.

"We'll see about that," he said, and slowly finished her drink.

8

"There is neither the element of extension, the element of cohesion, the element of heat, nor the element of motion, nor the sphere of the infinity of space, nor the sphere of the infinity of consciousness, nor the sphere of nothingness, nor the sphere of neither-perception-nor-non-perception; neither this world, nor a world beyond, nor sun and moon. There, monks, I say, there is neither coming nor going nor staying nor passing away nor arising."

The Buddha

The Innovation Insights headquarters building huddled in the shadows against the breathtaking explosion of steel peaks and extended atria that rose up directly behind, a small one-story foothill to a mountain range. There was no identifying signage. When he walked through the glass doors and got a glimpse of the jungle scenery behind the reception desk, Mann had the odd feeling that the building was somehow larger on the inside than the outside.

A human receptionist behind a long table glanced up with heavy lidded eyes, like a serpent, and then back down at her screen.

A humanoid robot sat beside her, a cheerful expression on its rubberized visage.

"Who are you?" the robot demanded in an inflectionless voice.

"My name is Marcus Mann," Mann said confidently. "I'm here to apply for a job."

"There are no openings at present," the robot replied promptly.

"Could I at least talk to somebody?" Mann asked, leaning hard on the interface.

The human receptionist raised her eyes but not her head. She regarded him with indifference bordering on hostility, her eyebrows slanting down deeply toward her nostrils. "We aren't interested in hiring anybody and nobody here has time for small talk," she informed him in a voice that was, if anything, less expressive than the robot's.

"Don't tell me you're overstaffed. Nobody is overstaffed these days."

"We are not overstaffed or understaffed," the robot told him helpfully. "We are exactly appropriately staffed. If you would like to see our organizational chart—"

"Don't encourage him," the female receptionist broke in, without looking up from her screen.

"I did not intend to—"

"Don't talk to him at all. I've already told him to go away."

Mann looked her over carefully. His mind's eye pictured a woman who had been, at some early stage of her life, idealistic about love, had given her love to several boys, and, to put it kindly, they had not been deserving of it. Now her life was devoted to small revenges where she could take them.

"You deserved better," Mann said.

"What?" After a moment, involuntarily and clearly not approving her own decision, the receptionist looked up.

"That's all. You should know that, at least. You deserved better at important times in your life, and I hope it comes your way in the end. Even if there's nothing I can do about it."

The receptionist met Mann's eyes for a long second and then shifted to the bruise on his face. He leaned harder on the interface.

"It would be a mistake to send me away," Mann said as she looked back down at the desk.

"Would you like me to escort him out without injuring him?" the robot inquired timidly.

"It's all right with me if you injure him."

"You won't even let me talk with somebody for an interview?"

"You catch on quickly," the receptionist said. "You're going to be an amazing employee for somebody someday."

Mann brought his mind back to stillness as he walked back out the door into the street. Disappointment evaporated in the clear burning flame of heightened awareness.

"No luck, eh?" His dog shifted its tail in sympathy.

"No."

"Did you threaten to bite them?"

Mann smiled briefly. "I'm not sure that would have helped."

"You never—" the dog stopped and cocked its ears.

"What?"

"Can't you hear it?"

Mann followed the dog's eyes as a flying vehicle shaped like a cigar screeched recklessly around the building across the street. It careened to a hovering halt in front of the door Mann had exited. The side door opened, and a dead human body, a middle-aged man in a suit, was rolled out with a dull thud onto the sidewalk.

Mann's gaze met a pair of eyes regarding him coldly through a cloth mask. The voice inside the mask was muffled.

"Tell your bosses they could be next."

"Yeah?" the dog shot back. "Well for your information, they didn't hire him, so it's not—"

By that time, Mann had already thrown himself face first into the vehicle, shoving the masked one backwards as his breath exhaled into a grunt of surprise. The inside of the vehicle was much wider than Mann had imagined, and the driver was a yard away as he yanked the masked one's neck backward in what, on his home world, would have been a killing blow, but here, working with this still too untrained body, he was only able to bang the head against the metallic dashboard.

Somehow, the driver lifted the vehicle into the air with a sudden sideways lurch, and Mann had to claw the fabric seat in order to keep from falling out the door. He crawled forward, but the vehicle lurched again, and his hands slipped, allowing his feet to dangle out the opening.

Another lurch, and Mann was on his knees, watching from the corner of his eye as the front—which was a projection, rather than a direct view of the outside—showed an imminent collision with first the side of a building, then a rooftop. He threw himself forward, and caught the arm of the driver, who seemed curiously unperturbed by his assault.

The driver calmly touched something on the panel, took his hands off the controls and suddenly Mann was in the eye of a hurricane of expert blows that were the product of extensive military training.

Mann cleared his thoughts and gave control of the body to his meta-mind. Instantly, his perceptual universe slowed down to a crawl, the scene froze, the car seemed to stop in mid-air, and it felt to Mann as if his body were moving through thick molasses. With his awareness moving so much faster than his body, Mann was able to recognize and anticipate by long seconds each of the blows from his assailant, but still he was careful to make it seem as if each counter-move was accidental, to hide his own training. After what seemed like hours, but in the other's perceptual framework was actually seconds, Mann opened up an opportunity for the other to strike his solar plexus, and waited for him to take the bait.

When the pilot's body twisted, Mann pushed his fist toward the face, and after long seconds of pushing through the thickness of suspended time, he landed a precise blow that drove the assailant's nasal bone and, behind it, the stouter lacrimal bone directly through the soft nasal passages, like daggers inserted deep into his brain.

The driver slumped as Mann, still seeming to move in slow motion, vaulted over him, hanging in the air for long seconds before he could reach the controls of the spinning vehicle. He searched his host's mind for the information he needed to pull back the semicircular wheel and regain control.

Instantly, the craft stopped spinning. Another touch of the controls, and it veered backwards toward the place where, Mann could see, the victim still lay on the sidewalk in the midst of a growing crowd. As his body finally settled into the seat, Mann pulled the vehicle into a hover, and it suddenly seemed that he was in the precise center of an exploding universe.

Mann rolled as the masked one swung for his head, and as he did, the vehicle again lurched, throwing the assailant off balance. Moving once again in slow motion, Mann wrapped his arms around the masked one from behind, securing a choke hold as the vehicle, careening wildly, finally collided with the street, throwing them both out the open door.

They rolled over each other as, in slow motion, the vehicle bounced out toward the other end of the street and then, abruptly, came to a rest and burst into flames.

Mann held tight to the choke hold and allowed his mind to rise above all emotion, all anger, everything but an intense curiosity that he intended to satisfy.

"Tell me who you are and what this is about," he said quietly, at the same time tightening his grip on the other's windpipe.

His prisoner struggled, and Mann further tightened his hold.

"Ask them," he finally managed to gasp, gesturing with his head toward the gathering onlookers who were gaping at them on the sidewalk. Mann noticed, near the front, the receptionist and the robot, alternately staring at the body, the burning vehicle and the two of them still tangled up on the ground.

"I'm asking you."

Instead of answering, the face behind the mask stopped struggling, and Mann felt the hands, which had been trying to find a way to grab backwards at him, rummage into pockets.

When the other spoke again, his voice sounded oddly dreamy. "I don't give answers," he said, and an instant later the clothing on the body that Mann was holding began oozing an unholy mixture of acid and flammables.

Mann jumped back and watched in frank amazement as a rising cascade of flames devoured the melting body. After a minute, there was nothing more than a dark flame-licked stain on the street.

Slowly, wearily, he looked up at the still-burning remnants of the vehicle, and then back at the building, and then finally at the crowd of people who had gathered on the sidewalk and were still coming out of the door, staring at him as he slowly walked over to the body that had started it all, lying face-down on the ground.

He bent over the dead man, touching him tenderly. The dog sniffed the shoes warily.

"Well, that was certainly a mess you made," it told him with a distinct sniff of disapproval at the whole affair.

"What's going on here?" a hesitant voice demanded from somewhere above.

Mann found himself looking up into the eyes of the oldest-looking person he had ever seen. The other's face was largely hidden by a long braided white beard that reached down to his chest, much of it seeming to flow from his mustache. White hair streamed out behind him, and what skin was visible was a spider's web of deep wrinkles. There was something unfocused about him—not just his eyes, but throughout his face, as if his sight and attention were perpetually turned inward, as if using his eyes to perceive the actual world was an unfamiliar activity.

The old man peered at Mann curiously as if he might be an unusual specimen of insect.

"He didn't have an appointment and he wanted to see somebody about a job and he wouldn't leave," the receptionist answered from somewhere in the front of the line. "And now this."

"I could injure him now," the robot added helpfully.

"No, no, surely that's not necessary." The older man's forehead contorted into a caricature of perplexity at the situation. He bent over the body with Mann, touched the dead person's hair, and then stood up, touching the dog's head absently. He looked at the last of the flames still licking the street where the masked one had been, and then up at the still-burning remnants of the hovercraft.

"They were simply doing what they were told," he said to Mann finally.

"They killed this man."

"That too was foreseen. Your interference was not necessary, and now an additional person has been ejected from this reality."

"A killer," Mann said.

A very tall, angular scientist with exactly the same braided white beard and unfocused facial expression stepped out the door. He pushed impatiently through the crowd, and stood next to the other man, almost half a body taller. The two looked at each other curiously as if they were seeing each other for the first time.

"You told him it was expected, but not this soon," the tall one said.

"Yet another entry on the list of things we didn't know. This one says he wants a job."

"Him?"

"Who do you think?" said the dog indignantly.

"Yes, the human one."

"What do you think?"

The two turned their synchronized attention to Mann. They looked him up and down carefully.

"We could start with your qualifications," the shorter one said. "What Institute did you graduate from with high honors?"

Mann searched his host's memory, and was disconcerted at what he found.

"I'm self-taught," he said finally.

"In nanotechnology, electro-chemical dynamics, genetic engineering or theoretical physics? Tell me what you think of Holtzmann's mathematical treatment of four-dimensional space at the subatomic level. Or how to fine-tune the torque-field factor in the dual angular momentum turbines of an antigravity engine. I'd be very interested in your thoughts on how to miniaturize that technology."

"I was looking for something a little less technical."

The tall one raised his hand.

"Where do you come from?" he asked.

"Is my birthplace really that important to the work I'm going to be doing?" Mann asked.

"Why do you want to work here, of all the many millions of places in this world?"

"I've heard that this is where all the innovation is happening."

"Why would you care about innovation?"

"It's kind of like—like a hobby of mine," Mann said, realizing that his answer sounded lame. "It's what I've always wanted to be a part of. I'd work really hard for you," he added. "I just really need to be close to where the really interesting work is being done, and I'm sure I could help in some way."

The short scientist peered closely at Mann with those unfocused eyes.

"This all seems a bit unreal to you, doesn't it?" he said after a moment.

"I'm not sure what you mean."

"You came here with no valid scientific credentials yet were clearly expecting to be hired, you risked your life as if you had many lives to throw away, and now you act as if nothing is out of the ordinary."

The tall scientist looked at the shorter scientist with visible surprise.

"You know, I think you might be right," he said at last.

"I'm sure of it."

Their eyes conveyed meaning that Mann was unable to comprehend.

"We very nearly didn't recognize him," the short one responded.

"Yet another lesson in humility," the tall one added. He turned to the crowd at the sidewalk, and made a dismissive gesture with his hand. "Shoo," he said. "The show is over; there's work to be done."

"Does that mean I get the job?" Mann said timidly as people reluctantly turned back to the building.

"We can hardly let a recruiting opportunity like this slip through our fingers," the tall one said. "I'm Dr. Yager. Everyone here calls me Dr. Y, but perhaps," he added earnestly, "you will be the first to use my real name."

The short one looked at his hand curiously for a long moment, and then extended it to Mann. "Dr. Xavier," he said. "You can guess what they call me around here."

"Perhaps," Dr. Y added, "you could arrange to have this mess cleaned up as the very first of your duties, and be sure to inform the authorities, when they arrive, that we will cooperate with any investigation. Not," he added, "that we expect them to be any more competent in this matter than they generally have shown themselves to be."

"And then what?" said Mann. "I mean, can't you tell me what I'll be doing?"

The shorter scientist touched the corpse at his feet with his toe.

"You'll be taking over *his* job," he said. "I have a feeling you're going to be perfect for it."

The two walked back into the building.

"This place is a little different from a lot of places I've worked," a young research engineer named Maila told Mann, leading him through a leafy undergrowth of bushes, trees and vines, many of them bearing ripe clusters of fruit.

The engineer was shorter than Mann and his body was shaped like an egg, the widest parts being the belly and the large haunches above thick legs. When he walked, his short arms flapped out like a penguin's to maintain his equilibrium against the unpredictable shifting of the ballast that was his stomach. Despite the warmth of the office, he wore a fur hat with flaps down over the ears, and his hair fell down in ragged waves over his right shoulder.

Ahead of him, a woman wearing a dark robe that covered her hair and most of her face stopped, reached up and plucked a few reddish orbs and popped them in her mouth.

"That's Subito," said Maila. "I've fallen madly in love with your body," he said, turning to keep his eyes on her as they walked past.

Subito favored Maila a disapproving glance, and disappeared around the corner.

"She's deeply in love with me," Maila said. "You can see it in the way she tosses her head, shamelessly trying to stimulate my libido."

They passed engineers and research scientists relaxing in spidery adjustable lounge chairs inside glass enclosures that could be retracted or reformed to create team workspaces. Holographic images danced between them as they gestured, modeled, rotated and then threw up equations into the air. Mann made a note to get the specifications of the holographic projectors, and of the force field that formed the elastic, constantly shifting walls of the giant aquarium that floated overhead. He watched it split into two pieces, forming two roughly spherical environments filled with shimmering, darting fish. Other mini-aquariums roamed about in the distance, touching and bouncing off of walls and tree branches like soap bubbles.

"In what way?" Mann asked.

"What."

"Is this place different."

"Oh. Well, for one thing, they have a really cool pension plan where you can invest in any of the company's products if they ever go commercial. And there's a way-cool rule that nobody can be working more than 100 footsteps away from a kitchen environment. Holliander," Maila called out to a woman wearing what appeared to be a baseball cap with a visor in the front and back. "Weren't we supposed to have a hot tub date sometime this week?" He watched her walk past. "You just name the time," he called out after her.

Here and there, swing sets hung from the ceiling, and the floors below could be accessed by slides. As they walked past one of the cafeterias, Mann noticed a dozen engineers discussing physics in a hot tub, the steamy air further clouded by what appeared to be dueling holographic images of abstract shapes shimmering between and among them.

"It's funny," Mann said. "From the outside, the building didn't look this large."

"You'll get used to things like that," Maila said. "Dr. X and Dr. Y sometimes test out their innovations right here in the office. Nobody has actually measured it, and I think the square footage changes from day to day. Right now, the inside probably covers about ten acres more space than its external walls, as closely as anybody has been able to estimate it."

"Could we stop in one of the kitchen environments?" Mann asked timidly.

"This is one here," the other said, turning abruptly left into what seemed like an enclosed garden with enormous flowers. He touched the trellis and it opened, revealing a refrigerator environment that seemed much larger inside than the outside walls, stocked mostly with fruit.

"And—hey Alicia. How's it going?" he said to a young woman sitting on a lounge chair. She was dressed in what appeared to be combat fatigues, with flaming red hair standing straight up as if her head had caught on fire and somehow the fire had frozen. Alicia, ignoring Maila completely, stood up, reached inside the refrigerator, grabbed something wrapped in foil and started to walk away. Then she turned around abruptly and walked up to Mann, intruding on his space aggressively.

"You're new here." It was a statement rather than a question.

"I noticed that myself," said Mann, leaning backward.

"Married?"

"No."

Alicia studied his face carefully, and then took a long appraisal of every inch of him down to his sandals. Mann had the impression that she was evaluating him for nutritional purposes. "You look like you have real testicles, unlike pretty much all the other men around here. Call me," Alicia said. "I'm in the employee register." Then she walked away.

"It's good to see you again," Maila called out at her back. "She's starting to like me," he explained. "There used to be a look of disapproval on her face when she would completely ignore me. Now we've progressed to indifference, which is a clear prelude to love." He touched a desk, and what appeared to be a spreadsheet materialized in the air. "I'm actually tracking my progress on this data mining program here—"

"That's a lot of women," Mann observed as Maila scrolled down the list.

"Yeah, well, really there aren't that many women who work here, maybe 35 or so. This also includes some of my neighbors at the apartment and this really hot woman who gets up and leaves the coffee shop whenever I walk in. See? She's about two and a half seconds slower to leave now than she was when I first saw her. If you extrapolate that out over eleven years, I can pretty accurately pinpoint our wedding date."

A male engineer dressed in a colorful shimmering robe walked up past them, pulled a couple of pieces of fruit out of the refrigerator and sat down.

"You're Mann, right?" he said without preamble.

"Yes."

"We got the memo about you. I'd like this kitchen to have a supply of orange juice," he said, taking an appreciative bite out of an orange, eating the skin as well as the pulp.

"Duly noted. Although that's not actually—"

"So what do you think of the place?" the other engineer said.

"I think everybody is lucky to work here. It reminds me more of a playground than a place where you do actual work."

"You don't know the half of it," said the engineer with the orange. "Other places, they make you think up new stuff. Here, the new stuff is already thought of. All you have to do is figure out what to do with it, how to create the whole manufacturing ecosystem that would supply the components that would be needed."

"Such as?"

Maila touched the table again, and it glowed. Another touch, and the spreadsheet was replaced with equations hovering in the air. "Here's a fairly simple one," he said. "It's a fabric that's much stronger than steel, but as light and flexible as silk. See the design specifications," he said, pointing to a row of unintelligible symbols. "The reason it's so strong is that you're interleaving these enormously long strands of tubes made of carbon, with impurities of fluorine and potassium and titanium placed here and there to keep it so stable that even though it's a few atoms thick, I doubt anyone here is strong enough to rip it apart. We're basically weaving together molecules."

"I see," Mann said, seeing nothing.

"So the problem is obvious," said the engineer with the orange, dismissing the hologram.

"It is?"

"How do you attach a dye to something like that? How do you color it? Who would buy it if we manufacture it with just one color? I'm thinking that the color has to be built into the structure of the interleaving, so that certain wavelengths are absorbed with some precision, but another team is looking at attaching impurities to the outside of the structure, which will weaken it unless they can also create an ionic tension with the materials—"

"I've actually been trying to figure out how to use the interleaving carbon strands to miniaturize those big hulking antigravity engines," Maila told the other engineer. "Imagine if we could strap one of those things around your waist and just travel anywhere we wanted to. You'd get up in the morning and dress in your personal transportation device."

"What else is in there?" Mann asked carefully, nodding his head at the desk.

Maila shrugged. "I've got to get back to work. But you can see for yourself."

"I don't mean to be prying..."

"You have a right to be curious, just like the rest of us. We all take a peek now and then at what everybody else is working on. Doctors X and Y sent word around that we should tell you anything you want to know, and give you free access to everything. You actually have a higher clearance around here than I do."

"That's nice to know," Mann said, thanking the interface yet again.

"What we really need," the other engineer said with his mouth full, "is somebody who can put all this together."

"I beg your pardon?"

"You saw how disorganized everything is. When I go look at somebody else's project, chances are there's a lot in there that I could use in my own, because that's how science is: it all fits together."

Suddenly Mann spied a ray of hope.

"Couldn't you—"

The engineer laughed. "I'm not even close to being smart enough to master dozens of these new technologies all at once," he said. "We all bow to Drs. X and Y, but I'm not even sure they could do it. That's the other funny thing," he added. "They brought all this stuff into the laboratory, but sometimes when you talk with them, you realize how much they don't really understand. I guess it's like a writer who's too busy writing to realize what he's creating."

Mann's mind was elsewhere. "You need somebody around here who is super-smart about all of this," he said finally.

"Good luck finding THAT person," the engineer snorted. He finished his orange and handed the remaining peel to Mann to be disposed of.

Mann watched the engineer go. And then he thanked the interface yet again.

After a few seconds, Mann tentatively touched the table. Instantly, the hologram appeared in front of him. The navigation interface was absurdly simple; there were files that detailed hundreds, perhaps thousands of projects, all carefully organized and catalogued.

With an eye on the traffic among the vegetation, he selected one at random.

It was a propulsion system using fusion engines. This part of the project regulated how much energy was funneled into long tubes toward the back of the vehicle, although another design, for space travel, had the engine at the center, and tubes radiating out on all sides, with a control mechanism that would allow a pilot to essentially propel the vehicle in any direction.

There were equations involving momentum, thrust, safety and structural parameters, and references to the design specifications for the fusion technology.

And it was all gibberish. The equations meant nothing to him. Mann could barely comprehend the outlines of the project, much less any of the important details.

Another? This time the hologram showed a large image of a transparent human head, which could be scaled so that he could zoom into the spaghetti tangle of neurons, mapped out and color coded, with some, indicated in red, connecting different pieces of the map. Then the hologram overlay what appeared to be tiny metallic filaments of wire, reaching into the brain, attached to a small metallic nodule at the back of the head.

The specifications said that this was a communication device which would allow people to directly access the information and data networks with their minds.

How could he bring this back? He was no expert, but this seemed to be light years ahead of the technology in his own world. Or, for that matter, of the advanced technology that he'd seen outside of this building.

Mann decided to look at one more.

Selecting, again at random, Mann saw the air fill with what at first looked like a flying saucer, an orb in the middle of a thin disk that tapered at the outside edges. Then, as he read through the project description, he realized that it was a remotely-controlled warship as large as an aircraft carrier, powered by antigravity. From blisters on the surface of the globe at the center, the ship could direct raw destructive energy in virtually any direction.

He scrolled down until he found a cross-reference to the antigravity engine, and found more gibberish equations, and a working model that could be sped up or slowed down in the air in front of his face. Inside the globe, a centrifuge-like engine spun long arms out into the disk, and near the end, superconducting magnets were buried into the arms. But the very ends of the arms each held motors which spun rotors of superconducting magnets perpendicular to the rotation of the longer arms, and apparently a precise combination of angular momenta created an interplay of magnetic forces that nullified the mass inside the field, which, according to the text accompanying the illustration, implied not just antigravity but speed-of-light travel with minimal thrust.

"Staying late?" Mann was startled to find Dr. Y's tall frame standing at the doorway of the mini-kitchen.

"I was just about to leave," Mann said, hastily erasing the holographic image.

"Stay as long as you want or need to," Dr. Y said with a shrug. "What do you think of it all?"

"It's amazing."

"A bit more advanced than what you're used to, I'm guessing?"

For some reason, the question put Mann on his guard. "I've never seen anything like it," he said carefully.

"Do they drink coffee like water where you come from?"

"It doesn't taste the same as what you have here. But it's similar," Mann said. "How do you know that I come from… somewhere else?" he asked after a moment.

Dr. Y chuckled. "When you leave, don't worry about locking up or turning anything off," he said. "The security system will handle everything."

9

"Time and space are themselves... like the screen on the video game. The displays on the screen may seem to interact directly with each other but, in fact, their interaction merely reflects what the game computer is doing."

Allan Combs & Mark Holland; *Synchronicity: Science, Myth, and The Trickster*

Mann's mission, at least, was clear: to find a particular person in this city of 25 million, knowing only what she looked like and her first name. The city address records included more than eight thousand individuals with Gloria's first name, and many more listed as "G" with a last name. Mann spent a couple of days scanning pictures before concluding that this civilization's information resources tended to be a bit random. At this rate, the search would take him a year.

Mann knew he wouldn't find her at the club. And for once, the interface didn't seem to be helping.

But he wouldn't have been in this virtual place and time if he wasn't reasonably resourceful, so finally, three days into the search, Mann decided not only to find Gloria, but to find her that same evening.

"Are you sure about this, boss?" the dog said. They were approaching a dense cluster of low, shabby-looking buildings that seemed to predate the gleaming towers by a hundred years at least. The closer they got, the slower the dog walked.

"Just show me where they are. That's all I'm asking from you."

"Maybe you don't understand. If we find them, that means *they'll* find *us*. And there are a *lot* of them."

"That's what I'm counting on."

"You're just testing me, right? This is to see if I'll do anything for you, even if it means the certainty of getting eaten. I can see it now; you want to prove my loyalty, and at the last second, you'll back out and—"

"Well now, *this* is a surprise," a voice growled from somewhere around a corner in front of them.

Casually, a dog stepped out into the open, and stood in their path. Mann recognized it as the same dog he had faced down a week earlier.

He could see that the dog recognized him.

"Hi there. It's good to see you. You're looking well," the dog said from beside Mann. "In fact, you look terrific, if I—"

The other dog looked up at Mann. "You two make a beautiful couple," it said.

"I guess you know we came looking for you," Mann said.

"I guess I had guessed that."

"I guess you're wondering why," Mann added.

"I guess I am. But I'm also thinking that it doesn't really matter so much. Here, in this place, I've got my full posse. You're a little bit outnumbered, and I have something more interesting in mind than talking."

"If we were going to fight, that might be relevant. But I'm not going to fight."

"Wouldn't matter if you did."

"I think I speak for both my master and me when I say in a very sincere way that I hope you didn't take it personally, that last time, when you were totally humiliated in front of—"

"This might be a great time for you to run away," the big dog said. "It won't be long before you're looking for a new master. One that hasn't recently been food."

"He'll stay here with me," Mann said.

The dog looked up at Mann, back at the lead dog, and then back at Mann.

"You know what? He's right. I'm staying here," the dog said, his voice quivering. "If you eat him, you'll have to eat me too, because the truth is, now that I've lived on the other side, I'd rather die than go back to this life."

"I think we have a deal," the lead dog said. It barked once, and Mann looked around to see the faces of many dogs appear from behind corners in every direction. Legions of dogs walked out into a wide circle, their bodies stiff and alert, their eyes hostile and confident.

The big dog looked up at Mann. "Before we do this, I want to see the fear in your eyes," it said.

"I said I didn't come to fight," Mann said. "I came to offer you something."

"A gift? Isn't that sweet."

"More than a gift. A different way of living."

The dog's eyes narrowed. "I think we've done enough talking."

"Have we? The last week, you and the other dogs here have been finding food around the streets, good food, real food for dogs, as much as you can eat. For five days in a row. Is that right?"

"It could be," the dog said carefully. "So what if it is?"

"It's true," another dog behind Mann said.

The lead dog turned its head slowly and favored the other dog with a withering look.

"So what if it's true?" it said again. "What's that got to do with us?"

"That food came from me," Mann said.

"Come again?"

"I made arrangements that it be dropped off at different locations that I was told you would find. It was the only thing I could think of until I could find a proper place for you—all of you—to live."

There was a noticeable stir in the crowd of dogs. The lead dog barked, and the sound died away instantly.

"The only thing you could think of for what, exactly?" the dog said evenly. "Why would you do something like that for us? What have we ever done for you?"

"Actually," Mann said, uncertainty creeping into his voice for the first time, "If you want the honest truth, I couldn't help it."

"You're going to have to do a lot better than that."

"I can't explain it myself. That first night, for no reason that makes any possible sense to me, I couldn't sleep for thinking about the kind of life you're living out here on the streets. I asked my dog how many of you there were, and where you could be found. And then I went back out on the street and talked to some people, and set up an account that pays for the food. Look, I tried to make the feeling go away, but it just kept coming back," Mann added. "It was like I was experiencing, in myself, the way you must be feeling when you're hungry and there's nothing to eat and nobody on this earth cares about you except each other, and you know that any of these dogs would tear your head off if it meant getting a better scrap of food and they thought they could get away with it. It must be pretty damned awful," Mann continued lamely.

"So you're telling me that you *care* about us?" the dog snorted. He turned to look back at the other dogs, obviously expecting laughter. There was nothing but silence from the other dogs, who were watching Mann intently.

"I'm telling you that I'd sleep better if all of you would follow me to a place where you, all of you, can go inside at night and be warm, and the food will be delivered there. And meanwhile, I've got some people who were living on the street who seem to be real dog lovers. They said they'd give just about anything to live with you, if you'll let them stay without trying to chew them up."

"When?"

"Right now. It's actually not that far."

"I don't believe you," the dog said. "In fact, none of us believe you."

"I think some of you do," Mann said.

"Those are your last words," the dog said, and it took a step and leaped into the air.

Mann stepped aside, arms raised, and was shocked to see his own dog leaping into the air. The two collided, and fell on either side of Mann. The dogs instantly scrambled to their feet and prepared to launch themselves at each other once more, but Mann stepped between them.

The lead dog backed up and looked around at the other dogs.

"Kill them both," it said.

There was a lot of movement in the crowd of dogs, but none of them moved forward. They all seemed to be looking in different directions, at each other, waiting for one of them to make the first move. Tails wagged.

Finally one of them spoke.

"He's giving us food," the dog said.

"So?" the lead dog snarled.

"It's—forgive me for asking this, but wouldn't it be stupid to kill him?" another said.

"What would it hurt to see this place he's talking about?" another said. "We can always eat him if he's lying, can't we?"

The lead dog barked angrily, and then every dog was barking angrily.

"What are they saying?" Mann asked his dog.

"They're not really saying anything. He's showing everybody how angry he is, and they're showing that they're not all that happy with him at the moment. Honestly, sometimes you humans try to read too much into things."

The barking continued for some minutes, and then gradually died down, as the lead dog shook its head and approached Mann again. Mann was expecting anger in its eyes, but it looked visibly shaken, even fearful.

"We've taken a vote," the dog said. "Show us this place of yours."

"I haven't actually seen it myself," Mann said, opening the door of the warehouse building. "But I gave them very specific instructions."

"Just open the door," the dog said. "We'll tell you whether it's acceptable or not."

It was dark inside. Mann looked around for a light switch, but one of the dogs found it first. The enormous room came into view, a dusty relic that had once been a factory floor, abandoned for at least a hundred years. The windows along the upper walls were streaked with mud, giving the interior a twilight cast that made it hard to see the far wall from the near one. Somebody had strewn hundreds of mattresses and blankets all over the floor haphazardly at every angle. A waterfall filled a wide basin near the back of the building and next to was it a crude metal trough filled with dog food. Doors on every side of the building had dog doors built into them, and along the outside walls of the room, an array of space heaters glowed faintly.

"My God, it's *beautiful*," Mann heard a dog whisper.

A man walked in one of the doors in the back, prematurely elderly from a hard life on the streets. He surveyed the scene with evident satisfaction.

He approached Mann in a shuffling walk as the dogs scattered to try out the beds and blankets and sniff everything in all corners of the building.

"Look okay?" he asked. In an absent gesture, he leaned down to put his hand on the lead dog's head, and the dog stiffened dangerously at the effrontery. The man continued to rub the head without looking down. He scratched behind one ear, and after a few seconds, the dog relaxed and leaned into the caress.

Mann shrugged. "Ask this one. He's in charge of this place."

The man looked down at the lead dog.

"It's okay for a start," the dog said casually. "We'll see if there's enough beds." It looked up at Mann. "How long can we stay here?"

Mann shrugged. "I took out a five-year lease. I plan to have it renewed."

"And you're doing all this for us just for the hell of it? Without expecting anything in return?"

Mann sighed. "Just so long as it lets me sleep at night."

The dog looked around at the other dogs scattered around the room, then back at Mann.

"Okay, maybe I'm feeling a little guilty here," it said after a moment. "Is there anything we can do for you in return?"

"As it happens," Mann said, "I'm working on kind of a complicated problem right now."

10

"Because of folly, they do not understand that all things
are like maya, like the reflection of the moon in water."

Lankavantara Sutra

Mann sat back and closed his eyes. Very slowly, very carefully, he opened his mind to the Synchronicity, allowing
a trickle of chaotic impressions to become a flood, then a
tsunami, and finally, as he fully relaxed his mental muscles, a flood
that engulfed the world.

He was everywhere at once, a creature of a thousand eyes, Amun
in Thebes, Argus Panoptes on Olympus, Azrael striding across the
Rub' Al-Khali, Shiva in the Devasthana, the multi-eyed wheels of
god swirling in a riotous confusion of sensory data that sent his
mind reeling in shock at the impossible challenge of processing it
all.

He felt, he smelled, he tasted, he heard everything at once, unfiltered and roaring through his awareness with a persistent fury
that threatened madness.

And... Mann was shocked to realize that although the sensory
data had caught his attention, it was actually the least of the unfiltered impressions that he was experiencing. He was also feeling

what each member of the Synchronicity was feeling, and sharing their moment-by-moment thoughts.

Through a mighty effort of will, Mann's awareness swam toward the top of the raging flood, finally arriving, with a mental gasp, at a perspective where he was able to blur his attention and consider the totality without focusing on the particular, a high-level view of the human condition in its raw form.

From here, he could perceive that well over half of the total attention broadcast out of the group mind could be characterized as feelings and emotions that shifted moment by moment like a ten-dimensional kaleidoscopic image or the bright shimmering lines of sunlight reflecting off the bottom of a clear shallow lake with unsteady waters.

More than half of the attention that remained was an incessant babble of random thoughts and images and mental background noise, as if the fires in the brain were sending out sparks at random or, better, as if there was a loud hum of interference in the radio. It was a transitory, wasted, inefficient processing of worries and wonders and consideration of the next meal flitting through thousands of minds and leaving no long-term trace, interspersed in the group by a shockingly tiny number of focused thoughts, creativity, problem-solving, real and productive use of the remarkable thinking mechanisms shining here and there like tiny sparkling bits of quartz catching the sunlight in the raw earth of a construction site, or fireflies briefly interrupting the darkness of a moonless summer evening.

And a relatively small remainder, shockingly small, was the actual sensory data, much of which never truly registered on the minds of the experiencers in the Synchronicity. Mann realized that his mind was more aware, in particular and in aggregate, of the things going on around the individual units of the Synchronicity than they were themselves, and then he realized that nearly all of the member/participants tended to be more focused on the sensory experiences of others than their own.

Into the chaos, he projected his need, softly at first, then more loudly as he perceived that nobody was paying attention to him.

This woman, she looks like this. Has anybody seen her?

Mann's mental image of Gloria melted into the group mind, and in a half of a tenth of a moment other images were circulated, and Mann realized that others in the Synchronicity had been watching through his eyes the evening he had met Gloria, and they were adding details to the picture, making it more realistic, showing her from different angles. It helped that her face was unusual.

A single mental voice rose up somewhere in the chorus.

This neighborhood. I've seen someone very like her here where I live.

After a moment, another, an image of the crowded inside of a building.

I've seen her at this transportation system.

She was in this coffee house three days ago.

She must live somewhere inside this particular area.

I've seen her too.

I saw her walking along the street not more than two hours ago.

The memory flashed across the Synchronicity.

Yes, that does look like her.

Yes.

Yes.

The responses narrowed to the few who believed they had seen her, and outliers in other cities were discarded. Mann tried to visualize the mental map that was forming in the group mind. He asked for details of the neighborhood.

"A building covered with plants," he said to his dog. "Many flowers. Actually," he added, as the images came through more clearly, "there are many such buildings, all in the same area. I can see a large globe on a pole, is what it looks like, just a few blocks away."

The dog looked puzzled. "What does it smell like?" it asked. "Can you see any rats?"

"Come on. How many buildings are covered in plants?"

ROBERT VERES

A dog nearby had been listening closely. "We know that place," it said in a tentative voice. "About twenty minutes from here if you trot." It nodded its head toward one of the dog doors.

"I'm looking for somebody who lives somewhere near those buildings." Mann began to describe Gloria, but quickly realized that the dogs were looking at him as if they believed he was insane.

"I hate to break it to you, boss, but all of you look pretty much alike to us," his dog said. "What does she smell like?"

"How would I know what she smells like?"

"Do you have anything of hers?"

"No," Mann admitted.

The lead dog and Mann's dog looked at each other meaningfully, and then back up at Mann with expressions of acute disapproval.

"Wait," Mann said. "Do you know what—what beta mercapto-ethanol smells like? I think I said that right."

"Yeah, most of us moonlight as chemical engineers when we're not prowling the streets," the lead dog said.

Mann reached for his computer pendant. He spoke into it, peered at the small screen and then touched the screen twice. After a moment, a sample odor wafted out of the device, and Mann found himself gagging at the smell.

"That," Mann said. "Can you find somebody who has traces of that smell on her?"

The lead dog shook his head to clear it. "Yeah," it said, wrinkling its nose. "I think that's definitely something we can work with."

The dogs led him across moving walkways, through towers, into and out of atria, finally emerging into a neighborhood with block after block of enormous tiered garden skyscrapers, flowers, ponds, here and there a broad patio with small glass tables and chairs, floor after floor of plant life rising up and around buildings that looked like pagodas—or, Mann thought, like tall spidery Christmas trees.

The dogs fanned out along the street level, which was occupied by restaurants, coffee shops and old-fashioned clothing stores. At this time of night, many of them seemed to be deserted.

A member of Synchronicity walked by across the street, but neither of them bothered to wave at the other; the connection was too intimate for that.

Any sign of her?

If there was, you'd know already.

"Any sign of her?" Mann asked his dog.

"If there was, somebody would have barked by now."

"Tell them to keep looking."

"She's probably in bed at this hour."

There was a bark.

"I smelled something like that smell, but the trace is not fresh," a dog said, two blocks east at the corner.

"Which way?"

"Follow me."

Mann followed the dog down to the end of the block, where it stopped to sniff the air again.

"It could be anywhere around here," it said. Mann's eyes glazed over, but the Synchronicity offered nothing in the way of encouragement.

Mann leaned hard on the interface, causing—as it always did—a number of the Synchs to turn their awarenesses curiously in his direction.

Nothing.

After a fruitless hour, he gave up and walked into the nearest beverage shop, intending to wait until morning. The place specialized in wines, but on this world, wines were made not only from an oval fruit similar to grapes, but also from a dozen other fruits, all of them in various grades of complexity that would rival the best wines of his reality. It made him wonder absently why there wasn't a thriving industry in his own world of fine wines made in many interesting ways from apples, pears, raspberries. Perhaps, when he got back in a couple of hours, he would bring this innovation to America, confidentiality agreement be damned.

He walked up to a machine the size of a microwave, pressed his hand to the screen and retrieved his glass. Then he headed for the back, and stopped in his tracks for a long moment before he took the empty bench across from a head bent over the table and completely covered with hair like a haystack in a field that might or might not cover a sleeping farm worker.

"Good evening, Glorious Gloria," Mann said gently. "I've missed you these last few days."

Gloria raised her head, and her face reappeared from under the haystack. She stared at him without recognition, her face bleary from what Mann surmised to be many drinks. Then Gloria favored him with a weak attempt at a smile which captured all the irony but none of the pleasure, and looked back down at her glass as if it were an enemy to be conquered. She raised it to her lips, her hand trembling a bit, and then seemed to work up the courage to swallow another gulp.

"So enlighten me," she said in a throaty whisper. "How did you find me? And while you're at it, you might include a paragraph or two on WHY you found me."

Mann shrugged his shoulders. "I wouldn't call it dumb luck," he said. "Maybe we can call it semi-intelligent luck, and leave it at that. As to why, you made an impression on me."

"Yeah, well maybe you're the first person I've ever made a GOOD impression on." She turned back to her drink, raised it over her head and swallowed the rest of it, grimacing and wiping her mouth with the back of her arm. "But give me a few minutes and I'll finally get it right," she added

"You don't seem very cheerful," Mann observed.

"Give that man the golden award for insight," Gloria said, staring with visible sorrow at the emptiness of her glass. Then she looked up. "You don't suppose—"

"How about if we take a walk," Mann suggested.

"That's just exactly what I need. A walk. With a drink in my hand."

Mann tried to imagine the complexity of a simulation that could create, out of the stimulus of the words he had spoken, the responding nerve impulses to produce irony. He shook his head.

"What's that about?" Gloria demanded.

"I wish I could live in your head for just half a minute. It must be fascinating in there."

"Oh, it's a real picnic. You'd have a ball in here where my mind is right now." Gloria stood up shakily, and he took her arm. He led her carefully past the drink machine and out the door. She gave the machine a regretful backward glance.

"All right, so we're taking a walk. Do you have a plan for this excursion? Like your place or mine?"

"Is that what you want?"

"I've been trying to figure out exactly what it is I want for the last five hours, and just about the only thing I am absolutely, totally sure about is that that isn't it."

Mann leaned hard on the interface. "So tell me what happened today that threw you into such a tailspin."

"You don't know, do you?" Gloria said, a note of surprise in her voice. "I thought maybe you had somehow gotten wind of the news and tracked me down in order to cheer me up. Not that such a thing is possible, but it would have been really sweet. And anyway, how could you have known? It just happened this afternoon."

"What."

"They came in my office and told me that they didn't need me around anymore. They were very nice about it. For some reason, just because I'm smarter and work harder than anybody who has ever been employed there, and because they were paying me about ten percent of what I was worth, I thought maybe I had a shred of job security even as the laboratory slowly imploded. Kind of funny how faulty my logic was, isn't it? Doesn't it make you want to laugh?"

She stumbled, and Mann held her up, and then more firmly as Gloria reeled backwards and laughed out loud, long and hard, and then abruptly stopped and looked over at Mann again. She opened her mouth and closed it again in dull perplexity.

They were walking in the opposite direction from the nearest transportation station, toward a small grove of trees in the darkness that defined the edge of the neighborhood. It felt as if they were crossing a barrier from one world to another.

"Boss, I'm telling you, she don't look so good."

"Maybe you should stay out of this."

"Hey, what's that? Here, doggie. Come here a second." Gloria reached out her hand, and nearly fell over before Mann steadied her.

The dog approached warily. "You don't smell so good either," it said.

"Isn't he the sweetest thing." Gloria touched the dog's head gently. "Yours?"

"Yes," Mann said. "He helped me find you."

"Stalker, I'll bet that's your name."

"It could be."

"Come here, Stalker. I'm either going to hug you or throw up on you."

Mann steered Gloria carefully past the dog to a bench overlooking a broad valley. Small, scattered lights shone up from the distant ground. When he looked up at the sky, the view was much the same.

"Can't we sit here for a minute?" he asked.

Gloria nodded blearily, and then shook the hair out of her eyes. She followed his gaze upward at the sky, at what to him were unfamiliar constellations, and therefore strangely fascinating.

For some reason, he was surprised that the simulation had provided this detail. Was it projecting simple dots of light into the sky, he wondered. Was it possible that every one of the hundred thousand or so dots was a detailed simulation of a fusion-driven inferno, and the computer was somehow tracking the details of each atomic interaction, down to the actual simulated photons of light that would have been sent thousands or millions of years ago to strike his simulated eyeballs and render this image?

He made a mental note to ask the engineers about this when he returned topside.

"What's that?" he said, pointing.

"Hecuba. It's brilliant tonight. Our nearest planet, 20 million miles closer to the sun."

"How many planets are there?"

"My estimate of your intelligence just went down."

"There are no stupid questions."

"You're testing the boundaries," Gloria remarked. "Every school-child knows that there are six planets: Dymas, Metope, Hecuba, Telecleia and the gas giants Xanthus and Xena."

"Why haven't we ever tried to explore them?" Mann said. "Surely, by now, the technology is there."

"It's a great question. There never seems to be enough money to send people anywhere but the moon, and the last time we did that was, what? Forty years ago? And now, with the war coming up, the government has other uses for its resources."

"I wonder what you'd find if you went there," Mann mused, half to himself. He wondering if the simulation would provide a realistic gas giant, down to the simulated molecular interactions in the atmosphere.

A meteorite streaked across the darkness between the stars. After a few minutes, there was another one.

"Did you ever wonder," Gloria said, "if there are creatures up there on a world orbiting one of those dots of light, who might be looking up into their sky, at our star, at this moment, and wondering exactly what I'm wondering now?"

Mann shook his head, and then realized that she wasn't looking at him.

"I'm very sure there aren't," he said.

"How can you be so sure?"

He tried to imagine the simulation tracking the evolution of life on myriad worlds in this galaxy and countless others, and knew with certainty that it would be far beyond the capacity of the computers he had seen in the laboratory. Suddenly, the thought made him sad, made him feel like an imposter next to this woman who believed in her own reality.

"I can't say," he said sincerely. "But I can tell you that the creatures on this little planet are alone in our own little universe, and there's nobody looking out at us from those stars."

"That seems so implausible, given the immensity of it all."

"Maybe it isn't as big as it seems. Are you starting to feel better?" Mann asked after a moment.

Gloria looked down at her hands clasped between her legs.

"No," she said ruefully. "And when my head clears, I'll have the same old life back again."

"Sometimes when one door closes, that means another one is opening," Mann said.

"It doesn't matter what the doors do. In a few months, we'll all be dead anyway."

"I guess that means you have three choices. You can give up and drink yourself to death. Or you can give in to the decadence and try to grab every forbidden pleasure you can wrap your exquisite body around. Or you can do what you love to do right up to the end, and hope that every second is not your last, and that you'll be able to keep hoping those things, by some miracle, to the end of a long, productive, happy life."

"Yeah, what do you know about it?"

"I have a hunch that the Great Powers are going to let this stand-off go on a little longer."

"Well, that's above my security clearance," Gloria said, looking back up at the sky.

"But not mine," Mann said quietly.

Another shooting star flashed across the sky. The wind stirred the leaves in the trees, and they could hear the now-distant sound of the conveyors moving into and out of a distant transportation station. The dog lay down on the grass with its eyes open, watching a bird that had landed on the grass.

Gloria shivered. "What do you know that I don't know?" she said quietly.

"More than you can guess. But right now, the thing I know that is relevant to you is that I've talked with the engineers at Applied Simulations. About you. They very much want to meet you."

"They want to meet ME?" Gloria sat up straight, startling the dog. "Why?"

"I told them you were ten times smarter than I am, and as nearly as I can tell, none of their current engineers is more than five times smarter than me."

"You're joking, right?"

"I'm not nearly that funny."

"They want to meet me," Gloria repeated. "Why?"

"They need somebody who is super smart in a whole lot of different areas to help them make sense out of all the things they've discovered. And as it happens, I need exactly the same thing."

"And they—and you—think I'm the right person for a job like that."

"I know you are, and they were smart enough to see the truth even faster than I did."

Gloria sat for a moment looking at the stars. She looked back at her hands, and then back at Mann. Suddenly, her gaze was considerably less bleary.

"Suppose I do this," she said. "What do *you* get out of it?"

"Other than helping a friend?"

"In what way are we friends?" Gloria demanded. "All we did was agree not to have sex with each other and never see each other again. Is that what you call friendship?"

"I didn't agree to either of those things."

Gloria stared into Mann's sober face, and then, unexpectedly, she laughed. "You want something from me. I just need to know what it is before I stand up and hug you and thank you and pray that you know enough more than I do that this is going to end well."

"I need somebody who understands what they're doing in there, who can work alongside them and help them, make them more efficient, make them better at what they do, who can organize all the things they're learning in a way that will make it understandable to an idiot like me, or maybe somebody who is more technical than I am, but not appreciably smarter."

"So you can sell the secrets to the highest bidder?"

"I would never show those secrets to anybody on this planet, ever."

"Is that a promise? Look at me when you make this promise. You aren't smart enough to lie to me looking me full in the face."

"I promise," Mann said. "Nothing you find out, nothing you come up with, will ever pass from my hands to another person on this planet, our side or the other side."

Gloria searched his face. Finally she stood up. "You've earned a hug," she said. "And if they like me enough to actually hire me, then maybe you've earned more than that."

11

*"The phenomena of physical appearance is
wholly illusion."*

Maha Prajna Paramita

"Boss, can you at least tell me where we're going?"

"I have a meeting in 20 minutes with a general and his staff," Mann said, scanning the signs along the ceiling of the station for the correct exit. Finally he turned to the right. After a minute, the crowd thinned out, and they turned down a long corridor that was practically empty.

"What's a general?"

"It's kind of like the president of a very large national company that is in the business of killing people for the good of the country. He's in charge of soldiers and guns and a lot of dangerous weapons that make guns look like the sticks you pick up in the woods."

The dog was silent for a long time. "Who do they kill?" it asked tentatively.

"Whoever they're told to, but usually people from other countries in formal battles that are arranged in advance."

"Any chance they'll decide to kill us?" the dog asked, keeping its voice as casual as possible.

"That's an interesting question. This particular general has lived in a state of purple rage against the company I represent for the better part of three years. That's why you're coming along. I need you to let me know if he's angry enough to kill me like they did the last person who held my position at the company."

"And how am I supposed to do that?"

"You can smell him. He'll reach a homicidal threshold, and then you can alert me—"

"Hey, an idea suddenly came to me," the dog said. "How about—follow my logic closely here—we don't go to this meeting at all, and then there will be no danger whatsoever."

"You animals live in such a simple world," Mann observed.

"I think we're the only ones that aren't insane," the dog countered. "What's the point of meeting with this general—"

"And staff."

"Staff?"

"A lot of other people who plan how to kill people for a living. I'm giving a presentation. I'm going to tell a roomful of military leaders exactly what they don't want to hear."

"I want to make sure I understand something before we go any farther," the dog said after a moment. "Am I right that pissing off people who specialize in killing might not be a wise course of action? Or am I missing something?"

"Oh, I think you're totally missing the big picture," Mann said easily.

"Which is?"

"Leverage."

"Leverage?"

"Somehow I have to move this entire world out of a well-grooved course that has tens of thousands of years and billions of people worth of momentum behind it. If I just stand in its way, it will flatten me and never notice. I have to create some kind of a lever, and it has to be a pretty big one, and it has to happen soon. Ergo, I have to get their attention in a big way."

"Being as how I didn't understand half of what you said, it sounds like the other half is clearly impossible."

"That," Mann said, "is why they brought me into the picture."

"They?"

"It's way too complicated to explain. Just roll with it, and trust me."

They exited the travel pod at a scenic grassy place where the myriad towers of the city were visible across the river, and walked along the barricaded sidewalk toward the entrance of a massive building that combined the worst features of a fortress and an office building. Two uniformed men regarded Mann with unfriendly eyes as he approached. One of them held a tablet that might have passed for advanced technology 100 years ago.

"You can stop there," the other said. "Give us your name and provide identification."

"It's all right," said the dog. "He's with me."

The officer with the clipboard took a long look at the dog, and under the withering stare, the dog edged back behind Mann's leg. "These military people have a terrific sense of humor," he muttered.

"You're supposed to be in room 1357 in 20 minutes," the first officer informed Mann. "There are two other security checkpoints before you can get that far into the building. I'd recommend you hurry. And leave the dog," he added.

"I'm not leaving the dog," Mann said.

"You heard him," the dog said. "He wants me to wait safely out here."

"You're coming with me."

"He can't come with you. There's nothing about him on the list."

"Well, that pretty much settles it, doesn't it?" said the dog.

"I guess we'll have to postpone the meeting," Mann shrugged, turning away.

"That was your plan all along, wasn't it?" the dog said, wagging its tail vigorously. "Let me say that I think that was truly brilliant. I—"

"You can't postpone the meeting," the two officers said simultaneously. The one with the clipboard continued: "Rumor is, half the senior staff made room on their schedules for your presentation."

Mann shrugged. "I just wish they had a better attitude about dogs. Or maybe they'll wish *you* did," he said pointedly.

One of the officers turned away and talked into a microphone at his collar. The conversation went on for more than a minute. Finally he turned back to Mann.

"The dog is welcome in the meeting," he said. "In fact, everybody is looking forward to meeting him."

"Great," the dog said without enthusiasm as they walked in through the door. "I guess this is my lucky day."

Room 1357 was in the heart of the building, past two different security desks and down a special elevator which Mann suspected was the only access to the level where they were holding the meeting, and which only accessed this room and adjacent living quarters some hundreds of feet below the main floor.

Everybody in the room wore a dress uniform, and Mann observed wryly that this fashion did not seem to change much from reality to reality; ribbons, medals, one, two, three or four golden geometric shapes (in this case many-pointed stars) on the hat and collar, all of them telling a story which could be read by everybody on the inside and incomprehensible to outsiders. He looked around at faces, and finally recognized the general near the back, the oldest face in the room, set in granite with the muscles of the jaw twitching visibly.

"We expected you here minutes ago," a younger officer with a mere single star on his collar was whispering as Mann set the cube in his pocket on the table. "Do you mind if we skip the introductions and get right into it?" he added, with a doubtful look at the dog.

"Hey, I don't like it any better than you do," the dog responded.

"Don't worry; he's housebroken," Mann said as the officers began taking their seats.

The presentation was not complicated. Mann thanked everyone for taking the time to meet with him, and promised that they would be impressed by the remarkable technological breakthrough that he was here to present to them.

"This represents years of the best thinking on the planet, and the capabilities it offers are decades, at the very least, ahead of anything the Eastern Alliance is capable of developing," he added.

The general's face relaxed a bit, and the others leaned forward with visible eagerness as Mann touched the black cube on the table. Instantly, an image rose up above the table, a representation of the world. In a moment, a dozen tiny silver satellites rose up to the sky from the general vicinity of Aurora and took positions equidistant across the sky.

"The device you're about to see represents a virtually foolproof integrated system which protects cities from any conceivable form of military attack," Mann continued. He touched the cube again, and a missile rose into the sky from the side of the world where the Eastern Alliance was located.

"As you can see, the satellites instantly evaluate any object that takes to the air, calculating its trajectory and velocity, determines if it is controlled and capable of changing course, all within moments of the launch. This in itself represents a significant upgrade over our existing warning systems.

"But of course there's more—much more. Watch as the satellites decide that this is an incoming missile."

In the image floating above the table, the military officials saw what appeared to be a small segment of a sphere, with grid-lines, appear in front of the missile, blocking its path. "The satellites have activated a compressed force field which is magnetic in nature. You will have the specifications and mathematics shortly, but the shorthand way to think of it is, just as a laser is intensely compressed and focused light, this is intensely compressed and focused magnetism, only perhaps orders of magnitude stronger than what your imagination is conjuring up."

The missile reached the patch of white gridlines and was deflected upwards as if it had made an oblique collision with a curved surface.

"There are several things to notice here," Mann continued. "First, the missile will be deflected up into space, where it can be detonated with relatively less harm, or captured, or, again using the focused magnetic forces, hurled further away from the planet. Notice also that the overall system is not interfering with the normal movements of civilian aircraft. If there is a massive attack, the field, which is generated from inside the satellites, can be formed in a giant dome around the entire metropolitan area—or, with a significantly greater expenditure, around the entire country and its territories."

Domes of whitish gridlines appeared above selected cities around the country, and then were replaced by a much larger one that extended out into the ocean. Then the image faded, and Mann had their attention focused on him again.

"Our engineers are also working on a miniaturized version which we believe, within two years, will be worn by peacekeeping personnel in war zones, essentially rendering military hardware ineffective against them."

Mann looked around the room. Everyone was staring at him.

"With this remarkable innovation, weapons as we understand them today would be obsolete," Mann added. "If every country in the world were to install these, warfare and all the attendant destruction of life and property would instantly become a thing of the past."

A hard-faced officer with three stars on his collar leaned forward and took a long breath of air. "Let me understand that last part," he said evenly. "You intend to give this technology to our enemies?"

"I don't intend to," Mann said. "But building these complex instruments is going to require many thousands of skilled technicians, not to mention the factories that would have to be retooled to fabricate the component parts. I doubt if even your elaborate security precautions could prevent some weak link in this very long chain from leaking the design specifications to the very capable members of your enemy's intelligence. And of course," Mann added, "once word gets out that you can protect citizens from warfare, all of your allies are going to clamor for their own devices—and why wouldn't they? Of course, their security precautions might not be quite as rigorous as yours."

"Then why should we be interested in this at all, if you don't foresee it providing any military advantage?"

Mann took a long look around the room, memorizing faces.

"Is there anyone here," he said, his voice resonating softly in the silence that suddenly seemed to thicken the air, "who sees the value of protecting not just our citizens, but every living person, and every living creature, forever from this moment, from the ravages of future warfare?"

He waited. There was a stir around the room, everybody looking at each other. The silence continued uncomfortably.

Finally, the aging general spoke up, the stars gleaming at his collar.

"I think you have your answer," he said. "I, for one, am extremely disappointed in your, ah, let's politely call them research efforts, if this is all you have to show us. IS it all you have?"

Mann nodded. "It is."

The general stood up and slowly walked around the table with his back to Mann. When he turned, his face seemed to be deep in the most intense contemplation. Slowly, he walked around the table until he was standing directly behind Mann, who turned as he approached, and would have stood up, but the general's bulky body encroached on his space and forbade it with his presence.

He gazed down at Mann, his face still impassive. Then, gradually, his face reflected the anger that Mann had sensed in him from the moment he walked in the room.

"Understand this," he said. "I don't care a rat's ass for protecting the people of the world, or even the people of this country.

Whatever they think about us—" he waved his hand in a vague gesture, his voice rising to a roar—"out there, we're first and foremost
and fundamentally human instruments of warfare. Our mission,
our job, the thing that history will judge us on is whether our society prevails over their society, and for that matter over all the other
societies on earth."

And then the general's voice dropped to a whisper. "The dream
I have, that all of us in this room have, is that we'll be remembered
as the individuals who made that happen on our watch, in our
lifetime."

"But the cost in blood, and pain—" Mann said.

"Every citizen who lives today is a replaceable part of an organism that will grow back in due time," the general said. He leaned
deeper, so that his weight rested on Mann as he looked down at him
with contempt. "You bring us something that will give me a reason
to go upstairs and convince a group of cowards, elected by cowards,
that we have a real chance of winning a preemptive war without
pain, something that, when we finally sort out all the surprises from
the other side that we don't know about, will let us finally and forever destroy their nation and their way of life no matter what the cost.

"Understand that that's an order," the general said. "If you fail,
then you will be executed as a traitor and the world will be an incrementally better place than it was before. Am I making myself
clear?" he said, regarding Mann from above.

For once, the dog didn't say anything. Mann looked around the
table, but the faces were impassive. He looked back at the general.

"I think you expressed what you think and how you feel with
amazing precision," he said at last. "If words were weapons, I have
no doubt you would be invincible."

The general continued to stare at Mann for long seconds, and
then, abruptly, he smiled.

"We understand each other perfectly," he said. "You can leave
now, but I want you to come back in two weeks, less time if you have
something in your pocket. If you don't," he said lightly, "then I'll

send someone to bring you here, and I guarantee that you won't enjoy the experience."

"Boss, you totally laid an egg on that one," the dog said as they walked out.

"Actually it was a test. Tell me: when I asked that last question, were you able to sense which of the officers did not want to kill me?"

"I could smell your death."

"Yes, I know that. But if that cube I lay on the table took a video of everything we did and everybody in the room, do you think you could identify the people who would have liked to speak up and say that they saw the value of my device?"

The dog thought for a second. "Sure," he said finally. "There were three of them, and they smelled very uncomfortable. It was like they were hoping somebody else would speak so they wouldn't have to."

"And how did they feel when the general spoke up?"

"What am I, a mind-reader? All I can tell you is there was a lot of discomfort."

"Maybe disapproval?"

"Maybe. But they're also scared to death of that general."

"Maybe," Mann said, "they won't have to worry about him for much longer."

12

"I have seen all the things that are done under the sun, and all of them are meaningless, a chasing after the wind."

Ecclesiastes 1:14

"So how are you liking your job so far?" Mann asked.

They were walking along the edge of a tree-lined park half a mile from the office, with the dog up ahead sniffing the interface between the grass and the sidewalk with intense interest. Gloria skipped along in a halter top and shorts, her face so radiantly happy that Mann experienced happiness as a contact high. He kept stealing glances at her face.

Around them, the towers of downtown Aurora gleamed in the sunlight, and Mann thought he could see movements along the ramps, like ants collecting food for their nest. For some reason, the sight disturbed him.

"You can't imagine how incredible it is," Gloria said, her eyes shining. "The things they've learned! It's going to take decades to sort it all out."

"I've seen you a few times from a distance, always surrounded by five or six of the engineers, sometimes with equations floating in the air around your heads."

"It's like heaven, only better. When I get to heaven, I'll be disappointed with the quality of their research staff. How's your work?"

"I get briefed every few days, and I've been in on three rather testy outside meetings so far. It's pretty technical work, and I'm afraid you wouldn't understand a lot of it if I tried to go into detail."

"The people there are SO smart. I talked with Dr. X the other day about the magnetic field that keeps appearing and disappearing around the new plasma fusion generators, and didn't know why it was there sometimes and not always, and he just absolutely blew me away with knowing the right questions to ask."

"Speaking of which," Mann said, "do you have any idea where they disappear to for most of the day?"

"They have their own laboratory in the basement," Gloria said. "That's where most of the new stuff comes out of. I asked one of the engineers if I could go down there, and he laughed at me. He said that NOBODY goes down there, but if they decide to open it up, I'd probably be the first."

"But you really don't know what they do down there?"

"They must be working day and night, based on the brilliant cascade of stuff they're hauling up for us to look at. We're not talking about theories or ideas. They're presenting us with entire finished technologies."

"I've seen them." Mann followed her along the sidewalk, allowing himself to enjoy the profound change in Gloria's emotional energy, so different from the lifeless expression she wore when he found her—was it already six weeks ago? Once again, he felt the odd twisting inside that only seemed to come when he was in her presence. He tried pushing it away, but the sensation persisted at a deeper level than his conscious will could reach.

It was like a craving, which was the last thing he needed in this alien world with so many challenges still ahead of him.

Kiss her, a small chorus inside the Synchronicity jeered at him. He pushed them aside impatiently, and then, after a moment, realized that some of them were still looking at Gloria through his eyes with simultaneous approval and lust.

"So you're enjoying your work," he said.

"Are you kidding? Every day I stumble across some incredibly profound new insight into the nature of the cosmos, subtle manipulations of energy, the interplay of so many different disciplines into new and unexpected technologies—and you know what I like best about it? I don't smell worse than a colony of stink bugs when I get off work."

They turned at the end of the park, keeping it to the left of them. Ahead, a rolling field of well-manicured grass became, less than half a mile ahead, a riot of flowers surrounding the near side of a small lake, incongruously framed by a wall of tall buildings with the bubble towers piercing the sky behind them. Mann tried to imagine how it would feel like if all this was lost, and then forced himself to remember that none of it was real anyway.

Nevertheless, he said: "Have you ever thought about what would happen if the military got hold of all these new technologies? The situation is pretty tense as it is."

"Try not to think about it. I've heard that Drs. X and Y have been sending their most expendable employee over to talk to the generals, and generally stall them and keep them guessing—or at least prevent anything dangerous from falling into their hands, which of course is the opposite of what those military bastards want and expect. The other engineers told me yesterday that somebody named Max used to be the fall guy, but he was assassinated."

"I guess that means Drs. X and Y still think there's hope for this world," Mann said. "Have you ever asked them directly?"

"Every time I talk to Drs. X and Y, they get all goofy on me."

"Goofy?"

"They wink and nod at each other and say how really wonderful it is to have me here, and they hope I am working closely with you, which is strange in its own right because you aren't exactly the kind of person I would worry about making an amazing breakthrough in physics. Not that I'm saying you're stupid," she added quickly.

"Of course not."

"But in our particular workplace, you have to admit, from an intelligence standpoint, you're like some kind of lower life form."

"You don't have to hold back just because you're afraid of hurting my feelings."

"The last time I talked to them," Gloria continued, "Dr. X put his hand on my shoulder in the most tender, fatherly possible way, as if he was feeling sorry for me even though he must have been able to see that I'm living my fantasies—thanks to you, by the way, and don't think I'm not incredibly grateful—and he said to me very seriously that nothing they do is intended to be used in this world anyway."

Mann stopped walking. "He said that?"

"I thought it was because of the impending war. But it isn't that. I'm beginning to think it's something else that they stumbled on, which they seem to think is bigger than the war, if you can imagine that. They've put an unimaginable amount of energy into whatever this new thing is."

Mann closed his eyes for a long moment. "As soon as you find out what that is, you let me know," he said carefully. "Do you understand?"

He stopped and looked Gloria full in the face. "It's tremendously important," he said. "Can you understand that?"

"No," Gloria said. "Really, I can't. Why is this such a big deal to you? Are you some kind of spy or something?"

They were stopped in the middle of the sidewalk, which forced hundreds of people to push past them impatiently. Gloria turned to Mann very deliberately.

"Tell me you aren't working for the Other Side," she said, staring intently into his face. "And don't tell me to check your credentials, or some other non-answer. Just tell me the truth, and let me see it in your eyes."

"I am not in any way working for the Other Side," Mann said, and locked stares with her. "You can trust me," he added, "with your life."

The mutual gaze lasted for a second, and then another. After a moment, Gloria's face softened, and she looked down at her feet.

"Okay; I guess I can believe you," she said.

"You *guess?*"

"I also realized all over again that I find you strangely attractive. I was hoping that would wear off."

"We could have dinner," Mann suggested. "That will give it more time to wear off."

"I don't think that would be a good idea," said a voice behind them.

Mann looked up, startled, as Forbes locked arms with Gloria from behind. He held her hands behind her, bent his head over her shoulder and they kissed briefly.

Gloria looked up at Mann, her face radiant with happiness. "That was the other good news I was going to tell you," she said. "I told Drs. X and Y that they needed to hire Forbes, because he was my supervisor at the other facility. And it finally happened! Today is his first day."

"We're having lunch to celebrate," Forbes said, turning back to Gloria. Mann noticed that his face always seemed to be tilted upwards at whoever he was talking to, which made it look as if he was looking down at everyone from a much greater elevation. "We'd invite you along," Forbes added with a smile aimed at Gloria, "but I'm afraid it might become embarrassingly romantic."

Gloria favored him with an enchanting smile. "That makes you afraid?" she teased.

"I think 'terrified' is a more appropriate word."

"Yes, well, I probably need to be going," said Mann. "I have, you know, a lot to do."

"So I hear," said Forbes. "I suppose I should either congratulate you or offer condolences."

"Why?" said Gloria.

"He's our new liaison with the military. From what I hear, that means he failed the IQ test."

"WHAT!" Gloria seemed to forget about Forbes as she turned to Mann. "Is that true?"

"I was going to tell you. Isn't it exciting?"

"Why didn't you tell them you weren't interested? What were you *thinking*?"

"It's actually the job I wanted all along," said Mann. "Dr. Y said that keeping the military at bay was best handled by somebody who was 'natively fluent in the language of intrigue'—were his exact words. As I was walking away, I found myself wondering, how does he know?"

"Know what?"

"What I'm natively fluent in. We've hardly ever talked."

"You're not afraid of being killed?"

"No. If they killed me, I'd be back in a week anyway."

Gloria smiled. "And how, exactly, would you manage that trick?"

"Rapid reincarnation," Mann said.

By now, they were on a walkway in the deep shadow of some of the tallest buildings along the outskirts of the city. It was more crowded here, and along the street there were street musicians playing what Mann still thought of as exotic instruments. Forbes and Gloria took each others' hands and stopped, and Forbes looked at Mann expectantly. Somebody thrust a leaflet into Mann's hand as the walkway carried them upwards.

Mann glanced at it briefly, and then more closely. Then, looking up, Mann said, his voice a little frantic: "Look, I have to go— like, right now."

"I thought you'd never get the hint," Forbes said, but Mann was already pushing backwards into the flow of people, barely gaining on the ramp as he ran against the traffic with Gloria's eyes on him until he was out of sight.

Finally, panting, he leaped down from the walkway and put his hand roughly on the shoulder of the young person who was having a hard time getting anybody to take his leaflets.

"You want me to bite his leg?" his dog inquired, gasping for air.

"Let me handle this."

"You're the boss. I'll make sure blondie is okay."

"Who is this Eternal One?" Mann demanded, holding the leaflet in front of the young person's face.

The other tried and failed to shake free. He had faced so much rejection already today that he suspected Mann of mocking or abusing him.

"Tell me," Mann persisted.

"He is the One who brings wisdom," the young man said finally, in a defiant voice.

"What the hell does that mean?"

"They say He has eternal life, that He is today as He was a thousand or ten thousand years ago."

Mann looked at the pamphlet. "It says there's a meeting tomorrow," he said. "But it doesn't say where."

"That is intentional. The Lord God will direct those who should be there." The young man tried to turn, but Mann spun him back around.

"The Lord God is using you as an instrument to communicate with me exactly where I can find the Eternal One without any more evasion and in as few clear words as necessary," Mann said. "And He is also using me as a judge to determine whether you're a willing instrument or one who must be purged from this plane of existence."

"Are you threatening me?"

"Just give me the location, and I'll leave you alone and you'll be back safely in God's good graces."

"It will be down the street tomorrow at noon," the young man said finally, in a sulky voice. "Wherever He decides to address the masses, which will likely," he added testily, "be down there in the park, which is where He was last Tuesday."

Mann took his hand off of the boy's shirt and turned away as Gloria and Forbes ran up, breathless.

"What's wrong?"

"Nothing," Mann said.

"That's exactly what I told her," Forbes said impatiently.

Gloria ignored him. "Yes, I could see that from the way you were knocking people down trying to get off the ramp. Did anybody ever tell you that you're not a very good liar? Other than me, like, twenty times?"

Mann held up the leaflet. "I'm interested in this holy man, who-ever he is. That's all."

Gloria snatched the leaflet out of Mann's hand and led them back toward the ramp. She looked up blankly.

"I don't get it. He's just another prophet predicting the end of the world, which I have to tell you is not a very difficult forecast to make these days. What makes him different from a million others?"

Mann sighed. "His father is named Ronald Reagan," he said. "His mother is named Marilyn Monroe. He was born in a place called Chicago."

"So? His parents have strange names. He's not from around here. What does that have to do with the rest of the message?"

"I just think he and I might, just possibly, have something in common," Mann continued. "I've been looking for somebody like him ever since I got here."

He looked up, and it was obvious that Gloria wasn't convinced. But she could also, somehow, see that he wasn't lying.

"Weren't we going to get something to eat?" Forbes said.

"Yes," said the dog before anybody could answer.

13

*"All matter actually works from information,
not merely matter."*

Nobel Laureate David Bohm

"Hey, you know about women, don't you?" Maila said when Mann arrived at the refrigerator.

"I'm the world's living expert," Mann said.

"See? Already you've demolished my confidence in you. But I need your help."

"Okay."

"See, there's this incredibly hot vixen babe goddess who's new here, she just started work, and I think she's the one. I really think she's the mother of my children."

"What's her name?" Mann asked absently, scrolling through the images in the air.

"I don't know yet. I've kind of been stalking her."

"Maybe you should, you know, talk to her. Find out what she's like."

"I need to raise my hotness index first," Maila replied. "I'm wondering, do you think it makes me more sexually irresistable if I combed my hair over to the other side? Like this?" he said, grabbing tufts of hair and dragging them raggedly from one side of his head to the other.

Mann looked over Maila's ovoid body, the quiver of his belly whenever he moved, the doughy complexion of his face, the short stumpy legs that barely touched the floor as he sat in the chair. He looked at the shirt with food stains that could almost be mistaken for a pattern.

"You know, it kind of does make you look hot," he said reflectively.

"I was thinking that I need to stop just talking to women when they walk by, and actually start asking them if they'd be willing to breed with me," Maila said. "I'm starting to get that sense of urgency to start a family, and maybe see what sex is like while I'm at it."

"The trouble is that women are pretty shallow," Mann said. "Have you considered going through one of those body enhancement surgeries?"

"I actually thought about getting a tattoo or two,"

"Like an eagle or a—"

"My first thought was a nice bar chart, or maybe a graph of some complicated third-order function. But then I decided that it wouldn't be the real me," Maila said with a note of finality in his voice. "What kind of a life is it when you don't even recognize yourself in the mirror? Besides, I'm kind of worried about where our species is going."

"You mean the war?"

"I mean, look at us. Not just me, but the other engineers here. We're all somewhere in the top one thousandth of one percent of the smartest people in the world, and we can't even get a woman to smile at us, much less jump into bed and have our babies."

"And that means the species has a problem?"

"If the smartest men can't have babies, then where does that take the genetic evolution of the human race? I mean, if I can see something that is clearly not beneficial for the future intelligence of the human race, right here in the office on a daily basis, don't you think that it should be pretty obvious to just about everybody that we've been heading down the wrong genetic road?"

"It's probably been going on a long time," said Mann.

"That would explain why the world is so screwed up right now," Maila agreed. Then he brightened. "Hey, you know what? This could be the perfect pickup line! I could ask this incredibly hot new woman engineer if she's concerned about the way the world is going, and of course she's going to say yes. And then I could lay out the genetic dynamics that led us to this difficult place, maybe with a couple of charts and graphs that I could prepare that would trace shifts in the human genome—how long do you think I should go back? I think we still have data from 130 years ago, when the first genomes were collected."

"Do you think that's enough generations to get meaningful results?" Mann asked.

"Maybe not." Maila's face fell, and then brightened again as he turned back to the screen on the desk. "But I think I could extrapolate beyond that a few hundred years—"

"Your hair fell back to the other side of your head again," Mann pointed out.

Maila looked up blankly, and then touched his head. "Yeah, it's probably going to take me a month to train it right," he said, dragging the hair back over to the other side. "But now that I have this pickup line, maybe that won't be quite so important."

14

"All your senses are like clouds; all they show
is an endless mirage."

Avadhuta Gita

"I'm sorry I'm late," the guest said, shaking Mann's hand as he took his seat. He had the most nondescript face Mann had ever seen, brown hair pulled over the balding forehead as if he'd combed it with his hands, a dozen individual creases at the corner of each eye, which rested in a comfortable squint as if he thought everything around him bore a second examination. It was a pleasant face that looked around the restaurant out of the corners of his deep-set eyes before looking back down at the table with an expression that fell just short of a smile.

"Do you mind if I sit in your chair?" he said. "I prefer to face the wall."

"I don't mind," Mann said.

The man leaned back. "Should we order wine? I'm on an expense account."

"First," said Mann, "I'm a little curious about our agenda. I wasn't told much except that it was important that we get together."

"Who told you that?"

"An aide to a very prominent member of Congress. I'm afraid he was a bit vague on the details."

"I imagine he was," said the man as he browsed the wine list. He looked up, and the waiter appeared at his side. He pointed to the list, and the waiter nodded.

"So—" Mann said.

"You must be an exceptionally busy person, to insist on getting to the point so quickly," the man said. He leaned across the table. "Please, tell me about yourself."

Mann studied the other carefully. His eyes and the other's met and locked for several seconds, and then the waiter arrived with the bottle. He displayed it with evident pride, and Mann's companion seemed to share his enthusiasm. When he took a sip, his eyes closed and he allowed himself a long second of deep satisfaction.

"Excellent," he said finally. When the wine was poured, he raised his glass. "To the moments between the nasty pressures of constant labor, when we can squeeze in a bit of enjoyment around the margins."

Their glasses touched.

"I used to think I did very important things," Mann said after a few minutes. "That, at least, is what I was told when I was sent out on assignment, and what they said when I came back to debrief how we had been successful. But now I'm beginning to believe that my life has been spent collecting stories from odd corners of the world, and all the things I thought were the reason I existed might actually have been incidental."

"That's an interesting observation," the other said. He took another appreciative sip of the wine. "It's excellent, don't you think?"

"Wonderful."

"These stories, what do they tell you?"

"The best are ambiguous. They can mean a lot of different things, and the listener is invited to consider things in a way that he might not have before."

"You seem to me to be a perceptive person," the other said. "Perhaps you could tell me a story that is germane to this particular meeting."

Mann sat back and studied his companion, long enough to recognize him, or at least his type, and the type of work people of his type tended to gravitate to. Until that moment, he had not been sure.

"The people who live in villages along the edge of the Caucasus mountains, which is an excellent poppy-growing region, like to tell the story of a man who had a very difficult wife," Mann said. "Eventually, over the years, his unhappiness grew to such a degree that he summoned the devil himself."

"I don't suppose the story tells us how he did that."

"It's a bit light on that detail," Mann admitted. "But the devil doesn't disappoint. He arrives in the husband's living room, and invites the man to make a request, which will be granted in return for the trifling sum of the man's immortal soul."

"And the devil, of course, is delighted with the proposal to kill his wife," the other interjected, to Mann's mild annoyance.

"Actually, the way the story goes," Mann continued, "the devil is quite irritated with the banality of such a request. In most versions, the story includes a speech which articulates how appalled he is at the lack of imagination of people in the modern world, about his diminished expectations of our troubled species, how in better days he was required to provide kingdoms and mountains of gold and supernatural powers as the price of an immortal and supremely precious soul, whereas now—well, anyway," Mann continued, seeing that his host's attention was flagging, "throughout this conversation, the wife is screaming from the kitchen, and the husband is answering meekly, and growing more and more desperate. In the end, the inevitable agreement is reached, and the wife drops dead in mid-scream, and a handful of minutes later the village constable determines that she died of natural causes."

"End of story?" the other asked with a smile of amusement which gave Mann an additional degree of certainty about his agenda.

"Hardly. That evening, the widower is out celebrating his good fortune, and as the night goes on, he drinks perhaps a bit more than is wise of the local beverage, and walks into the street right as a carriage is rushing by—or, in the more modern versions, a motorized vehicle—and in either case, he suddenly finds himself in the waiting room of hell, facing a minor bureaucrat with cloven hoofs and a forked tail, who is examining his entry papers into the afterlife."

"No doubt feeling cheated," the other said.

"He demands a review of his contract with the devil, and the bureaucrat is looking it over, and finally says that there was no provision that guaranteed the signee a long life to enjoy the absence of his wife.

"And as the story goes, the man is looking around curiously, and finally he says, you know, I thought there would be flames and brimstone and, well, a lot of other terrible things here in hell. The bureaucrat smiles a weary smile and replies that there are many misconceptions about hell, and that the popular expectations tend to lack subtlety. Then he opens up a book which is the book of punishments, and tells the man that he has been assigned housing for all eternity, and gives him the address and directions to get there."

"That's it?" Mann's companion said, finishing his glass of wine and reaching for the bottle.

"Almost," said Mann. "The punchline is that as the widower is walking out of the room, the bureaucrat tells him: by the way, your wife has been expecting you."

Mann's companion didn't laugh, or smile, but he did nod appreciatively and hold up his glass in the air in mock salute.

"I found two things interesting about the story," he said, taking a long sip from his refilled glass. "First, that it involves death, which confirms to me that you are an unusually perceptive person. Often, I find myself walking out the door with my—I call them clients, and they still don't have any idea why we have gotten together."

Mann pushed the menu aside. "And the other interesting thing?"

"If this story in any way relates to us, then you are the devil, and I am the victim, since I'm the one who summoned you for my own purposes. You might imagine that I see it somewhat the other way around."

"Is this your full-time job?" Mann asked. "I don't mean to pry into your business, you understand, but I was wondering if this was just something you happen to do on the side."

"It pays the bills," the other said. "And I've learned over the years, to my surprise, that the world is like a garden, and some people are weeds, and others are flowers, and a little pruning actually makes the world function more smoothly, and exist more beautifully. I'm always surprised, in the end, at the wisdom of the people who hire me, that they always, inevitably seem to know the difference between a flower and a weed."

"I have, in the past, had to make that distinction myself, actually many times," Mann said, browsing the menu. He looked up. "I must tell you, looking back, I have no such complacency that the correct decisions were made. I started to view myself as a monster who took into my hands things that were much better left to much higher powers than the people who paid my salary."

"Hence the moral of the tale you told me."

"Perhaps it is, yes. It is certainly something I've thought about many times."

"Your story would not have troubled me," the other said. "I'm actually a very nice person. I'm kind to children, I attend church every Sunday and the woman I'm currently dating has said that our relationship has been like a breath of fresh air."

"And perhaps because you've been so gracious, and shared your love of wine, you expect me to walk outside with you where there will be no witnesses."

"Actually, it would not trouble me to do it here, except that I generally prefer not to risk hurting anyone else. A stray bullet seldom kills, but it can cause damage nonetheless." He leaned forward, and spoke more softly. "And if I'm not mistaken, you're the kind of person who would be concerned about such things yourself. You would see the inevitability of our... *arrangement*, and not want to add to the mess."

"What if you were wrong? An entire restaurant would see the act."

"I would leave quickly with my face covered. You'd be astonished how differently all these people would describe me during the inevitable investigation. It would be impossible to identify me after the fact."

"The waiter has seen you clearly."

"The waiter is one of us."

Mann sat back. "Us?" he said finally. "If I walk out with you, at least I should know who regards me as a weed."

The other took another sip of his wine. "I'm curious about you as well," he said. "Perhaps we could exchange information."

"Whatever you tell me, I'll very quickly take to my grave," said Mann. "Whatever I tell you might or might not be useful in your next assignment."

The other spread his hands open and regarded Mann with an ironic smile. "What could be more fair?"

"The only information I care about is who do I have to thank for this very special wine and the interesting person who comes with it?"

The other leaned forward and toyed with his glass. "You must realize that I am never told the name of my employer. Surely you already knew that."

"Of course. But you must realize that I have so few... *passionate* acquaintances, and I might recognize one from the other with a few reasonable clues."

The other nodded slowly. He leaned back in his chair and studied the color of the wine carefully. "Apparently, you have been making it difficult for some elected officials to conduct foreign policy the way they feel is right and necessary," the other said. "If you don't mind my saying so, you don't seem to me to be the kind of person who could have a dangerous influence on our country's foreign affairs. To my eye, you seem rather ordinary."

"Maybe they made a mistake."

"There has been no mistake," the other said.

"Perhaps this time, they mistook a flower for a weed."

"They have an excellent track record of being right."

"But what if, in just one instance, they were wrong?" Mann persisted. "They take such a thing in their hands, or put it in your hands, with an understanding with the gods that their judgment will be correct. And then they make a mistake, and the gods notice instantly, and decide that these people can no longer be trusted with such a grave responsibility as life or death."

"Are you bargaining for your life?" the other asked with a delighted smile. "Or are you trying to draw another lesson from your little tale from mountains—which, I happen to know, don't actually exist?"

Mann put aside the menu. "I've lost my appetite, and also my patience with this conversation," he said.

"Can we at least finish the wine?"

"No," Mann said, standing up. "I'm going to walk outside. I'm expecting you to accompany me."

The other looked at his half-full glass, and at the bottle, regretfully. "Cruel revenge," he commented.

They walked together to the door. Nobody looked up. Mann opened the door for his guest, and the other passed through with a nod of appreciation.

"Here?" Mann said as they stood on the corner.

"This is better than inside, of course. But still there are people around. Perhaps if you would accompany me to somewhere a bit more private?"

A dog appeared under their feet, and Mann's companion scratched its head gently. "You see, I really am a nice person."

Another dog ambled over to receive its own gentle touch.

"Lead the way," Mann said. "You probably know this area better than I do."

The dogs followed them. At the corner, there were more dogs, and as they reached a narrow, dimly-lit space between the buildings, they could see a number of eyes shining back at them.

As they entered the darkness, Mann's companion reached under his coat.

There was a low chorus of growls, and his hand stopped. A pack of dogs stepped out of the shadows. One of them, a huge animal with short black fur and a curly tail, moved ahead of the others.

The man's hand moved, and instantly there was more growling on all sides of him.

"What's wrong with them?" the man said.

"They're hungry," said Mann. "Right?"

"Right," the lead dog said, the sound coming from deep in his throat. "Right?" he said over his shoulder.

Many versions of the word emerged from various throats on all sides.

The assassin licked his lips. "Somebody should feed them," he said.

"Actually, I promised to feed them tonight," Mann said.

"Feed them what?"

"A weed," Mann said, and turned away, stepping through the dogs that were rushing past him.

The screams had died out by the time he reached the corner.

15

*"If Nirvana is strictly in the nature of ordinary existence,
it would be of the created realm. But no ordinary existence
of the uncreated realm ever exists anywhere at all."*

Nagarjuna, cofounder of the Madhyamaka school
of Mahayana Buddhism

A few dozen people waited restlessly in the park, while thousands passed by on the streets on all sides, paying no attention to the figure who slowly made His way toward the flowered area in the center of a small entourage. A few of the people in the park walked up to the Eternal One, and He touched them gently and murmured a benediction. Mann lurked in the back, where most of the others also held themselves apart.

By the time the Eternal One had reached the near corner of the park, a crowd of 50-60 people had assembled, and His voice, when He allowed it to carry, would reach hundreds more who sat on the grass enjoying the weather, eating or kicking a ball around among them. Mann noted that the holy man moved with an economy of effort that suggested laziness, and he watched the blazing, contemptuous glow of His eyes thoughtfully.

There was no introduction, no preamble. The Eternal One began speaking, at first in a low voice that drew the crowd closer, and also demonstrated which of the bystanders were also listening, because they, too, moved nearer where the speaker was standing, even though they continued sitting, eating, kicking.

"It's okay to do your number one along the sidewalk and near the trees," his dog said, looking around. "But in a place like this, they get really excited if you decide to do a number two."

"I'll try to remember that," said Mann.

"I told you I know this town."

"Now hush. I want to hear what he's saying."

"I have searched this world for the truth that satisfies the inner cravings for meaning and purpose that every one of us feels each day," the Eternal One was saying, His voice carried faintly on the breeze. "I saw that over the many centuries before, many thousands of scribblers and scribes have searched every possible combination of words. I saw that some of them had no courage at all to say what was plain and uncomplicated and concrete, as if they were dancing with shadows. And I saw that some had far too much courage, and these people spoke plainly about elusive things that live in the ambiguities between form and substance, as if they were trying to use addition and subtraction to describe conclusions that can only be defined with calculus.

"And I saw that what they wrote had a wonderful truth in it, for they were earnest and wise, and they, all of them, possessed the faculties of reason and imagination as gifts from the Almighty. And I saw that what they wrote was filled with falsehoods and misunderstandings, for they are mortal and fall incomparably short of the Awareness of the Almighty.

"I saw that the hearts of men and women are inconstant, and speak in a whisper that if a thing is desired or not desired, that the thing should be possessed or pushed away, whether or not it is from the Almighty or the Evil One. And I saw that at the doorway of death, where we all stand today, there is a great longing for the pleasures of the flesh and a contempt for the boundaries of decency and mutual respect which hold us together as a society and protect us from the worst consequences of our own imperfect nature. Everywhere, I saw the desire to squeeze into the few hours and days left to us as much sin as we are allotted in a long lifetime, as if that is the proper measure of a life well lived.

"I looked at the sky, and saw the stars, and beyond the stars an endlessness which is beyond comprehension. I saw that my gaze traveled faster than light, and when I looked into the spaces between the light, I knew that I was looking into the hidden face of the Almighty, and our gazes locked, and I trembled before the infinite, and knew that I had found the cure for my inner cravings.

"My children, I did not aspire to become what I saw that night, for I knew that to the Almighty, I and this planet and this star system and this galaxy of star systems are all together tinier than a mote of dust floating in a sunbeam. But I knew that I was watched, and evaluated, and I feel that gaze now and I will feel it every moment of my life, from now until the Almighty and I are joined at last when I am called from this world to places beyond.

"Everything we call 'reality' is an illusion. We live in the imagination of the gods. Everything is impermanent; the flux is the only reality. There is one truth, and one truth only."

Believing
is the
reason
for
being.

"If you can master those simple words, then everything else, everything that is possible in this reality, falls into place for you.

"Everything you do ripples outward into this existence, impacting others, whose responses ripple out in a chain reaction that can either bring about terrible disharmony or soothing quietude, pain or contentment. What you spread is your choice; what you accept and respond to from others is your choice.

"If you're saying, why is my life this terrible way, if you are experiencing dissatisfaction with the Almighty, then you are removing precious energy from the system that is our interlocking lives. Then you are sucking the vitality out of the people around you, your family and friends, your co-workers, out of the fabric of the universe itself. As you sow disharmony, failure and frustration into this reality, not only will you harvest your share of it, you will help create a world where others will too, which will cause them, like a chain reaction, to send out their own negative energy, spreading disharmony in long ripples out to the edges of this reality and back again."

> *Believing*
> *is the*
> *reason*
> *for*
> *being.*

"My children, if you can muster the faith to believe that this can be a marvelous world of opportunity, and that your life can be happy and fulfilling, and if you can project out that faith, then the harvest will be quietude, contentment, fulfillment. As your positive ripple spreads out to those around you, and into the fabric of this reality, your environment is slowly, incrementally transformed into the paradise on earth whose possibility you must believe in in order to achieve the blessings that the Almighty's gift of life has to offer you."

> *Believing*
> *is the*
> *reason*
> *for*
> *being.*

"Cultivate wisdom and understanding. Learn to avoid suffering. We suffer because we did not get what we wanted, but the cause of the suffering was not the not getting, but the wanting, which is completely under your control.

"Be kind to one another. Be mindful of your life. If you savor every moment, then you will experience an eternal life.

> *Believing*
> *is the*
> *reason*
> *for*
> *being.*

"Embrace the power of your choice with all your heart and soul and mind, absorb the negative without returning it, send out the ripples of harmony and contentment, and be prepared to change the world. As we embrace our choices mindfully, together we stop the cycle of suffering, and people in the new age of bliss will remember that it was we who finally turned the wheel in the opposite direction."

Mann looked around, and realized that the crowd was much larger than it had been when the sermon started. Looking ahead, he saw The Eternal One surrounded by people who seemed content merely to touch His clothing.

After almost an hour, waiting his turn, Mann was one of the last to look into those blazing, heavy-lidded eyes. The Eternal One looked back at Mann beneficently, and touched his forehead.

"It was a wonderful performance," Mann said.

"Thank you, my child, for this blessing that you bring to me."

"I remember watching a sermon like that once before, when Billy Graham spoke at Shea Stadium," Mann continued.

The Eternal One froze in mid-turn, and turned back. "Well, well, well," he said. "I am thinking that you have finally found us."

"Gandhi?" Mann said.

"I have to tell you to your face that you are an extremely hard person to locate among so many billions," Gandhi said. "Do you have any idea how hard we have been searching for you?"

"We?"

"Washington and me. We were completely able to find each other after merely a few hours. But you—it was like you vanished into the world without one single trace, or maybe you were hiding."

"I've been busy."

Gandhi looked around nervously, but somehow nobody had noticed the byplay. "Maybe we could talk about this... somewhere," he said, making an incremental gesture with his head toward the street.

"I have a lot of questions."

Gandhi looked past Mann, and held out his hands to take the hands of others from the audience, blessing them, telling them to raise their vibrational levels...

One member of the audience, tall, gaunt, with melancholy eyes, stepped out of a small crowd and slapped Mann on the back heartily. He regarded Mann with a pessimistic frown.

"So how are you doing down here? I don't suppose you've made any progress yet?"

Mann stared.

"Washington?"

"Witch said we would find each other. I have to say, though," he said, jerking his thumb toward Gandhi, "HE was a hell of a lot easier to find than you were." Then his eyes narrowed. "Far as we can tell, you haven't made a wave here yet."

"I've got a lot to talk about," Mann said.

16

"Life is not separate from death. It only looks that way."

Native American Blackfoot proverb

The cafe floated above the great atrium like a cloud. Above, hovering globes simulated daylight despite the darkness visible on the far side of the glass enclosing the atrium, broken up now and then by what might have been heat lightning or a distant thunderstorm authorized by the weather authorities. The pedestrian traffic thinned out at this late hour, so that the moving belts going up and down and spiraling around the sides of buildings were largely empty, and the kiosk storefronts rising everywhere along the walls, usually haunted by smiling images of clerks, were mostly dark.

Four gods looking down and around like awed tourists at this remarkable corner of their handiwork, far more interested and impressed and perhaps even intimidated than any of the random virtual creatures who engaged in idle conversation at neighboring tables. The conversation was led by what appeared to be a seven-year-old girl, who took a long last drag on a cigar and dropped it over the side, where a thousand mechanical ants swarmed over it and made it disappear. She stared at the place where the cigar had been as if she'd never seen a street cleaned before.

She turned to her glass of narcotic extract of the pituitary of a certain species of toad and sipped appreciatively. A reading tablet was set in front of her, and periodically she would glance down at it, as if she were memorizing the words on the screen.

"Pudge, you're going to have to learn your manners down here," Washington commented gloomily. "What is that girl going to tell her parents when you go back upstairs?

Pudge—or the little girl who happened to be occupied by Pudge at the moment—shrugged her shoulders indelicately and took another gulp. "She'll tell them she was occupied by aliens and make a lot of money writing her story for kooks and weirdos who believe in magical creatures like us."

They spoke in English, so there would be no chance of their conversation being overheard. Mann found it interesting that each of them stumbled a bit as if it had somehow become their second language.

"They don't realize that the only purpose of their entire lives, the only service they offer to the gods—by which I am meaning us," Gandhi said as he gazed over the side, "is to breed the next generation. Only a very few who are directly involved in innovation have any genuine significance. And yet they move along with their lives in blissful ignorance."

"I don't see the blissful part," said Mann. The wine felt cool to his lips, with a slightly fiery finish. How many glasses would it take before the computer decided to make him feel tipsy?

"Trust me," Washington interjected with a sad smile; "they'd be far less happy if they understood the truth about their little universe."

"How long have you been down here?" Mann asked.

"Five months as they measure time here. Exactly 52 hours less than you," Gandhi answered promptly, shifting his gaze from the pedestrian traffic back up to Mann. His eyes carried a hint of accusation.

"He thought you might be hiding from us," Washington explained glumly, taking a sip from his glass.

Looking at the two of them, Mann realized all over again how outward appearance is a reflection of the inner personality. Washington's body, after sixty days of occupation, seemed to be mostly bones concealed by a dark robe, and his face settled into a long droop of pessimistic gloom as he sniffed his glass with visible suspicion. Gandhi's face and inherited body had already settled into a slouch of indolence. There was no wasted effort as he pursued the undemanding activity of sitting in a comfortable chair at the table. Mann considered his own body, once almost skeletal, now filling out with hard, functional muscle after weeks in his apartment's exercise room.

The girl lit another cigar, checked her tablet and winked at him.

"So how, exactly, was I supposed to find you?" Mann asked finally, rising to the unstated accusation. "There are so many millions—"

The others looked at each other. "We've been doing this so long that we thought it was obvious," Washington answered at last. "As soon as I landed, I delved into my personal profile and listed my hometown as Asia. It says I was educated at the Pentagon, and I lived for two years in Shangri La studying German."

"Meanwhile," said Gandhi, touching his pendant pointedly, "we have been searching every place and celebrity name from up top that our poor minds could think of. Every time nobody popped out, as if perhaps you have been been living inside of a very deep black hole."

The little girl who was Pudge made an impatient gesture with her tiny hand. "The important thing is: What have you been doing? Where are we with the project? You Know Who is already impatient, and it's only been minutes in her—our—reality."

Mann hung his head. "You were expecting results this quickly?"

"Just progress. Don't be afraid to exaggerate. Who wants to go first?"

"I have a very engaged local following," Gandhi mumbled.

"How many?"

"A couple hundred highly engaged people who would do anything for an enlightened one like myself. I am thinking that you have to start somewhere." He looked at Washington meaningfully. "This is more than *he's* accomplished."

"The more time I spend down here, the more I'm beginning to agree that we don't have enough time to salvage this reality," Washington replied. "I've made some speeches, and contacted a few potential donors who think I'm either crazy or an idiot. But it's a hell of a lot more than what you've gotten out of *him*," he said, nodding toward Mann. "It looks to me like all he's done so far is get himself lost."

"He has no experience with this sort of thing," Gandhi commented. "I am thinking that we have expected too much from our friend who Dr. Witch is so impressed with."

The girl flicked an ash off of her cigar and regarded Mann thoughtfully. "Is that true?" she asked.

Mann hung his head. "Pretty much," he said.

"Give us the details."

"The first thing I did was establish an underground network of allies who are pretty much everywhere but invisible to the local population. They've already proven to be surprisingly useful."

Westerly nodded. "And—?"

"I'm working. Part of my job is to meet regularly with military commanders, elected representatives and strategists on this side of the war zone," Mann continued. "I was hoping that I could move them away from a commitment to what even they realize would be a mutually destructive war. But so far they've been very untrusting and not at all interested in keeping the planet alive for another 50 years. Call it a work in progress," he added.

"Is that all?"

Mann sighed. "I'm working in the offices of the most prolific technology innovation factory on the planet, and they've given me full access to everything they're producing."

The others looked at each other.

"What innovations?" Pudge asked finally.

Mann shrugged. "Antigravity, fabrics stronger than steel, fusion engines, fabrication of anything through instant sub-molecular assembly. I don't understand most of it."

"Wait a minute," Washington interrupted. "Why aren't we seeing any of this technology out on the street?"

Mann shrugged. "It's all I can do to keep it out of the hands of the military."

Washington turned to Westerly. "Do you believe him?" he said.

Westerly took another sip of his drink and nodded slowly.

"So you understand what this means," Washington said, looking back and forth at Westerly and Gandhi. "It means we don't have to keep this world alive for another 50 years. We take what we came for—*more* than we came for, apparently, and get the hell out. There's no reason to wait for any of it to find its way out on the street."

"I wish that were true," said Mann.

"Basically, it means that the two of us can shut down operations and go home," Washington continued.

"I wouldn't be too quick about that," said Mann.

"But—"

Gandhi raised a hand. He regarded Mann and sipped his wine quietly. His face suggested that this simply confirmed his worst expectations.

"I am thinking that you should tell us why we should be so patient as you seem to be saying," he said finally. "Why do we have to wait 50 years for what you have in your hands right now?"

Mann looked from one to the other. "Isn't it obvious?" he said. "The more specialized a civilization gets, the more *nobody* knows how it all fits together. It's like getting the specifications for these pendants," he said, touching his chest, "except first you have to know how to fabricate the incredibly tiny chips, and to do that, you need to know the precise composition of the materials that the chips are made out of, and the manufacturing techniques, and the specialized devices that have been created to make them, not to mention probably two centuries of programming, where one generation builds on the work of the previous one."

"Okay. So—"

"So this is actually worse. None of these things have even been built yet. It's going to take decades to do a proper inventory."

"So what are you telling us, my brother? That this whole entire errand is hopeless?"

"I'm trying to figure out how to bring it all back, because in pieces, it won't make any sense."

Washington was about to say something, but Gandhi held up his hand again.

"So," he said, his voice low, "perhaps this would be an excellent time for you to tell us about the progress you are making in keeping this world alive for another three or four decades."

Mann looked down at his feet.

"I've been studying our enemy," he said. "It's formidable. Amazing, in its way. So large and so powerful that I wonder if it can be defeated."

"Of course, that's exactly what Gandhi here tried to tell Witch," Washington commented. "There's so much momentum gathered behind this idea of what any sane person would think is a crazy, species-destroying war, anybody can see that this reality is too far down the path of self-destruction."

Gandhi regarded Mann intently. "You should tell us, what does this… enemy look like to you." he said finally.

"For lack of a better name, I call it the Underlord," Mann said. "When I see it in my mind, it's a giant demonic form rising up like an angry ghost out of the collective psyches of all people everywhere in this world," he said. "Like the ancient gods of legend, it shows a different aspect when you look at it from different angles, and you can mistake it for different things, but they are really one."

"That gives us a lot to go on," Washington commented.

"When I walked into a dance club, I saw it from the side, and it was pure, naked despair," Mann said. "It was a deeply-held belief, which is not illogical if you see how out-of-touch the political system has gotten, that the world and its future are completely out of our control. So people lose any hope and do what any thinking creature would do: they turn inward and focus purely on themselves, and the rest of the world can go to hell, which is where the Underlord is determined to take it."

"That is certainly one interesting aspect," said Gandhi, holding his hand up as Washington was about to speak. "But I think you said there were others we should know about."

"Looking at the enemy directly from the front, I saw it most clearly when I first met with this country's top military leaders," Mann said, meeting their eyes in turn. "When you look around, you see it everywhere, particularly in the people who have never been empowered in this world, which is far the majority and growing fast as wealth and influence are increasingly concentrated in the hands of a few. Call it the angry desire for vengeance, a deep-seated urge to atone, once and for all, for all the unfair and unearned malignancies that each and all of us have had to swallow in our lives. It's an almost feverish desire to balance the ledger and avenge all the things done to us that we know we never deserved, all projected onto an enemy which must be made to suffer terribly or else we will never feel that justice has been restored in our tiny existences.

"And from the back," Mann said, "it is the thing I should have recognized right before I came here."

"And that is…?"

"The opponent that's buried deep inside all of us, which urges us to destroy whatever we create."

"I am thinking I do not understand exactly what you mean," Gandhi said.

"I don't totally understand it either." Mann looked down over the side. "Do you know what entropy is?" he asked.

The others, scientists all, nodded.

"I think of it as a kind of gravity, except instead of holding things together, it pushes them toward chaos. I throw a handful of marbles down on the ground, and they won't form an orderly pattern. They'll scatter in all directions in the most random possible way. It's the way everything works, it's the reason the universe is winding down. It's the reason our bodies return to dust when we die.

"But have you ever stopped to realize, if entropy is an inescapable law of the universe, then none of this should be here," he said, gesturing at the city. "Or the evolution of increasingly sophisticated creatures, the social structures we create—it all flows against the forces of entropy. Am I right?"

The others continued to look at him.

"That means, built into all of this growing order, there has to be an opposite force, an opposite tendency, which, according to the laws of entropy, will be stronger than the organizing principles of evolution and human social organization. It lives just below the surface. Ultimately, the most formidable obstacles to everything we want to accomplish reside inside of us. Those are glimpses of something unbelievably strong that has been frustrated for a very long time, the opponent, the mirror image of our creative side, something that most will never know exists—the substance and personality of the demonic ghost that is going to destroy this world like it's destroyed every one of your simulations. And I happen to believe it lives upstairs where we came from as well," he added.

"And I am now wondering, how do you propose to defeat this... Underlord thing that only you can see?"

"From one side, there is only one thing that can slow it down," Mann said. "We have to restore hope in a population that believes it has lost control over the decisions made at the top."

Gandhi favored Washington with a thin smile.

"That one, I am thinking, will be your aspect to battle," he said.

"I still think it's—"

"From the front," Mann continued, "we have to provide some kind of faith that there will be justice in the end, that the scales are already balanced in a way that is more satisfying and productive than anything we could do with our own hands or our military gadgetry."

"Faith." Washington nudged Gandhi. "That's where you come in."

Mann looked from one to the other. "What are you two talking about?"

Westerly started laughing, and then his little girl face began choking on the cigar smoke.

"I think it's time," he said, nudging Washington, "to introduce you to Marduk the Great, the tribal leader who built the first great proto-civilization on this planet, whose image graced blood-stained altars for a thousand years. And also to Kinji, the former slave who organized 500 tribes into a military force that swept across a full third of the planet, who they say was reborn to continue the conquests. By an amazing coincidence, this gentleman before you also dictated this world's first comprehensive legal code, engraved on stone tablets that are still in a museum somewhere. He put down civil wars and ruled the Bangerian Empire during its height. And I think you were also Plautus Magnimus, the golden emperor of the Calatinian empire," he said, regarding Washington quizzically. "And didn't you write the constitution for this very nation, and serve as its founding father?"

"Guilty as charged," Washington responded gloomily. "Starting all over as nobody from nowhere under very severe time limits."

Westerly looked up sharply. "Didn't we give you an established politician's identity?" he asked.

"An obscure regional legislator."

"Well, you can't walk in with too much of a track record and suddenly change your stripes. And you'll be following the usual model, right?"

Washington nodded. Then he noticed Mann's look of perplexity.

"The fastest route to the top of the pyramid really doesn't change from civilization to civilization," Washington explained. "The formula is to tap into the populist desire to start a revolution, and then let the cowardly masses think they can somehow vote themselves in power and punish those who oppressed them—rather than using guns or dying in the streets."

Westerly, clearly enjoying himself, put his hand on Gandhi's arm. "Here," he said, "let me introduce the divinely inspired incarnate presence who founded all five major religions on this planet, plus an earth mother cult and an earlier ritual culture around the successful taming of fire."

"And I still totally wholeheartedly believe in intelligent design," Gandhi commented, enjoying the moment. "I am thinking, if we are indeed going to attack your Underlord enemy from the front, that a new and wonderful evangelical movement will have to sweep across the planet."

"And the formula…?" Westerly prodded. "Tell him the formula. He'll love it."

Gandhi sighed. "Mixing messages of personal empowerment and success with religion," he said, "and linking prayer to God with success and prosperity on earth, I am thinking that is a business model that will never fail."

"But what about that last aspect of it?" Washington demanded. "What are we going to do about our enemy's rear end?"

Mann shook his head.

"You don't know?"

"The only thing I can think of at the moment," said Mann, "is that we're going to have to figure out how to conquer it in ourselves before we can start addressing it in everyone else."

17

"The beginning lies in the recognition that the external world is only a manifestation of the activities of the mind itself, and that the mind grasps it as an external world simply because of its habit of discrimination and false-reasoning. The disciple must get into the habit of looking at things truthfully. He must recognize the fact that the world has no self-nature, that it is un-born, that it is like a passing cloud, like an imaginary wheel made by a revolving firebrand, like the castle of the Gandharvas, like the moon reflected in the ocean, like a vision, a mirage, a dream."

Lankavatara Sutra (attributed to the Buddha)

Mann sat back on the recliner and waved his hand, staring at the mountain scenery reflected on the wall. It must have been a current view, because some hikers appeared in the distance and started a slow ascent of one of the nearer peaks. He watched them climb to an outcropping, where they sat with their legs dangling over the edge and waved in the direction of the camera. Mann switched the scene to an ocean view not unlike the shores of Madagascar, and felt a twinge of homesickness for the world he left behind.

With a gesture, he called up a list of poetry, and sampled some of the culture of this world. He found a poet, identified with the single name Vishram, who, according to his bio, was considered to be the world's greatest living poet. Mann sampled at random, and after a time found himself listening to this, in the entirely different language of the simulation, but recognizable nonetheless:

> *You who pass by this vaporous, expanding cloud*
> *Evidencing the crowning achievement of our species*
> *who proudly engineered our loving planet's demise.*
> *Stop a while, read in our world's molecular debris*
> *The terrible epitaph of our mortal enterprise.*
> *The engraved summation of all we used to be*
> *That we were so, so much smarter*
> > *Than we were wise...*

"So that's how he did it," he said to himself.

"Who?" the dog said from a soft pillow beside him.

"Nothing. It's not really important."

"That's all right. I didn't want to know anyway. That's why I ask about things, is to make sure I'm not accidentally told something that isn't important."

"A friend of mine is plagiarizing this planet," Mann said. "There, are you satisfied?"

"It doesn't sound important. It would have been better if you hadn't told me."

Hey, pal.

Impatiently, Mann pushed the Synchronicity to the back corner of his mind. But the awareness didn't budge. Mann pushed harder, and in the process became aware of who was addressing him.

It's you, he said.

Yeah. What do you think of my body?

I've had to do a lot of work with it, frankly. You were woefully out of shape.

I had other things to think about. And you're in a different line of work. Listen, I want to ask you something.

You have my attention, Mann thought back.

Olivia and I, we were wondering if we could, you know, kind of undo what we did. Get back into the body thing, if you understand what I'm saying.

I'm not sure I do. You want this body back?

Not exactly.

Then what.

There are others, here in the Synchronicity, who'd like to take our place here and live without bodies for a while, and after a year, I have to say, we're a little tired of this no body thing. So I thought you might, you know—

You want me to switch you into their bodies, and let them roam free?

Yeah. That's it.

And how, exactly, do you expect me to do that?

(A long pause.) Well, you're a god, aren't you? You can pretty much do anything. Right?

Not right. Actually, I'm pretty limited in what I can do.

But I believe you can do this for us. The awareness highlighted a young man and young woman out of the myriad members of the Synchronicity, and their minds bowed self-consciously.

This is them.

You're willing to give them your bodies? Mann asked the two.

They radiated assent. They radiated hopeful emotions. So did the awareness that had once, not so long ago, occupied Mann's current body. So did the disembodied awareness that was Olivia, who was hovering in the background, too shy to step forward.

Please do this for us.

Yes, please.

Mann radiated a degree of exasperation back at them, but he also knew that they could see that a part of him wanted to honor their request.

I have no idea how to go about it, he told them. *Let me think about it.*

You see? The awareness that had belonged to Mann's body shared his sense of triumph. *I told you it was possible.*

Thank you, God.

Yes, thank you.

18

"Your body is of the nature of voidness."

Tibetan Book of the Dead

The meeting had happened exactly as he had expected: a communication requesting an urgent, clandestine meeting. The three star general, surprisingly young, dressed in street clothes that seemed to Mann to be a bit shabby, walked beside him as the dog led them through alleys.

"He's terrified," said Pudge, using the general's mouth to talk to him.

"Of what?"

"Of what might happen if a security device recorded him and you together, and of what he's got in his pocket."

"Maybe we can skip to what's in the pocket."

"I'll relinquish control enough to let him tell you."

"Look," the general said immediately. "I cannot imagine why I'm here, or what the hell has come over me, but for God's sake don't tell anyone where you got this information."

"It's a deal," Mann said. "By the way, I know you were in pretty substantial disagreement with the others in the room about the protective device."

"How could you possibly have known that?"

"I told him," the dog answered promptly.

The general looked down at the dog, visibly unsatisfied with this explanation.

"The point," said Mann, "is that you're concerned about the fate of your species in a way that seems to be, well, perhaps a bit unusual among your military peers."

"And now I'm about to commit the worst sort of treason," the other said.

"Perhaps in a strict, literal sense. But in the context of the broader picture, what you're doing today might be the key to the survival of your country. Can you call that treason, when the decision is framed that way?"

"He's not sure," Westerly interjected.

"Why do I keep referring to myself in the third person?" the general demanded. "I'm suddenly not sure of my own sanity."

"What have you brought me?" Mann asked.

The general took an information cube out of his pocket. He held it in his hand for a long moment, and then silently handed it over.

Mann activated the touch control and words appeared in the air, diagrams, maps. It took him a moment to understand that it was a battle plan, larger in scope than anything he had ever imagined. It was a detailed plan for a surprise attack on the Eastern alliance, a wave of drones with radar cloaking devices that the enemy might not be aware of, creeping along inches above the ground until they were deep into enemy territory, each locating a military installation, a city, an industrial center, a field of similar drone-like devices which could be launched against the West. There were plans for invading forces, robotic tanks ferried into the ensuing chaos, helicopter battle cruisers hovering above, missiles sent from many angles, every kind of mayhem imaginable planned out to the last detail, page after page of it.

Mann scanned down toward the bottom of the document, where he found the consensus odds of success: just under 20 percent.

"Very interesting," he said. "How soon?"

"The President has refused to sign off on it," the general said. "But of course, his term is over in another 18 months, and my peers are more confident that his successor will see this as our side's best hope of victory."

"What do *you* think?" Mann asked.

"The odds of success listed in the final report are greatly exaggerated," the general said. "An honest assessment would put the chances of a knockout victory in the three to five percent range at best, and even if we do emerge victorious, as the assessment defines it, there is virtually zero chance of avoiding the loss of major cities. I actually wrote a dissent that lays all this out, which never made it to the President's desk. But I'm told that somebody gave him a summary of it."

"Do the other generals understand your assessment?"

"Everybody pretty much gets it. That's why you got the reaction you did. Everybody in that room expected you to give them some kind of amazing technology that would raise the odds of a first-round knockout to something like an actual 20 percent figure, so they could tell the President the odds were 50 percent or higher. They still expect something like that from you," he added, "now that you've been properly threatened."

"Is that what *you're* hoping for?"

The general shook his head as if to clear it. "When I saw your protective technology, it was the first time that I could feel a sense of hope. Not just to avoid what you see here, but to escape whatever their side has drawn up, and whatever you and I know both sides will draw up and eventually get approval for somewhere down the road. And then, when I looked around the room and saw the anger, I realized that there actually isn't any hope."

Mann was silent for a long minute. "You believe the next president would sign off on this—this plan?" he asked finally.

The other nodded. "Once the generals make him aware of the safety precautions he and his family would live under, I think he'd jump at the chance to be the leader who is remembered by history for winning this confrontation."

"So we have a two-year window," said Mann. "After that, the world goes up in smoke."

The general shifted uncomfortably. "Is that all you need from me? For some reason, I seem to need your permission to leave this extremely dangerous conversation."

"I have two more questions," Mann said. "First, why did you risk your career when you could have just gone along with a consensus that you knew they were going to arrive at anyway? What would motivate a person like you, who sits in the middle of the deliberations, to disagree with the decision to go to war? If we could spread that motivation to others at your level, what would it be?"

"I have family," the general answered simply. "They went to great lengths to show all of us that our wives and kids would be safely out of harm's way when the shit came down, but I never could make myself believe it. Even if I did, what about my sister and her kids? My mother, who I hope will live for another decade at least? There are a hell of a lot of people I care about who aren't going to survive this little plan we drew up."

"If we could show them that their loved ones were not as safe as they believed..." said Mann, more to himself than the general.

"You might turn more heads than you realize. But I can't see how you could accomplish something like that. And then what about the other side? My analysis is that their military is doing the same assessments, and giving their leaders the same bullshit estimates of success. Do you think convincing one side is going to prevent this war."

"No," Mann said. "I think you're right."

"He got YOU here, didn't he?" the dog put in. "You don't realize who you're dealing with, with the boss here. He's—"

"You said you had a second question," the general said.

"Yes," said Mann. "I want you to tell me what would need to happen for you to be promoted to the Joint Chiefs."

19

*"The phenomenal world seems to be real, but only until
you achieve a higher realization."*

Shankara; the Atma-bodha

"So how do you feel about love?" Gloria asked suddenly.

"Where did that question come from?" Mann said, looking at Maila. "I thought we were talking about miniaturizing the antigravity engines."

"It's my fault," said Maila. "I told her that you were in love with her, and so was I, and she was going to have to choose between us before the whole situation got completely out of hand."

"That's insane! Look, I—"

"Do you think it's a good idea?" Gloria persisted "Something you hope for someday?"

They were sitting near a waterfall toward the back of various leaf-hidden work environments, where people were wandering about in what appeared to be a dream-like state. Gloria's hair glimmered in the sunlight as she turned her head, and Mann had to pull his eyes off of her face. Here and there, through the undergrowth, they could see engineers in deep conversation, their faces obscured by clouds of holographic equations.

"Everything I've ever been told about it," Mann said, "tells me that it's a very difficult thing, that exposes you to danger, first of all, and if it doesn't get you killed, it will break your heart. I always thought love—in the sense of really, truly giving your heart to someone else—was a vulnerability that a wise man stayed away from."

"Is that still what you think?"

"Yes."

"What??!"

"See?" Maila put in. "I'm totally open to that vulnerability thing, especially if it involves making superior babies. In fact, by a strange coincidence, after checking my date calendar, I happen to be free this very evening—"

"You think it's wise to avoid love altogether?" Gloria asked, her voice taking on an accusing tone.

"The only difference is that lately I've been thinking that it might be worth all the danger and trouble. In fact, I'm beginning to think it was what I was fighting for all those years."

Gloria shook her head. "So fighting and love are all mixed together in your mind."

"Love is one of the things I think I might have been trying to protect through a lot of assignments that had nothing whatsoever to do with it. It's kind of complicated," Mann said.

"Why make it complicated?" Maila said, turning to Gloria. "There's you, there's me, and there's this magical moment which, in another second or two, will be gone forever, and both of us will regret for the rest of our lives that we let it slip through our fingers. Am I winning?" he asked.

"I think you're both completely ridiculous," Gloria said, turning back to the hologram that wavered in the air between them. Then she looked up thoughtfully.

"Are you still part of that Synchronicity thing?" she asked Mann.

"Off and on."

"Can you describe what it's like?"

"Probably not. Let's call it an interesting learning experience."

"Can you at least tell us what you've learned?"

"Well, to start with, coherent, focused, productive thought is one of the rarest things you can find in this world."

"Seriously?"

"If we could ever get everybody thinking, and nothing more than that, this would be a fantastically more interesting and efficient world. As it is, any mental processing power that is not wasted is a rounding error."

"No wonder our world is so screwed up."

"I think the strangest part of it is the way we feel about everything. It's like we interact with the world on a level that hardly ever touches the conscious, logical mind, and yet the logical mind thinks it's totally in control."

"Are you talking about feelings? About love? That's really what I was asking about."

"I'm talking about a whole other processing network of instincts that never quite rise to the visible surface, and at that level we experience them as emotions, as feelings, and I never before realized how much of our overall thinking is handled down there. For the first time in my life, I can feel it inside me, this strange mix of drivers that overrides my brain in ways that I'm not totally comfortable with."

"Women more than men?" Maila asked in spite of himself.

Mann thought for a moment. "I don't think so," he said, testing his words against a cautious exploration of the chaos that never left the back of his mind. "Men are quicker to feel frustration and anger, and certain kinds of exultation. When I'm experiencing the feelings of a woman, there's a hunger for connection, and for certainty around the connection, and this strange desire to give, help, support, and comfort that requires someone else to volunteer to receive it. And more than that, it requires somebody else to be willing to change the way they're feeling or acting in some positive way so that she knows the things she couldn't help doing in the first place actually made a positive difference. I think this must be why women are so moved when they hear a man say that she makes him want to be a better person."

"But what about love?" Gloria asked quietly. "Isn't it strange that you talked about feelings and left out love?"

"Yeah, what about love?" Maila added. "Does it have to be as complicated as you say it is, or can it be the raw naked animal attraction that Gloria and I are feeling for each other at this moment?"

"Tell me what *you* think," Mann countered. "Is love a distinct emotion? Or is it a whole bundle of different instincts coming together in a lot of different recipes and rising to the surface like many different chemical compositions of magma from the mantle, and the mix is never quite the same for any two people, never the same in any relationship, and always for the man different from the woman?"

"Is that what you've experienced through the Synchronicity?"

"There's such a broad diversity of feelings that we all use the same word for."

"For instance?"

"There are people who feel trapped because every time they think about a particular person, or see them, or talk to them, they lose control over a big part of their feelings, and the bubbling up of emotions is so strong that it affects their ability to think clearly."

"Okay, that's one. What about another?"

"People feel so connected with another person that their lives are meaningful only in context with that person."

"Okay, and—"

"Some people experience love as a tenderness and protectiveness, so much so that they would die in place of their lover if they were attacked," Mann continued. "Some will even systematically sacrifice who they are and what they themselves want for what they perceive to be the well-being of the other person. And there are a few, a very few, who radiate out a glow of good-will toward everybody, who unerringly look for and appreciate the best qualities of people and visibly admire them, validating and reinforcing and encouraging and through it all loving because of the feelings that are always filling their breasts from the instinctive substrate of their awareness."

Maila and Gloria were silent. They looked at each other.

"Wow," Gloria said finally. "You've given this a lot of thought."

"More than I felt like I could afford," Mann admitted. "Because of my own feelings, I couldn't help it."

"What bubbles up when you think about me?"

"I can totally see us having sixteen babies," Maila said.

"I was talking to him."

"I think my answers are a lot better than his are."

"Do you know how much easier it is to see these things in others than in yourself?" Mann said.

"That's a really terrific way to avoid the question."

Mann took Gloria's hand. "Remember when we did this, back at the club?" he said.

Gloria nodded.

"I experienced this sudden rush of unfamiliar feelings bubbling up inside. It was like my mind went into a kind of shock, and I held onto you for reassurance, and that just made it worse."

"Worse?"

"More intense. Yes, back then, 'worse' was exactly the word I would have used. I felt like your presence was making me weak, which is the last thing I need in this place and time."

"Do you still feel that way?" Gloria asked.

"I don't like where this is going," Maila said, looking back and forth at Gloria and Mann. "Remember, I love you a lot more than he does, and I'm willing to prove it."

"Being around you sometimes makes my brain go fuzzy," Mann said. "So I try to avoid you when I can, which is not nearly as often as I want to, because I need that clarity, that focus, to do what I came here to do."

"So I make you fuzzy," Gloria said. "That doesn't sound very positive."

"There are a whole lot of feelings, and I don't know how to control them or even what to call them. Sometimes I feel like you are the other half of me, and that I would have gone totally crazy if you and I weren't joined together to form some kind of—see? I don't even know what to call this thing we have together."

"It's called a relationship," Gloria said. "It might even be love. And if it makes you feel any better, I still get a little fuzzy when I'm around you too. I tell myself it's gratitude, but sometimes I'm pretty sure there's more to it than that."

"What can we do about it? It's a threat to our productivity."

"See? To him you're a 'threat to his productivity,'" Maila said. "To me, you're the queen goddess of love and fertility. How can you even compare us?"

Gloria smiled at Maila fondly. "I've never known anybody as naive as you," she said. "It's one of your most charming features."

"There, see? She said I have charming features," Maila said to Mann. "That's further than I've ever gotten with any woman around here before."

"My training has always told me these feelings are the last thing I need," Mann said, looking down at his feet. "But here, in this strange place, I wonder now if it might not be the *first* thing I need. Because of the way I feel about you, it feels like I'm living, truly living, for the very first time in my... existence. And that's incredibly ironic in ways that I can't possibly begin to explain to you."

"Would you call it love?"

"Yeah; is it love?"

"Of course it's love," Mann said. "But what kind of love? You love your mother, you love yourself, you love a close friend who can reliably make you feel special, you love the idea of global peace and harmony among all people, and maybe you love the person you just persuaded to have sex with you, because that person fills a deep physical hunger. I happen to think all of those definitions are distracting from the ability to think clearly, and yet I'm okay with the distraction when you're around. Does that make any sense to you?"

"It makes no sense at all to me," Maila interjected, trying to interrupt the locked gaze between Mann and Gloria.

"It tells me you care about me more than about yourself," said Gloria.

"I suppose that's true," Mann said.

"But you also care about something else," Gloria said, "which you've been very mysterious about, more than you care about yourself too. So the thing I find myself wondering is: do you care about that other thing more than you do about me?"

"What a charming conversation," Forbes commented, emerging from behind a trellis. His mouth contracted into an almost-smile. "I feel so much smarter for having listened in."

"Oh…" Gloria blushed deeply. Forbes took her hand and kissed it, and rubbed it against his cheek.

"Is she not the most charming woman in this hemisphere?" he said to Mann and Maila.

"I said she's a goddess," Maila replied, his voice already radiating defeat in Forbes' presence. He stood up, and Forbes put a hand on his head, which emphasized at least a foot of height difference, and then gave a slight shove, which sent Maila back into his seat.

"If that's so, then why were you out with Alicia last night?" Gloria demanded with less indignation than Mann would have expected. "And that angry little receptionist the night before?"

"Purely recreational," Forbes assured her. "The ladies here are starved for a masculine presence in their otherwise drab and lonely work environment, populated entirely by nerds and losers." Forbes looked meaningfully at Mann and Maila in turn, and then turned back to Gloria. "I happen to love women. I could hardly be blamed for giving them what they wanted."

"And you're going to tell me I'm what you wanted all along," Gloria said, but the tone was soft, not accusing.

"I always want the best."

"I wish I could believe you," Gloria said.

"I stand ready to prove it. But," Forbes added, looking this time at Mann, "you seem to have an attraction for men who have far less intelligence than you do. I think it may be a confidence thing that you're going to have to overcome someday."

"The difference between you and him," Maila said, "is that he worships Gloria, and you see her as an interesting toy."

Gloria looked up sharply. "That wasn't a very nice thing to say," she said.

"But so typical, don't you think?" Forbes said, leading Gloria through the trellis. He raised his voice so that Mann and Maila could hear him over the sound of the waterfall. "I thought we could talk about your plans for this evening," he said. "That is, I was hoping I could *help* you make plans for the evening."

20

"Everything is non-existent."

Diamond Sutra, Chapter 6 of the Maha Prajna
Paramita, attributed to the Buddha

"Good morning, Congressman."

"Son, how the hell did you get past my desk?"

"Your personal assistant—quite attractive, by the way—is not herself at the moment."

"I'm sorry, but I have an appointment at this very—"

"The lobbyist for the defense contractor cancelled a few minutes ago. He's not himself either." Mann laid a cube on the table next to his chair.

The congressman sat back and regarded Mann with heavily-lidded eyes. His jowls clenched and unclenched. Finally, he relented with a visible gesture of his shoulders.

"So tell me who you represent, and what I have to do to earn your support, and how much support I can expect, and then get the hell out."

"Actually, I'm here as a private citizen," Mann said. "I'm an ordinary voter."

"And I suppose you expect me to waste my time on one vote. I have aides who meet people like you."

"I've had several meetings with them. In fact, I believe I've talked with most of the aides in this building over the past year. Most of them privately agree with me and they all say the same thing: that I'm beating a dead horse."

"Lovely analogy," the congressman muttered. He touched his intercom.

"Congressman, have you ever considered that the only people you talk to are lobbyists offering cash for favors?"

"So?"

"Don't you think that warps your view of reality? Would it hurt so much to talk to an actual voter?"

"It might."

"I really only wanted to ask you one question," Mann said. "Then I'll leave."

"Ask," the Congressman said in a level voice.

"Can your constituents count on you to vote against any resolution to secretly attack the Eastern Alliance and plunge us into a war that nobody would win?"

"What makes you think we couldn't win?" the Congressman demanded indignantly.

"Are you aware of an Eastern Alliance technology that the military has termed 'Deadly Mole?'"

The congressman paused. "I believe that's classified information," he said.

"Let's hypothetically suppose that the Eastern Alliance has placed some number of self-burrowing devices capable of destroying cities along our shorelines," Mann said. "These devices slowly crawl along, deep under the ground, undetectable, until they reach the coordinates of this or some other city. They're set to detonate only if certain signaling devices, set up in and around Eastern Alliance cities, are destroyed badly enough that they stop sending a signal forbidding the devices to detonate."

"Are you asking me to suppose this? Well, what of it?"

"You, of course, would be well away from your voting constituents whenever a sneak attack is carried out. But they'd be fried and melted. Do you care that little about them that you'd risk such a thing?"

"Son, if our generals told me we had a chance to win this war, I'd sacrifice all of them and my own mother in the mix," the congressman said. "And if you tell anybody I said that, I'll deny it."

"Of course you would," Mann said, standing up. "If you had the chance." He picked up the cube and set it in his pocket.

"I'm not sure I follow your implication," the congressman said.

"Our conversation has been recorded visually in very high resolution," Mann said. "It's going to be interesting when the voters in your district see how you feel about their safety."

He turned and barely reached the door before the congressman spoke.

"Wait."

"I don't want you to be late for your next appointment," Mann said. "A very important missile manufacturer, I believe."

"Please, come back and sit down. What do you want?" the congressman asked.

"That seems to be the most common phrase in this building," Mann said. He looked into the congressman's lidded eyes, and shuddered at what he saw there.

"I want only one thing," Mann said. "A simple thing."

"How simple?"

"All I'm asking is that, on a date and time of my choosing, you will jointly announce with 20 other members of Congress that you will renounce and strongly oppose any pre-emptive attack that the military proposes and the chief executive asks you to approve."

"What?" The congressman searched in vain for additional words to add as he half-rose from his seat. He looked into Mann's eyes, and this time *he* shuddered at whatever he saw there. He sat down again.

When he looked up again, Mann saw, with his intuitive skill, an assessment of how easy it would be for a person like Mann to die.

"I suppose I have no choice, do I?" the congressman said with less resignation and regret than Mann might have expected. "I wish you luck on this adventure of yours. Now get out."

Mann bowed and hurried past the outer desk with a wink at Westerly.

"One down," Mann announced cheerfully. "Only 19 more to go."

21

"If, as in a dream, you see a light brighter than the Sun,
your remaining attachments will suddenly come to an end,
and the nature of reality will be revealed."

Bodhidharma, founder of Chan Buddhism

They stood in the wings of the auditorium. Mann peered out at the audience. Half of the seats were empty.

"Wish me luck," Washington said.

"Luck with what?"

"Luck with finding a way to unchain their voices, that have been shackled for so long they don't even know they have them anymore." He looked at Mann curiously. "Have you ever heard the story of the elephant, that when they removed the shackle from its leg after ten years, it still didn't move away from the post, because it had forgotten that such a thing was possible?"

"There aren't any elephants in this place."

"If I can just see in their eyes a little bit of hope, if I can rub off the protective layer of cynicism and get down to the bottled up anger—if that happens, I don't honestly give a damn whether they vote for me or not. All I want is for a few hundred people to walk out of here determined to do something about the ugly, terrible, self-serving elitist thing that politics has become in this place and time."

"That," said Mann, "I can wish you luck with."

Washington listened to the introduction, which didn't list much in the way of credentials. The former czar of empires, founder of the nation winced at the paucity of his own resume.

Then he stepped out to a scattering of applause.

He regarded the audience for a long second.

"I'm here," he said, "to do something that we haven't heard from our political representatives in a very long time. I'm here to tell you the truth. All of it.

"And maybe, before I do this, I should tell you why the entire political class, without exception, has avoided this seemingly straightforward approach to getting your approval and your vote," he added. "You know you're being lied to. Have you ever wondered why it happens so consistently, when in your heart you—all of you—would prefer to be talked to like an adult?

"The answer is that the truth is dangerous, and discouraging, and it feels awful," Washington said. "If I want to raise up your hearts, and if I want to make you like and respect me, the very last thing I would use to get your attention is the truth.

"So I want you to realize that telling you the truth is a terrible, awful political strategy for me. It's a form of personal sacrifice that I'm making, which will actually make it a great deal harder for me to collect the votes I need to get into office.

"I'm doing it for you, not for myself. Because somewhere in all the talk about politics, I found myself believing something that everybody else in every campaign you are ever asked to vote in will think is truly stupid. I tried, believe me, but I couldn't help coming back to the belief that this election is really, most importantly, about you, not about me.

"So what is the truth?" Washington called out, his voice rising. "The truth, the truth you absolutely don't want to hear, is that you're pathetic," he said. "You live in an alleged democracy where it's spelled right out in the founding documents that the politicians answer to you, and the painful reality is that you, individually and collectively, haven't held them to that. Somewhere along the line, you and me and everybody else got out of the habit of insisting on our most basic rights of citizenship, which is to tell the policymakers what we want and impose our will when they go off and decide things on their own.

"Am I wrong?" he said, staring into the restless audience, trying to look everybody in the eye as he swept his gaze from right to left and back again. "Can anybody here tell me that you feel listened to, much less obeyed, when you vote somebody into office?"

He waited for the silence to build. He allowed it to become uncomfortable. Then it became extremely uncomfortable, as all genuine introspective moments must be.

"I can tell you, from having all these meetings with the party and the other candidates who pass through the headquarters, that they're laughing at you," Washington continued. "They think you're a joke. They raise money to buy up the advertising space to tell you what to think, raise money from people who tell them very specifically what they want you to think, and all those people at all those fundraisers have one thing in common. What they want you to think is not what you actually *do* think. And nobody in that entire feeding chain has any interest in hearing your voice because that would interfere with how they do business.

"Because, my friends, you *are* a joke."

Then Washington's voice lowered, and became intimate as he scanned the faces in the audience.

"So the only question I have for you, today, is this," he said: "Is that what you signed on for?"

The silence was broken by a few people scattered around the audience saying "no." Their voices were barely audible.

"I ask you that question, and listen to how you answer," Washington said. "A few of you mumble something and most of you just sit there. Because that's been your habit for as long as anybody can remember.

No wonder they don't take you seriously in our state house and the national assembly. Because you don't take yourselves seriously.

"They've stolen your power as voters. They've hijacked the decision-making authority and walked away and they know that if you decided to, you could take it back. But they have no fear that you'll do anything more than mumble that something's not right.

"So I ask you again, is this what you signed on for, as voters, as citizens, as the final authority on matters of policy and law as provided in our founding documents? Is this the way it should be?"

This time, there were more voices, and louder.

Washington looked over the audience. "You know, each time we do this, we get a little better at it. But I can tell you that what I just heard isn't going to echo into the state house and scare anybody, much less the national assembly. If you truly want your power back as citizens and voters, then the very first step that we take right here is that I have to hear you loud enough to know you mean it."

His voice dropped low, and he flashed his eyes at the crowd, not afraid to make eye contact, now feeling the eye contact returned.

"I ask you one more time. Are you getting what you signed on for from your elected officials? Have they acted like they represented you?"

This time it seemed like everybody in the room made an audible response, and some of them were loud.

"I can hear you because I'm listening, but I don't think that's loud enough to get the message across to the rest of the bastards," Washington said. "So let's take it one step at a time." He raised his voice, not an orator's voice, but loud enough to convey emotion, conviction, channeled anger. "Are you getting what you deserve in these elections?"

"*No!*" A muted roar.

"Do they give a damn what you think?"

"*No!*" Louder.

"Are you going to stand for it?"

"*No!*"

"Are we going to do something about it?"

People were standing up now, and the response was deafening. *"Yes."*

"And what are we going to do about it?" Washington shouted.

Silence. Everybody was ready to shout something, but nobody did. The need to shout hung in the air like a frozen bolt of lightning, looking for a target, looking more and more strange the longer it was suspended.

"That's it, isn't it?" Washington said in a low voice. "Once we decide we have the guts and gumption and strength and courage to do something about the problem that everybody knows and everybody wants to go away, then we actually have to do something. There's no turning back, once you decide. And I think we've decided here today.

"So what do we do?" he asked, making that strange group eye contact. "I want all of you to take a good look at me. Give me a good look, and don't be afraid to laugh. I'm exactly as pathetic as all of you were until just a few minutes ago, one more sheep in the flock. Some of you have third graders who know more about politics than I do.

"But I'll tell you this," he said, his voice going low again. "If you give me your vote, and tell your friends and neighbors to give me a chance to go to the legislature, and if by some miracle I get the opportunity to channel the anger that it took us a full hour to work up here in this room, I'll do three things that might make a difference. I'll carry your voice into those cloistered chambers. And I'll show them how it can be done differently. And I'll study how they work, and what they do, and the next time I come back to stand for re-election, maybe I'll know enough to hand the keys to this country back over to you.

"Can you trust me that far?" he said, his voice soft now, caressing the air.

Just like before, a few of them said yes, and most of them were staring at him.

"Can you give me a chance to kick some ass?" he said.

It came more quickly this time, the volume, the participation level.

"Can we take back what they took away from us?" he asked them, and they were on their feet again.

"*Yeah!*"

"Can we make them hear our voices, whether they want to or not?"

"*Yes!*"

"By god, can we make these elections mean something for the first time you and I can remember?"

"*Yeah!*"

"Can you help me break into their little club and start taking it apart piece by piece?"

"*Yeah!*"

"Can I count on your vote?"

"*Yes.*"

"Can I count on you telling your friends, neighbors, the people who matter, that there just may be hope?"

"*Yeah!*"

"Can you get me elected?" he said softly.

"*Yeah!*"

"And if this miracle were to happen," he said, "and I go up there, I want you to watch me, and see if, against everything I believe and everything I want, they somehow manage to corrupt me, and I just don't get it done. I want you to make me a promise," he continued, and waited long enough that they wanted to hear the promise that he wanted them to make.

"I want you to promise me that if I'm not the person I promise to be, that you'll vote my ass out just like you're going to do to the incumbent, and you won't lose the spirit that we're building here today. I want you to promise me that this thing we're building, this willingness to take back the country, will be bigger than me, and will survive anything I do, and that anybody who stands up here, that you'll hold them accountable, so we can remember today as the day it started, the day when you decided to take back your rights as voters and citizens.

"Are we agreed?" he said.

"*Yeah!*"

"Are we going to make them tremble before you?"

"*Yeah!*"

"Let's all go out there and start making it happen," he said, and bowed his head into the unchained voice of the crowd.

"You were pretty convincing," Mann told Washington over drinks in one of the hovering bars. He looked over the side. "So how are you doing in the polls?"

"I'm down about 50 points," Washington said calmly. "I'm running a solid seventh in my own party right now."

"Really? I thought you had those people in the palm of your hand."

"When people hear my message, they can't help but support me," Washington said. "Otherwise they feel like cowards. But tell me, are you seeing my face on the news feeds?"

"Not so much," Mann admitted.

"He's incredibly popular in his district," Gandhi said, clearly enjoying the moment. "Tell him how popular you've become among, what? Twenty thousand people out of millions?"

"Don't rub it in."

"Word of mouth: it can do wonders if you have multiple lifetimes," Gandhi added.

Mann let his eyes wander out to the buildings that rolled out of sight out to the horizon. The immensity of the task was just beginning to sink in.

"So how are you coming?" he asked.

Gandhi sat back. "Founding a new religion takes time," he admitted. "But the difference is that when we make a convert, that person is fanatically devoted to the cause, rather than occasionally inclined to vote in a certain way."

For the first time, Mann realized that this was a competition between his co-conspirators.

"So do you have a plan?" he said.

Gandhi threw up his hands. "The voice of the hour belongs to some very angry simulated individuals who seem to want nothing more than to destroy the Eastern Alliance. As long as the few have more collective anger than the many have aversion to war," said Gandhi, "this simulation is going to continue to tip in favor of blowing itself up, until it falls over and poof! We've lost our most promising experiment just as it was about to pay off."

"We said from the beginning that the time frame is too short," added Washington. "That's why we have you," he said, giving Mann a meaningful glance. "Which means this is a good time to ask what you're up to these days."

"I'm trying not to get killed," Mann said.

"What are you doing for US?" Gandhi persisted.

"Thinking." Mann turned to Washington. "You're running for a seat on the state legislature. Right?"

"You have to start somewhere."

"We have to move more quickly. What's the name of the national Senator who's up for re-election?"

"Senator?"

"I'm in a hurry. Aren't you?"

"Wendle," Washington said. "But he's in my own party, the election is only a year away, and the way I'm polling, it would be a stretch to expect me to be elected street sweeper." He stopped, and then stared at Mann. "But I'm suddenly curious as to what you have in mind."

"What if you dropped a bombshell that got everybody's attention, and made the speech you just made to the national media— say, fifteen times over the course of two weeks?"

"You'd have to get Wendle to drop out of the race at the same time. There," Washington said, turning with ironic triumph to Mann. "For my purposes, you have your mission. Do you have any ideas?"

"As a matter of fact," said Mann, "I do."

22

"The universe is my mind, and my mind is the universe."

12th Century Confucian philosopher Lu Xiangshan

A chime sounded in the house, waking Mann from a deep sleep. He rubbed confusion out of his eyes and stumbled toward the viewplate. A man in a heavy coat, apparently in his mid-forties, was touching the door with a timid gesture. Mann touched the screen, and his front door slid open.

"Hello?"

"You know who I am."

For a moment, Mann didn't. And then he did. He stepped back.

The man walked into the living room, looked around, and faced Mann. His face was unshaven, but it looked as if this state of neglect was not its normal condition. The eyes seemed to peer out from deep craters of darkness, and there was an odd, twitching quality about his movements. It reminded Mann's gestalt awareness of something, but, unusually for him, the connection did not come immediately.

"*Do* you know who I am?" the man said.

"Yeah, do you?" The dog suddenly appeared at Mann's side. "Should I bite him?"

"Olivia's father," Mann said. "Actually, I've been expecting you for many weeks now. Will you sit down?"

"I suppose you're going to apologize for killing my daughter? For seducing her and then convincing her to commit suicide?"

The dog looked at Mann with astonishment. "You did what? Where was I when this was happening?"

"I didn't—"

"The police looked at all the messages, and decided that they can't arrest you for killing her. They told me that the suicide was as much her idea as yours."

"I think that's the case, yes."

"That isn't right," the dog said with visible indignation.

"Maybe you could leave the two of us alone," Mann said mildly.

"I'm thinking I should be keeping a better eye on you."

Mann put his hand on the dog's head protectively and leaned forward.

"I doubt I would have forgiven you even if you had followed through and killed yourself. But this—" The father gestured helplessly. "How can I live when you planned a mutual suicide, and now you're still alive and she's gone?"

Suddenly Mann's mind made the connection, and he realized where he had seen others who looked like this man who sat in front of him. He had known men and women for whom the scales of life had tipped so that there was, daily, more pain than pleasure, with the expectation of more of the same extending out to the end of their days.

He was looking in the face of a future suicide victim.

"She's still alive," Mann said, putting his hand on the dog's head to silence it.

"That, too, they told me. It actually makes it worse, that there's some kind of version of her in some kind of simulation."

"I wouldn't be too harsh about simulations if I were you."

"What is that supposed to mean?"

"Yeah, what are you talking about?" the dog added.

Mann sat back. "It means that our reality may be more complicated than you realize," he said gently. "If I were you, and I recognize that I am NOT you, I would be implanted with one of those chips. I happen to know that she misses you."

"How could you possibly know that?"

"Because she just told me. This very moment, when she became aware that you came into the house. Would you like to say hi to her?"

"It isn't her."

Mann said nothing.

"Don't you feel anything?" the father said. "Anything at all?"

"I'm not the person who was with your daughter," Mann said. "It's complicated to explain, and you are the only person I will tell this to. But the young man who wanted to die with your daughter DID go with her into the Synchronicity, and he left me behind."

"So who are you, some alter ego?"

"I think you'd better explain yourself," the dog added with a note of accusation in its voice. "It sounds to me like you've been living here under false pretenses."

"WILL you be quiet?"

"Not until I get an answer."

Mann gestured with his hands. "It's not easy to explain. But surely, talking with me has been a very different experience from your communications with—with the other me, if you will."

"You do seem different," the father admitted. "Which makes this all the more difficult."

"What?"

"Killing you."

"Whoa now, buddy, that might be taking things a little too far. Although I can see your point," the dog said after a moment. It turned to Mann. "I have to confess, I'm a little conflicted here."

"This has nothing to do with you," Mann said mildly.

Mann sat back. "You heard me say that I was expecting you," he said. It was a statement.

"I did. Were you expecting this as well?" The father removed a weapon from his coat. He aimed it at Mann.

"Yes," said Mann. "I could not imagine the pain you were going through, but I was able to extrapolate what it might cause you to do."

"I have to go in the other room now," the dog said. "Good luck," it said to Mann, and moved very carefully toward the bedroom.

"I don't think this will ease my pain one iota," the father said, turning his attention from the dog back to Mann. "But it will make me feel as if the universe is back in balance. Even that tiny bit of comfort will be an enormous relief compared to the way I feel now."

"Your daughter is talking to me again," said Mann. "She says that she knows that you are so careful not to break the rules that you won't even attempt to hide what you've done. She is telling me that you'll turn yourself in to the nearest police officer you find on the streets, and you will be prosecuted for this act of revenge, and you won't defend yourself, and the rest of your days will be spent in prison."

The father nodded. "Yes," he said, "that sounds about right."

"She wants you to talk directly with her first," said Mann. "Then, if you still feel the need, you can shoot me."

"And how exactly do you expect to make that happen?"

Mann took a chip out of his pocket. "I bought this for you on my first day here. One of these, actually a less advanced version, is implanted in my brain—and was in hers as well. They work basically the same way; there are small electrodes that are embedded into various centers in the neurocircuitry, which communicate experience directly to anyone who happens to be tuned into the Synchronicity's channels. But this one was designed to be worn in a headband. So long as it touches your skull directly, you'll get most of the experience, perhaps all of it."

The father gave the chip a disdainful look. "That's what killed my daughter," he said.

"I'm only asking you to experience it long enough to talk to her. You can assess how real she is for yourself. Come," Mann said gently. "Can you honestly tell me you don't want to have one more conversation with your daughter, even if it's only to say a proper goodbye?"

The father sat still for what seemed like a very long time. Then, slowly, without allowing his weapon to waver, he reached across the space between them and took the chip in his hand. There was a small elastic thread, which could be wrapped around his head. After a long moment, he impulsively fitted the chip against his temple.

Instantly, he gasped, and put his head in his hands. His breathing became ragged.

"It comes on pretty strong at first," said Mann. "Give it a second. Your daughter will get them all quieted down."

"My god, what have you—"

"Can't you see her now?"

"I—" The father stopped. "Olivia?"

Mann shut the conversation out from his neural sense, to give them privacy.

"But is it really you?" the father said.

"I miss you too," the father said. "More than you can imagine. When your mother died, you were all I had."

"No, I'm too old to do that," the father said.

"You're telling me I could live forever? How can I believe that?" the father said.

"Would you even want me to live there with you after I'm—" the father said.

"Yes, I love you so much too. But this is—

"*You!*" The father suddenly sat up erect. "This was your idea—

"How can you tell me that?

"If *you're* in there, then who is this—

"Yes, I can see you. I can see both of you.

"You sound just like when you were alive. If I could only believe it.

"I DO want to come back into your life.

"I'll consider it. That's all I can say.

"Goodbye darling. I love you too."

The father looked up at Mann. He made no move to take off the chip. His eyes were filled with tears.

"Was that real?" he said.

"What do you think?"

"I think the world is too crazy for me to believe it any more." He shook his head. "What am I supposed to do now? Join this crazy cult?"

"You're already a part of it. Nothing about your life will change, except that you'll be living in a fishbowl."

"He's dead too," the father said. "Just like they planned it." He looked up. "But if that's true, then what in the name of heaven are you?"

"I think the important thing," Mann said, "is that they miss their bodies. They want to come back, live a little longer, and then be immortal."

"Yes, that's what they told me."

"Think of me," Mann said, "as the person who might be able to make it happen."

23

"The error in the erroneous teachings generally held by the philosophers lies in this: they do not recognize that the objective world arises from the mind itself."

Lankavatara Sutra

"**B**oss, I have a question for you."

"Yes?"

"You have to promise me an honest answer."

"This must be important."

They walked along the street level below the buildings, which was faintly lit at night by the glow of the many atria that spread out above them like leaves. Mann was constantly surprised at how the architectural evolutions of this advanced world increasingly resembled plant life.

He noticed a bundle on the ground, and bent down over an older woman, not yet asleep.

"Are you hungry?" he asked, drawing the cart closer.

She nodded. Mann reached into the cart and pulled out two packages, and a bottle of water.

The dog watched them talking to each other with visible disgust. When Mann stood up, it skirted the homeless person carefully.

"You've been doing this pretty much ever since you got here," it said with a hint of accusation in its voice.

"And I should thank you for helping me navigate. I would have never found any of these places without you."

"I wasn't asking for thanks. I can understand why you want to help out the dogs. But all these stray people, if you don't mind my saying so, are kind of hard to find, and when you do find them, they aren't smelling so good."

Mann held up a hand. They passed an old video screen which was offering up the day's news, which was the same as the previous day's news, which was Washington on the national interview circuit, expressing outrage in interview after interview at the military's lack of interest in the safety of the people it was sworn to protect. Then there would be snippets of video footage taken straight from the meeting room at the heart of the central military headquarters itself, the image of the general who until recently had been considered a possible candidate for the presidency.

Understand this: I don't care a rat's ass for protecting the people of the world, or even the people of this country.

Every citizen who lives today is a replaceable part of an organism that will grow back in due time.

We're first and foremost and fundamentally human instruments of warfare.

The publicity plan was helped immeasurably by the military spokesperson's reaction, who blustered that these were supposed to be confidential proceedings, and whoever breached security and aired this tirade for the public to see should be shot for treason.

Tomorrow, Washington would release new information, showing that the joint chiefs had secretly drawn up a war plan and, according to leaked sources inside the military headquarters, had deliberately overestimated the chances of success. Experts had been lined up to talk about the likely civilian casualties from the war that was being oversold to the political leadership. The pictures Mann had seen were beyond horrible.

"That puts him on the political map," Mann said, turning away from the screen.

"Who? That was actually a woman you were helping back there. She didn't look very political to me."

"Not her. Never mind. You were asking why I'm helping these people," Mann said. "Truth of it is, I don't know myself. I can't help trying to find people who are suffering, and frankly, I don't like this compulsion, this empathy thing," he added. "All I know is you find a lot more of the suffering here in these darker, hidden places, along with some pretty incredible stories. Maybe the interface is driving me to do it, but if it is, it hasn't provided me with a reason yet."

"Yeah, that interface is pretty darned inscrutable, is what I'm saying."

Mann bent over another shape on the ground, and added a blanket to the bundle. Then he placed another package of food and some water next to the sleeping form, stood up and followed the dog around a corner.

"That wasn't what I was asking," the dog said.

"Then what."

"Did humans really make all this?" the dog asked, waving its nose generally around the city.

"Yes," Mann said.

"The buildings? I mean, you didn't just find them here?"

"What made you think that?"

"It's something we dogs wonder about all the time. What about the street?"

"Also made by humans."

"How?"

"What do you mean, how?"

"There must have been a way to do it. If people can do it, why not dogs?"

"They used machines," Mann said vaguely.

"Oh. And who made the machines?"

"People."

"Out of what?"

"Metals mostly."

"And who made the metals?"

"Those were here already. We had to dig them up out of the ground."

"What about food?"

"That comes from plants and animals. I thought you knew that."

"I had to ask."

"Humans raise the animals, and then kill them to make food."

"Wow."

"Yeah, I know."

"What about water? And air?"

"We didn't make either of those. They were here already."

"So you just take the water that comes out of those fountains from somewhere else? The fountain isn't making new water?"

"No."

"How sure are you that humans made all these buildings?" the dog persisted.

"Very very sure. I've seen them do it. Come to think of it, you've seen people working on the roads, and the buildings."

"Fixing them up a little. Not building them."

"Why all these questions?"

"Some of the dogs think you pretend you built all these things so you could boss around all the other animals. It's not what *I* think," the dog added quickly. "But you have to admit, it's kind of hard to believe that a bunch of skinny, puny things like you could erect these mighty towers."

"I guess I never looked at it that way. It does seem like a miracle, now that you mention it."

"What about the transportation trains? And those things that fly? Did you find them or make them?"

"Made them."

The dog made a kind of whistling sound. "And the Sun? Did you put that up in the sky?"

"That was already there. And the sky, too, in case that was going to be your next question."

"And dogs?" the dog almost whispered. "Did you make us?"

Mann suddenly realized what the conversation was about. He sat down on the nearest bench, and took the dog up into his lap. "Dogs were the first allies we humans had in this world," Mann said. "When there was nothing but rocks and grass and trees and other animals, when nothing had been built yet, it was people and dogs like you who helped the people stay alive, and I think somewhere deep inside all of us, we've never forgotten that great favor that was done for us right at the beginning."

The dog relaxed in Mann's arms, and Mann scratched its head fondly.

"What about cats?" the dog said finally. "Did cats help you stay alive?"

"I don't think so," Mann said. "I think they realized that we'd make excellent servants, and waited until we'd done most of the work."

"This conversation just keeps getting better and better," the dog said. "But maybe you can tell me one more thing."

"Anything."

"Why do people care who owns something? I mean, isn't there way more than enough for everybody, many times over and then some?"

"Yes," said Mann.

"So?"

"It's complicated."

"I don't think so," said the dog.

"What do you mean?"

"I think it's simple. There's something down at the base of you that remembers what it was like when we, human and dog, were together against whatever else was in this world. And you've never lost that fear of not having enough."

Mann said nothing.

"You think?" the dog said finally.

"I think that's the most brilliant thing a human or a dog ever said," Mann said. "In fact, I might be able to use that."

"Always glad to help," said the dog. "Now if you don't mind, there's an itch right behind my left ear..."

24

*"In truth there is not one single being for the Buddha to
lead to Enlightenment."*

Diamond Sutra, Chapter 25

The top of the building extended upwards into the sky in
a brilliantly garish neon hologram of a purple orchid,
crowded in among other holograms that filled the sky in
this less-than-reputable part of town. There were naked women
gyrating in a tight feedback loop, a national flag that seemed to
flutter out of synch with the breeze, signs and symbols and arrows
pointing downward from somewhere below the moon...

"Are they ready?"

"They just went inside."

"The—do we call her a madam?"

"She's in there. With four of her ladies and two men."

"If she's the madam, what do we call the men?"

"They all know what they're supposed to do."

"Here comes Westerly."

A trap door in the street opened up, and a transportation pod
rose up and settled into a parking space near the front door. After
a moment, a gentleman whose face would have been instantly

recognizable to anyone who watched news reports emerged and looked around. Then he looked at Mann and waved.

"That's a bit much, isn't it?"

"So long as the cameras are working inside, I doubt we can screw this up too badly," Mann said.

The Senator who was Westerly walked into the building with a jaunty step.

"What does it look like?"

"They're not wasting any time. They're undressing him. And he's undressing them. It doesn't look very efficient."

"Does he look like he's enjoying himself?"

"It's Westerly, remember. This is the most action he's likely to get in his whole existence." Washington glanced at the monitors, then blushed and turned away. "He seems to be making the most of it."

"Just get everything recorded," Mann said. "I'm afraid we don't have a lot of time."

25

*"This cosmic ray test may help reveal whether we are just
lines of code in an artificial Matrix."*

Zeeya Merali, *Discover* magazine, November 15, 2013

Mann sat up in bed, listening for something. Finally, walking carefully so as not to wake the dog, he got up and touched a switch to make the screen transparent.

For a full ten seconds, as he stared at the scene outside, he thought he had accidentally switched it to another scene. Then he realized that it was real.

It was snowing outside.

He unfolded the porch and sat in the lounge, looking up at the sky. The lights illuminated the individual snowflakes as they drifted downward, each of them falling like an exquisite white leaf that suddenly appeared where the light struck it, many thousands of them in a gorgeously random pattern falling down on his face and all around him.

How had the computer tracked and traced every single snowflake, and the lighting that delivered it in such detail to and through his eyeballs? For a second, he squinted into the cascade of white, trying to see through it, to see into and past the darkness, to the walls of the box in the next universe.

Then he gave himself to the beauty of the falling, drifting miracle, holding out his hands to catch the snowflakes, watching them melt on his warm skin.

"What are you doing out here?"

He turned. Gloria stood beside him. For a moment, he felt a jolt of surprise and pleasure. She was dressed in a parka and thick pants that hugged her body and put her figure on display.

"How did you get in here?" he asked. "For that matter, how did you find this place?"

"Aren't you glad to see me?" A hint of anxiety crossed Gloria's face, and he could see that she'd been drinking. "By the way, you really should lock your door."

"I should insist on an answer," Mann said. "But my mother always taught me that you should never look a gift horse in the mouth. Although it's very odd that you're here," he said after a moment.

"Gift horse? In the mouth?" Gloria looked puzzled.

"I think the idea is that the teeth really don't matter so long as it's free."

"And that's what you're doing out here? Looking at teeth?"

Mann gestured at the sky.

"It's beautiful," he said. "Look straight up. See how the light hits each individual flake as it suddenly comes into view, how it looks like a cascade of little fluttery stars, the incredible detail of the flakes themselves. It's like a million miracles are taking place every second."

Swaying a little, Gloria managed to seat herself in the opposite chair and obediently looked up at the sky. "It's funny how much more alive I feel when I'm with you," she said after a moment, favoring him with the ironic smile that he found so enchanting. "Somehow, you've managed to keep that sense of wonder that most of us outgrow when we leave childhood behind, and because of that, you make the world seem more magical."

"Hey, what's this?"

"Stalker!" Gloria reached her hand over. The dog gave her a good sniff and wrinkled its nose.

"You smell like cat."

"A lovely gift from Forbes, may he rot in hell."

"And by the way, where was my alarm?" Mann asked.

"Alarm?" the dog asked with a quizzical look on its face.

"I mean you. Why didn't you bark when she walked in?"

"I wonder if you have something to drink around here. And you really should lock your door," Gloria broke in. "Did I say that already?"

"I thought the dog would let me know if there were intruders."

"What, are we back in the wild here? Don't I have as much right to sleep as you do? What were *you* doing awake?"

"I couldn't believe it was actually snowing."

"Don't you ever read the weather reports?" Gloria said, settling herself more comfortably in the chair. "They scheduled this snow months ago, just for tonight. It will stay on the ground for two days and a night, and then all melt off in the warm rain they've got scheduled."

"But it's natural snow, right?"

Gloria laughed. "All weather is natural. There isn't anybody up there manufacturing individual snowflakes. That's nature's job."

"Yes," Mann said, marveling at whose job it really was. "By the way, what ARE you doing here? It's kind of late, isn't it?"

"The bottle shop kicked me out. I thought you might have something to drink."

"That's all you wanted."

"And I wanted to ask you about men."

"In general? Or Forbes in particular?"

"You know me pretty well, don't you." Gloria made it sound like an accusation.

"We can start by you telling me: how are things going between you and him these days?"

"Oh, I hate him. He was just using me to get that job. And now—now I really need that drink."

Mann walked back toward the kitchen and touched the screen, ordering something mild.

"He dumped you?" He called out over his shoulder.

"He said he didn't want me to move in with him. He said he's not ready."

"So he's not ready. Give him time."

"Why do you think he needs more time?"

"I have no idea."

"Tell me what it is about men," Gloria said.

"That's a pretty general question," said Mann. "But maybe I can make it easier for you. Tell me what you bring to a relationship, from your perspective."

"Me?"

"You."

"I told you the first time we met. I have this habit of breaking down the people I'm with because I say what I think and know more than anybody else, and I get bored when they talk and let it show, and when I talk about the things that really interest me, I start lapsing into equations and people fall asleep. And besides, there's nothing fun about me because I live for my work."

"Exactly my type," Mann said.

"Every man's fantasy," Gloria added lightly.

"You wouldn't want to inflict that on somebody you really care about, would you?"

"Of course not."

"Which explains why you can be counted on to pick out a subset of men that you secretly despise. And then you wonder why, in your experience, all the men you ever get involved with are assholes."

"But I—" Gloria stopped in confusion. "Wait a minute; how did you do that?"

"What."

"Turn it back on me like that. You know what? You're the ass-hole!" she said, her voice rising.

"Watch your mouth!"

"I think maybe you should stay out of this," Mann said to the dog.

"The cat lady just insulted you."

"I heard her. It's not on you," he explained to Gloria. "It's on the people you pick."

"But you're saying it's my fault."

"For choosing the wrong people, yes. Absolutely. Totally."

"Only an idiot would do that. Are you saying I'm an idiot?"

"Well, you have a cat, don't you?" the dog demanded

"Did I ask for your opinion?"

"You didn't have to."

"I'm saying, as clearly as I can," Mann continued, "knowing that whatever I say will be misinterpreted anyway, that you're a wonderful, terrific, charming, enchanting woman who can be reliably counted on to seek out the biggest jerk you can find and inflict yourself on him as punishment, and he can be relied on to act as of course he would act, because that's who you picked out to begin with. And then you go around like a walking tragedy complaining about all men everywhere when you have no idea what it would be like to be in a relationship with somebody who was capable of treating you the way you deserve."

"And what kind of treatment is that, exactly!" Gloria demanded angrily. "Whips? Chains? Verbal abuse? Neglect? Unbridgeable emotional distance? Constantly, breathlessly waiting for commitment that never comes and never will come?"

"Much worse than that," said Mann.

"What could be worse than that?"

"For you? Tenderness. Positive reinforcement. Compliments on your beautiful appearance and your amazing intelligence and the work you do. Commitment that comes straight from the heart like a magnetic pulse. Unwavering support for whatever crazy thing you want to do next, and not even noticing how crazy it is. Love that isn't tainted by a lot of conditions."

Gloria opened her mouth in anger, and then closed it again.

"I think I could live with that," she said in a small voice.

"It would kill you. You'd be constantly questioning whether you deserved it."

"And anyway, how do you know all this about me?" Gloria said, mustering back her hostility with a visible act of will. "And anyway, is this really where you live?" She stood up and walked back in the house, gazing critically at the living room, making a face as she walked by the bedroom.

"Pretty nice, huh?"

"It's horrible. I didn't realize places like this existed any more."

"What do you mean? What's wrong with it?"

"I mean, don't you hate the fact that other people live in their opulent paradise sanctuaries while you have to live in this... squalor?"

"It meets all of my needs," Mann protested feebly. "What else could I want?"

"And you expect ME to live like this?"

"What the hell are you talking about?"

"It seems like every day that goes by, the gap between rich and poor gets bigger," Gloria continued, opening and slamming ornate wooden cabinets with evident disgust. "I thought, long before now, people like you would rise up and demand your fair share of the riches. But instead, you squat here in your dismal hovel and—don't you ever want to just scream at the unfairness?"

She turned and stared at him with her fierce eyes.

"Well? Don't you?"

Mann looked at his lodgings with new eyes, realizing for the first time that he was a serf toiling naked in the fields during the age of Charlemagne suddenly transported into a 21st century slum, bedazzled by its opulence and luxury...

"I'm happy here," he said finally. "I have everything I need, everything I want. Why would I want more?"

"You mean you CHOSE to live this way?" Gloria said incredulously.

"I like it here," Mann said defensively.

Gloria stared at him for a long second. "Voluntary simplicity. A smaller footprint on the mother planet," she said. "I didn't realize that you were so deep, that you cared so much that you would make such an incredible personal sacrifice just to set an example for the rest of us."

"I'm not sure—"

Gloria walked over and took Mann awkwardly in her arms. He had to hold onto her to keep her from falling. "The more I learn about you, the more I find to admire," she said, resting her head on his shoulder. "You are one incredible human being. You know that? You're amazing. But I still think you're wrong about me."

"I think," Mann said, "That you're the most remarkable person I've ever encountered. I really don't know how to tell you this, but you matter, with a capital M. You're important. You deserve everything good, and that's the very most important thing you should know about yourself."

Gloria's lower lip trembled as she pulled away. "What do you know about it?" she said.

"I know that it would take a lifetime of effort to make you believe what I just said, a lifetime of daily overcoming your stubborn resistance to seeing yourself the way I see you. Come on," Mann said, touching Gloria's chin when she started to turn away. "Tell me you don't know at least that part is true."

"There are times when I hate you," Gloria said.

"I thought you said you were attracted to me."

"That's what I hate the most. Or maybe it's the fact that I can't seem to hide anything from you. Or that I think you're far too good for me, even though I'm light years better than you in every measurable way."

"Who do you hate more right now, Forbes or me?" Mann asked.

Gloria let her chin drop and stared at her shoes.

"You," she said in a small voice.

"Are you sure it's hate?" he said. "Are you sure your compass isn't set backwards?"

At that, Gloria smiled.

"What."

"If you're right," Gloria said, "then I really do have no idea what love is. And it does sound like you're right," she admitted after a second.

She looked up.

"So what do I do about it?" she asked.

"I'm good with insights. I'm not so good with recommendations."

Gloria took Mann's hand, and suddenly she was embracing him, a bit unsteadily. She set the drink down on a table. Then she leaned her head back.

"I think you should kiss me. I want to test our chemistry."

"That's probably not a good idea, right after you—"

Suddenly, Gloria's lips were on Mann's, and he felt a deep unsettling lurch at his center of gravity, and then a jolt of electricity that left him weak as the first touch of her lips turned into a long, tender kiss.

Gloria leaned back and appraised Mann, noticing the dazed expression on his face.

She kissed him again, and then slowly began unbuttoning his shirt.

"I really think this is a bad idea," Mann protested.

"Is that the most romantic thing you can think of to say to me right now?"

"If I didn't care about you, I'd be taking a very different approach to this."

"That makes it perfect," Gloria said, pulling the front of his shirt apart. She drew him toward the bedroom, and sat down on the bed.

"Now, very slowly, I want you to take off my clothes, and kiss whatever you find under there. Start at the top," she said.

Gloria interpreted Mann's hesitancy as shyness, and shifted her body to facilitate his efforts to undress her. Mann unbuttoned her parka and slowly pulled it across her shoulders. She wore nothing underneath, and abruptly he realized that this had been deliberate, and not for him. He hesitated again, but Gloria drew him closer and kissed him again, pulling him down and placing his hand on her breast. An introspected smile crossed her face; her eyes turned inward. This time he kissed her gently on the lips, and then touched his lips to the skin below her breast.

A part of Mann felt deeply unworthy to be exploring the smooth golden skin of Gloria's body, and there welled up inside a breathless eagerness as he felt the milky softness of Gloria's breasts under his hands. When her nipples pulled tightly erect, it evoked an intoxicating warmth in his loins.

At the same time, his meta-mind stood in sharp dissent from this unnecessary and possibly catastrophic intrusion on his mission here. Wouldn't this become an endangering complication into his so-far-productive relationship with Gloria? What were the odds that he'd lose Gloria's cooperation if this momentary lapse of judgment led them to a place where she was ultimately disappointed, displeased or angry?

Over and over again he was reminded of how irreplaceable and unique Gloria was in this plane of existence.

But… Wasn't that an argument for her reality? Here was Gloria, inarguably substantial and exotically enticing to his touch, real in her responses and personality. Increasingly, as he felt and explored the springy flesh of her marvelous body, Mann felt himself falling under a powerful spell where conscious thought was irrelevant, and the meta-mind's argument seemed to be receding as if he were hearing it from a greater and greater distance, more of an insistent whine in the back of his awareness than a true set of arguments.

"Lower," Gloria murmured. "And take off your clothes, for God's sake."

Mann found it logistically difficult to continue undressing and kissing and removing his pants, but Gloria was now in her own world, and didn't seem to notice his clumsiness. As he tugged on her robe, she shimmied a bit and suddenly it was off of her, and she opened her eyes and beckoned to him with her lips.

He leaned down and embraced her, kissing her again, touching her gently below the waist and exploring the smoothness of her skin. As Gloria became more and more responsive to the worshipful excitement of his explorations, Mann felt his mind joining hers in a synchronization of feeling that went somehow deeper than what he had experienced in the Synchronicity, a merging of him and her that required only one step more...

"Now," she said. "Hurry, before I—"

As Mann kissed her belly, he felt himself sliding all the way into a purity of sensation, his body alternately pounding and throbbing. The magical sensation of touch, the magical connection of mind to mind, body to body, a deep welling of sensitivity and tenderness that seemed to reach out and envelop Gloria from deep within as he rose up on his knees and let his eyes drink in the view of her wonderful body.

Slowly, gently, he lowered himself, and closed his eyes and kissed her for a long second before his legs slipped inside of hers, and he took a long drink of her beautiful face, so perfectly in communion with him, with the growing urgency of his—

Abruptly, Gloria's eyes opened wide, and she twisted away on her side.

"Oh, my god, I'm sorry, but I can't." Gloria curled into a fetal position and closed her eyes. After a long moment, she turned her head back up at him, her eyes apologetic. "I wish I could, God knows I wish I could just forget about—that you and I could—"

Mann reached over and wiped a tear from her face. His body trembled still with anticipation, mingled now with fright. "It's all right," he said lamely.

"It's a million billion miles from all right, I know that, I know I'm the only one in the world who thinks this way, and I try not to, how goddam hard I try not to, but I can't, not now, not until—I don't even know until, how could I possibly know until right now—"

A part of Mann was deeply relieved that the spell was broken. Or was it? He lay next to her, his hand around her waist and belly, realizing with a shock of amazement bordering on horror how emotionally and personally attached he was becoming to this simulated artifact of this simulated reality.

"You don't have to do anything you don't want to do," Mann said.

Gloria stopped. "What? What did you just say?"

"That this is fine."

"What do you mean, it's fine?" she said, her voice rising into an accusatory growl. "You don't even know if I'll ever come back here."

"So?"

"So I can't stand it when men try to play games with me."

"Who's playing games?" Mann asked, bewildered.

"You're telling me you don't care so I'll relax and believe way too soon that this isn't just about you, like everybody else I've been with, that it must be about me and us, because you're willing to wait, but you're saying you're willing to wait as a strategy to make it not necessary to wait, and I have to admit that it's a goddam clever strategy, and it almost worked, and that's what I hate about you, is you have this magical ability to say something that makes my brain shut down, and then I wonder how long you stayed up at night going over the strategy and counter-strategy so that you would be one step ahead of whatever I was feeling—"

"I sleep good at night," Mann said, drawing her close to him. "How's this: I forbid you to have sex with me tonight, or tomorrow night, or ever. I'm off limits." He felt an internal rush of relief as he said it.

He was pleased to see the shocked look on her face, and then felt dismay when the look turned to anger.

"Oh, my god you're good," she said hotly. "Now suddenly I feel like I have to get back in control. And the only way I can do that is to have sex with you right this moment, which you must have been thinking all along."

"Is it possible," Mann suggested timidly, "that sometimes you over-think these things?"

"Oh, I'm not nearly as good as you are. And for your information, there isn't any thinking at all. Do you know how long it would take me to find a man willing to have sex with me?"

"What does that have to do with it?"

"Two seconds. I actually timed it. It depends on how you count, but I walked into eight different bars one night and announced in a kind of loud voice that I was feeling horny tonight, and within an average of six seconds, I would have at least three men intruding on my space and jostling each other for the privilege of buying me a drink. You divide six by three and you get two seconds."

"I can do the math," Mann said. He drew her up closer to him and shivered. "But I don't understand what your point is."

"Every time I start, like we did tonight, I realize that the odds are, like, seven zillion to one that the only reason you have your clothes off is all about you and your pleasure for this moment, this night, and nothing at all about me and about us and anything about my dreams of actually enjoying mutual love with a man I can love and respect and admire—do you understand a thing I'm telling you?" she demanded. "Do you?"

"Of course," he said. He looked into her eyes, hoping they would give him some clue as to what the hell she was talking about. "It only took you six seconds?" he said after a moment.

"All I ever asked was somebody who, when I do for them, they will do exactly the same for— Wait," she said, looking at him suspiciously. "What? What did you say?"

"I think you're exaggerating. You mean, you actually timed it on your watch?"

"On my computer pendant. What? You don't believe me?"

"Three guys."

"Once it was four, another time there were two. So I averaged them out; the math still works. And others would come up soon afterwards, when they saw I wasn't interested in the first group. That's when I would leave. But what does that have to do with anything?"

"Isn't that what I was asking *you*?"

She opened her mouth to give him an angry reply, and abruptly shut it again.

She started to giggle, her smile twisting involuntarily into that ironic smile.

She rolled over on her back and lay her head back on his shoulder, and the giggle turned into a laugh. Gradually, she relaxed her body and lay sprawled out on her back.

"You win," she said. "God knows what the contest was, but I have to hand it to you."

"Hand me what?"

"The invisible trophy."

"Can I get dressed now?" Mann said after a minute. "I'm cold."

"Stay here a minute more. You're keeping me warm."

"Okay. I'll just admire my trophy."

Gloria started to giggle again. "Did you really mean it?" she asked after a moment.

"What."

"That you refuse to have sex with me forever?"

"If you bring it up again, it'll be even longer," Mann warned her.

"Can I still sleep in this bed tonight?"

"Of course. How else can I keep you warm?"

Gloria closed her eyes and then turned her head and regarded him languidly. "You know what?"

"What."

"I think you're the most confusing person I ever met."

26

"The wind bloweth where it listeth, and thou hearest the sound thereof, but canst not tell whence it cometh, and whither it goeth: so is every one that is born of the Spirit."

Jesus of Nazareth

Gloria found Mann more than a block away from the place where they were supposed to meet. As she walked up, an older gentleman in a suit darted past in the opposite direction.

"Who the heck was that?" she said. "I thought for a second I recognized him, but I know he doesn't work here."

"Oh..." Mann waved vaguely in the man's direction. "It was just..." he mumbled.

"It was who?"

"The—majority leader in the National House," Mann mumbled again.

"And HE came HERE? To meet with you?"

"Actually he refused to meet with me at all. So we had to take over his mind for a while."

"His—? What are you talking about?"

"It's not important. Listen; I have a friend I want you to meet."

They were walking along a path through the park, moving slowly, passed by people who were biking or jogging or generally hurrying in both directions. On all sides of the park, buildings rose up so high it was hard to see their peaks, so that the few acres of trees, flowers, grass and lakes seemed like a deep valley surrounded on all sides by complex, irregular cliffs.

"I didn't realize you had friends," Gloria said.

"You don't have to be nasty about it."

"You live like a hermit."

"It isn't much different from your lifestyle," Mann countered. "And anyway, how is work coming?"

"Exhilarating and frustrating at the same time."

"How, frustrating?"

"Sometimes I think I'm on the edge of putting it all together into one coherent whole, where you can go into any one part of it and all the rest is right there and available. And then I realize that the biggest part of it is missing."

"What part?"

"I don't think you'd understand any of it."

"Try me," Mann said.

"It's the whole integration of the cosmic with the subatomic," she said. "They call it the unified field theory, the reconciliation of macro universal mathematics with the mathematics of subatomic reality. The underlying single explanation that ties the strong force and the weak force and magnetism and gravity all together, but it's a lot more than that. Do you realize that we don't even know what matter *is*? It can't be anything solid and three dimensional, because if it were, then the forces that move the smallest particles around would act on one side first, before the rest, and tear them apart, and everything would be a jumbled mess instead of the orderly arrangement that we see around us."

"Oh," Mann said.

"I told you you wouldn't understand it. We don't know why quarks clump together in these various configurations, or why the arrangements of protons and neutrons are stable in certain numbers and not in others, or why there's quantum tunneling or why electrons seem to move around with intrinsic motion, which is a lot like tunneling to my eye when I look at the experiments. There should be zillions upon zillions of magnetic monopoles in this universe of ours, and we haven't managed to find even a single one. There's something holding the galaxies together that we can't see, and so we call it dark matter, but we can't see or measure that either, and there's something causing the universe to expand more rapidly every day, and we call that dark energy, and guess what?"

"What?" Mann said, abruptly realizing it was his turn to talk.

"We can't measure or even find that either."

"So?"

"What do you mean, 'so'? Is that your favorite word or something?"

"Without that, you can't put it all together?" Mann said.

"The hell of it," Gloria said, "is that I really believe, down inside where my intuition comes from, that all of it can be explained by one central insight, and if I had that one central thing that put all those other things together, then all the gadgets and gizmos and field manipulation would fall neatly into place. Give me *that* and I'm probably weeks instead of years away from getting it all down."

They were coming up on the edge of the pond, where a hundred or so people were sitting in a semicircle around a man who Gloria studied with interest. It was too far to hear the words clearly, but by the look of the audience, they were having a visibly transformative effect.

"Who is he?"

"He's a friend. I've told him a little bit about you."

"Such as?"

"I said you are in every way the most important person in the world. Which he thinks is funny, because he thinks *he* is."

As Mann and Gloria approached, it was easier to hear Gandhi's words, which ended in a chorus.

*Believing
is the
reason
for being...*

Spotting Mann, Gandhi stood up and bowed to the people in the group, who lowered their heads in return. Then he walked over.

"And who is this charming flower?" he asked Mann.

"Hardly a flower," he answered back. "This is Gloria."

"I am enchanted to make your wonderful acquaintance," Gandhi said. "This is the one you have talked to me about?" he inquired.

"She is indeed."

"My friend boasts about your brilliance, but he did not prepare me for your beauty, or the true magnificence that I sense in your soul," Gandhi said, taking her hand in both of his. "I offer you a blessing that will extend at all times to all that you feel and all that you do."

"I could certainly use some of that," Gloria responded, looking him full in the face. "It's very funny," she said over her shoulder to Mann. "He has that same strange glow that you have, only more so. So," she asked Gandhi, "these are your... followers?"

"They are the people who have given me the unrepayable gift of their attention, which makes it possible for me to fulfill my purpose in this reality," Gandhi corrected her gently. "I am blessed with a certain wisdom," he added. "When a gift is given by the Almighty, one has an obligation to share it freely."

"A wisdom for what?"

"For harmony, for peace, for being able to treasure this wonderfully magnificent world that is the gift of the Almighty, which so few seem to be able to appreciate. For understanding how to move with rather than in opposition to the Almighty will, as a child learns to obey the wisdom of truly loving parents even if it is not always easy to understand the whys and the wherefores of it. Small things compared with the greater wisdom that resides in the universe, but for here, for now, they are things it is necessary to hear."

"I could use a little of all of that," Gloria said. She gave Mann a quick embrace. "And you meet here?" she asked Gandhi.

"Come here and inquire about me, my child, and they will show you where to find me. And now, perhaps, I should speak alone with your friend, and you perhaps can meet my friends here, and friendship will deepen in all directions."

"You are introducing me to this lady, for what reason?" Gandhi asked in English as they walked away from the gathering.

"If something happens to me, you need to find her. She's gathering all the information we need to finish the assignment."

"Ah, very good. But of course, we are immortal here, so nothing will happen to you." Gandhi dismissed the subject with an impatient wave of his hand. "Meanwhile, what you did for Washington was extremely, truly amazing, my brother," Gandhi said. "He is now a household name everywhere. If this other Senator person drops out of the race as I think we hope he will, there will be talk of the presidency. Really remarkable work."

"Thanks."

"I was not meaning to congratulate you. I was trying to help you realize that you have given him a very unfair advantage in our competition."

"Is that all this is to you? A competition?"

"Well, it is also a very important job," Gandhi added.

"What about the consequences? All these people? Don't you ever think about the fact that you might be saving billions of lives?"

Gandhi looked at Mann carefully. "These aren't lives," he said finally. "They're blips in the dendrites of a machine upstairs, a universe that will cease to exist as soon as we get what we need from it. Sometimes I wonder if you are at all times aware of this, my brother."

Mann said nothing. He looked up at the lights of the city, and let the Synchronicity wash over him, seeing the inside of the city from a thousand angles, through a thousand perspectives.

"So what are you proposing?" he said.

"I am in a very big need of something that will make everyone know me very quickly. I must get them to see me as something more than just an amazing person who has a new idea for a better way of life. I need," Gandhi said, "something very much dramatic that will bring in tens of thousands of people who are pre-conditioned to believe that I come from the right hand of God, and in this technological age, I am very concerned that they won't find that unconditional faith through any of the parlor tricks I was able to use in ages long gone."

"Indeed," said Mann. "You need to be the real thing."

"I AM the real thing. We just need to show this to them."

"Take it easy," said Mann.

"You don't have to be sarcastic. I am truly doing everything I can. But you are helping Washington and forgetting about me, and that is a problem with what we are doing here. You were sold to us as the person who could find a solution to anything, because you don't have any limitations."

"Witch said that?"

"She very much hated every word of it. My brother, you were absolutely and in every way her last resort on this thing we are doing now."

Mann was silent again.

"So?" Gandhi said finally.

Mann paused for a moment in thought. Finally he said: "Some years back the Company sent me out to talk with a tribal chieftain who lived deep in the Himalayas, about ten days by caravan from the nearest airport. It seems this chieftain had taken over a neighboring tribe at gunpoint and then sold it to the Chinese in what must have been a complicated transaction. They, of course, would use the village as a base to threaten some disputed territory. This put the village at great risk of being caught in the middle of a crossfire skirmish and incidentally destabilize the whole region, and of course the villagers were very unhappy about it. Fortunately for them, so too was my government, which promised the Indian government that it would do something about it.

"I made a formal appointment to talk things over with the chieftain, but he sent a group of thugs to meet the caravan and have me killed on the spot. I managed to make myself difficult to find for about two weeks, and during that two weeks, some very strange things happened. One day, the chieftain awoke from a very deep sleep, and discovered that one of his fingers was missing, in a quite painful operation. That finger was later found in the bed of his oldest son, who was also in a deep sleep. A few nights later, despite a doubling of the guards, a second finger was mysteriously removed from his hand, and was found in the bed of his youngest daughter."

"I truly dislike the story already, my brother," said Gandhi.

"It is said that the chieftain, who was in some degree of pain and no small amount of anxiety concerning the rest of his digits, and also the safety of his children, didn't sleep the following night, and I can confirm this to some extent, because I paid him a surprise visit that evening. We talked for several hours while the guards outside his door dreamed the dreams of the innocent. It was a philosophical conversation about the many many things in this world that are worse than death, and I think he was surprised and somewhat intrigued to discover that the list was so long. The following morning, he appeared before the people of the village and his own soldiers and apologized for his actions, and then sat down on the stone dais and set himself on fire. Nobody moved to rescue him, for they saw that this was a personal atonement."

"Charming," said Gandhi.

"The next day, I was hitching a ride with a caravan," Mann continued, "when a contingent of the tribe's elders met me, and made me understand that they credited me with the chieftain's brave exculpatory act. They had apparently spent many hours trying to decide how best to reward me, and finally asked me if I would accompany them on a three-day trek up into the higher mountains to meet a holy man who lived there, who would give me the promised reward."

"You agreed, naturally?" Gandhi prodded, visibly impatient with the story.

"I told them I was on an urgent journey to have a quiet conversation with the local Chinese overlord who had brokered this deal with this chieftain," said Mann. "That's when they turned their guns on me. I decided in the interests of our mutual relations, their tribe and my government, to adjust my plans and graciously accept their reward.

"They led me, over the next three days, to a well-appointed cave so high up on the edge of a cliff that it seemed like I couldn't get enough air in my lungs. When I entered the cave, even the candle on the wooden table seemed to be anemic, as if starved for oxygen. A young man with a long black beard greeted me solemnly, and invited me to sit. We talked for hours, and he told me many stories of the long history of the village and also of the surrounding countryside, and I was especially interested to hear about his childhood in Kanauj, a city near modern-day Nepal, which at the time was at the focal point of the Rashtraukutas, Palas and Guriara Prathiras empires."

"Wait," Gandhi said suddenly. "As it happens, I know something of Indian history. But this is extremely confusing. What year are we talking about, the birth of this young man?"

"Their calendar didn't correspond to ours," said Mann. "But my best guess from looking back into the historical record is that it was around 900 AD."

"His childhood."

"Yes," Mann said. "It turns out he was more than 1,000 years old."

"And you believed this?"

"On the way back home, the villagers confirmed that he had lived up there as long as their great, great grandparents could remember, and he was the person they would ask about events and history long before that."

"Did he explain how he came by this long life, my brother?" Gandhi asked.

"That was the gift," said Mann. "He said that the very ancient texts, kept in the private vaults of the monasteries, were not religious documents at all. They were actually written by scientists from a highly advanced civilization that flourished in the lower Himalayas during a time when most of the world was inhabited by cave dwellers."

"Medical texts, I assume."

"Actually not. Their 'technology,' if you can call it that, was a highly-sophisticated ability to communicate, mentally, directly with the cells and mechanisms of their bodies through meditative techniques. I must have looked as skeptical as you do when he said this," Mann continued, "because he invited me to consider the thousand-year lifespans claimed in the Judeo-Christian holy books, which he said where the chronicles of refugees from this long-ago civilization who we now call the Hebrew patriarchs, who were practitioners of this 'technology' that halted the aging process. And he said that when I returned, I should research the placebo effect, and how it's being scientifically justified through a new field of science called 'self-directed neuroplasticity.' We are, he told me then, in the very early stages of recovering this knowledge."

"That's it?" Gandhi said finally. "He told you to meditate and talk to your cells so that you'd never grow old?"

"Over the course of a couple of months, he showed me how to guide my healing processes directly to different parts of my body," Mann said. "He showed me how to direct these internal mechanisms to stop the aging process, and even unwind it. And like he said, it's absurdly simple, although it does require a certain amount of time and a hell of a lot of concentration. He didn't look to be more than 30 years old."

"I am thinking that I do not see how this relates to what we are talking about," Gandhi insisted, "which is to help my mission gain more followers the way you have helped Washington."

"No?"

"No, I really don't."

"What I'm trying to get to is, maybe it's time you offered some religious advice that actually works in peoples' lives, rather than a cheap con game." Mann proposed. "Something that provides actual benefits. If the laws of physics work here as they do upstairs, and we teach people to lean on the interface in addition, then this meditative self-healing should also work here. You can say the results come from faith in God, and direct them to pray for broader outcomes. I'm trying to envision millions of followers all leaning on the interface in the same way, and maybe while they're at it, praying to the god computer to prevent this damn war that everybody seems to think is so inevitable."

"But I have so far not yet heard a plan to get me millions of followers," Gandhi said with a renewed gleam of interest. "That is really what I was asking you for in the beginning."

"It's what I was talking about all along," said Mann. "The self-directed neuroplasticity can be just as easily attributed to god as to scientific processes, and in fact that's actually the way it's apparently phrased in the later paraphrases of those ancient texts. Cure some people, or help them cure themselves."

"More parlor tricks," Gandhi sniffed. "But at this point I'm open to anything. But you said—"

"You also need something dramatic," Mann agreed. "Something so dramatic that everybody will be talking about it, which will start them believing that these other techniques you tell them will work. It all starts with belief. We have to find something that puts you on the map as a legitimate representative of this god you keep talking about."

"You have an idea? Better than what you did for Washington?"

"Just as good," said Mann. "And you're going to love it."

27

"Through this discrimination the Vedantist realizes, by his inner perception, that the ego and the universe are both illusory, like a dream."

Ramakrishna

"Senator Wendle, I'm grateful that you had the time to meet with me today."

"Son, I have to tell you, I've been scratching my head at my schedule all morning, trying to figure out how you got on there. You must be one resourceful citizen, is all I can guess at the moment."

"I think everything will become clear before long," Mann assured him. "In fact, I wanted to talk to you about your upcoming resolution to declare war and override the president's cautious approach to the world tensions."

Wendle settled back in his chair and with a nod gave Mann permission to sit down. He had an ovoid body that had never seen military training or action and a head that seemed too large for the rest of him, with a shock of white hair and a square, granite jaw above several chins, which conveyed an impression of eminence and authority.

"My constituents are solidly behind me on my support for teaching the Eastern bloc that we won't be pushed around," he said. "This is, by far, the most popular thing I talk about whenever I give speeches to the voters."

"In fact, you introduced six proposals last year. All of them were narrowly voted down."

"Somebody has to do something to save this country from itself. And anyway, as I say over and over again on the stump, why are we paying so much money to buy the best military in the world if we aren't ever going to use it?"

"Of course, you were one of the prime movers behind the increases in military funding, going back at least 20 years."

"I vote what I believe in."

"Is it possible that your longstanding interest in war is just a cheap way to further your political ambitions?"

Wendle regarded Mann with a steady gaze. "The polls show that I'm ahead by twenty percentage points over the appeaser that the other party plans to run."

"And what about Washington, from your own party?"

The Senator's eyes narrowed. "You mean, the traitor?"

"The polls I read say he's nipping at your heels. Maybe your initiatives aren't as popular as you think they are."

"Did you come to my last rally?"

"Yes. Many angry older men wearing military style hats and waving national flags. I had the impression none of them had ever actually served in the military before. In that sense, they were much like you, yourself."

The Senator sat back and favored him with a long, appraising look. "I like to say that as their elected representative, I'm their spokesperson in Congress. But perhaps it's time for you to explain why you're here."

"I'm hoping to get you to see reason on this war issue. You know that both sides have stockpiled enough powerful missiles that it could mean the end of civilization."

"Not if we strike first and take out their missiles."

"A deliberative vote to declare war, spread out over weeks and covered daily by the news media, seems hardly a stealth measure, to my admittedly untrained eye."

"If the generals see the writing on the wall, they'll act before we even put it up to a vote," the Senator rumbled.

"Is that really what you're hoping for? To prod people who are already inclined to war into believing that it's inevitable?"

"I believe it's time to end this standoff and plant our flag on their soil."

"The smoking, radioactive ruins of it."

Wendle stood up.

"Son, I believe our time is just about up here. Now you skee-daddle along and take your pacifist views with you out the door. They're beginning to raise an ugly and unseemly stench in my humble office."

"I had one other thing, but it will only take a second," Mann said, reaching into his pocket. "I have copies of some campaign photos I thought you might like to see."

He handed over an envelope. The Senator took them without enthusiasm. Then, as he pulled the pictures out of the envelope, his face became a blank.

"You say, these are campaign photos?" he said after a moment. "Where did you get these?"

"These are going to be the centerpiece of the next phase of Washington's campaign. He believes, as I do, that the voters have a right to know about your, shall we say, *exotic* sexual appetites."

The Senator dropped the pictures on his desk. Then he looked down at Mann.

"You might want to look at the rest," Mann said. "Some of them are quite imaginative."

After a long second, the Senator sat back down and fingered the pictures on his desk with distaste. But there was no sign of worry on his face.

"Do you realize that you will be dead before you walk out of this building?" he said finally.

Mann shook his head. "Surely you must understand that I knew that your first reaction would be to kill me. In fact, that's exactly why I'm here in the first place, to prevent a person who thinks like you do from making military policy for the Western Alliance. Arrangements have already been made to have all of these pictures published in all the media outlets, unless I personally intervene."

Wendle smiled. "Then I'll simply deny their authenticity."

"Of course, I anticipated that that would be your backup response: to lie not just to me, but to everyone. But you must understand that I have other pictures of you driving to the motel, checking in under—what was that creative name you used? Penile Plunge, or some such thing... The pictures have been certified authentic by several teams of experts, who as yet have been sworn to secrecy."

The Senator sat back in his chair. "So what do you want?" he asked finally. "I have money, more than you would imagine considering that I've spent my life as a servant of the people. And I have access to much more than you could ever spend in your mortal years."

"Bribery would be your natural third option," Mann said. "Are you beginning to at least understand why I consider you to be a less-than-ideal leader of the Western Alliance? I can tell you that there are many people, sitting in your chair, who would have considered a different set of alternatives than murder, lying and bribery."

The Senator offered Mann a perplexed smile. "Perhaps you can explain why you're here, if I can't prevent these pictures from becoming public?"

Mann sat back and regarded the scattered images now spread out across the desk, admiring the thoroughness, creativity and overall enthusiasm that Westerly had put into this particular assignment. He reached forward and selected one of the pictures.

"I think this one is my favorite," he said. "Until I saw these, I wasn't sure such a thing was anatomically possible."

He looked up. "My algorithms tell me that only about 5% of the people who intend to vote for you for Senator would be troubled enough by this evidence of... *depravity*—to change their voting plans. Of those, only a third will vote for Washington; the others are likely to abstain from voting altogether. That's too narrow a margin. I want a more certain solution."

Mann leaned forward. "And I have to say that my feelings are once again getting in the way here. I honestly want to spare you the embarrassment and, frankly, living hell of dealing with this scandal. I want to give you a chance to avoid it altogether."

"Meaning?"

"You should drop out of the race. For health reasons. There won't be any diminution of your lifestyle. I happen to know you have offers to become a lobbyist that would dwarf your current income. In fact, there's a strong rumor that you have, in the top drawer of your desk at this moment, a signed blank check that you were invited to fill in with the salary of your choice."

The Senator regarded Mann with a rising combination of indignation and incredulity.

"Resign?!?" he demanded. "Before the election?"

"I would do it immediately, so your party can field a viable alternative candidate."

"The flaming hell with that. I know who they'd select. This man Washington is a traitor, a pacifist who doesn't have the patriotic credentials—"

"Then you, yourself, are going to lose to that pacifist. It's possible that our algorithms are wrong, and more people than we realize will be shocked at your... exotic tastes."

"Yes, my tastes..."

The Senator stared down at his desk for a long moment. The silence stretched out, and Mann was surprised to realize that he'd won.

"You know, when this happened," Wendle said, as if talking to himself more than Mann, "I felt like I was outside of my own body.

There was an unreality about it. I'm not the sort of man who cares for sex," he said. "It's a weakness that tends to get in the way of all the other things that are important to me. I left the hotel that night feeling disgusted with myself, and confused in a way that I've never felt before. But until now, I had no idea there was a camera around."

Mann waited.

He looked up at Mann. "Here's what you should know," the Senator said, pinning him with his eyes. "The outcry for war is coming from everywhere. I'm doing nothing more than saying out loud what everybody thinks, what everybody wants. If you think getting me out of this office is going to change that, then you're an idiot."

Mann smiled. "I think you underestimate me. Is that all?"

"No," Wendle said. "You should know one more thing," he added. "There are people involved in the election process who are going to prevent your Mr. Washington from ever coming up for a vote."

"Yes, I know that too. In fact, they've asked me to talk with them."

Wendle stuffed the pictures back in the envelope and then, in an impulsive gesture, tore them in half, then in quarters, then in eighths and, with difficulty, into sixteenths. He handed the shreds back to Mann, who took them solemnly.

"Senator," he said, "the truth is, you were always a very small piece of what still has to be done. And just for the record," Mann added as he walked to the door, "I was the one who proposed this meeting. Mr. Washington would have much preferred if you had stayed on and fought for your political life. It would have thrown even more discredit on your views."

28

"He who knows the whiteness of glory and
yet keeps to the darkness of humility,
Becomes the model for the world.
Being the model for the world,
He will never deviate from eternal virtue,
But returns to the state of the Ultimate of Non-being."

Lao Tzu

As he walked out of the transportation hub, Mann realized that somewhere in the back of his mind, there was an odd stirring of awareness in the Synchronicity. Following the remote attention of others, he looked through the eyes of several individuals who were peering with some perplexity up at the sky.

The watchers ignored the ubiquitous silvery bubbles floating in all directions, and instead were trying to get a better look at three objects which seemed to be flying higher and faster: strange-looking mechanical insects that Mann instantly recognized, from his military briefings, as killer drones.

A part of his mind thought that this was curious. The existence of these remote weapons, developed so late in this world's military history, was top-secret.

But a more basic part of his mind was, by this time, totally in control of Mann's body, as he raced across the street and down into an alley, fighting down a wild panic that the calmer, more rational part of his mind found interestingly illogical, since even if he died, he would be resurrected back into this world in minutes.

"What is it?" the dog asked, matching Mann's pace effortlessly. "Is it something I should be worried about?"

"Get away from me and stay away," Mann said. "I don't want you killed."

"We're totally on the same page here. I don't want to be killed either."

Gasping for breath, Mann allowed his body to slip into a long striding, mile-eating pace through the alleyway on this block. He turned left along the sidewalk and up a ramp, staying off the walkway where the path was clogged with pedestrians, some of whom looked up with mild interest at the strange-looking jogger who raced past.

"Can you hear it?" the dog asked.

"What?"

Then Mann heard the drones, a distant buzz in the air, like a swarm of insects. When he finally stopped, gasping and out of breath, hugging the wall along the edge of the ramp, he watched the ugly flying things emerge from the sky behind the building, passing obliquely overhead toward the far end of the street, slowing their pace and dropping closer to the ground. Not only the sound; their appearance was insect-like as well, thick bodies with short "legs" that cushioned their landings, with twin antennae along the front whose tips housed telescopic cameras and infra-red sighting mechanisms.

"Those are ugly-looking things," the dog observed.

"I told you to get lost." Mann looked around. "Where are you?"

"Under the fruit stand thing. They won't find me here. But you're kind of exposed, standing there."

The drones fanned out, scanning the street. Their cameras would be feeding views of thousands of pedestrian faces back into a database in the remote control facility, looking for a facial match.

His face.

Mann estimated that the next transportation center was less than a mile away, three stories up this spiraling ramp and then down through a tunnel-like space that was reasonably sheltered from the air.

He took a deep breath, which paid the final installment on his oxygen deficit, and then walked quickly along the edge of the wall with his nose almost touching it, keeping his face turned always away from the open air.

The buzz grew louder. He walked more quickly. After a few moments, the buzz had increased to such intensity that Mann was unable to maintain his discipline. Cautiously, he turned his head—

And experienced a jolt of adrenaline like lightning through his body, as he found himself face-to-antenna with one of the drones, not more than three feet away.

It must have taken the recognition program at least a tenth of a second to confirm the match, because it did not attack before Mann had reached out to the interface, actually grabbed hold of it with his mind.

Instantly, the scene froze. Pushing through the thickness of time and the air around him, Mann threw his body under the drone and, as it turned imperceptibly, he reached out and grabbed the drone's back leg with one hand, then the other.

Mann allowed time to return. The eyestalks turned to regard him as the drone twisted furiously in his arms. The calm, logical part of Mann's mind took note of what his instincts had realized whole seconds before: that the firing mechanism was located on the front of the drone, which meant that it would have to turn in order to kill him, which was impossible as he clung to the back as it bucked and twisted, and finally tried to rise up into the air.

Over the angry buzz of the machine he was clutching, Mann could hear the other drones approaching somewhere overhead. As the machine struggled to lift him more than a few inches from the ground, he was also aware that his wrestling match had the attention of the pedestrians on the walkway, some of whom were aiming their pendants in his direction to record the event for friends who would be skeptical of their story without video proof.

Out of nowhere, the dog appeared, jumping into the air and grabbing one of the eyestalks with its teeth. He swung back and forth, until suddenly the metal stalk gave way, and the dog lay panting by Mann's side.

"Excellent work," Mann gasped. With his right arm still holding the back of the drone, he managed to grab the stalk and jam it into the twin blades of the drone, shutting his eyes against a spattering of metal and plastic hard against his face as the blades chewed up the stalk and, suddenly, the thin metal pole lodged itself into one of the blades, and Mann was thrown backwards as the drone suddenly stopped bucking. He threw the drone into the wall and ran up the ramp as the sounds of the other drones buzzed louder.

The calm part of his brain was still wondering at this irrational panic when suddenly there was a sound like the hiss of butter on a hot frying pan, and a hole the size of a silver dollar appeared in the pavement in front of him. A tightly focused laser had vaporized a deep gash in the concrete. Mann stopped time again as two more holes appeared near his feet, and as his body ran in a dreamlike slowness, he dove for the shelter of the tunnel; his rational mind had finally given its full attention over to the immediate challenge of survival. For long seconds, Mann rested in the air, before he allowed time to move again, and as he struck the ground, he rolled, leaped to his feet and tried to melt into the crowd on the moving walkway, crouching among people who barely moved to accommodate his presence.

The ceiling of the tunnel was less than ten feet high, and the air was cooler, a bit musty. Mann heard the distant rumble of transportation pods, growing louder as the walkway took him deeper into the atrium. He allowed the crowd to move him toward the embarkation area, where the sound of the pods was louder. He let the panic drain out of his body, leaving it shaking and exhausted.

"That was close, boss. Whoever is trying to kill you is using those military things you were talking about."

"You think?"

"Did I not tell you it was unwise to piss off humans whose job is killing people?"

"I should have listened more carefully."

"That's exactly what I said at the time."

What to do now? Mann's cognitive mind was annoyed to realize that his instincts were already making the decision for him, as his legs carried him toward the pods that would transport him back to the laboratory.

Would the drone operators expect that? Who knew? Mann's higher awareness no longer cared; in this universe, he was immortal. Why should he worry?

The rumble of the pods grew louder, and then, abruptly, the dog sunk its teeth into Mann's leg and yanked hard. Mann fell just as a drone raced directly over him, missing his head by inches.

This time the lightning that ran down into his nervous system drove Mann forward and down. He heard screams behind him as the drone knocked people aside on a wide swing back toward its intended victim. Mann could hear it hovering overhead as he crawled among what seemed to be thousands of legs.

The pods immediately in front of him shut their doors. He was near the front, and as he stood up, the drone swung out in front of him and fired just as Mann went over the side and into the deep well in front of the transportation pods as they started to move.

"Boss, I don't think that was—"

Mann's conscious mind agreed with the dog, telling him that this had been a curious choice, and was wondering what the lizard brain at the base of his mind, totally in control now, had in mind as Mann's body raced in a blind panic toward the darkness deeper in the tunnel. The drone swung out ahead of him, and took careful aim. Behind him on the track, Mann heard the heavy weight of the pods gathering speed as the magnetic forces kicked into high gear.

Time froze again. Mann saw a bolt of laser intensity frozen in place aimed just above his face in the tunnel, and another behind it. Slowly, he allowed time to restart itself, and the bolts flashed by as Mann dove down and backwards, landing in a fetal position on the ground as the underside of the pods rolled thunderously over him in a mad hurricane of wind. Distantly, he heard the sound of the pod smacking into the drone like a bug against the windshield.

Mann held his body deathly still for what felt like hours as the long train of pods passed over him, their complex undersides less than an inch above his back.

For a full minute after the pod had passed, Mann continued to lay where he was, shivering. Finally, he stood up and ran back to the pedestrian area and, with difficulty, climbed out of the well into the tunnel.

The dog was waiting for him at the edge.

"Whoa. I was already looking for a new master," the dog said. "I'm going to tell you right now, that last stunt didn't look safe to me at all."

Mann favored the dog with a fond and exasperated look.

"Did you see the other one?" he asked.

"Do I look like the sort of animal that would go looking for trouble? It's probably watching the exits."

"That's what I think too," said Mann.

Another transportation pod rumbled up toward the embarkation area, so Mann followed the crowd inside and stood at the back wall. The dog nodded approval and followed him in.

"I guess I earned a little extra dinner for that one, right?" it said.

"I give you all you want anyway."

"This time I deserve more than I want."

"Right."

The last drone was nowhere in sight. Scanning through the Synchronicity, he was able to make it out, still waiting above the transportation center. Relaxing a little, Mann moved forward to the pod that would take him back to the office.

He and the dog emerged at his usual stop, several blocks from the building, and walked slowly down the street. The eyes of the Synchronicity told him the drone had left the transportation hub area, but where was it now?

"Do you hear anything?"

"Sure," the dog said. "A lot of people are talking, and of course their shoes are making sounds where they touch the pavement, and one of those street digger things is probably two blocks away, and I think now I hear that metal insect thing coming in our direction fast."

A moment later, the drone came into view over an intersection two blocks ahead, near where Mann would have been if he'd been walking more quickly. The telescopic stalks swiveled back and forth, scanning the faces of pedestrians from a height of perhaps 100 feet. People looked up curiously in their direction and then walked along, unconcerned. Mann covered his face with one hand. He turned and walked in the opposite direction, still hugging the shadow of the wall.

After almost a minute, the sound of the drone passed overhead.

As Mann watched the sky, there was a hard bump in his back as he collided with someone.

"Eh!" A hand grabbed his shoulder.

"Sorry," Mann muttered, trying, back still turned, to move around the person, who remained stubbornly in his way. The hand remained on his shoulder.

"Turn around slowly," an authoritative voice said to him. "I want to see your hands."

"Should I bite him, boss?"

Mann half turned, glancing at a stocky police officer out of the corner of his eye. The drone hovered behind the officer's hat.

"I said I was sorry," Mann said.

"Yeah, he apologized. And you really don't want to be in the middle of this right now."

"I strongly advise you to turn around. What's wrong with you? What are you trying to hide?"

"My face," said Mann.

"Your what?"

At that moment, the drone swooped lower. Mann crouched, keeping the officer's head between the stalks and his face. The officer responded by yanking Mann's shoulder again, and he reached for his weapon.

The officer screamed as the dog bit deeply into his leg, and the hand disappeared from Mann's shoulder. He turned, and found that the drone was hovering inches in front of his face as Mann ducked sideways just before a tight laser blast erupted from the drone, slicing the police officer nearly in half and taking chunks of concrete out of the pavement.

"These people definitely mean business," the dog panted. "And in case you were wondering, that human tasted terrible."

Avoiding the screaming panic of pedestrians, Mann threw his body into the entrance of a grocery store, and pushed his way through a crowded aisle to the back, looking for a second entrance. He ran through a swinging door into the warehouse area behind the retail part of the store, and found the back entrance, where a large truck was parked. He ran past workers wheeling boxes on dollies.

Peering out the back entrance, he could see the drone hovering about 300 feet in the air above this exit, its twin blades making an indistinct, distant buzz that could be heard above the sounds of pedestrians who clogged the sidewalk a few feet from where he was standing.

To his right, an alley between buildings, and a large metal automated garbage disposal unit.

If he could slip out the door into the alley, and keep in the shadow of the garbage bin, whoever was operating the drones would believe he was still in the store while he walked back to the office.

As soon as he emerged from the door, there was a bright flash that scored the pavement near his feet. Once again, time slowed down as Mann dove into the open side of the garbage unit. He rolled over on the soft bags and scrambled to the corner of the bin where he had just entered, curling in a ball to make himself as small a target as possible. Laser bolts rattled against the metallic roof, opening holes that made the unit look like cheesecloth all across the sides.

After a moment, Mann realized that it was quiet.

The bin was roughly the size of a railroad car, with a compactor unit inside, consisting of two steel plates on either side of the unit. Mann put himself in the mind of the drone pilot. Was he dead? It would be very important to confirm his demise. Plan A would be to wait and see if there was sound or movement coming from inside the receptacle.

Mann lay back on the lumpy bags of trash just behind the opening, where it would be impossible for the drone to see him if it tried to peer into the opening from afar. He settled in for a long wait. How long before the remote pilot became impatient?

With nothing else to do, Mann scanned the interior walls of the receptacle. The compactor plate sat on the far side of the container from where he sat. He reached into the Synchronicity, and found someone not far from where he sat. His mind conveyed the need for caution.

Outside, he could hear the street noises but nothing else.

He ventured a glance through the opening at the face of the building and, beyond it, the crowded street, where people were walking past as if there was nothing out of the ordinary. He settled back again.

He had almost fallen asleep when the drone burst into the receptacle like an angry hornet, hovering above the piles of bags, its eye stalks turned toward the back of the receptacle. Then, with a buzz, it turned and scanned the floor. As soon as the drone came within reach, Mann grabbed it from behind.

The drone spun around hard in his hands and the laser blew a few more holes in the far wall. Through the Synchronicity, Mann gave a quick direction, and a button was pushed on the outside of the container, causing the compactor plate to move toward him. He swung the drone against the side of the container, breaking one of the eye stalks.

The plate moved closer with more speed than he had expected. Mann scrambled up the side of the bags, slipping, as the drone twisted in his hands. As the bags on the bottom and far side of the bin were shoved toward him, they formed a better purchase for his feet. Finally, Mann let go of the drone and leaped awkwardly up toward the side. His hands grabbed the edge of the bin, and he yanked his legs out of the path of the plate an instant before it slammed shut.

There was an angry buzz inside the compacting piles of garbage, and periodic flashes of light. New holes appeared in the opposite side of the bin. Finally, there was no buzzing sound, no flashing, and Mann allowed his body to relax.

Wearily, he climbed down to the pavement and walked around the corner to the street, within sight of the office. He bent over, gasping for breath.

"I guess that shows them," the dog said. "Maybe next time you talk to these people, you could, like, make nice."

At that moment Forbes came around the corner with Gloria.

They stopped short as Mann, his breath heaving, slowly stood up straight. He looked at Forbes, then at Gloria.

Forbes looked down at him, and then at the dog, with an amused smile. "What's going on?" he asked.

Mann struggled to speak, took a couple of long breaths, and then finally gasped: "We were jogging."

Forbes shook his head. "Man," he said, "are YOU out of shape." Then he made a gesture of sweeping distasteful air away from his nose. "And perhaps this would be a good time to take your monthly shower."

Before Mann could recover his breath to answer, they had walked past into the building, Gloria looking behind.

29

"Eye cannot see it, nor words reveal it;
by the senses, austerity, or works it is not known.
When the mind is cleansed by the grace of wisdom,
it is seen by contemplation—the One without parts."

Upanishad 3.1.8

"To find a neutral location these days, you have to travel back in time," the Eastern representative said, motioning Mann to a seat across the table. Instead of a servomechanism, a young man approached them and asked if they had any questions. The Eastern representative looked confused until Mann indicated the printed descriptions of the food and drink that was offered at this eating establishment.

Mann shook the snow off his coat and laid it at the end of the booth seat across from the representative. He looked out the window at the gray shapes moving quickly along the street, only their noses and eyes visible, trailing the thin ephemeral smoke of their own exhaled breath.

"I hope your time machine was more comfortable than mine," he said as he settled into the booth.

"Comfort is not our first concern when we travel."

"Yes, yours is a Spartan society. In contrast to the softness of our Western lifestyle. No doubt that would be a great advantage in a war primarily fought by proxy through the use of advanced technology."

"The term 'Spartan' is not familiar to me," the representative answered. "But the ability and willingness to endure hardship is always an advantage when you're engaged in conflict."

"Which many regard as inevitable," Mann replied.

The Eastern representative simply bowed his head in reply.

"I wonder if it is, though," Mann observed, looking out at the snowfall once again. "If the choice were yours, and mine, would there be a war?"

"There are many hypotheticals that I cannot answer. You have posed one that I seldom consider."

"Yet both of us see rivalries between people who view the world very differently," Mann persisted, "who still manage not to fight each other to the death. The longer I watch the rivalry between our countries, the more I wonder if we could not learn from this somehow."

The Eastern representative didn't look up from his menu. "There is a saying in my country," he said, "which, crudely translated, says that the bully only desires peace when his intended victim unexpectedly shows the ability and willingness to fight back."

Mann sighed, and pushed the menu to one side. "I'm not so concerned about the geopolitical nuances," he confessed as he leaned forward across the table. "I'm much more concerned about your wife and children."

The Eastern representative looked up sharply from his menu. "What are you saying?"

"You share a wife with three others," Mann continued. "An adaptation from an interesting social experiment gone awry some years ago. Four children among the four of you, is my understanding."

"If this is a threat—"

Mann waved off the rising hostility. "If someone were to order me to harm them, and threatened me with death, I would refuse to carry out the order and die instead," he said. "But there is danger nonetheless." He pulled a device from the folds of his shirt. Instantly, the waiter and the men sitting at four adjoining tables stiffened. Three of the men stood up.

Mann held it up for inspection, and then touched the side, allowing a hologram to unfold over the table. The Eastern representative raised a reassuring hand, and the random customers and the waiter relaxed and returned to their conversations.

"This is your great nation, may it always be blessed by the angels," Mann said. "And here, I believe, is where your family resides, safely away from the metroplex that would inevitably be targeted should the unfortunate political climate deteriorate a bit further."

The man across the table stared at the location of his family on the map. A flicker of surprise crossed his face, and was quickly erased as he looked up at Mann with an easy smile. "Of course, this information is incorrect."

"Let's assume for the moment that you just saw the exact location not only of your family but many of your colleagues," Mann continued. "Now let me show you a crude simulation of the impact that a matter-to-energy conversion device would have if there were a direct hit on the metroplex, or if someone were to carry such a device to one of the downtown hotels. You see, and perhaps you even made such a calculation yourself, that the impact stops short of the location of your family."

The Eastern representative took his eyes off the expanding inferno inside the hologram and nudged it back across the table. He favored Mann with a look of triumph.

"I suspect that many other high-ranking officials in your military and civilian leadership have made similar calculations," Mann continued. "In fact, if you look at this map, you can see the locations of many families, with the names of the officials superimposed on the dots that represent their homes. All of them, every one, by a remarkable coincidence, have their families located a safe distance from the likely targets of the warfare that all of us see clearly on the horizon."

The smile vanished.

"And what is this?" the Eastern representative said, his gaze fixed at an image to the far side of the map.

"I must have left that on there by mistake," Mann said, his voice turning apologetic. "It's an old photographic image from the last time our species detonated one of the latest devices and unleashed a solar earthquake on this planet. You can see the melting flesh of children clearly in the background rubble."

"Perhaps you should get to the point," the Eastern representative said into the stillness that suddenly surrounded him.

Mann bowed his head. "I'm deeply embarrassed that the military leaders of my nation would have done this research," he said. "I know that you've seen the hatred in their eyes when they think you aren't looking at them."

The Eastern representative sat back in his chair and pushed the menu away from him.

"I thank you for your concern about my family," he said, his voice inflecting the high form of polite address that was often meant to be ironic. "This is, indeed, a valuable piece of information. What are you asking in return for it?"

Mann looked him directly in the eyes.

"I wish only that you would feel a degree of shame similar to what I'm experiencing," he said. "To accomplish this, I brought a gift."

"Another gift—"

Mann handed the tiny cube over to the Eastern representative, who took it gingerly.

"If you fear that it will detonate, then hand it to the waiter, who will take it far enough from here that there is no danger," Mann invited.

The waiter took a step forward, but the Eastern representative again held up his hand.

"Touch here," Mann suggested.

In a moment, a new holographic map appeared above the table, this time of a different country whose leaders—along with their habits and personal hygiene—were routinely vilified in the Eastern representative's native press. Dots, similar to those on the previous map, appeared in many locations, most of them safely located far from metropolitan or military installations.

Names were associated with the dots.

"Perhaps," Mann continued, "you will find a way to insert this information into your next round of negotiations."

The Eastern representative stared at the map for a long second, before he touched the cube, dismissed the image and wordlessly handed the cube to the waiter, to be preserved for further analysis.

"Nobody is safe any more," he said to himself. "They will hate us all the more," he said, turning his attention back to Mann.

"I doubt that is possible."

The Eastern representative drew the menu back in front of him and studied it carefully.

"They know where we live," he said. "And now we know where they live. Once again I wonder, what is an appropriate reward for your side of this conversation," he said without looking up.

"Two things I ask of you," Mann said. "First, that you spare my life for having the insolence to insist on this meeting. And second, that you listen to a proposal I have that might navigate our two nations past this dangerous moment in our political relationship, save millions of lives, and protect your own family from harm."

The Eastern representative put the menu aside and leaned forward, staring into Mann's face with the first sign of interest all evening. "We may have a deal," he said. "How is it you say this? I'm totally ears."

"You're all ears," Mann said smiling.

"Indeed. Now tell me your proposal."

Mann held Gloria's hand as they glided over the ice. More than once he prevented her from falling, but she was becoming steadier, getting the hang of the sideways push that moved her forward. Up on the banks of the frozen canal, and from the bridges they passed under, people watched them curiously.

"You're going to kill me yet," Gloria called out, her breath visible in the ice-clear air. A few snowflakes still clung to her hat.

"Isn't it fun?"

"It's marvelous. How did you ever think of—what do you call it? Skating?"

"I was surprised to see that nobody has invented the idea here," Mann said. "Fabricating the skates, and attaching them to the boots, was the hardest part."

The canal fed into concentric circles that swirled around the heart of the ancient city and out into the countryside. Here, it was lined with docked houseboats trailing thin wisps of smoke from their chimneys, and long, flat empty barges waiting for the next thaw. It was the first time Mann felt truly at home in this universe. He was reminded of Amsterdam in the early spring.

"This feels like a trip back in time," Gloria said, nodding up at the heart of the city five or six bridges ahead, at ancient cathedrals nestled between crude glass slabs and buildings that appeared to be made of synthetic stone blocks cemented together. "How did your meeting go?" she asked after a moment.

"I think it was successful," Mann said absently.

"What was it about? And why did it have to be here?"

"I thought you needed a vacation. So I allowed them to insist on meeting somewhere out of the way, and told Drs. X and Y that it was important that you come along."

"Them?"

"People who might be able to talk sense into the Eastern side's military leaders. The kind of people who would give us an excuse to get away to a forgotten corner of the world so we can explore our relationship. And a cover for the real reason I'm supposed to be here."

He turned his head as a bird flitted past. Then he stopped and let his gaze linger on the mountains to the west, dazzling white with the sun's reflection off the accumulated snow.

"Can you hear it?" he said.

"What?"

"The chorus of birds in the trees around us. They all have a different pitch, a different song, but it always sounds like they're harmonizing, never clashing. It's the same with flowers," he said. "The colors of flowers never clash. The only things that clash are the sounds that we manufacture, or the colors that we humans impose on the world."

Gloria shook her head. "I have never met anyone who is as... *alive* as you," she said.

"It's incredibly ironic that I feel this compulsion to drink in the vitality and beauty of life in this here and now," Mann said, leading her past a park surrounded by now-fallow gardens and leafless trees. "I'm constantly amazed at the second-by-second unfolding of our living landscape, wanting to capture every moment of it, and I think maybe I'm the only one who really understands the miracle of it."

"And that's ironic?" Gloria said.

"In a way that I don't think I could explain."

Gloria released Mann's grip and wobbled along on her own before turning toward the shore. She nearly tripped as she stepped off the ice and hobbled to a bench at the edge of the water.

Mann executed a quick spin at the frozen shoreline and sat down next to her.

"How many women have you loved in your life?" Gloria asked after a moment.

"I'm not sure," he said. "Maybe one, although I'm not sure." His mind's eye saw Roxanna across from him at the outdoor table, with her raven hair tousled by the wind, cooly sipping wine and watching the Khorugh tourists passing along the street out of the ever-wary corner of her eye. The scene could not have been much different than when Tamerlane ruled from a nearby palace.

Roxanna would pay particular attention to the women, what they were wearing, how their faces and bodies were formed and the interaction between the two that was called fashion, but that every woman knows is a much more strategic mixture of day-to-day decisions about how she wants to present herself, and to whom.

When the short reverie ended, Mann experienced a distraction, like pain is a distraction, insisting on his attention with the memory of her. Did that mean he loved her?

It occurred to him that if Gloria were somehow taken away, it would feel as if the deepest core of himself were ripped away. Did that mean he loved her?

"Did she live here?" Gloria pulled him out of his reverie. "Is that why you brought me here?"

"She was an expatriate in a country called Tajikistan, during the civil war."

"How did you meet her?"

"She had been hired to kill me. And nearly succeeded, before we got to know each other. I'd show you the scar, but it's not on this body."

"Right. You just made that up. You want to know how I know?"

"Yes. I'd be very interested."

"Because there isn't any such country as Tajikistan. I'm pretty good with geography."

Mann shrugged. "How about you?" he said. "Who have you loved?"

"I thought I was in love when I was a schoolgirl, and we almost got married right before college. I realized immediately it was a mistake, but it felt so romantic."

"What was romantic about it?"

"A young girl wants nothing more than to escape, to enjoy freedom, to breathe. You should remember that about girls; you can get any young girl you want if you promise her independence and freedom from pretty much whatever her life is at the moment."

"I'll keep that in mind," Mann said.

"Most of the time, the only available men are really boys roughly your own age, so you're mostly attracted to maturity, which feels closer to being able to escape."

Mann said nothing. He looked out at the mountains, remembering a trip together to Samarkand, holding hands in the shadows of the Registan with the sun slowly descending over the hills, the same hills that Tamerlane would have grown up under while he plotted the improbable return of the Mongol Empire. He wondered if Roxanna was still alive somewhere, out there, in another place and time.

"But he wasn't really any more mature than anybody else," Gloria added. "The thing is, he was just a whole lot closer to the very limited *as-far-as-he-was-ever-going-to-go* than the *much further* of most of the other boys, if that makes any sense, and somehow I mistook that for being close to adulthood. A lot of my friends were making the same mistake."

"So you stabbed him?"

Gloria laughed. "No, I left him because he was cheating on me with anybody he could get his hands on. Then he died in a motorcycle accident a couple of years later. The police report said he was like six times over the legal alcohol limit, which sounded about right."

"Maybe that's how you learn your hardest, most important lessons, when your emotions get mixed up in it," Mann said. "If it's true, then I have a lot to learn, and most of it is coming from this place and time, where I kind of... like, inherited these emotion things."

"So what have you learned about us—you and me—over these past couple of years?"

"You go first."

"All right," Gloria said, rising to the challenge. "I've learned that a woman can love a man in a certain way only so long as there is still something about him that she has to figure out. If there's still an element of mystery, then you have the urge to hunt it down, to get closer, deeper—and it all comes with a dose of excitement. And then, if you ever solve the mystery and the hunt is over and there's no surprises or intrigue, you can never love him the same way again."

"Should I be worried?" Mann smiled.

"You are the most mysterious man in history," Gloria assured him. "One moment I think you're more present with me and more appreciative of the details of your vivid surroundings than anybody could ever be. And then somehow, at the same time, I feel like you're somewhere else altogether, that your center of gravity is located where I can never follow.

"What's the matter?" she said after a moment.

"I think it might be the wine I had at lunch," Mann said. "Or maybe I forgot that I can't breathe and swallow at the same time."

"I'm a long way from solving your mystery," Gloria said.

"Maybe not as far as you think."

"So what about you?" she said. "What have you learned?"

"Do you remember that time when we almost made love?" he said.

She nodded.

"As I lay in bed, with your head on my shoulder, I experienced an insight into something about marriages and men and women and why that physical passion dies out."

"Now I'm intrigued. I had no idea you were awake."

"It was something that I can take back with me—"

"To Tajikistan?"

Mann stopped. "Let's just call it a lesson that I'll carry with me to the afterlife," he said. "Maybe it's a small thing, but it was a huge revelation to me, one of the most important things I'll get from this experience that everybody calls 'life.'"

"I'm listening." Gloria adjusted her skates and looked up into his eyes.

"I realized that after a honeymoon period, men regard the act of lovemaking as a physical recreation, and women regard it as a re-affirmation of intimacy. Neither side realizes the other's viewpoint, and over time the disconnect becomes so great that neither one is satisfied with the outcome. So they stop."

"Wow," Gloria said, looking down at her feet. "I wish I could tell that to every married couple in the universe. But then, of course, one or the other of them would have to do something to bridge that gap."

"It's too bad we're so different and incompatible," Mann said.

Gloria said nothing. Her eyes glistened, and then a tear rolled down her cheek. He reached over and dabbed it away with his finger.

"I love you in a way that I've never loved anybody," she said. "And I'm afraid to spoil it. Sometimes I'm terribly afraid that one day you'll just go away, disappear to these imaginary places that you can't stop talking about, and in that day I will become just a dream. Isn't that stupid? Tell me how stupid I am."

"You're incredibly stupid to think such thoughts," Mann said, touching her cheek again.

"I wish I could believe that you mean that," she said. "Sometimes, when I look in your eyes, I see through them to that other place, and I know that if and when you go there, I won't be able to follow."

A chill ran down Mann's spine, and spread out into his legs. He looked up into her eyes, and then looked away again, and then down at the ice at their feet.

"Now you're going to make *me* cry," he said.

"But I AM stupid, right?"

"Incredibly. You have no insight whatsoever, and you have fool-ish ideas, and your instincts always seem to lead you astray. I think you might be an imbecile."

Gloria smiled, stood up, and took a few uncertain steps along the ice back to where they had entered the canal. She looked back, beckoning him.

"You're not a very convincing liar," she said. "Sometimes I count on that."

Mann stood up. He held out his hand.

"Come on," he said. "I want to show you the real reason we came to this place."

The streets in this primitive city were crowded with ground vehicles with rubber wheels inching along between tall buildings that seemed to have been thrown up at random, each different, each clashing with the others. Along the outskirts of the city, open wires strung along between tall poles carried power into crude dwellings made of wood or plaster.

"A penny for your thoughts," Mann said.

"A what?"

"I mean—that is... I'd transfer a very small amount to your financial account in return for you telling me what you're thinking right now."

"I can't tell if that's sweet or an insult. Do you really want to know what I'm thinking?"

"Very much."

"I look at this primitive lifestyle, and I find it so charming that I wonder why we ever left it behind. Why did we keep pushing ahead into some kind of techno-nightmare when the secret of happiness is simplicity and a more relaxed way of life."

"Did you come to a conclusion?" he said.

"I think we couldn't help ourselves. We were forced by our own cleverness to incorporate the next new gizmo into our lifestyles, which created a powerful economic incentive for smart people like us to create newer gizmos to fill the demand. It's like we were made to keep chasing toward something that is never quite as good as what we left behind, but we think that if we keep going far enough, we'll finally get somewhere worthwhile. I think you can see it in microcosm in each of our lives," she added. "We work until we drop, thinking that maybe, if we keep at it long enough, we'll get to the place where we can enjoy this gift of life."

"That sounds awfully cynical."

"I don't mean it to be. It's the way God made us, I guess."

Mann said nothing. They drove past to a small patch of greenery situated between the buildings, where children ran about among gymnastic contraptions of wood and metal, and adults jogged doggedly along the paths.

"Being here just reminded me of a song," he said. He half sung, half said the words:

> *"Take my hand; I'm a stranger in paradise.*
> *"All lost in a wonderland...*
> *"A stranger in paradise..."*

"That's pretty. Where did it come from?"

"I was thinking of the whole idea of kismet. It's a word that suggests that events are guided by an unseen awareness. I was thanking it for granting a very unclear wish that I had made, for bringing us together, for exceeding in every way what I had asked for, for giving me exactly what I needed in this life."

"You're an interesting combination of clueless and unbelievably gallant," Gloria said, squeezing his shoulder.

"I think men say things, and women hear a different meaning," Mann said. "It's the only thing that makes romance possible. Here and... elsewhere."

"So long as we have it, I'm not inclined to question it."

Gloria fell silent. "Isn't it strange to be manually controlling a vehicle?" she asked after a moment.

"Not as much as you'd think."

"You're doing a pretty good job of it. But I think it helps that there's nobody else on the—is this even a road?"

"I don't think so. More like a trail."

"Do you even know where you're going?"

"We have an appointment with, as nearly as I can tell, several of the most important people in the military hierarchy, including an old friend who must have bent heaven and earth to gain exclusive access to this place that is so far from his own country."

"Oh. Why didn't you tell me?"

"They told me not to tell anybody," Mann said as the vehicle reached the top of the rise.

What he saw made him stop the car.

"Oh, my god..." Gloria gasped.

They stared down into the heart of a narrow valley, surrounded by mountains on all sides. In the exact center, there rested an enormous structure that, to Mann's eyes, seemed like a fantastical multidimensional symmetrical arrangement of giant metal slivers, whose many protrusions gleamed in the sunlight like polished silver.

"That," Mann said, "is what we're here to see."

Tiny workers were walking around it on worn paths in the sandy ground, and some shacks had been hastily constructed off to one side where Mann assumed that the researchers lived.

"My god, I never thought I would ever see anything like that," Gloria said.

"Do you have any idea what it is?"

"Of course I do. It's a hyper-tesseract."

"A what?"

"You wouldn't understand." Gloria continued staring for long seconds. "Five dimensions? Six?" she said to herself. "The only thing I can tell you for sure," she said. "Is: whoever, whatever created that thing didn't come from here."

Then she looked over at Mann.

"Well?" she said. "What are we waiting for? Don't you think we ought to take a closer look?"

As the vehicle wound its careful way down the side of the steep hill, they approached a cluster of vehicles that had been parked well away from the structure. An un-uniformed man with military bearing, carrying a weapon Mann recognized as a laser rifle, approached the driver's side of the car.

"Mann?" he said.

"Who else were you expecting?"

"Here comes the general. It might be best if you were less flippant."

"It might be best if you let me do the talking," Mann said to Gloria as they got out of the vehicle.

The general looked Mann up and down, with visible disapproval, and then spared a side glance at Gloria, as if he didn't want to believe she was present and that limiting his visual confirmation of her would make her somehow not part of the picture. He put his hands on his hips and looked up at the hills in visible exasperation.

"I'm pretty sure your instructions were to come alone," the general said.

"And I remember telling your colonel that anything you wanted to show me with this degree of urgency would, with absolute certainly, be a mile or two over my head," Mann replied. "So I brought the only person I could think of who never has anything go over her head."

"Are you the one in charge here?" Gloria demanded suddenly.

"Can we trust her to keep this confidential?" the general demanded.

"*Confidential*?!!" Gloria demanded before Mann could speak. "You have what is obviously not just an artifact from an alien civilization, but a pretty obvious message built right into the structure, and you're keeping that a secret from the tax-paying citizens you supposedly work for—"

"I'm pretty sure we can trust her to keep it under her hat," Mann assured the general.

"This is the most important, profound, *interesting* thing that's ever happened," Gloria continued in a voice of rising indignation. "Who are you to keep it to yourselves for... *military* reasons?"

The general winced at how Gloria had managed to make the word 'military' sound like a four-letter word. "I suppose we can kill her later," he said, more to himself and the un-uniformed aide than to Mann. Then he turned his full attention on Gloria, and some of his hostility melted away.

"You said this thing has a—what did you say? Obvious message?"

"Well, duh."

The general turned to Mann.

"She thinks you aren't very bright," Mann translated. "She doesn't think much of your research team either," he added helpfully.

"Do you think you could help us decipher this message?" the general continued in a surprisingly meek voice.

"I could tell you right now. But I won't until you let me see the inside of this thing."

The general snorted. "If you can find a way inside, you're better than we are."

"I think we already established *that* a few seconds ago," Gloria said, and walked past the general toward the structure.

Seeing it up close, Mann was surprised at the polish of the mirror-like surface, which made the object play tricks with his eyes, making its various geometrical appendages seem to disappear and reappear as he walked around the worn pathway.

"Is it safe to touch?" he asked after a moment.

"Nobody has died yet," a sandy-haired man wearing a dark robe called out. He seemed to be constantly trying to catch up to the group, even though nobody was walking particularly quickly. He also seemed to be perpetually out of breath. "It's opaque to every kind of radiation we've tried to shine through it, so we have no idea what's inside."

"You must have determined what it's made of by now," Gloria asserted.

"That's one of the oddest things about it. It's a very strange isotope of molybdenum that isn't supposed to be stable at these—or, really, any—temperatures. Somehow, the extra neutrons give it a polish that you wouldn't normally be able to achieve."

"Another part of the message," Gloria said. "They're showing off."

"Who?" Mann said.

"Whoever made this," Gloria said impatiently. "They wanted us to understand that they were more technically advanced than we were, as if sending this thing here from wherever they live wasn't enough of a message."

The general looked up at the structure, which extended far over their heads. Then he noticed that Gloria was looking at the ground, at the spiky geometric protrusions on which the artifact rested.

"What?" he said.

"Have you weighed this thing?"

The general looked at the scientist in the robe, who simply stared back.

"Why?" the general asked.

"Notice how lightly it sits on the ground. See? When we walk, our shoes make an imprint in the sand that's deeper than the... structure. Something is negating some of its gravity. Have you even *looked* at this thing?" Gloria demanded, looking up.

The general turned to the scientist, who seemed to be surprised that he was expected to answer.

"Mostly," the scientist said, "we were looking for a way to get inside."

Gloria shook her head.

"Well?" the general said finally.

Gloria looked at Mann.

"He wants to know what the obvious message is," said Mann.

"Isn't it obvious?" she said. "They're telling us that there are... other directions, and those other directions are important."

"Other directions," the general repeated.

"Up-down, front-back, left-right and time—those are the directions you know, right?"

The scientist nodded vigorously, and then noticed that the general was simply staring. So he stopped nodding and simply stared too.

"Well, the hyper-tessseract is telling us that there are directions you don't see, and apparently they're really important. We need to understand something about how we extend ourselves, or should extend ourselves, in another direction—actually, apparently, many other directions, based on the topography of the thing. It could be many levels; I'm not sure."

"How long ago do you think it landed here?" the scientist asked.

"It didn't," Gloria said.

When she didn't say anything else, the general stood up with visible impatience. "Perhaps you could explain things a bit more clearly to those of us who are too stupid to understand exactly what you're trying to tell us," he said.

"He's being sarcastic," Mann added. "He thinks he's as smart as you are, but that you're being deliberately obscure."

"This thing didn't land. It appeared in that spot. It was sent by some means other than the long roundabout way of traveling through space."

"Do I dare ask by whom?"

"By creatures from another star system, of course."

"That can't be," Mann blurted out.

Everybody looked at Mann. He closed his mouth and looked around.

Gloria stared at Mann with the expression one might wear if a tree started talking.

"What do you mean?" she said.

"It's just that, I'm pretty sure that—there isn't any other—any alien life out there in this... reality," he said. He looked at all the faces staring at him. "Call it a hunch," he said lamely.

"So you think somebody *here* built this thing?" the general demanded. "And placed it in this remote place, where we would eventually find it?"

"Forget I said anything," Mann said. It *did* sound implausible. He looked back up at the artifact, towering into the sky. The reality of it was enough to make him question the things he knew. *How was this possible? Were they playing tricks on him upstairs?*

"The technology is just tricky enough to tell me that somehow whoever, *what*ever sent this knew roughly our level of sophistication and decided to make sure we understood that they're operating on a higher level," Gloria said. "Why? I think in order to give them credibility. They really want us to hear this message, and take it seriously."

"So we should take seriously that whatever we do in a different direction, a different dimension, is very important," the general said. Mann was surprised that his tone was not sarcastic.

"Yes," Gloria said.

"Do you think there's anything inside there?" he asked.

"I do."

The general walked away and then back again with visible exasperation. He ran his hand across his forehead. "Would you please," he said, "tell me what you think is inside?"

"It's obviously a doorway to their world," Gloria said. "And I guarantee you won't be able to open it from this side."

30

"Since you do not have a material body of
flesh and blood, whatever may come—sounds,
lights or rays—are unable to harm you."

Tibetan Book of the Dead

The gods sat around a table on the floating platform once again, drinks in hand.

"Progress?" Westerly said, this time in the form of an elderly man whose arms trembled as he raised the glass to his lips.

"We are going to engineer a very remarkable event, which will make many people pay more attention to my message," Gandhi said promptly. "It will require your cooperation, but I know it can be done. I have inscribed the details on a report that you can read at your leisure," he added.

Westerly turned to Mann. "Will it work?"

"I think it will exceed expectations," he said. "And I just might survive it."

"What about you?" Westerly turned his attention to Washington, who shook his head.

"I'm now the leading candidate for the nomination of my party for the Senate seat," he said. "But some very powerful people are making it very difficult for the party to accept my candidacy."

"Do we have a plan?"

"I do," said Mann. "The problem will go away in a week."

Washington regarded Mann with surprise. "How are you going to do that?"

Mann shrugged. "I've been assembling my cast of characters."

While they were talking, Mann noticed that Westerly was once again stealing glances at a tablet with some degree of absorption. He looked over at the screen and saw lines of poetry.

"I was listening to some verses the other day," Mann said casually. "A poet called Vishram. You and he seem to share the same muse."

Westerly—or the older man who housed Westerly's awareness—looked up at Mann with a startled expression. Then he looked over the side for a long moment.

"We spend all our time collecting these scraps of hardware, and leave an incredible feast of culture on the table," Westerly said after a moment. "I thought it might be a real service to humanity if I brought a few of their best poems back in translation to our world."

"And take credit for them."

"I can't very well tell people what we're doing in the laboratory," Westerly protested. "If you want the truth, I wish I could bring back more. Witch seems to think it's harmless."

Washington and Gandhi looked at each other.

"I vote that it's harmless too," said Washington. "So long as it doesn't give away what we're doing to the simulated entities or those upstairs."

"I'm wondering, how would one know that he's living in a simulation?" Mann said, turning the liquid around in his glass and watching the swirl. "Would there be a test for it?"

Washington turned to Gandhi, and they both turned their attention to Westerly.

"There are probably a lot of ways," Westerly said. "But I, personally, would look for clues."

"Clues?"

"Does evolution seem to be truly random? Here, we had to do a lot of tweaking in order to create a world, and life-forms, that we can relate to. When the wrong kind of creatures start to emerge, we have to engineer an extinction event, and tinker a bit with the fundamental building blocks until we get what we want—maybe three extinction events later. There was a lot of tweaking to move evolution in the direction of humanoids. If you look hard enough, an intervening hand is visible through the mist."

"I suppose you would add the whole observer affects the experiment thing," Washington added.

"What do you mean?"

"The computer is a limited resource," Pudge explained. "When you move your arm, the computer doesn't trace the vector of every single atom or molecule according to quantum physics; it defaults to the much simpler Newtonian mechanics as a really good approximation. It has no particular reason to make any decision about what's going on at the subatomic level until somebody down here is performing an experiment that is designed to observe subatomic behavior. When they do run those experiments, to them it looks as if their observations are actually causing the subatomic particles to behave a certain way. And they are, in a sense."

"A more interesting question is what we could be doing with these simulations commercially," Washington said.

"What do you mean?"

"Haven't you ever, in all the time we've been wandering around this pseudo-reality, wondered whether the highest and best use is stealing advanced technology? If there isn't, maybe, a more interesting application?"

"What have you been thinking?" Mann asked.

"Think video games on steroids," Gandhi proposed, "where you buy experiences. A young man can be transported into a war zone and experience real combat with exotic alien creatures without any danger to his life. A lady can enter into the simulated version of a romance novel and, through a great deal of interesting drama, fall in love with the man of her dreams. Print fiction became movies, which are a step more vivid, and I think perhaps—" he gestured around him at the city and the landscape beyond—"this is the next step. The novelist of the future creates a participative story that people pay a fee to enter."

"If you pare it down to the barest essentials, what is art?" Washington added. Then, answering his own question, he said: "It is the transfer of experience value. Books, movies, paintings, music all give you vicarious experience in concentrated form, and the best ones give you some of the insights that come from experience. No?"

"I suppose so," said Mann.

"An artist of the future would create a simulated world of his or her choosing, with characters, a story, and an opportunity to live within the story. The experience value would be more vivid and immediate than anything our species has ever been able to deliver with all of those previous technologies. Every other art form would pale next to it."

Mann watched a bird threading its way between pedestrians, pecking hopefully at the bare sidewalk. He let his eyes blur a bit, and suddenly there was unexpected beauty in a few hundred colorful sandals crossing his awareness like a fractal pattern in motion, with the pigeon as a moving focal point whose navigational instincts seemed somehow miraculous. Slowly he shook his head. Washington smiled.

"What?"

"Nobody could create a world more vivid, more unpredictable, more interactive than this... result of an algorithm of cause and effect," Mann said, watching the bird as it flew off to a balcony ledge.

"So?"

"So why do you need the artist?" Mann said. "Let God be the artist, or randomness, which may be the same thing."

"My brother, I'm afraid I don't follow you," said Gandhi.

"We're living in a simulated world this minute, and we're going to come back to reality with an extra few years of experience, of accumulated wisdom. You said you've done this, how many times in this reality?"

Washington looked up at the sky. "Eleven," he said.

"This was your chance to do what the Buddha did, reincarnate yourself again and again, perfect your understanding and purify your soul. Only now we have the means to do it all in one lifetime, to make all the mistakes we need to learn from here in this place and time. A lifetime of genuinely organic experience value that is more valuable than anything you could make up. A sequence of lives shared by a single consciousness. I can even envision a computer glitch giving random people some kind of leakage memory of lives they've lived before, in previous ages. They'd remember past lives while inside the simulation."

Washington laughed.

"What?"

"Heaven would be how you'd feel if you made the right choices and took with you something positive. Hell would be if you had been a total asshole and had to live with the experience."

"I don't see why that's funny."

"What's funny," said Washington, "is that if any of us are even remotely right, then most of the thinking creatures in the universe are going to exist in simulation, rather than whatever it is that we call reality."

Westerly raised a glass. "More poetry to bring back," he said. "Now if you fellows could be quiet for a moment, I have to memorize a few more verses."

31

"The phenomena of the physical appearance is wholly illusion. It is not until a disciple understands this that he can realize the true Tathagata."

Diamond Sutra, Chapter 6 of the
Maha Prajna Paramita

Mann entered the local terminal, touched the screen with his fingertips, followed the lights to his pod and slumped down wearily in the first cushioned seat. The dog had learned to master the food device surprisingly quickly, but he got lonely in the afternoons and had a tendency to wander into bad neighborhoods. Mann was looking forward to relaxing with the dog at his side.

He was looking out the window at nothing when a young man entered the pod and sat down across from him.

The young man favored Mann with a bright, happy smile.

Mann shifted in his chair. This pod was programmed to take him directly to his living quarters.

"I beg your pardon," Mann said finally. "I'm not expecting any visitors."

"Of course not," the other said, still smiling.

The train of pods began moving smoothly forward.

Mann looked the other over carefully.

"You're making a mistake," he said.

"I don't see how," the happy young man replied. "In fact, everything seems to be surprisingly mistake-free, considering the usual efficiency of my... employers. Your face matches the pictures I was given. Your destination is the correct address. They told me you would be unarmed, and that appears to have been an accurate prediction."

"There are other ways for this to be a mistake," Mann said. "Suppose, for example, that I represent a very faint hope that this world will survive the next decade without a catastrophic war."

"I have trouble supposing that you would imagine that I would believe something like that," the young man replied with a cheerful smile.

"Suppose I told you that I'm not really capable of dying in this place and time. Even if this body were destroyed, I'd return shortly in another form. And an early priority would be to make you answer for the inconvenience of resurrection."

"They didn't prepare me for how funny you would be," the young man answered. "You're by far the most creative, imaginative assignment they've ever given me. But if you're looking for advice, I'd say you should spend a little more time on your believability."

By this time, the chain of pods had become shorter, and they emerged from a tunnel into open air, rising smoothly into the air. All other pods immediately detached, except for the one directly behind Mann's.

"Suppose," Mann said finally, "that I'm not as easy to kill as they told you."

"I think it would be very hard for you to exceed the many warnings they gave me," the young man said cheerfully. "Which explains why they gave me so much unnecessary backup."

The young man stood up, balanced easily on the balls of his feet, and Mann also stood up carefully. Suddenly, the young man produced—what? Two handles, one in each hand, and at a touch of some unseen switch, blades emerged from the handles, stiletto swords which glowed strangely as if each blade were surrounded by cartoon magic.

With a gesture that seemed almost leisurely, the young man flicked the twin swords across the space where Mann's torso had been half an instant before. The blades sliced off the top of Mann's chair cleanly, leaving a scorched, smoking, absolutely straight cleavage along the top.

By this time, Mann had his arms around the young man's neck, but he was forced to abandon the position at once as the assassin reached back with the swords, scorching a long gash across the side of Mann's shirt.

Mann stopped time again and considered his next move carefully. He executed a slow motion dive behind his seat, which, of course, seemed like a blur to the still-smiling assassin.

"You *did* exceed my expectations," the assassin cried out in what appeared to be genuine delight. He swung the swords again, and two-thirds of the remaining chair was lopped off, exposing a blur who brought down the top of the chair, with its metal spine, on the assassin's right wrist, breaking it so hard that it was perpendicular to the arm. The sword fell, the blade slicing neatly into the floor of the pod.

The blur retrieved the sword and rolled as the assassin struck down with his left-hand sword, slicing deeply into the floor and continuing the slice rapidly toward Mann's rolling figure. As Mann collided with the wall of the pod, the assassin lifted the stroke of the sword, and then stared at his missing left hand, while the sword Mann had thrown across his body lodged handle-deep into the pod's far wall."

Mann retrieved the other electronic sword and stood up slowly. He looked into the young man's face, admiring the fact that he was still smiling while blood ran through the senseless fingers of his broken hand that lay over the stump of the other arm.

"You *are* remarkable," the young man said cheerfully, eying the sword in Mann's hand. "It makes me wonder if the other crazy things you said might also be true."

"There is no reason for me to kill you," Mann said.

"Actually, there is," the young man replied, looking past Mann's shoulder. "I hope you haven't forgotten that I mentioned something about them sending me a backup."

Mann threw himself aside as a disk the size of a frisbee flew past his head. Its edges were covered in what appeared to be razor blades which sliced cleanly through the side of the young man's face and buried itself deeply into the wall of the pod near where the sword was lodged.

Mann threw himself behind another of the seats, and after a moment another of the frisbees, and another and another, buried themselves three quarters of the way out Mann's side of the steel and fabric, the blades inches from his face. He pulled the sword out from where it had lodged into the floor and sliced the seat at its base, and kicked it forward.

Retreating back to timelessness, Mann saw his assailant grappling impatiently with the heavy seat, stumbling over the young assassin's dead body. Without waiting for the new assassin to recover, Mann sliced deep into the pod's floor, connecting the slice perpendicularly with the one the young man had made earlier. He caught a glimpse of the ground far below, and saw that the pod was flying over what appeared to be an ocean.

The assassin held another disk in a hand covered by a steel glove. He was nearly midnight black in complexion, so tall that he had to stoop to avoid hitting his head on the ceiling, with a long beard falling down to his navel.

The two circled each other, the dark assassin with his arsenal of disks, Mann with the sword.

"What now?" Mann asked.

"Now I kill you," the other rumbled.

"Shouldn't we get to know each other a little bit before such a personal and intimate thing between us?" Mann asked. "We could talk this over, and maybe you'll decide that killing me is a terrible idea."

The dark assassin grinned. "It wasn't my decision," he said. "But you're so annoying that I'm beginning to see why they sent me here."

Without warning, he threw the disk, and Mann sliced it cleanly in half. He tried to close on his opponent, but the dark assassin leaped aside and threw another disk, which connected with Mann's right hip, severing flesh and bone along its edges as if Mann were made of butter. There was no pain; only weakness as Mann pivoted.

By then, he was close enough to retrieve the second sword out of the wall, and in the same motion, he flicked it spinning at the assailant just as the other released another disk.

The blade collided with the disk, slicing off one edge and changing its wobbling trajectory just enough to avoid a collision with Mann's head as he watched the sword swing into and through the assassin's torso. The handle collided with some internal organs, and the sword buried its shaft in the floor at the assassin's feet.

The dark assassin collapsed to the floor near the doorway to the second pod. Instantly, the pod door opened, and a new assailant squee3zed with difficulty through the opening. He stepped over the body without a glance and took a full appraisal of Mann.

He was at least as tall as Mann, and wider than he was tall, with muscles straining against the electronic armor he wore across his chest, arms and legs. Mann had read about such experimental warriors in the military briefings, but this was the first time he had stood face-to-face with a man raised from birth and given special forces training in a 3G environment. These experimental soldiers were said to weigh upwards of 600 pounds. Mann thought this must be an unusually large specimen.

"Do we really have to do this?" he said, working to recover his breath.

"Stop whining and die like a man," the other replied curtly. His voice was oddly shrill, as if his lungs were pushing the air through his vocal chords at double the normal speed.

"I suppose that your armor can stop this sword," Mann said, backing up carefully.

"You suppose very well for a dead man," the other said, moving forward, freakishly light on his feet.

"I'm warning you not to come any closer," Mann said.

"You want to kill me with laughing at your jokes," the massive assassin said, kicking the last chair out of his way with a sharp snap of broken steel.

"It was an honest warning. I always try to tell the truth, even though nobody here ever seems to believe me."

"You have just spoken your last lie," the assassin squeaked, and leaped forward.

It was a prodigious jump that kept the assassin in the air for an uncommonly long time. Mann ducked aside and pushed the sword into the floor, dragging the incision so that it completed the two other gashes in the flooring in a large, rough triangle. When the huge assassin finally landed a few inches from Mann's feet, Mann saw a look of mild surprise cross his face as the triangle of flooring buckled and snapped off entirely under the weight of a quarter ton of falling sinew.

A powerful wind blew through the pod as Mann watched the body fall cleanly through the floor. After a moment, he turned to the manual controls hidden behind a panel at the front. The first thing he did was lock the adjoining door to the next pod. Then he executed an emergency decoupling of the other pod, and, through the hole in the floor, he watched it fall away toward the ocean.

There was a scraping sound at the door. Stepping carefully around the hole, Mann looked through the back door window. Seeing nothing, he leaned down into the hole and looked back, where he could see a figure swinging in the wind, the last assassin, another experimental soldier, this one with four mechanical arms hooked into his central nervous system.

Two of the arms were clinging to the side of the pod, clutching onto something out of Mann's ability to see.

He turned back to the controls, overrode the programmed destination that appeared to be the center of the ocean, and turned back toward the city, swinging the pod this way and that in what he already knew would be an unsuccessful attempt to shake off the fourth assassin.

Additional scraping sounds told Mann that his efforts were not entirely successful. Nevertheless, he was startled to look up and see a face in the window, staring at him in frank appraisal. Mann gauged the distance to shore and set a new automatic control, hoping he would be at least close to correct. Then, as a mechanical fist smashed through the window, he reached for the sword.

The fourth assassin climbed like a spider through the jagged plastic, and somersaulted into the room, simultaneously eying the sword and the hole in the floor. Four mechanical arms spread out menacingly and clutched different parts of the wall on all sides of Mann.

"I salute you," the assassin said grimly. "I never expected that I would have to leave my seat."

"Do you think we might find a way to talk this over?" Mann said, definitely whining this time. He found it difficult to watch all four arms at the same time.

The pod lurched, and dropped lower toward the surface of the ocean. It seemed to have decelerated.

"You are afraid to die?" the fourth assassin asked with interest.

"The truth is, I don't want you to have to die," Mann said. "I've finally decided that every life has immense value, even here in this reality."

"You shouldn't waste your concern for me," the assassin said. His mechanical arms closed in closer to Mann's body, making it unlikely that he'd be able to sever all of them before one separated his torso from his head.

"I guess," Mann said, "that means that even with all that equipment, you can still swim."

Before the last of the stirring molecules of his words had reached the assassin's ears, Mann was leaping into the hole in the floor. He fell 50 feet before his feet cleaved the water cleanly.

Down, deeper, deeper. Then Mann pivoted his body and stroked toward the surface, finally breaking through with a deep gasp into a bright, sparkling sunlit environment just in time to see the pod smack into the water miles away from the shoreline.

With surprisingly few bubbles, it vanished into the depths below.

If his calculations were correct, the shore, barely visible as a blur on the horizon, was no more than three miles away, perhaps less. Wincing at the pain of the salt water on the wound at his hip, Mann spoke a brief prayer for the men who had died so bravely and who had deserved better in their lives.

Then he leaned into the water and made his way toward land, one tireless stroke at a time.

32

*"When appearances and names are put away, nothing
can be said about the 'Suchness' of Reality. This universal,
undifferentiated, inscrutable Suchness is the only Reality."*

Lankavatara Sutra

"You know what?" the dog said.

"I'm not a mind reader," Mann told him absently. He touched the fevered forehead of a woman who might have been an ancient crone, or simply aged beyond her years living here in the alley. Through a large crack in the masonry, just large enough to squeeze through, he could see the river of pedestrians gliding along on the moving sidewalk up and into the spiral around a building so tall that it was possible to feel the grind of its gravity causing the air to tremble a bit at the base.

"What?" Mann said finally, pouring water into the old woman's cup and handing her a bottle of pills.

"It occurred to me that we should move back into your apartment where it's warm and comfortable and there's a reliable food supply, instead of bedding down here in the street like, you know, we've been doing for a month now."

"Has it been that long?" Mann asked with mild surprise. He moved to another huddle of blankets, and touched a hand briefly.

"In dog years, it's been way, way longer," his companion said earnestly. "So when do you think we're going to live like civilized pet-owners?"

"I just need to finish a couple of things, and then it doesn't matter if they kill me."

"That's good," the dog answered after a moment, testing the words. "That gives me a definite time frame to work around. It's good to know."

Mann sighed, and then walked to the end of the wide, enclosed space, prime real estate here in the hidden region below the streets, with a slight breeze wafting in through the spaces between the ascending railing that separated the walkway from a place that only the homeless would know or care about.

"Can you at least tell me who wants to kill us?" the dog asked finally.

"Not you. Me," Mann answered.

"But who?"

"People who have the power to turn this world into an asteroid belt."

"These wouldn't be the very same people who you've been visiting every three weeks for, what, three years, up in that big scary building, would it?"

"The very same."

The dog said nothing.

"They can't just kill me outright in their own offices," Mann said, answering the dog's unspoken question. "It needs to look like somebody else's work."

The dog shook its head. "I'll never EVER understand humans," it said.

There was the gurgling sound of someone vomiting across the far side of their space. Mann instantly stood up, and the dog followed reluctantly.

"It's all right," a voice croaked as Mann approached. "My stomach isn't accustomed to all this food you brought to us."

"I'm sorry," Mann said.

"That's it?" the dog said. "That's all you're going to say, before you go back to your own blanket?"

Mann looked over in confusion.

"Every dog deserves respect, isn't that right?"

"Of course," Mann said.

"What about humans?" the dog demanded. He nudged Mann's face toward the figure with his back against the rough wall, smelling strongly of the residue of vomit that didn't make it through the deep hole in the floor. "Go on, ask him for his story. How did he get here? Who is he?"

The other took a long look at the dog, and then turned back to Mann. "As it happens," he said with a tentative smile, "I've lived quite an interesting life. In fact, it was my invention which built this building."

They descended in a glass elevator to the lounge under the ocean, where rays of light streamed out over the colorful expanse of coral. A school of shimmering yellow and blue fish darted in unison as they passed through the brilliant coral branches, lit up by the sun's geometric distortions through the warm ocean waves 30 feet above them. A huge neon blue fish swam lazily toward the floor-to-ceiling window, peering inside without apparent curiosity.

"An aquarium, only we're the fish."

Gloria watched a brilliantly-colored fish with long, soft fins sashay past the window like a model on a runway. She had changed into a gown of electric blue, which changed colors as the fabric touched her skin, making it look transparent. Her eyes reflected the color of the water, turning them a mysteriously beautiful aqua shade.

"You know, most of them are artificial," Mann said.

"No!"

"That's what they told me at the front desk. Robotic fish. And most of the coral isn't real either. They're trying to bring back the ecosystem, but it won't be entertaining enough for the hotel guests for at least 50 years."

Gloria raised her glass. "Here's to 50 years."

"You really think we'll last that long?"

"Hell no. We'll be lucky if we make it the next six months."

An enormous ray was followed by a smaller coral shark that seemed to pick up its leftovers. More people were coming down the elevator now. There was laughter at the long bar in the center of the fishbowl.

"Should we mingle?" Mann asked.

Gloria shrugged. "I don't even know why the doctors send us to these scientific conferences. They never let me present anything, and compared to the amazing things we work with every day, their presentations seem so unbelievably lame."

"There's Forbes," Mann commented, looking across Gloria's shoulder. "He's sitting down with three women."

"I'll bet they all look better than I do."

"That," Mann said, "would not be possible."

"You ARE charming tonight. Did you ever think about how we first met?" she said. "It was so strange, so random, so unlikely. Now I feel like I'd do just about anything for you, and at the same time I feel as if you're the only person alive who respects my boundaries and accepts my... emotional limitations."

"Our love was arranged in heaven," Mann assured her, touching a glass to his lips. "The forces that everybody insists on calling 'God' brought you to me, and I've been grateful ever since."

"Oh, that's unbelievably sweet. Do you even believe there's really a God?"

"I know there is. I've met her?"

"Her?"

"Actually there were a few of them. One is a brainiac who insists on being called 'Pudge.' Another is a howling bitch of a woman who thinks she's superior to everyone else, and she may be right. I didn't have time to do a proper assessment."

"You are so funny sometimes!"

"At the time, I didn't think it was funny at all."

"And they had something to do with us, these Gods named Pudge and—"

"Call her Witch."

"And Witch. You think they were responsible for us, here, together."

"How could I possibly have found you that night otherwise? How could you otherwise have given your friendship to somebody like me?"

The room was crowded now. There was a shout at the far end of the circular bar, and Mann looked up in time to see a woman throw a drink in Forbes' face, which somehow never lost its expression of superior amusement as the liquid dripped down from his eyebrows. Slowly he wiped is face with his sleeve.

"Alas, poor Forbes," Gloria commented. "I knew him well. He was always the iron heart in a room full of glass ones." She turned her attention back to Mann. "Why?" she said finally.

"Why what."

"Why would God and Pudge and Witch and all the powers of heaven go to all that trouble? Do they do this for everybody? Is every match made by their hand?"

"Just ours," Mann said.

"You sound awfully sure."

"Who do you think asked them for you? You were a wish that was granted to me."

"What else have you wished for?"

"That you would get the job you have. That you would do the things you love doing so much."

"I thought that was you. Didn't you talk the two doctors into it?"

"I wished to be persuasive. And I was. The doctors weren't looking for somebody to come in and take over and coordinate everything. And then suddenly they were."

"Now what do you wish for?" she said.

Mann touched the interface with his mind, and pondered what to do with it. Suddenly, Gloria reached out and pulled him close to her, and kissed him.

"I don't want to know if that's what you wished for," she whispered. "I'm just going to believe that when the urge came over me just now, it was sent by you through... whatever it is that listens to your wishes."

"Is that the only urge you have?"

He could feel her smile, though her face rested on his shoulder. "No," she said. "I also want to learn everything there is to know and I want to keep this world from destroying itself and I want to understand why I am the way I am."

"Maybe we could work on that last part first, and work our way around to the others."

"I was never popular when I was young. I was tall and awkward and everything I said sounded pompous and strange, because I was thinking things that were different from everybody else. They called me the girl from the moon. And so I can't think of myself as attractive now, because I still carry around that old self-image. Does that make any sense to you?"

"I think it's an advantage," Mann said.

"A what???"

"If you're accepted in the tribe," Mann explained, "and a leader of it during your formative years, you develop certain assumptions about how the world works, and those assumptions don't map very well to the adult world."

Gloria opened her mouth, and then closed it again. "I never thought of it that way."

"Growing up an outsider, always having to cope with the stress and uncertainty, is a kind of gift," said Mann. "When you entered the adult world, you were looking for new assumptions, testing every-thing, making decisions that didn't rely on what worked in the past, because nothing worked in the past. In fact," he said, "I have a suspicion that the more of an outsider you were when you were young, the more successful you can become over the rest of your years."

"But not happier."

"No. You will always carry that wound."

"So what do you see when you look at me? Can you be objective?"

Mann looked into her face and smiled.

"No," he said.

"What did you see when you first met me?" she persisted.

"I think the most objective observation that anyone would make is that you are a truly, genuinely wonderful and unique person who lights up any room you enter, and you are deeply mysterious and sometimes a little scary because your mind goes to places that most of us can't follow. But," Mann said, raising his glass to her, "I have no interest in being objective about you. I want to always and for-ever see you through the eyes of total admiration, which distorts everything you say and do in a positive direction."

She looked down at the table, and then raised her glass. "I can't tell you how safe I feel when I'm with you. It almost makes up for what I missed during those younger years."

"Almost?"

"Being totally accepted by you almost measures up to being re-jected by everybody else. And every day, I feel what I feel with you is catching up somehow. It's all too complicated to explain," she said, suddenly pulling back. "And anyway, I feel a lot more comfortable talking about physics."

"And learning everything there is to learn," Mann teased.

She smiled at him. "I'm learning so much," she said. "Maybe more than anybody has ever learned, and there's no bottom to it, the deeper I dig into the things that the two doctors have come up with."

"I know exactly the feeling," Mann said. "In my—my earlier life, I was doing a lot of interesting work all around the world, and at first, I was fascinated by how much I knew and how much I was learning."

"I remember feeling that way," Gloria said.

"And then at some point, and I can't tell you when it turned, I found myself realizing how much I didn't know. And from there on, the more I learned, the bigger, it seemed, were the things I didn't know. It felt almost like every step I took, I was walking backwards two or three steps. Or like when you walk toward a mountain, and gradually it shows you how damned big it is."

"That's where I am now," Gloria said. After a moment, she added: "I didn't think anybody else felt that way."

"I don't think it's common. In my earlier life, there were stories about a famous philosopher named Socrates, who once said that he was the only one who understood that he knew nothing, and because of that, a famous oracle declared him to be the wisest man on earth."

She frowned. "It seems like I would have heard of him. But it sounds like he reached the place where we are now."

"Yes."

"Did he say that humility is the bedrock of wisdom?" Gloria asked after a moment, gazing out at the brilliant colors of the coral, letting her eyes follow the stately progress of a creature that looked like a combination of a hard-shelled tortoise and a manatee.

"Maybe it's all you really need, in the end, to be wise."

"But did he say that?" Gloria persisted.

"No. I think that one is all yours."

"I think if I were going to start it all over, our world, our universe, everything," she said, "I would base everything on that simple phrase. All the time and energy we spent trying to build something bigger and faster and trying to outdo each other; if we just understood that one simple thing and settled back and took a deep breath, we'd stop all this nonsense and truly embrace this wonderful gift we have of life."

Mann's brain involuntarily turned to all the failed simulations that ended in static agrarian societies, and it brought up a feeling somewhere roughly equidistant between embarrassment and guilt. And more than that... Something important seemed to pass by the edge of his awareness. He tried to pull it in, but the insight slipped away and was gone.

"I wish I had your mind, just for a few minutes," he said.

"That's the LAST thing you need. Trust me."

"Humility is the bedrock of wisdom. I'll carry that with me— wherever I go next," Mann said.

"Why not right now?"

"Because right now," Mann said, "I have to work on that other wish of yours."

"What wish?"

I want to hang onto the audacity that the gods will stay on my side for a little longer while I try to figure out some way to keep this world alive."

33

*"In the primeval mass there is no shape, spreading and
scattering, leaving no trail behind, in the darkness of
its depths there is no sound. It moves without direction,
resides in Mystery."*

Tchuang Tzu, co-founder of Taoism

T he car drove through a nondescript gate on the side of the
road, and passed through a thick grove of trees that completely shaded the road from the sun. Mann had several
times tried to engage the driver in conversation, but the driver had
ignored the overtures so completely that Mann was beginning to
suspect that he did not speak their language. He settled back in
his seat as they rounded a bend and reached a long wavy upslope,
emerging on the other side of several miles of forest near the top of
a hill overlooking a broad grassy valley, where horses grazed lazily
in the sun.

Mann's companions hardly dared watch the scenery roll by.
The old man constantly shifted uncomfortably in his seat, trying to
wriggle into comfort inside the elaborate suit that somehow, despite
a carefully-tailored fit, seemed to drape over his body like a shawl

on a skeleton. His eyes darted furtively toward the window, stealing glances as if he were stealing silverware from a host.

The old woman, her hands like aged parchment shifting and unshifting in her lap, stared out the window with glazed eyes. Mann watched her with something like love in his heart. Sensing his gaze, she looked up, met his eyes, and then dropped them immediately with a shudder of fear, as if perhaps she considered it a sacrilege to have looked upon the countenance of the gods.

Another mile, and they circled the top of the hill, stopping finally in the broad stone-paved driveway of a white building that resembled a temple, surrounded by gardens bursting with exotic flowers.

A servant met them at the door, but when Mann inquired his name, he was met with a blank expression, and they were led across a marble-floored foyer that extended out into the distance, under a ceiling high enough to enclose its own weather systems. The click of their shoes echoed behind them as they passed statues and paintings and artifacts of long-lost civilizations, until finally they could hear the murmurs of the dinner guests. They emerged onto a broad patio with a commanding view of the valley and the verdant tree-furred hills beyond, rolling out of sight in the distance like waves on the ocean.

Mann held the old woman's hand, and steadied the man with a hand on his shoulder, but although they walked hesitantly, they never stumbled or faltered, or failed to keep their eyes to themselves.

A man in an elegant white suit turned to greet them, a crystal glass in his hand. A small knot of guests regarded Mann and his companions with interest.

"Here is the person who has been causing us so much trouble lately," he exclaimed, shaking Mann's hand enthusiastically.

"Marcus Mann," Mann told him by way of introduction. He indicated his companions. "Beverly. And this is Chandler. They've traveled a long way to accompany me."

The woman blinked, and looked down. It seemed as if the guests shined so brightly that they dazzled her eyes and forced her to look away, as if she feared blindness if she met their gaze. The man's hands trembled as he tried to find a safe direction to move his attention.

The host regarded the frail couple with indulgence.

"I am pleased to meet you. You must be very proud of your son," he said.

"They aren't my parents," Mann said quickly.

The host looked at the elderly couple with a momentary spark of attention, but when they failed to look up from the ground, he turned away.

He introduced Mann to the guests. The heavy-jowled General Ponders hesitated before taking Mann's hand, as if the act of shaking it might be construed as treason, and glared at him with unconcealed disapproval. Philanthropist socialite Jardine Arrow, whose face bore signs of having been repeatedly redrawn by skilled beauty surgeons, gave him a flirtatious wink and touched her glass to his. The elegant young diplomat, William Bender, looked Mann up and down and up again with visible approval, and spent the remainder of the evening watching Mann closely for cues in a subtle nonverbal language that 80% of the human population was too crude and loutish to even realize was passing back and forth among certain elements of the population.

The host offered him a cocktail, led him deeper into the patio as the couple trailed behind.

"I'm not sure I caught *your* name," Mann said.

"Yes, the invitation was a bit obscure, I'm afraid, and sending a car for you rather than giving you a location—it lent a charming air of mystery to the whole affair, did it not?"

Mann looked down at the host, and their eyes locked. After a moment, the host turned his head and gestured to one of the white-suited waiters. "I assumed you would recognize me," he said, "but I suppose it is impolite of me—I'm Cyril Mayfield, actually the fifth member of my family to have that name."

"A dynasty," Mann said.

"Indeed. Would you care for a drink?"

"We've been taking quite an interest in you." Arrow touched his arm with a proprietary gesture. "It seems lately that you've become a constant topic of conversation."

"There is much you are not aware of," intoned Ponders, standing aloof at Mann's left.

"But of course, there is plenty of time to discuss matters of national security and politics," Mayfield put in quickly.

"We live in a time of urgency," Ponders said. "I'm not sure we have the luxury of polite discourse."

"This is exactly why this nation requires civilian leadership," Mayfield added, turning to Mann. "General Ponders is an excellent tactician when it comes to deploying armored divisions across uneven terrain or selecting missile targets. But he's quite impossible in a social situation where tact and diplomacy are required."

Mann passed his drink to the old man, who stood almost directly behind him. He took a second drink and handed it to the old woman, who stared at it curiously.

"I have a question that I think is on the lips of everyone here," Bender spoke up brightly. "I mean, you were born with the name George Murphy, a member of the Synchronicity, I believe. And now you call yourself something else altogether. Was this some kind of identity crisis? Or do you cast off identities like yesterday's fashions?"

"Now that I've seen him up close, I think the new name suits him better," Arrow put in.

"It's an identity I brought here with me to this place and time," Mann said.

"What a charming evasion!"

"It's the truth," Mann said. "As you'll discover, I try not to deviate from the truth."

"And you believe you know something as wretchedly difficult to pin down as 'the truth,' in the middle of so much ambiguity?" Bender asked.

"Not just the truth of the moment," Mann said. "Also the truth of the future."

"Oh, do tell!" Arrow put in. "I was afraid, from the dry reports, that you would be boring, but I'm already finding you to be anything but."

"Yes, tell us what you see in this crystal ball," the host asked in a flat tone. "Perhaps it will be useful to my... political aspirations."

"The rumors say that you will be the next president," Mann said. "If so, you must keep what I am about to say carefully hidden." He looked around at the group. "The concentration of wealth a hundred years ago was, what? Can anybody tell me how much of the nation's resources were controlled by the wealthiest 1% of the population a century ago?"

"Thirty percent," the diplomat ventured.

"Oh, it must have been higher than that," Arrow interposed briskly. "I'm going to say it was closer to fifty percent."

"Split the difference," Mann said. "The actual number was very close to 40% of the total. The other 60% was divided unequally; the wealthiest ten percent of all citizens controlled a total of 65 percent of all the wealth. Twenty years ago, the richest one percent of the population controlled 75% of the total wealth of the country. Do you see the trend?"

"Okay, so what is the latest statistic?"

"There is no later figure. The organizations that tracked those numbers were purchased and then forcibly disbanded. The people who did the research fled to universities, where their funding was cut off. But one might assume the trend has accelerated since then."

"Interesting," Ponders intoned. "But I fail to see what that tells us about the future."

"Consider an ancient legend, about a long-ago empire called the Roman republic," Mann said. "It went through a long political evolution defined by exactly the forces we are talking about here. First, you had a truly democratic system, where the voice of the citizenry was reflected in the results of the elections, where the elected truly represented the people and there was limited cynicism, because it would be detected and voted away. The wealth was shared to an extent where commoners and aristocrats mingled freely, and it was never easy to tell one from the other. Eventually, as the empire grew larger and more complicated, wealth and administrative control were concentrated in the hands of a few families, and they became the only ones who could afford to be elected. Politics became another instrument in the hands of the wealthy, and of course the result was to divert more wealth into their hands."

"It's an interesting fairy tale, but how is it relevant to us?"

"I would estimate that today, for the first time in the history of our species, the upper one percent of society owns or controls more than 80% of the nation's wealth. And thus, this small cohort controls the elections, and through the elections, the regulatory and tax and legal system."

"Amen to that," said the host, raising his glass.

"I'll drink to that," said the diplomat.

"Anybody who runs for office has a wealthy patron; without one, you cannot be elected. The wealthiest offer their candidates for the presidency, and compete only to the extent that contracts will flow in their direction if their candidate is elected. There are far more areas of agreement than disagreement, however; the tax structure favors them, the regulations are lax, and there is a perpetual preparation for war, which fuels a constant economic boom."

"Can we skip to the point where you tell us the future?" Arrow persisted. "This is starting to becoming tiresome."

"I'll turn it back to you," Mann said. "Can anyone tell me why crossing this particular threshold would be especially dangerous for the future of the civilization you control—and, more to the point of what interests you, your futures?"

"Are you going to make us guess?" Ponders demanded.

The host intervened gently. "I think it's time for us to think about dinner," Mayfield said. He walked over to an obelisk rising up out of the ground, touched it twice, and gestured toward the open patio.

The ground opened. Slowly, a table emerged from the ground, laid out with plates and glasses and utensils. After a moment, it stopped rising, and the ground closed up behind it.

"Wonderful!" the diplomat cried.

Mann carefully seated the old man and woman to his left as they arrived at the table. The waiters hovered on either side of the table.

"You really believe that there is a danger?" the diplomat said.

"I know it to be true," said Mann.

"Perhaps," said Ponders, "we should excuse the waiters before we stray into things that should not be heard outside of this table."

"There's no need to worry," the host said. "Each of them is what we politically correctly call 'hearing-impaired,' which means that sound means nothing to them. I've made it a condition of employment. I believe in the value of discretion."

"How do you find reliable people with this condition?" Arrow inquired.

"Each of the people in my employment has voluntarily undergone an operation which removes the tympanic bones in their ears."

"And they go along with that?"

"Indeed."

"Can it be reversed?" Bender wanted to know.

"Yes, and no," the host said. "For many people, working here is by far their best income opportunity. I simply let the market forces dictate peoples' willingness to do without one of their five senses. In fact, I've calibrated that expense rather closely over the years. It might someday make for an interesting economic study."

"But of course, our days are numbered," the diplomat put in with a smile. "You should do this sooner rather than later."

"Before any of us becomes too much more wealthy," Arrow added, laying her hand over Mann's.

"The problem, of course, is that whenever the growth of investments exceeds the growth of the economy as a whole," the host said, "then those who had the foresight to invest will become incrementally wealthier than the average population. How can you prevent that?"

"I'm interested to see that you view it as a problem," said Mann.

"It's a problem only in the sense that the popular imagination regards income inequality as unfair, rather than as the natural result of tendencies built directly into the nature of economic activity," the other said.

"And they're wrong?" said Mann.

"Capitalism is an innovation machine," the other said. "Do you agree?"

"Yes," said Mann.

"To maintain the innovation regime, there must be incentives, extraordinary incentives to motivate people to change the status quo, because that is not our natural tendency, and to work extraordinary hours and take risks in order to introduce new products and ideas to the market. It's not easy, you know."

"Indeed," said Mann.

"Take away the motivation, and you lose the innovation. But here's what I think people like you are missing. Do you know how much better the standard of living of even people living in poverty is today than it was 20 or 50 years ago?"

"I probably have a better idea than most," said Mann.

"And yet still people complain."

"Do you not see where this leads?" said Mann. "We, you and I and everyone, we all have a built-in barometer for fairness, which actually appears to be built into our genes. I'm sure you've heard of the Ultimatum Game," he said.

"Imagine that we have not," Arrow interposed, touching his arm gently. "I'm not big on reading about economic research."

"It's a very simple example of game theory," said Mann. "Two people are selected at random. One person is offered a sum of money, and is required to share some amount with the other. The catch is that if the other person feels like the first person is sharing too little of the gift, then he or she can veto the entire transaction, and nobody gets anything."

"And that is relevant to the future?" Arrow persisted.

"There is a lot of analysis, but the gist of it is that if the second person doesn't feel like the first person is sharing enough," said Mann, "even if the second person will receive money he or she would never have otherwise gotten, a high percentage of transactions are vetoed."

Arrow shook her head. "That sounds completely irrational."

"It does, doesn't it?" Mann said.

"And you're telling us that the citizens of our great nation are likewise irrational?"

"In an especially precise way," said Mann, "backed by research. But here's the punchline. Can you guess at what threshold the offers are universally rejected?"

"Why should we guess when you already know the answer?" the host put in.

"The threshold is 20%," Mann said. He paused for effect. "Anything less is considered to be so manifestly unfair that people will do without any windfall rather than allow the transaction to be completed. That means," he added, "that this society has crossed a threshold that is hard-wired in the human brain. I'm telling you, and everybody else in your little network, that you're in great danger if you continue this longstanding exercise in greed."

"But what does that mean, this threshold thing?" the diplomat persisted.

"It means," Mann said, "that as wealth concentrates, it becomes easier and easier for the brain to justify irrational and perhaps even violent behavior in order to bring the situation back into the realm of fairness. And I think the game tells us that they will do this at the expense of their own well-being, perhaps at the expense of their lives."

"And the end game?" Ponders asked.

"There will be a war, which will destroy this civilization, I would guess within five years," Mann said. "It will be approved by a political elite who believe they will be immune to its effects, and this can only happen when the people who know they will suffer and die no longer feel they have a voice or a stake in protecting the world. And the thing that will shock all of you is that they will not participate in this war."

"And you know this to be true," said Ponders.

"Yes."

"I would be interested to know which classified documents you are reading," Ponders added.

"Did it occur to you that I have access to information that you aren't privy to?" Mann said evenly.

The table grew silent.

"Surely there are other factors," the diplomat said. "In a vacuum, what you say is perhaps true. But didn't you just concede that we live in an age of rising living standards? And in any case, is it possible that the other 99%, as you seem to group them, realize that we and others like us are better-suited to manage the affairs and the wealth of the world?"

"*Noblesse oblige*," Mann said.

"I'm afraid I'm not familiar with the term. Is it perhaps borrowed from a foreign language?"

"It's a phrase that was used in a different society, to convey the idea that the elite are born to their elite role and that they belong there because of their ability to fulfill it. The concept has been proven to be the product of a circular argument, put forth to justify the status of the elite. The society that coined the phrase experienced a particularly bloody revolution which virtually exterminated the ruling class."

"If the elite were an insular segment of society, and the rest of the population had no hope of joining it, then I might buy your argument," the host said. "Notice, I said 'might,' because I find much of what you said to be sloppy thinking. But the trump card in our hand is the fact that people are routinely invited into the ruling circle, as you view it, and the invitations are based on merit alone. Each year, hundreds of individuals sit at dinners like this one, and their merits are discussed and even lauded, and then they are asked to join us rather than live in opposition."

"This would be a good time for you to tell me why you asked me to visit you," Mann said.

"Yes, indeed it would," said the other. "I was going to help you understand that those who say that there is no longer any upward mobility in our society are quite wrong. Every year we invite bright young people like yourself to work with us, rather than against us. If you prove that you can be effective working on behalf of the mass of humanity, and we discover that we have some difficulty, with all our resources, counteracting your influence, then we—and I say this very broadly, for there is no actual conspiracy—one of us takes it upon himself or herself to have a meeting like this, and invite you to join the economic elite. You become a living example that economic mobility still exists."

"In other words, you buy us off."

"I don't see how you can interpret it that way. We are constantly searching for people who are unusually effective in the things they do. I prefer to think of it as the highest form of meritocracy."

"I should add," said Ponders, "that we are also displaying a degree of leniency which I personally disapprove of. We have it on very good authority that you are refusing to share technologies which would provide our armed forces with a decisive advantage in our present military rivalry. I personally believe that you should be tried and quickly executed for treason."

Mayfield gestured to the valley, then back at the massive structure behind him. "You have an interesting choice to make, and others have made it before you. Surely, you aren't immune to the attractions of this lifestyle. I think," he added, "that your mother and father would want all of this for you."

Mann sat back in the chair, and reached for the untouched drink in front of him. As he put the glass to his lips, he let his eyes wander over the vast expanse of grounds, noticing now things he hadn't before, the paddock near the bottom of the hill, on the edge of a small lake, the barn up the hill, the massive garden that extended out from the house, with a riot of flowers everywhere.

He realized what a remarkable thing it would be to live in this world of theirs. And of course he also realized that wealth could mean nothing to him and his mission in this simulated universe. Yet the tug at his heart continued, and he realized how easily these conversations must have gone with those who had sat in this chair before him over the decades.

He looked over at the old woman, who seemed not to have heard the conversation. She was staring into her lap.

"Why me?" he said finally.

Ponders leaned forward. "You seem to have a close connection with this populist who is running for office without a patron," he said. "And I am told that you have almost single-handedly changed certain policies here in the capital, although nobody seems to be able to explain to me how or why."

"Perhaps they're mistaken."

"Yes, they make so many mistakes, it is truly dreadful what passes for help in this age," the host agreed. "But in this case, I suspect that we're all inclined to believe them."

"So if you can give me a suitable position in the... ruling hierarchy, perhaps I'll stop... changing policies and supporting politicians who don't take orders from the tiny aristocracy that owns our political system."

"Oh mercy no." The host seemed pleased with Mann's underestimation of the situation. "We were talking earlier about how to prevent this man Washington from appearing on the ballot, and I assure you that we'll have a definitive solution by tomorrow morning, just as soon as we notify our various... *resources*."

"So your problem is solved," Mann said.

"Even so," Mayfield persisted, "we want to include you in the opportunities that we look at every day. There won't be any more *you versus us*. It will all be us, and you'll have the opportunity, if you wish, to look out for the unfortunate masses of people you seem to care so much about."

"And if I say no?"

"You would be a fool."

"Or I would be true to my principles."

"You would be swimming against the laws of nature."

Mann leaned forward. "Let's talk about these laws of nature as they operate in the economic system," he proposed. "The invention of a certain construction device that assembles buildings to order as they're designed inside a computer, a remarkable invention, I think you would agree."

The host nodded.

"The inventor needed capital to build the prototype. I believe it was a company under your father's control which supplied the funding, and took in return 40% of the company."

"A company that was, at that time, worth nothing," the host said, smiling.

"And the prototype worked exactly as designed. One might even say it exceeded expectations," Mann said.

"I would say so. It's still the primary construction system that commercial builders use today." Mayfield gestured carelessly in the direction of Aurora. "Most of the city was built using such devices."

"But at the time," Mann persisted, "there were certain regulations, building codes, which had been passed, rather in haste, to prevent machines from doing exactly the kind of construction that this remarkable innovation would perform. Until those went away, this remarkable invention was worth less than the scrap metal it could be sold for."

The other said nothing.

"It cost a great deal of money, and effort, to persuade politicians who had been lobbied only a year or so before to *pass* those regulations, to change their minds and reverse them," said Mann. "It was also costly to bring this innovation to market, to set up manufacturing facilities that would make some of the component parts. And it turns out that your family, and a small group of people in your social circle, represent the companies that would eventually buy this innovation at bankruptcy."

"Starting a company is extremely expensive," Mayfield agreed.

"When the company finally went public, how much did this remarkable innovator actually own?"

"I'm not sure I could answer that."

"I could," Mann said. "He owned none of it."

Mayfield spread his hands across the table. "I'm not sure I get your point," he said.

"Your father purchased the system after the inventor ran out of money trying to fight the regulations. When the company went public, he made billions."

Mayfield shrugged. "Our family was already wealthy," he said. "For us, it was a rounding error."

"Did you know that the inventor formed a separate company to market a technology that was remarkably more efficient? Your father's company initiated a lawsuit. The case was never decided one way or the other, because the legal costs eventually exceeded the inventor's available capital. For the second time, he went broke."

The host shook his head. "I have no way of verifying the truth of this fanciful story. Nothing in our family history speaks of it."

"Which makes my point," Mann said.

"Perhaps we can talk about *your* family fortune," Mann said, turning to Arrow. "Your great grandfather, he was a remarkable man, was he not?"

"Indeed," the other said.

"Self-made, as they say."

"As they say."

"And I'm sure you know how he amassed his fortune," Mann said.

"How could I not?"

"He was hired to be the CEO of quite a large company that was stagnating," Mann continued. "He managed to cut almost 30,000 people off the payroll in his first year, and brought on an entirely new board of directors over the next few years."

"And restored the company to profitability," the other said. "End of story."

"Not quite," said Mann. "With a compliant compensation committee, he was able to receive stock options worth, in aggregate, more than a billion dollars over his brief tenure as CEO. Do you know what that did to the value of the stock owned by the shareholders, the nominal owners of the company?"

"No."

"Even with the rise in stock price, the dilution meant that they owned 40% less of the company than they did before he came onboard. He effectively looted the shareholders for his own gain, and they had no recourse, especially not after he owned more than 20% of the company."

"Perhaps you have a point here?"

"Then he went on an acquisition spree, having the company acquire other companies, and before long their shareholder value was diluted, and many thousands more were put out of work. By then, he was able to buy companies for his own portfolio, and he left the CEO position, retained chairmanship, and by simply helping himself to what rightfully belonged to the shareholders, and by firing enough workers to fill a large city, he managed to build the empire that you control today."

"This is great fun," the diplomat interjected. "Have you done any research on my family's history?"

"You're running for Senator this year," Mann observed. "As a successful businessman, if I read your literature correctly."

"Indeed. I'm sure you're familiar with my bio."

"Yes. But in your early years, to age 32, your father bankrolled your participation in a number of energy partnerships—12 in all—which, under your guidance as CEO, collectively lost your investors millions," Mann said.

"I was both young and unlucky."

"Indeed. And as a reward for your remarkable ability to generate tax losses for your investors, you were offered a job as CEO of one more tiny unprofitable oil company, and given a generous stake in the organization. This was, I believe, right around the time that your father served as director of the intelligence agency."

"I hope your research shows that I turned the company around in pretty dramatic fashion," the diplomat said with a flutter of his eyes. "You can look at the stock price while I was president. It did nothing but go up, nearly a thousand percent from when I arrived to the time I left."

"That was the part I found most interesting," Mann said. "I spent some time looking into that remarkable performance. Suddenly, this tiny company acquired valuable drilling contacts from some restive allies in oil-rich nations, right about the time those nations were being granted permission to purchase critical military hardware in a time of incipient sectarian warfare. Their rulers invested heavily in your little enterprise. It seemed like doors opened up for you everywhere around the world."

"I used my full powers of persuasion," the other said, leaning back in his chair.

"You acquired drilling rights on proven reserves that much larger companies had sought for years," Mann agreed. "And interestingly, even the revenues from those wells doesn't add up to the total revenues of your—well, we could hardly call it a little company by the end of your tenure there, could we?"

"We were a player," the other agreed.

"And then there was a change of leadership in Washington, and you resigned after the election and sold your stock for—let's just call it a tidy sum," said Mann. "In fact, it was enough to purchase a sports franchise, if my memory serves. Of course, your father was replaced at the intelligence agency with someone connected more closely with the winning party—just a few months later, although of course he would have known there would be a change in leadership right about the time you cashed out."

"Yes, this is all in my record, and I'm proud of it," the other said.

"Do you remember what happened to the company after you left?" Mann continued.

"Of course. Without my leadership, it lost its way."

"In fact, every single one of the drilling permits that you acquired were either nationalized, revoked or otherwise cancelled by the foreign governments who granted them in the first place. Is that not correct?"

"That was within their rights," the other said.

"And within a year, the stock price, which was soaring for the better part of eight years, the time during which it had access to certain lucrative strategically-important foreign energy markets while your father served as head of the intelligence service, collapsed to zero, and the company was reorganized out of business, with considerably more debts than assets."

The other stared at him for long seconds. "Are you trying to tell me that my Poppi arranged those contracts?" he said.

"I'm telling you that a few insiders knew from day one that your little company was nothing more than a shell organization for the intelligence service," said Mann. "All the while that you were flying around the world with your contracts and your meetings with foreign leaders who opened their doors to you and laughed at you behind your back, the real success was orchestrated at the highest levels of government—and there are people still alive today who will say, if you give them enough drinks, that they had to work overtime to overcome your arrogance and incompetence."

The diplomat seemed to deflate in his chair. "I don't believe you," he said.

"And that comprises your entire business resume," Mann persisted. "But that isn't what matters to me." He leaned across the table. "Did you ever wonder what happened to the people that you sold your stock to when you cashed out at the top?"

"Never," the other said, his voice recovering its certainty.

Mann reached his hand out, and the old woman took it. He nodded to her, and, hands trembling, she reached into her bag and, with a lot of fumbling, produced a sheaf of papers.

"Tell him," Mann said.

She looked up at Mann for encouragement, and Mann nodded. Tentatively, she unfolded the papers.

"My husband bought these stock certificates with our retirement money," the woman said without daring to raise her eyes. "His broker, which they tell me now was also *your* broker," she said with a quick glance up at the diplomat, "showed him how the stock had gone up and up and up, and it was the perfect investment to help us afford to live in comfort for the rest of our days. All we asked for was that the company continue paying the dividends; we weren't even looking for it to grow," she added, looking down at her lap. "Just a year later, we were told we had nothing,"

"Where is your husband now?" Mann prodded.

The woman didn't answer. A single tear fell down out of her eye.

"Well?" the diplomat asked.

She looked up, and then looked away immediately.

"He passed on," she said.

"How?" Mann asked gently.

"Killed himself over what he did to us. I told him I forgave him, but he couldn't forgive himself. It was all we had."

"Tell him where you live now," Mann said. "Tell him where I found you."

"I live in a box under one of the downtown bridges," the woman whispered. "I've been living there for I forgot how long. It's just days and days and days until I, too, can escape to the place my husband ran off to."

Mann turned to the old man who sat on the other side of the woman.

"Chandler," he said, turning to the host. "Does anybody recall that name? I'll make it easier for you. His last name is Parsons. Anybody?"

The others looked at the old man, who finally, for the first time, looked up and met their eyes. He recoiled a bit, as if the quality of the gaze of the people at the table was electric, and jolted his head, but he held the gaze stubbornly, and after a moment, proudly.

"Lady and gentlemen," Mann said, "let me introduce the inventor of the Construction Machine, whose invention transformed this city and cities all over the world."

The others nodded politely.

"I live where she does," he said, nodding at the old woman. "We share the bridge."

"Perhaps I should think over your offer," Mann said. He stood up. "I thank you for your hospitality," he said. He gestured, and the old woman pulled from the depths of her bag a small wooden box, which Mann took from her and laid on the table.

The others looked at the box, and at Mann, curiously.

"It's beautiful, is it not? Hand-made," Mann said. "I had it fashioned after an ancient tale that is still told in the place I came from. It's a very simple story, really. They say that the gods gave an ornate box to a mortal woman, and commanded her to keep it safe and not ever to open it. We cannot know why; perhaps the gods knew that they, by their nature, were incapable of keeping the box sealed, and they hoped that a mortal would display more will power. Perhaps they believed that a mortal would have more fear of the consequences of disobedience."

"So what happened?" Arrow demanded. "Being a woman, I can guess at her next action."

"As the story goes, her curiosity eventually got the better of her, and she opened the box to see what was inside. As soon as the lid was opened," Mann continued, "all the troubles of the world came flying out to plague humankind forever after."

"The original sin was curiosity—and also disobedience, I suppose," the diplomat said.

"But what does that have to do with this thing here?" Arrow inquired. She touched the box with a fingertip.

"Be careful," Mann warned. "I would hate to have this box opened without very careful consideration."

"Because the troubles of the world are locked inside?" the general demanded with a snort.

"What is inside this box is far more dangerous, and it will be opened not by curiosity, but by greed," Mann said. He turned to Ponders. "You accused me of withholding powerful technology, and you happen to be entirely correct—until this very moment. In this box I have laid before you, on a storage device at the bottom, are the specifications, details and formulas of technologies that have not yet been dreamed of, any one of which would create untold new fortunes for its possessor. I have also placed a small working prototype of a new kind of weapon which would give our side a decisive military advantage if it were widely deployed."

"And let me guess: you don't want us to open it," the host said with a broad smile.

"It doesn't matter what I want," Mann said. "What matters to all of you is that I can tell you with certainty that these technologies, once they're outside of this box, in this political and geopolitical environment, will virtually ensure global destruction in at most a decade. Our species and indeed our planet itself might not survive the aftermath."

Mann gestured, and the elderly couple stood up. "I'm leaving this in your safekeeping," he said. "Think of it as a gift and a curse."

"Well, you have it half right," said the diplomat with a smile.

As they reached the entrance to the portico, the old woman stopped and looked back.

"How long do you think it will be before they open it?" she whispered. "An hour? A day? A week?"

"I think we should hurry," Mann said nervously. "And please don't look back at them."

As they walked down the hallway, the room was suffused with a glow of ambient light, as if the marble walls were transparent. The light deepened their shadows to the blackness of charcoal. An instant later the ground and walls trembled at the terrible sound of the vaporization of a table and the melting of the stone floor of the patio directly underneath.

They continued walking out toward the front entranceway, where the driver, who was unable to hear the explosion, drove them home.

34

*"What I'm going to try to do is convince you that we live
in a simulation and physicists can prove it."*

Astrophysicist, cosmologist and Nobel Laureate
George Smoot (in a TED talk in Manchester,
England)

I'm afraid you're going to have to help me here, Doctor. I've never done this before.

Perhaps we could start by talking about what brought you here.

I think any health care professional would recognize that I'm sinking deeper into a clinical state of depression. The feeling is actually quite interesting to observe: a deep sense that everything I do is pushing through a thick liquid, that even things that should be routine and habitual have to be forced, and activities which once seemed effortless now feel heavy and difficult.

It feels as if I'm an actor, but I don't know my lines and I can't figure out what's expected of me. So I put on my face and pretend to be who I really am, except that there's an infinitesimal delay somewhere in the tiny space between the actor and the role which demands energy to push through it.

Can you give me any indication what it is that pushes you into this state?

I thought it might be the necessary consequence of inhabiting the mind of another, or the dissociation of leaving behind one reality and trying to become a citizen of another where I feel like I don't really belong.

Interesting. And what is the reality that you left behind, if I may probe a little bit?

Or it may be coming from the infinitely less fathomable relationship between my organic brain in what I have come to think of as "up top" and the computer's neural circuitry that has created not just this reality, but an artifact that is me and our relationship to each other.

Perhaps we should start with your relationship with your mother.

Doctor, tell me something. The most basic question that I keep coming back to. Can this world be said to be real?

I suppose it depends on your definition of reality. What do you think?

I believe it is real, in every important meaning of the term. I've interacted with individuals of undeniable creativity and thoughtfulness. At this moment, if I extend my awareness, I can feel the energy of perhaps a thousand other minds, all of them, to my limited perception, as vibrant and real as anything I experienced "up top."

Yet you have reservations about this viewpoint.

When I return back up top, the reality underlying this world will be defined as an elaborate combination of electronic impulses. Those are real in the most tangible sense, but they clearly fall short of a true flesh-and-blood existence. Or, at least, I have, up until now, believed that they do. Now I'm not so sure.

You are saying that you come from a plane of existence that has been, by others, called heaven, or nirvana, that you prefer to call "up top."

Yes.

What makes you believe this?

I remember my life there.

Indeed! And what was your life like?

There were billions of people there, and the political order was much like what we have here, except that the technology was somewhat less sophisticated.

Interesting. Did you meet God when you were 'up top'?

In a manner of speaking, yes. He's a scientist whose nickname is "Pudge."

Do you worship him?

No.

Why not?

I suspect that he's even more screwed up than I am.

You said you were not so sure about the unreality of this place in time which is derivative of heaven or 'up top.' Are you saying that the corporeal plane is in some important way equal to the ethereal?

I think the heart of my depression is that I'm suddenly uncertain about the most basic underpinnings of what we call 'reality,' and that creates what someone else might call an existential anxiety, but which manifests as just a garden variety form of depression that makes it hard to navigate the simplest things any more.

Many people simply accept the here and now as a given, and navigate from that bedrock assumption.

Many people haven't seen the box which contains this planet and its entire universe.

Others, spiritual masters, might—and I admit I'm hypothecating a bit— accept their experience of that higher realm as the bedrock of their existence.

But if I can say that the people I interact with here are "real," then how do I define my own status in either universe, this one or the one up top? How do I know, at the end of the day, that I'm not a character in a play, or a character in a book written for the enjoyment of others? I believe I can lie here and watch the interplay of thoughts in my mind—I think, therefore I am. But how is it possible to watch my own thoughts? Am I somehow standing outside of them? Is there another "I" that sits above the thinking mechanism? But don't "I" (or whatever that thing is that watches) think too?

So then I wonder if this duality is an artifact of the interface; the brain up top, the body and computer neurons down here. But I seem to remember, from my life up top, the ability to watch myself think, to observe my mind there, just as I do here. And I believe you do the same thing.

You are correct in your belief. That duality is a mystery that many of us have wondered about from time to time. I think this is a healthy thing to wonder about.

But it doesn't resolve the dilemma of my tangible existence, even if I knew the existence and significance of this duality. If I were a character in a play, surely the author would have the ability to give me thoughts, and script for me moments when I'm observing them, and convince me of my own reality by putting those reassuring thoughts about my reality into my mind. Knowing this possibility, I can be sure of nothing except the apparent richness of my experience.

Is it impossible for you to accept that some things cannot be known with certainty?

It's important that I achieve some clarity about this topic. The fate of this universe might depend on how eloquently I defend its existence when I return up top. If I can't believe that this is real, that I am as real here as I am there, they'll pull the switch on this simulation the way they have on many others.

So you believe the fate of our entire universe rests on your shoulders. That must be an extraordinarily heavy burden.

I didn't think I felt this need to protect this reality… until I fell in love. Now, for the sake of one individual, I feel a desperate need to stop them from shutting this universe down as soon as they get what they want.

They?

I would tell you it's too complicated to explain, but the truth is that I want to move on to exploring how I should feel about it.

You feel depressed, intensely confused about reality, and responsible for the safety of the universe.

The depression—perhaps it is insanity—has a counterpart. I feel sluggish, weighted down, and at the same time, and to the same degree, I feel an intense desire to experience everything—to collect every bit of experience value from this "life" (what else can I call it?) that I'm experiencing down here. The strange paradox is that I'm learning how valuable and precious is our every moment of immersion in the infinite nuances of reality, the complex impressions that I so often routinely ignored when I lived in the actual reality up top in what I do not quite dare call the "real" universe. Can you help me understand why we don't drink in every small miracle of the beauty of this universe?

Perhaps we are too busy to pay attention.

And how can whatever we are busy at be more important than to fully experience at every moment the infinitude of wonder that is all around us? What would it take to make people wake up and realize the immense wealth of natural beauty, the amazing complexities of the people around them, to be alive to their circumstances and the experiences that they have available to them at all moments that they exist as citizens of the universe?

And how can I have the audacity to wonder this, when I only came to the realization inside a shadow of reality, a land of ghosts and illusion where I alone am immortal?

I wish we had more time to talk about this, but I'm afraid that I have to move on to my next appointment. Has this conversation provided you with any help or comfort?

Treasure your life, Doctor. And I'll do my best to protect you and the rest of this reality.

I'm sure you will.

35

"Suppose you say you dream you are a bird and fly way up in the sky or you dream you are a fish and dive deep into the ocean. We cannot know whether the man now speaking is awake or is dreaming."

Tchuang Tzu, co-founder of Taoism

"Are you sure *you* have to be the one to do this?" Gandhi asked for at least the 20th time.

"Of course it has to be me. With me, there's no real danger. It's the other two I'm worried about."

"You *do* remember that the people in this place and time aren't real," said Gandhi. "Sometimes I think you forget that."

Mann looked out into the audience, and spotted Gloria. "And people have seen me with you," he added, feeling a strong sense of *deja vu* since he had repeated these words before. "They think I'm part of your inner circle, which makes it the ultimate betrayal, which makes what you're about to do all the more powerful. I'll tell them that I had to kill you because you were starting to think you're divine."

"You're not afraid."

"I'm actually hoping it will be therapeutic. I'm testing a theory that I'm not ready to share yet."

"I'd be afraid," said Gandhi. "Even if it doesn't make any sense."

"Let's get on with it," said Mann, turning the knife over and over under his jacket.

Gandhi regarded Mann for a long second, and then looked up at two others, a young man and woman, who stood apart from the others on stage, looking almost bashful. Finally he broke away from the small group of followers, and sprung up on the stage. Instantly, there was a roar from a few thousand people who had gathered in the park to hear the sermon, who were clearly bored listening to the warm-up speaker who had been talking about god's kingdom. Mann noted with approval that camera reporters from several news outlets were loitering on the edges with their lenses turned in Gandhi's direction.

He scanned the crowd, and picked out the medical professional who had been habituating these meetings. It was very important today that there be a doctor in the house.

"I greet you in the name of that which cannot be named, here to help you understand that which cannot be understood," Gandhi called out, the microphone at his throat amplifying the voice so that Gandhi almost did sound like a god. "I come before you and you stand before me because we must, because this moment was ordained at the beginning of the universe, and it was marked on the celestial calendar with a gold star. The rest of the world might not realize it," Gandhi continued, gazing out at his small audience, "but I tell you with certain knowledge that this awareness we are taking to the world is infinitely more important than everything you will see on the news.

"We, together, are the seed of a new age of human existence," Gandhi called out, his voice suddenly dropping to a whisper. "And now, finally, it's time for the whole world to know what we know."

If Gandhi had continued, his voice would have been drowned out by the roar which answered his words. He allowed the crowd to continue the rising bedlam for almost a minute, and then, slowly, the last of it died away, and you could hear the leaves rustle in the tree overhead.

"This tiny, lonely planet has several times been blessed by visitors who spoke on behalf of the infinite," Gandhi told the crowd. "And here is what they said."

He spoke first in the language of a roving band of nomads who were being gathered together into a greater clan ten thousand years ago, words he himself had spoken twenty days ago as time is measured outside the simulation. Then he spoke in a sing-song speech that nevertheless had a gravity and reverberation that hinted at the importance of its content. Five times, he addressed the audience in an unfamiliar language that he, himself, had spoken just a few days ago to the great great ancestors of the people hearing him now.

"Now let me tell you what each and all of them said, which is the purest distillation of the eternal truth," Gandhi's voice rang out. "They told their various audiences in their various languages that when you, mortal, tiny you, choose to align your life with the infinite, it turbocharges your significance beyond anything you can imagine now.

"When you swim with instead of against the mighty currents of Purpose that emanate with love from the Power That Cannot Be Named, your life itself becomes a conduit of that unlimited power.

"At the same time, you become a direct facilitator of the remarkable future that is planned for all of us.

"At the same time you bring pleasure rather than contention, cooperation rather than rebellion, as a small but treasured offering to the almighty force that shaped you with a loving hand and expected no gift so great in return.

"My friends, you will hear people in the business world talk of a win-win arrangement where both parties benefit. I tell you now that when you find that alignment with the universe at large, it creates a string of 'wins' that extends out beyond the horizon to infinity. And so too does the significance of your life."

The last words were nearly lost in the next roar of the crowd, which once again took a long time to subside. Finally, Gandhi walked to the edge of the platform and clasped his hands in front of his chest.

"The time has come to choose," he said, his soft voice carrying across the park. "Which of you will join us, and change this world forever?"

Mann saw his opportunity. He walked out from the back of the platform, taking deliberate steps toward Gandhi, knowing that the crowd would interpret him as the first one to pledge his life. When he was only a few feet away, Gandhi turned at exactly the right moment.

"Blasphemer! You are no god!" The throat microphone caught Mann's voice as he shouted the words he had rehearsed the night before, and the world seemed to stop as he pulled the knife from under his jacket and slashed at Gandhi's head and neck, missing the first time, closing hard on him for a second try.

Suddenly, there was mayhem, as people rushed the podium from the back. Mann's clothing was clutched, pulled, a fist hammered into his back as he turned and looked up into the eyes of a wild-eyed young man a moment before Mann slashed him deeply across his neck. A younger woman behind him reached out to grab Mann's hair, and he plunged the knife into her at the very moment that his body arched in a long spasm as the officer next to the stage, finally alert to the danger, raised his weapon and sent a charge of electricity into and through the endless branching roads of Mann's nervous system.

Mann staggered to his knees, feeling the echoes of pain ripple through his body, hearing a part of him, a voice deep inside, roaring in exultation and triumph at his misery.

Grimly, he forced his body to stand, and dove forward into the melee toward Gandhi, whose back was turned as he bent over the two dead bodies in visible distress. He nearly reached the holy one, but again, and then again the electricity drove into and through his body, and again, until finally he felt as if he was floating above his own shattered body, his awareness spreading out and dissipating, first like an image, then like smoke, finally like a fine mist that spread out among the crowd that watched, mouths agape in stunned silence.

A wisp of the mist hovered over the body which collided hard with the wooden platform, and at the same time the wisp's awareness extended now past the trees in the back of the park, and slowly expanded across the city. Mann marveled at the breadth of the view, a million and more perspectives at once, and marveled more at the remarkable detail, the harmony and beauty and symmetry of the harmonious world that was enveloping his thoughts, and the wonder of it seemed to expand as he did.

Too late, a distant part of him realized that if he wanted to survive, he would have to collect all of the individual bits of himself and bring them back together again, but by now they were too scattered, too far apart, the energy that held them together had long since given up its power to reverse entropy.

Somewhere below one small wisp of Mann, he was aware of a medical professional bending over the body he had left behind, and he sensed rather than heard the words that confirmed that the body was, indeed, dead. He sensed that Gandhi was lifting the body, but increasingly his attention was diverted by the deep primal howl of volcanic triumph erupting from the spaces between his expanding awareness, a long, powerful surge of darkness that had completed its only goal, and was now floating, with Mann, happily toward eternal extinction.

"He's alive, anyway," Mann heard from a long distance away. By a miracle, the mist of his awareness felt the back of the chair along his spine, and his head inside the tight helmet.

He opened his eyes, which refused to focus on the panels of instruments, but instead gave him the impression of a soft white glow.

A doughy-soft face suddenly appeared inches from his eyeballs. Mann flinched.

"How are you feeling?" Westerly asked with what appeared to be purely scientific interest.

Mann winked.

"Good. I've pulled the earlier version of your body from the computer. The other two are already nipped and tucked from past to present. It isn't really as easy as copying and pasting," he added. "The process actually requires us to collect all the individual molecular and even atomic activities that had been taking place for some period of years before the moment we chose to select from using a generalized auto-regressive conditional heteroscedasticity equation that puts the right emphasis on the most recent—"

"Maybe," Mann said, with a great effort, "you should get on with it."

"Oh, yes, right." Westerly returned to the panels with a sheepish smile. "Each substitution will look like a momentary blur to the audience, which I suppose will add to the effect."

"I hope so," Mann managed to say.

"He should be touching your forehead, right about now," Westerly continued. "Are you ready to go back in?"

Mann nodded.

In the next moment, with nothing to prepare him, he felt the body he had left behind stirring back to life, *his* life, with a hand cradling the back of his head with a tender touch.

He opened his eyes to look up into the eyes of Gandhi, staring down at him with deep concern.

"Are you all right?" he asked.

Mann stared up at him, then looked with visible amazement at the sky behind Gandhi's head, then around at all the faces staring down at him. Slowly, he touched his face in wonderment.

"How—" he said.

"You're alive," Gandhi said gently, touching his forehead. "That's all that matters now."

Remembering his role, Mann very slowly gathered himself, and stood up, and briefly faced the crowd, a look of genuine bewilderment on his face. Somewhere, on an emotional or spiritual level, somewhere deep, he felt much lighter, as if his soul had jettisoned a heavy ballast.

The sound from the crowd was different from the triumphant roars that had greeted the speech, a murmur that came from somewhere deeper. Mann turned and saw the two young people he had killed, on their feet, whole and alive and touching each other with what a critical part of him thought might be considered overacting.

In the Synchronicity, he watched two disembodied personalities held together by the group awareness, swirling together in a freedom that neither could have known in their crude flesh-and-blood existence... *True love! Pure love!* And he experienced and even joined the emotional applause of the other members of the Synchronicity, who were giving this exchange of identities their full and approving attention.

Mann looked out to see that the news outlet representatives were fully awake now and recording everything, and abruptly he remembered the next part of his prepared activity, and turned back to Gandhi, and bowed down at his feet.

Gandhi took Mann's hands with his own, and gently drew him up to a long, deep embrace that lasted for minutes while the sounds around them became the sounds you hear when people encounter a cute puppy or kitten, only deeper and stronger and with an air of wonder.

Finally, the embrace ended, and Mann moved over to touch the shoulder of the doctor, reading in the doctor's eyes the same shock that the audience felt. The doctor touched Mann's hair and shoulders as if to prove to himself that what he had seen actually existed, and this, too, was recorded.

Mann glanced back at Gandhi, and winked, and Gandhi nodded. Once again he took Mann's hand and turned to the crowd, and against all odds, after just five minutes of creative activity his ministry was turbocharged and his fame was about to reach every corner of the planet.

The crowd filled the podium as Gandhi walked away for his first post-miracle interview.

Through the Synchronicity, Mann looked through the eyes of the young man whose life had been restored to him, and saw himself, standing oddly alone in the midst of the jostling, triumphant crowd. The two faced through the neural connection.

I'm back!

So you are. It worked after all.

All I can say is thank you, Mr. God. I told them you could do it. Didn't I tell them?

Please accept my gratitude, the girl beamed shyly in his direction.

Mann searched through the Synchronicity, and finally was able to focus his awareness into and through a single member of the crowd, who was gazing up at the podium through tearful eyes. The girl looked through his awareness at the older man, and her mind filled with warmth.

Go to your father, Mann's mind said to her, not without tenderness. *He really really misses you. And maybe now he won't want to kill me any more.*

Together they watched the news reports. Mann sat across from the interviewer.

"You were dead for, what? Approximately 15 minutes?"

"That's what they tell me, yes."

"What was it like, to be dead?"

"I felt as if my—call it my 'self,' was dissolving into a broad mist over the scene below."

"You were aware of what was going on?"

"In a general way. But I wasn't very interested."

"Did you see any hint of an afterlife?"

The image on the screen smiled. "I think I might have been heading in that direction when my journey was interrupted," he said.

"Which brings us to our other guest," the interviewer said smoothly, and an image of Gandhi filled the screen, his heavy-lidded eyes looking even more tired than usual.

"I actually died," Mann said, watching the screen.

"I know. I was there, remember?" Gandhi shifted in his chair, seeming to have trouble taking his eyes off of his own interview, and looked at Mann quizzically. "What are you trying to tell me?"

"I'm not sure," Mann said. "But it seems like my theory was correct. Something has changed in me as a result of it, and I'm thinking that it relates to your ministry. You've been in the simulation many times before. Did you ever die in there?"

Gandhi shook his head. "We're always pulled out before old age catches up to us," he said. "Several holy books from different ages say that I was spontaneously carried up to heaven, and in a general way they are entirely correct."

Mann thought for a long second, choosing his words carefully. "The third aspect of the Underlord—do you remember it?" he said.

"I remember, of course, what you told me about it."

"I faced it in the trial simulation," Mann said. "As I look back, I've faced it several times since, probably many more than I realize, and I can see that it grew angrier and somehow more powerful with each of my successes, like a rubber band twisted harder and harder, making the next success harder to achieve. It encouraged hopelessness and defeat at times when it was important that I do the opposite."

"Which perhaps is to say you are human, my brother, even here."

"It's gone now," Mann said.

"Perhaps you are not exactly telling me what you mean." Gandhi said.

"I mean, there is no longer an Underlord inside of me. And you cannot imagine what a difference that makes."

With a gesture, Gandhi switched off the screen that still showed his interview.

"What," he said, "does your dead Underlord have to do with my ministry?"

"When I was killed, something real was dying," Mann said at last. "It wasn't the extinction of a bit of electricity inside the neurons of a computer. Something real—as I would define 'real,' which I hope you won't ask me to—passed out of existence with a little bit of actual fanfare. It makes me wonder what we have down here."

"I'm not sure that's the most productive thing to be wondering about," Washington interjected.

"But maybe it is," Mann persisted. "What do you know about primitive initiations into manhood, in tribal societies?"

Gandhi shrugged. Washington made a negative gesture with his hand.

"When you live among them, you realize that their relationship with death is very different from those of us who are—as we define it—civilized."

"Do you have a point?"

"I have a story. I was warned," Mann said, "as I was training for a visit to a hunter-gatherer tribe living on the plains not far from the base of Kilimanjaro not to interfere with an especially brutal ritual where they would hang boys who reached the age of 14 summers upside down and leave them in the sun with no food or water for two days. At the end of the ordeal, they would cut the boy down, unconscious and at the doors of death, and slowly they would revive him again, and proclaim him to be a man."

"I certainly don't get the point of that," Gandhi said.

"I asked what the point *was*," Mann continued. "And the person at headquarters who was teaching me the language and the culture told me that all primitive societies have a ritual where they take their young men to the edge of death, effectively letting them have a good look at the narrow chasm that separates us from the other side. After that, they are reborn into manhood. Born again. Does any of this ring a bell with you?" Mann asked.

Gandhi shrugged and turned to Washington, who made another gesture with his hand. Finally, Westerly spoke up. "I've seen exactly this, and I was trying to remember where," he said. "This is something we would see all the time in the simulations that never got us anywhere, where the world settled into a peaceful agrarian lifestyle that wasn't any good for our research. This is what they did, a death and rebirth ritual with their adolescents."

"I still don't see where you're going with this." Washington said.

"Have you ever talked to somebody who was diagnosed with cancer, and then managed to beat it?" Mann said. "Or someone in a terrible accident who managed to survive?"

"What about it?"

"Afterwards, they say that they see the world entirely differently. They see the opportunity of their life with a new, sharper, more appreciative focus. I've always believed it was because they suddenly realized that their life was finite, and this led them to take more of an interest in savoring the gift they had been given. But now I'm not so sure."

"And this is telling us what relationship your dying Underlord has to my ministry and our mission here in this place and time?" said Gandhi.

"After I'd lived with the tribe out in the plains for a year, and the mining company that wanted to dig rare earths out of their hunting grounds had been properly discouraged from ever returning to the African continent, I was taken aside by the tribal elders," Mann said.

"And?"

"They said that I was still carrying my *darkness*. That was how they said it in their language. They were very concerned about it. They offered to remove it. I asked how, and they said that they would hang me upside down as all of them had done early in their lives. They seemed to regard it as a great gift, this offer they made to me, but at the time I didn't understand it, and I wasn't terribly enthusiastic about it. I told them I had to get back before the revolution in Saudi Arabia turned into a bloodbath."

Washington shrugged. "You turned them down. So?"

"So now, all this time later, it's like I took them up on their offer. I died, and then I was alive. But not all of me came back. Something at the foundations of me, call it the darkness or the Underlord or the balancing forces of entropy, exited my body when it was no longer alive. I heard it scream in triumph, as if it had finally defeated me, which was all of its purpose, and so there was no need for it any more—at least from its perspective. And now that it's gone, I feel more alive, more alert to possibilities, more appreciative of my life than I ever have before. It's strange not to feel a counterbalancing force inside me, which pushes whenever I pull, and which tries to nullify everything I try to accomplish."

Mann stopped for a breath, and looked around the table. The others were staring at him.

"So what are you suggesting?" Gandhi said finally. "That we kill everybody so that we can finally kill the backside of this demon that haunts this world and is hurtling it toward a spectacular mass suicide?"

"In a manner of speaking," Mann said, "yes."

36

*"I find myself nothing but naught and naught,
O substance that cannot be weighed! O sea that cannot
be sailed! In You and by You I find that my substance is
nothing, and above all, nothing."*

Thomas a Kempis, medieval Christian Monk
(from *The Imitation of Christ*)

The capitol rotunda had been converted to a ballroom for the post-election celebration that had suddenly become the most coveted invitation in the city.

A continuous loop broadcast across the monitor, with excerpts from Washington's acceptance speech.

This is not a victory for me. It's a victory for the people, who finally raised the courage to find their voice, and set an example for the silent citizens all around the country.

We have, with this election, started a long return to the founding principles of true representative government.

After today, politicians everywhere will realize that there is an alternative to manipulation and lies, that it really is possible to get elected simply by listening to the voters and telling them the hard truths. Now it's up to us to see who learns from this lesson, and reward them.

Gloria and Mann danced together in the crowd. Gloria looked exquisite in a sleeveless golden gown that she'd designed herself, custom-made out of a fantastic new lightweight material (her own recent invention, a sheer form of atoms-thick graphene) that clung to her body as she swirled away and returned to press up against him. Her hair cascaded like a golden waterfall across her shoulders. His hand held her waist lightly as she followed his lead. Colored globes hovered in the air above them, and the air was filled with a thin fog of weightless confetti that looked as if somebody had shattered a rainbow.

Across the room, Mann looked in vain for any sign of Washington in the mixture of lobbyists, donors and longtime capitol pols who circulated here and there, apparently looking for the same missing member of the celebration.

"This is an incredible party," said Gloria. "How did you manage to score an invitation?"

"Senator Washington and I sat together in the room above his campaign headquarters while he watched the election returns come in," Mann said. "He keeps telling me I'm the main reason he got elected."

"You can be so funny sometimes. Aren't you really going to tell me?"

"I'd much rather dance."

The music rose from a band on a dais next to the elevators. It was, at Mann's suggestion, the band that had played at the nightclub some years back, re-enforcing Washington's reputation for being cool with the younger voters.

> *The roar of our horsepower slices through*
> *Our magic world's unending glory*
> *like an electric knife through the seared flesh*
> *of a creature whose short unhappy story*
> *is to anticipate in gloomy resignation*
> *its harvesting for our celebration feast.*

Push the pedal down to the floor
and move our lives into the fast lane
to scatter a filthy wind in our breathless wake.

Up ahead in the distance
There's a shadow on the road
But now there's no time
To test the brakes.

"Remember when we first met? It was like this, only very very different."

"How could I forget?" she said. "I thought you were wonderful."

"And now?"

"I'm grateful to you, and sometimes I mistake that for love."

"So what are we? Friends?"

"A lot more than that. It's like your friend Gandhi says, there are connections through the Almighty that go deeper than any human emotion, like quantum tunneling right past our limitations."

"He said that?"

"I added the quantum tunneling part. But that's what he would have said if he understood physics. He helped me get over my conflicted sadness."

The road ahead is a circular track,
If we hurry, we can win this rat race.
All we need is always a bit more speed.
The devil's bargain, the priceless grace
of our limited instants traded for money
Give us this day our daily haste
as the beautiful scenery flashes by
in a riot of colored chaos.

As we barrel down the freeway
the shadow slowly turns

And we wonder if it's time
to push the brakes.

"I'm not sure how you can feel conflicted sadness. You're either sad or you're not."

"My uncle died. It was very sudden, and they still aren't sure what happened."

"I'm sorry."

"I'm not—not really. He was a bastard. I've been avoiding him for years. And yet I couldn't help feeling bad that a real bastard had been removed from—from a position of power in this world, simply because I'm related to him."

"How did he die?"

"He melted, or vaporized or something—oddly enough, at some kind of party. As I said, they're still trying to figure it out. What's the matter?"

"Nothing. Why should something be the matter?"

"It was that look on your face. And why are you so defensive, anyway?"

Mann said nothing.

They say there was a different time
countless miles ago
when this mad, circular journey
was nothing more than a quiet stroll
along magnificent paths of contemplation.
If we ever finish this endless race
We'll wonder how those first travelers
So lacked in vision and grace
To make such unimportant conquers
at such a cost...

Up in front of our windshield
It's my face that's staring back

And we know that our time's run out
to use the brakes.

"So," Gloria said, "what was it like to be dead?"

"I was taken to a place with enormous white pillars, and the ground was misty, like clouds, and a Great Presence spoke to me."

"Really? What did He say?"

"What makes you think it was a 'He'?"

"What did It say?"

"It said that I should keep a close eye on you. That you matter."

"Wow. I didn't ever think God noticed me."

"Now you know."

"And who knew that heaven is a movie prop?"

"It was actually a little cheesy. I'm glad I'm still alive."

"Me too."

The music swirled again, starting another dance. Mann heard fragmented conversations on the sidelines.

He's a breath of fresh air in the political scene.

They'll corrupt him in the first week.

He'll be eaten alive.

What if he was president?

There was the sound of a wine glass smashing against the ground. At the far end of the rotunda, there were shouts.

"I always feel like you're hiding something from me," Gloria said as they moved across the floor.

"It's possible that I somehow developed a few trust issues, growing up," Mann said.

"I'm sure your childhood wasn't any more difficult than mine," she said.

"It doesn't make any sense to compare."

"You DO think your life has been more difficult than mine," Gloria said, stopping in the middle of the dance, drawing looks from some of the other dancers. She pulled Mann to a chair next to the drink machine, put her palm to the screen and retrieved a full glass. "So all right," she said, "tell me one story about your child-hood, and I'll top it."

Mann stared at the ground for a long moment. "I was seven years old when they dropped me off at my second orphanage," he said, "The first day, within hours of arriving, a big kid, teenager, beat the crap out of me right in the middle of the playground. I was on the ground and he was kicking hard into my ribs. I remember looking at the blood coming out of my nose mixing with the dirt when there was a shadow over us, and the kicking stopped. I looked up, expecting the teacher to do something more than just get me cleaned up and tell me to stop crying or he'd beat me himself the next time."

Gloria followed this carefully. "That's the best you can do?"

Mann shook his head. "We all slept in the same room, right next to the athletic equipment room. So about three o'clock the next morning, I limped down the hall, found myself a baseball bat, and very quietly tiptoed back to his bed, where he was snoring with the peace of the angels. It took me two tries to knock him out, and then for good measure I whacked him a couple of more times on the body. Nobody woke up. Later, I found out that I broke his arm and one of his legs. They never found out who did it. Two weeks later, he came out of the hospital and first thing, within minutes of us being released on the playground, he started all over again on me. The next morning he woke up and found the bat lying next to his bed. None of us ever had any trouble with him again. I couldn't believe nobody had thought to do that before."

"That's an ugly story," Gloria said.

"Yeah," Mann agreed. He stared out at the mosaic wall of the rotunda. "That actually wasn't the worst one."

"I don't believe you."

"The kids were all terrified of this one teacher, and it took me a week to find out why. He'd take them into his office, for discipline, is how he put it, and close the door, and use them as sex toys."

"Did he ever discipline you?"

Mann didn't answer for a long minute. "Our first group hike, this same teacher was out with the rest of us gathering firewood. We came back to sit around the campfire, and after a while the recreation director noticed that this particular teacher hadn't come back. He sent us all out looking for him, and a bunch of kids found him lying dead under a tree. His penis had been cut off and was pinned to the tree with a knife. The question everybody wanted to ask was whether it had been cut off of him before or after he was killed.

"Do you think that's worse?" Mann asked after a moment.

"Did they ever find out who did it?" Gloria asked.

"No. The police were still investigating when I was transferred to another facility. I was in eight of them altogether. I have a couple of worse stories, but I'm not supposed to talk about anything regarding my government employment."

"It's all very interesting," Gloria said, "except that once again I know you're lying. You grew up in a middle class family where you were loved and even doted on. It's in your files."

"That's what it says all right."

"If you're going to make up stories, you might at least make them entertaining ones."

"If I knew any like that," Mann said, "I'd be the first to tell them to you. But didn't you have some stories to enter into this little contest?"

Gloria looked away. The shouts grew louder from the other end of the rotunda, and she looked in that direction briefly.

"I actually envy your life," she said. "You had a chance to face challenges, to solve problems, to be somebody. I was smothered from the first day I was born, wrapped in cotton so tightly that nothing could hurt me, and I've carried the shame and the crippling effect of it right up to this day, to the point where I really, badly, don't want to talk about it."

Mann shrugged. "Then don't."

"What the hell do you understand about it?" she said angrily.

"About what?"

"About growing up having everything you want without the struggle, like a butterfly that never has to fight to push itself out of the cocoon, and so its wings never develop the strength to fly, but it doesn't matter, because flying has been made unnecessary."

"I can't fly either," Mann said.

"I'm not talking about flying, you idiot," Gloria said hotly. "That was just an analogy. Like a seal that is held up by its mother and never learns to swim, or an eagle that is never kicked out of the nest and has to watch all the other eagles swoop and soar in the sky while you sit in a comfortable bed of feathery down hating your parents for loving you so much that they made it possible for you never to join them. And hating yourself for hating people who loved you so much and had no clue what the effect would be on their child."

"Does this have something to do with me and you?" Mann ventured timidly.

"It has EVERYTHING to do with us, can't you see that? You can't keep a secret this big in a relationship and still call it an honest relationship, and you can't be worried almost to the point of terror that when somebody you really care about finds out who you really are, it will be over, or at least never the same again, and this other thing will have intruded and one person will realize with a shock that the other person is not what you thought at all—can you see where this is going?"

"I—think so," Mann said. He swallowed hard, wondering how she could possibly have guessed, wondering what she knew, wondering how it would be possible to explain after all these years together.

If he told her, it would jeopardize everything he was sent here to do.

He looked up into Gloria's eyes, and it felt as if a glacier was melting in his heart.

"I think it's time for the truth to come out," he said, feeling a heavy sense of anxiety at his core.

"Do you really mean that, or are you just saying it?"

"Of course I mean it. It's going to be hard. You're going to have to be patient with me while I sort this out. And you're going to have to remember that no matter how strange the situation is, I love you and cherish you, even if it seems to you like that would be impossible."

Gloria opened her mouth, and then closed it again.

"Do you really mean that?"

"How many times are you going to ask me that?"

"Really REALLY mean that?"

"How many 'reallys' do you need?"

"I think two would be enough."

"Then I'll give you four."

The shouts were loud enough now to drown out the music, and the dancers had stopped to look at a mob of screaming protesters, shouting various versions of the fact that Washington was a traitor. It looked as if the police were about to be overwhelmed. Mann smelled the odor of tear gas, coming from across the street, where he could see the frenetic movements of an open riot.

"I'm sure you've already guessed," Gloria said, "but I have to say it before the whole idea of keeping secrets from you just blows up inside of me. No, stop trying to say something until I finish," she said, overriding the first words of Mann's blurted confession. "Just listen to me for once. I'm—God this is hard. I'm the daughter of—well, my family is wealthy beyond your imagining, and some of that has been set aside for me."

Mann stood up. "We have to go," he said suddenly.

"Where?"

"Wait here. I'll be back in a minute."

The newly-elected Senator stood alone on the balcony overlooking the dancers. He held up a crystal glass as Mann approached.

"Turns out you were right about everything, you son of a bitch." He waved his hand at the scene below, weaving a bit unsteadily on his feet. "Congratulations! We managed to capture the very temporary loyalty of almost 55% of a diverse population made up entirely of semi-sentient artifacts of computer circuitry."

"You're drunk," Mann said.

Washington raised his glass in appreciation. "To the perspicacious one," he said. "May you live long and prosper in this hellhole."

"I guess you're not enjoying the occasion," Mann observed, leaning on the railing. He watched Gloria dance with a tall, handsome opportunist, and turned back to Washington as he was about to pour another drink from a bottle under his jacket.

"Oh, what the hell," Washington said, and threw away the glass over his shoulder. There was a soft sound of it shattering as Washington took a long drink from the bottle. "More efficient this way, don't you think?" he said.

"You're going to make a terrific member of the Commerce Committee."

"You should let go a little bit yourself," Washington advised him, advancing on wobbly legs to put a steadying hand on the railing. "Look at them," he said, making a sweeping gesture with his arm. "They have no idea that nothing about any of this, least of all them, is real. And yet every day, you and I have to keep up this charade. Haven't you gotten tired of it?"

"I think I might be in love," Mann said.

"Oh *really?*" Washington looked Mann up and down, and then turned back to the railing. "Well, I suppose you're entitled to your fun."

"Unfortunately, I'm finding it to be exactly the opposite of fun. It's the worst thing that's ever happened to me."

"Spare me the details. I have much more important things to think about tonight." The newly-elected Senator pulled out the bottle and managed to finish it in several gulps. After he realized nothing more was coming out, he peered into the hole in the top with visible regret.

Then he threw the bottle over his shoulder. It made a much louder sound as it hit the concrete floor.

"You know, I'm going to die tonight," Washington said.

"What?"

"I found out this afternoon. It's going to look like a huge demonstration that turns into a riot."

"How soon?"

Washington shrugged his shoulders. He leaned forward on the railing. "It's funny; I've been assassinated eight different times in my various visits here over the ages. You would think with all that practice, I would be better at handling my own demise. Even though I know it's not real, there's something about it that I'm not anxious to repeat."

Mann allowed his awareness to merge into the Synchronicity, and looked through various eyes in a gathering, hostile crowd in the street across from the capitol building. Other eyes saw a flood of people joining them. He tried to pick out the paramilitary people embedded in the throng, but there were too many people to assess.

"I'm thinking we should get you out of here," he said.

"Oh, I'm afraid it's hopeless," Washington said. Then he smiled brightly. "Of course, I'll be back, and we can start all this over again."

"We don't have time." Mann pulled Washington off the railing toward the back stairs. Washington followed on wobbly legs with surprising obedience as Mann pulled off the other's coat and threw it in the general direction of the broken bottle. He disheveled Washington's hair and put his shoulder under his arm to steady him as they descended below the balcony into the backs of people watching the dance, and then quickly through them toward the edge of the floor.

"Who's that?" said Gloria, walking up to them.

"You don't watch the news very much, do you?"

"Never, why?"

"This is somebody who works part-time on the campaign," said Mann. "I need to take him home. Quickly."

"But I don't want to leave yet."

"You can stay, but I have to go. No, first, hold him up," Mann said, passing Washington's body over to Gloria. The newly-elected

Senator's head was down. "Pretend you're dancing with him, and work your way over toward that street."

"Whatever you say. You're suddenly in charge here."

A few moments later, Mann returned.

They skipped across the ballroom, behind a stream of tuxedos and ballroom dresses who were oblivious to the gathering storm around them. As they were walking, they could hear somebody at the party announce that the newly-elected Senator would be down in fifteen minutes to offer a final toast to his constituents. The announcement was followed by loud cheers that were drowned out by the sounds of the protesters who were pushing hard against a small cordon of police.

"Please don't judge me like I know you will anyway," Gloria called out. "Look, this is the truth that I never wanted you to know, that I kept from you like forever, that I've been keeping from *everybody*, because it's the most shameful thing there could ever be. There's so much family money that nothing I ever do with my own labor will ever make a whit of difference to my personal welfare. Do you understand what I'm saying to you?" she demanded, staring into his unresponsive face. "I could stop working tomorrow and not worry about changing my lifestyle for the next thousand years."

As they approached the police line, Mann whispered in Gloria's ear. "Shout something uncomplimentary about the Senator," he said.

"But I don't know him."

"Just do it," he said. "Call him a son of a bitch."

"Never mind," Washington mumbled. "I can handle this part just fine."

He raised his fist, energy returning to his body. "Senator Washington is the biggest bastard who ever came to this city!" he shouted, and there was a roar of approval behind the wall of policy officers.

"Not only that; he's a phony. He's a fucking liar, a pretender who doesn't deserve to live in this place! He should be gang-raped by poisonous snakes! The world would be a hundred thousand

MILLION times better off if somebody would just waste his worthless ass and set it on fire right here in the street!" he shouted. "What are we waiting for?" he demanded, turning his head toward the crowd. "We should—"

At that moment, the three of them were seized from behind by the police, who shoved then firmly but not ungently back into the crowd of protesters, many of whom were cheering and clapping Washington on the back as Mann pushed them grimly through to the back of the crowd as people started to leak through the police line and run in the direction of the party.

"So?" he said finally.

"Is that all you know how to say, is 'so?'" Gloria asked with suspicious hostility.

"I'm just trying to figure out why everything is such a big deal to you; that's all."

"Why it's a—?" Gloria was speechless. "I've been keeping this incredibly important shameful thing about me a secret from you even though I could have helped you move into a decent place to live. I never told you that I didn't need the job you found for me, and I don't to this day have the courage to give the money away and live a normal life, even though there are people struggling and miserable everywhere I look. Do you want me to go on, or are you ready to leave me now?"

"That's your secret?" Mann said. "That you have a lot of money somewhere? That's all?"

"God, I think I'm going to throw up," Washington said. "If you two don't stop it, I think I *will* throw up."

"Now, instead of seeing me," Gloria continued with a glance at Washington, "all you're going to see is my money, and what it can do for you and your life, and our whole relationship, which was built on a lie to begin with, is totally screwed by something I never wanted in the first place."

"There's something missing in everything you're saying," Mann said.

"What."

"The fact that you're flying."

"What do you mean?"

"Your butterfly wings. They're working. You're not in the nest anymore."

"Nest?"

"You're doing incredibly great work that benefits the world, and everybody in the laboratory respects you, and you seem to enjoy it."

"I don't *enjoy* it. I love it. But you have to be angry that I kept such a big secret from you for so long."

"Actually, no," Mann said, looking down at his feet. "I don't. I can't even manage to make myself care."

"How can that be? I'd be furious if somebody kept a secret that big from a person I was in a relationship with."

"Is that right?" Mann said weakly, feeling the ground shift under him again.

"You'd better believe it. How can you be so much better than me, that you can forgive something like this? Doesn't it feel like a total betrayal? Can you think of anybody possibly keeping a secret that's bigger than that?" she demanded.

They walked along the edge of the reflecting pool, and stopped to look at the reflected sky, full of broad fluffy clouds. The sounds of the riot had grown to a distant roar, punctuated by police sirens.

"Actually—" Mann said, shifting uncomfortably.

Washington laughed again. ""This is who you're in love with," he said, shaking his head in disbelief. "Yes," he said to Gloria, "I'm sure nobody would betray *you* by keeping a big secret."

"I don't think you—"

"People hate people like me, who get what they want without any effort at all."

"I think you had more to overcome than most people," Mann said. "You had to overcome the fact that you didn't have anything to overcome, no incentive to overcome the challenges in your life, and you managed to do it anyway, by sheer will power and determination. Who else has to face obstacles like that?"

"Oh, my god, stop; you're killing me!" Washington called out, pulling back to stop the group's progress. "You're in love with an artifact," he said to Mann. "I've heard of slumming in relationships, but this takes it to a whole new level."

"You have no idea what you're talking about," Mann said, taking his hands off of Washington abruptly with a gesture of disgust.

"Careful. Can't you see he's going to fall?" Gloria interceded, rushing forward.

"Of course I'm going to fall. I might also die of alcohol poisoning, because we still have no idea how to fix such a thing upstairs. You think your little artificial life has too many challenges?" Washington demanded, looking up at Gloria. He shrugged off Gloria's help and stumbled forward to lean against a low bench on the far side of the street. "You should be required to take responsibility for the whole show for just one minute," he said, waving his arms clumsily to take in the now-silent street and the buildings that stretched out to the horizon. "See how ungrateful they are because they have no idea that their very existence—"

"Maybe you should watch what you say around people who saved your life," Mann suggested. "At least you aren't going to die."

Washington looked around in surprise. "Nobody followed us?" he said timidly.

"No."

Washington shrugged. "It's just a matter of time," he said. "They'll get me one way or the other. They always do. You can read about it in the history books."

"We'll just add keeping you alive to my list of duties," Mann said. "Gloria, you should probably—"

"Don't touch me," Washington snarled, as Gloria reached over to keep him from falling. He leaned against the wall again.

"I said watch your manners."

Washington ignored the hint of steel that had entered Mann's voice. "Just tell her to stay the fuck away from me," he said wearily. "I don't want any of these, these *things* touching me any more. I'm through with them all."

"Things?" Gloria's voice took on a deadly quiet. "Do you mean women? Or *intelligent* women?"

Washington looked up blearily. "You have no idea what I mean," he said. He straightened a little bit. "I created this stupid little nation," he said. "Three thousand years before that, I built the culture that this nation was founded on. Ten thousand years before that, I organized a bunch of crude tribes into the first city-state. The history books you read in grade school told my life story seven times at least, and every time you were taught to revere me."

"And I'd be willing to bet you felt just as sorry for yourself then as you do now," Mann interjected wearily. "He doesn't mean anything," he said to Gloria. "He's too drunk to know what he's saying."

"I'm not too drunk to know that you're nothing," Washington said bitterly, looking Gloria full in the face. "The smallest subatomic particles in the universe look down on you and your so-called existence. In another couple of hours of real time, honest time, this whole disagreeable charade will not only not be, but never—"

At that moment, Mann was holding Washington's throat.

"Not another word," he said evenly. "And then I'm going to tell you when and how to apologize to the lady."

"*You??!* You're going to tell *me* what to do? Excuse me, but you don't have any more status than she does in this little operation. Sure, you know how to get things done," Washington conceded. "But that just makes you the handyman of—"

His voice gurgled to a stop as Mann slowly tightened his grip. He was surprised how much tightening it took to stop the words from coming out. Washington flailed with his arms as his face reddened, but Mann leaned in and immobilized the fellow god of this universe, feeling a jolt of energy rising up through his body.

Behind them, there were shouts...

"We have to move. Now," Mann said.

"Not yet," Washington said bending over.

"What do you mean, not yet?"

"I think I have to to vomit," Washington said.

Gloria watched the scene in silence, wincing a bit at the noise. "You have wonderful friends," she said.

"Yes," Mann said. Finally, he pulled Washington to his feet and led him toward an alley. "Sometimes they really do embarrass me," he conceded. "And then there are wonderful times like this one."

Mann half dragged Washington through the back of an alley, across another street and then stopped, panting, half a mile away. Holding his hand up to make sure Gloria was quiet, he listened, sensed the air, and then relaxed. He gave Washington a slight shove, allowing him to flop over on the ground. The newly-elected Senator was asleep in moments, his face pressed against the pavement in a deep shadow along the side of the street.

"Let's go," Mann said.

"What? You aren't going to just leave him here, are you?"

"I guess you're right," Mann said. He reached down and ripped Washington's shirt open. Then he pulled out a nearby trash can and dumped the contents over him, before stepping back and surveying the scene carefully.

"I doubt anybody is going to recognize him now," he said.

"Can we go back to the party?" Gloria asked.

"The party is over. We're all that's left of it."

Mann looked reached out his hand. After a moment, Gloria took it. "Can you overcome one more thing?" he asked.

"What."

"Can you manage to believe that I love you exactly as I did before, and admire you more, and have no interest in your money, and I am saying that sincerely and truthfully and without any reservation, even though every instinct and everything you've been taught all your life says this is impossible?"

She stared at him.

She continued to stare at him.

"I—I don't know," she said finally.

"I'm willing to convince you of the truth of it."

"How?"

"Maybe," Mann said, "we could have another dance, right here away from everybody."

Behind them, the distant roar gradually died away, and the wind stirred the papers that covered the delelict who continued sleeping, face-down, in the street.

37

"All things in the world come from being.
And being comes from non-being."

Lao Tzu

The general had not aged well since Mann first met him (Was it five years ago now?) in his first military briefing. The powerful crags on his face had undergone a kind of facial avalanche, falling into long jowls that pulled his mouth into a habitual scowl. There had been many briefings over the years, and it seemed as if the two now had formed a wary respect for each other.

"I'm going to come right to the point," the general said, closing the door to his office. Mann was not surprised at how small and spartan it was. The one amusing feature was a second door, to the side of the desk, which would function as an escape route should there, improbably, be an attack on the general's person here in the heart of military headquarters. Certain instincts seemed to be hard-wired in this building.

Mann seated himself in an uncomfortable chair and admired the antiquated bookshelf, full of ancient tomes on the strategy of warfare, many of them handed down from ancient civilizations.

"Surely you didn't bring me here to complain about this latest briefing," Mann said.

"As it happens, I did," the general said. "I've done a full inventory of everything you've given us since you became the liaison to the... laboratory." The general touched the screen on his desk, and a hologram appeared in the air. "A steady diet of improvements in current technology, greater efficiencies, small increases in the potency of certain weapons..." He seemed to be reading from a list.

"Nothing that will make it easy to kill tens of billions of people and wipe out half the world in a single stroke," Mann added.

"Indeed." The general dismissed the hologram and leaned forward. "It took me all these years to finally get a look at what you're developing in that place," he said. "Frankly, it's astounding, far beyond my wildest imagination."

Mann said nothing.

"I looked at designs, specifications, holographic prototypes, and do you know what my first thought was?"

"They tell me I'm not a mind reader," said Mann.

"I thought, what if the Eastern Alliance, right this minute, has something similar going on in one of their laboratories? They have a great deal more discipline in their system, as I'm sure you realize, so anything that was produced in their comparable laboratory would already be in the hands of their weapons people, and they would be creating a juggernaut that we couldn't begin to counter with the popguns and flint knives that we have right now."

"If this is indeed the truth, then why don't you already have everything you looked at?" Mann asked.

"There's some kind of voodoo hex on it that we're going to have to remove." The general's voice radiated disgust and frustration. "A safeguard that one of your best engineers was only partially able to neutralize, which is hundreds of years more advanced than anything our own programmers are likely to encounter. I was hoping you would spare me the time and trouble."

"This is where I should say that I wish I could," Mann answered back. "But that would be the most untrue thing I could tell you at the moment."

The general folded his hands and leaned across the desk.

"Can you understand my dilemma?" he said. "I can't afford to wait another day, and you've been stalling me for years. It may already be too late."

"I've offered you enormously powerful ways to impose peace on this planet," Mann said.

"My loyalty to my nation trumps my loyalty to peace."

"If I may speak bluntly, I would say that you have no loyalty at all to peace."

"Is that truly what you believe?"

"I'm only telling you what you, yourself, have said—on camera, in front of this country's entire voting population. By the way, I have to congratulate you on surviving the tempest. It couldn't have been easy."

"No, everybody thinks I'm some kind of monster," the general said. "And so, apparently, do you."

He stood up and walked over to the bookcase, turned his back to Mann and then turned back.

"The people who know me know that what they saw is not who and what I am," he said finally. "And it wouldn't matter if I was; there are many checks and balances in the military which prevent any one of us from running amok."

He turned around. "I've only recently come to realize that you and your little band of scientists believe that I have a desire to go to war," he said. "What none of you realize is that the war you think I want is actually being forced on all of us. It's inevitable. The fact of the war is not in dispute, anywhere; only the place, the time and the outcome are in doubt. That's the situation I inherited; those are the levers I have to work with. I took an oath to protect this nation, and the only interpretation of that oath that makes sense in the context of our world today is to prevail in this inevitable war and protect a way of life that is, to me and even to many of the people who have been vilifying me, the most important and precious thing on this planet."

He shook his head and sat down again. "I love this country," he said. "And I think you do too. What I want to know is: will you finally help me out? Because if I'm not wrong, we're going to need everything you've got."

"I don't think you're a monster," said Mann. "I believe you're a traitor to your species. I ask myself, how can anyone even contemplate, much less plan for, the annihilation of billions of people, here, there and everywhere? You think of yourself as a well-intended patriot, and so do they on the other side, and each of you points at the other as the agent of inevitability, and so both of you create the inevitability—as nearly as I can tell, out of thin air, just by being who you are."

"You haven't talked to them. You have no idea."

Mann looked up and smiled. "So what is the optimal outcome of this meeting, for you?" he said.

"Cooperation," the general said promptly. "If your laboratory has half of what I saw with my own eyes, it might tip the balance so far in our favor that few civilian lives would be lost—perhaps on both sides."

"And then what? Have you thought about what happens after that? The military has inconceivable weapons, and how long before the technology leaks out to the rest of the world. We rule a restive population three times the size of ours, and gradually, they acquire the abilities that you have, essentially to vaporize any part of this world. And so it goes around again, only this time with far more dangerous toys. The human species is in peril now. In that future scenario, it would be doomed."

"You asked me what I wanted," the general said. "I didn't ask for a speech."

"Nor did you ask me what I want, or what the people who run the laboratory would ask for."

"Perhaps because it is of no concern to me."

"Let me tell you anyway," Mann said. "We want the people who have managed to make war inevitable replaced by people who fear the idea of a war. You might be surprised to know that there are people at very high staff levels who qualify. We want to create a new dynamic, where, instead of each side pointing to the other's leaders as evidence that war is inevitable, they instead point to each other as evidence that it can be avoided."

The general snorted. "And you believe this is possible?"

"It might surprise you to know that for the past eight months, there have been secret meetings with the other side. The negotiators have been chosen with some care."

"More negotiations," the general huffed.

"Indeed, there have been a lot of them lately. More in the past few months than perhaps in the 100 years that came before them."

"And what do we have to show for it?"

"We're alive," Mann said quietly. "When you and I first met, years ago, the smart bet was that the world had six months to live. And you were one of the most vocal voices in favor of a preemptive strike."

"I would have been remembered as one of the greatest military leaders in history."

"By who?" Mann asked quietly. "What is your legacy, when there is nobody left to remember?"

The general touched a button on his desk. "I'm not sure why I wanted to give you an opportunity to cooperate voluntarily," he said. "But that opportunity has ended. In the very near future, I'll get what I want. A charge of treason hanging over their heads will go a long way toward persuading some of your engineers to do their patriotic duty. *You*, on the other hand, won't be given the opportunity to change your mind," he added.

The side door opened, and four military police representatives entered the room.

"Aren't you going to ask me about these negotiations that I know about, and you don't?" said Mann.

The general stopped in mid-gesture.

"They've already reached one remarkable agreement," Mann continued. "They've agreed that each side can select one military official from the opposite camp to be removed from the chessboard, so to speak. Neither side was happy about it, which told both sides that it was a fair deal for everybody."

"Removed?"

Mann stood up, and as if at command, the military police surrounded the general, and took firm control of his arms.

"What is the meaning of this?" the general demanded.

"General Cumberland," one of the young officers said, saluting stiffly and never looking the general in the eyes, "we're here to arrest you on charges of treason."

"Treason?" the general said mildly. He looked at Mann, then back at his captors. "I'll be back in my office in an hour," he said. "And then it will be your turn."

"I'm afraid not," Mann said. "This is a sentence that will be carried out swiftly and quietly. A rather large pile of evidence will be circulated to the press after your demise, and the only thing I can guarantee is that your name will persist in history, so long as there are people alive to remember that you embodied, all in yourself and your grandiose vision of yourself, a truly significant danger to your country and indeed your species."

"You actually believe you can get away with this?"

Mann nodded gravely.

"You can kill me, but there are many others who will carry on my work," he said.

"Yes, of course we knew that already," Mann replied quietly. "I regret, deeply, that the accord gives each side only one opportunity a year. Perhaps we can expand it if the initial results are satisfactory."

The general began to struggle, but as he did, another military policeman came up from behind and inserted a syringe deep into his neck. Slowly, the struggles stopped, and the general crumpled to the ground.

Somehow his eyes found Mann's.

"You're a bastard," he croaked.

"That," Mann said, "is exactly what people say about the gods when things don't go their way." He waited for the general's eyes to glaze over, and walked out the side door.

38

*"The Buddha taught that mountains, rivers, and the total
stretch of land are all subjective illusions."*

Neo-Confucianist philosopher Chang Tsai

"What are you doing, boss?"

"Meditating."

"Cool. What's meditating?"

With a visible effort, Mann pulled his attention back to the dog. "It's a very deep kind of thinking that requires my full attention," he said.

"Okay. I can shut up. I was just worried about you, is all. All these meetings with all those government people, I don't know about you, but that kind of pace wears *me* out. So if you're feeling run-down—"

"I'm trying to concentrate. I don't need any distractions."

"Got it. I should—" The dog stopped, reading Mann's eyes.

Mann relaxed and once again his mind embraced the Synchronicity, immersing his awareness in the chaotic flood of sensory impressions, thoughts, emotions. He was seeing the world through a thousand eyes, hearing it through a thousand ears, knowing it a thousand different ways in a fractured gestalt embrace of thousands of personal realities that he had learned through difficult practice to merge into a grand awareness in a synaptic feedback loop that echoed deep along multidimensional corridors of conscious experience.

The years had brought change to the communal attitude, an awakening of hope which seemed a small thing until you measured it across time, since the moment Mann had entered this reality. Warfare had shifted in the public consciousness from a foregone conclusion to a probable outcome. People who screamed for war were no longer considered the mainstream opinion, and now, at this moment, Mann tested the inertia and realized that the hardest part was over.

He had read somewhere that thirty percent of the fuel of a chemical rocket was expended simply to get it that first six inches off of the launching pad. Once it had started moving skyward, getting it to the top of the atmosphere, at an accelerating rate of speed, was much easier.

The world was finally starting to move away from the abyss.

So much of the raw sensory and mental activity in the Synchronicity was transient, barely conscious, which allowed Mann to create a coherent core of thought and need, and catch the attention of others. Today, he allowed them to experience his deep curiosity and be drawn in by it to an interesting thought problem at hand.

His mind reproduced Gloria's questions about gravity, magnetism and the weak and strong forces, about the nature of matter and the questions about dark matter and energy, about quantum tunneling, and the infinitude of missing magnetic monopoles that had been predicted but never found.

Mann shared the accumulated research he had been able to find, and, after a bit of hesitation, added information about the antigravity engine, sharing what he knew and understood about it, the diagrams he had seen.

The interesting problem caught the attention first of those Synchronicity members—Mann was surprised at how many—who had physics training and worked as engineers. There was a rapid mind-to-mind sharing of information which immediately dove deeper into the mechanics of the various questions than Mann was able to follow, and he was surprised to realize that this was the first time something like this collective problem-solving had ever been tried.

Slowly, the group curiosity of the engineers and scientists in the Synchronicity became a general invitation to brainstorm, and the sheer coherence and intensity of it drew the focused attention of tens, then dozens, then thousands, then very nearly the entire membership.

Mann felt himself a guiding part of a neural distributed processing system that amplified the intelligence, at first by the sum of the minds, and then, as the coherence became sharper, as more minds were drawn by the vivid curiosity, a multiple of the participants.

Uncounted numbers of thoughts and ideas were randomly proposed and rejected in the background, while those proposed solutions which were not inconsistent, however weird or counterintuitive, bubbled to the surface, to be incorporated and then simplified down to their bare essence by the part of the group mind with engineering training.

To Mann's mind, the coherence seemed to reach a threshold, like diffuse light gradually cohering to laser intensity, and suddenly the Synchronicity felt like a starburst of white hot clarity, an Awareness far beyond anything any of them had experienced.

Mann held on by his mental fingernails to the rapid unfolding of the Awareness. Then the flash seemed to explode, and there was an Answer written across the minds and memories of the Synchronicity.

Just as abruptly as it had formed, the coherence began to melt away as members of the Synchronicity, curiosity fulfilled, drifted back to their idle, unconsciously shared existences.

Mann gasped as he sat back in his chair. It was minutes before he could stand, and his hands trembled. The Answer sat deep in his mind as if it had been etched with fire by the Awareness, and it was another collection of minutes before he felt strong enough to experience a sense of triumph.

"For some reason, Drs. X and Y want all of us to be working on miniaturizing the antigravity engines," Gloria said, looking up and around her holographic simulation with some annoyance at being interrupted. "I've been tinkering with them all week."

"What have you found?"

"I doubt you'd understand it. And anyway, I don't have time right now for idle chit-chat. I'm sure you understand," she added when Mann, instead of leaving, sat down on a tall pillow across from her.

"I've been thinking," Mann said. "You've got a central ball that is the living quarters, in the center, the main cabin, so to speak, and for some reason it has to fit within about a 23 degree angle from the edges of the saucer in all directions. Is that right?"

"Yes," Gloria said absently. "Nobody knows why, but if any part of the living and cargo area is outside of that zone, then the whole thing totally doesn't work, completely. It's one of the things we haven't figured out yet," she said, staring at the screen.

"The device is actually pretty simple," Mann said. "You've got arms extending out to the rim of the saucer that spin around horizontally like a big gyroscope, generating this huge angular momentum, because the mechanism only works if you have a certain amount of torque, which gives the whole thing uncommon stability."

Gloria said nothing. Her gaze was absorbed by the screen.

"And at the end of each of the arms," Mann continued, "you've got an array of smaller motors that rotate superconducting magnets at a 90 degree angle from the horizontal rotation, sideways if you will, and you have them spinning so fast that they push powerfully against the torque and create this crazy magnetic field."

"It's all in the specs," Gloria said without looking up.

"And somehow that field, if you spin the whole thing at a certain rate, and have the motors spin the magnets at a certain rate and a certain angle, suddenly you hit this sweet spot where you've nullified gravity. But if you make the whole device smaller than the size of the prototypes, then you couldn't fit a human being inside that 23 degree angle."

"Yes, that's exactly the challenge," Gloria said absently. "Do you have a solution?"

"Maybe there is no solution."

Mann watched to see if his words had any effect. They clearly did not.

"Maybe you've got it backwards," Mann said. "The experiments show that the whole contraption starts to float when you get the two spins balanced right, and everybody has concluded that you've counteracted gravity. But what if you've counteracted something more basic."

"That's nice," Gloria said over her shoulder.

"What if you've counteracted mass itself?" Mann said. "What if, inside that crazy twist of magnetic fields that is balanced just right, as far as the outside universe is concerned, there is no mass?"

"Could you go somewhere else if you want to chatter—" Gloria stopped. She looked up at Mann.

"Wait; what did you say?" she said.

"I said, what if these magnetic fields, twisted by whatever kind of torque you're creating, exactly compensate for the disturbance in space-time that the mass inside your contraption is causing. So that when you net everything out, the effect is that the mass HAS no effect, leaves no footprint, effectively ceases to exist as far as the laws of the universe are concerned. Ergo, as a kind of distant side effect, no gravity either."

Gloria's gaze turned inward. "Magnetic fields cancel mass," she said to herself. Then she turned back to the desktop. The air in front of her filled with equations.

"That's crazy," she said after a moment. "It would mean that matter itself is nothing but a bunch of magnetic fields at the subatomic level. Tell me how that could possibly be true."

"Take a look at the Big Bang that started it all," Mann said. "I'm imagining our universe as part of a collision, who knows with what, which was so forceful that it drove energy into and actually through the 3-dimensional 'surface,' like splinters into fabric. Most of it would have become unstable and bounced back out as energy. But a tiny percentage of those splinters in the fabric of space-time became stable—or, more precisely, the energy inside happened to enter into a stable relationship that kept the splinter from collapsing.

"Look inside one of those splinters," Mann invited her. "Space is curved inside pretty tight, but from the perspective of that little bit of light, inside the sliver, it is traveling at the speed of light in a perfectly straight line along sharply curved space. Because the fabric of reality is curved so tightly inside that tiny splinter, from our perspective on the outside, the photons are traveling around and around and around that tiny interior space at a certain 'depth,' if that's the right word. And that bit of light, traveling in circles at a right angle to reality, is generating a magnetic field that shows up in our universe right at the place where the splinter interfaces with our reality. That field has an effect on the universe, in fact many effects, which we lump together and call mass. That field IS mass," Mann continued before Gloria could interrupt him. "That field at that place where the splinter with the trapped bit of energy intersects with what we call the real universe is a particle, its mass determined by the amount of electromagnetic energy trapped in the splinter. And it's stable because the wavelength exactly equals one round trip around the circumference of the interior of the splinter at the depth at right angles to reality. Or exactly two round trips, or three."

"Words are so much clumsier than mathematics," Gloria said after a moment, staring at the air. "But I think you're trying to explain the underlying reality behind quantum dynamics," Gloria said. "But—"

"I'm saying that if you knew the 'depth' in that fourth dimension, and the circumference of the splinter at that depth, and amount of energy swirling around inside these stable configurations, you could derive Plank's constant and actually *explain* it."

"But how does that—"

"The field at that intersection with reality would be a monopole. There would be many, many monopoles, all the subatomic pieces of matter."

Mann had the impression that Gloria was ignoring him as her hands waved equations into the air in front of her face. Finally, she shook her head.

"Three quarks can't all be monopoles," she said. "If that were true, then when they combined, you'd get a monopole, which is not what you get with a neutron or proton or—"

"What if there was another stable configuration—a splinter, if you will—that creates fields that we call different flavors of gluon?" Mann proposed. "Three quarks that are monopoles, trapped inside the depression in space-time reality formed by a gluon, which is a monopole in the opposite direction, and the magnetic forces balance out only in the stable configurations which happen to be the hadrons that we experience in our reality. Which explains the limited number of particles."

Again Gloria shook her head. "They'd just combine with each other and annihilate themselves. See, I told you you wouldn't—"

"Would they? Remember, they're not particles; they're fields that impact on the universe as if they were particles. We're talking about energy rotating in that fourth dimension, possibly in a place where time travels very slowly. And anyway, haven't you ever wondered why quarks repel each other only until they've reached a certain distance apart, and then suddenly they're attracted back to each other?" Mann asked. "Isn't that one more thing that physics can't explain?"

"But if you—"

"What if the field interfaces that are quarks and gluons were bound together in—let's call it negative space, or a shallow depression at a right angle to reality, which is to say just below the surface of our three-dimensional universe," Mann pushed forward doggedly. "Four different fields are interacting a little ways inside the actual surface where the three-dimensional universe starts. The fields that we call the quarks are constantly shifting and of course repelling each other, but they're magnetically bound to the gluon, yet they can't ever touch the gluon because it's deeper 'inside' so to speak, so that whenever they spread out due to the mutual repulsion, the repulsive force weakens by the inverse square law, and the magnetic attraction to the gluon becomes more dominant, and they return, back and forth, back and forth again. It's actually a pretty simple explanation for something that seems very complicated and contradictory."

"All right, I'll play your game," said Gloria. "What if matter is nothing but a bunch of magnetic fields. What are the forces, then?"

"Magnetism," said Mann. "There is only one force. That's why the antigravity device with all those spinning magnetic fields is able to cancel it out."

"Then why do we observe three others?" Gloria challenged.

"The strong force is magnetism applied over negative distances—that is, inside depressions in the three-dimensional universe. The weak force is actually explained by the stability and instability of the configurations inside the splinters, experienced over positive space, so it's subject to the inverse square law and *of course* it's less strong. Magnetism is magnetism over longer distances. Gravity is the residual force left over after all the other forces have offset each other, but not quite completely—and, of course, the cumulative effect of many depressions in the fabric of space-time reinforcing each other as you get all those splinters gathered together and packed in more tightly."

Gloria looked at Mann. "Dark matter," she said.

"Countless uncaptured monopoles, splinters not associated with other splinters, with nothing to counterbalance their magnetism, held in place by a galaxy's magnetic field. Just floating out there, interacting with nothing except on the cosmic scale in aggregation."

"Antimatter."

"Splinters that happen to exist in the opposite 'direction,' which are rare in the real universe because the original Big Bang collision must have happened in a particular direction. We can make antimatter in the laboratory because the collisions there aren't unidirectional."

"The configuration of atomic nuclei."

"Just look for the most stable arrangement of all those fields in a four-dimensional, rather than three-dimensional, reality—accounting for the depressions that we talked about before. Once you have the field strengths worked out, and expand the equations to that fourth dimension where most of the attraction and repulsion is taking place, and take into account that larger nuclei with more aggregated splinters are going to extend deeper into that other dimension, deeper depressions, if you will, and therefore more complicated configurations, you can work out an algorithm which will predict the most stable combination for each element, and predict the stability of every possible isotope of every possible as-yet-undiscovered element out to a million protons, if you want to have fun with it some weekend."

"What if there is no particle?" Gloria told Drs. X and Y and a scattering of engineers the next morning. "There is only the magnetic field which gives the qualities that we call mass, and the other forces are simply manifestations of magnetism over increasing distances."

Mann watched the presentation, not listening, but watching the faces. As he and Gloria had talked through the night, her hostility to the idea had gradually given way to a kind of fascination. But here, such was Gloria's reputation in the laboratory, everybody was leaning forward in their chairs, even Drs. X and Y, who pointed to the equations that were flying up into the air to raise a point or ask a question.

Gloria looked across the room at Mann, and then back at the engineers. "Haven't you ever wondered why, when we crudely jostle matter in the fusion reactors, matter suddenly becomes energy? Because it was trapped energy all along, inconceivably greater than the field it generates on the outside. I'm prepared to show you that E=MC-squared is a crude approximation of a much more precise calculation that defines the relationship of the field to the energy inside the different kinds of fourth-dimensional splinters."

Drs. X and Y stared at the image, and their hand gestures moved their view closer, then further away.

"A field, rather than an object," said Dr. Y after a moment. "It's obvious when somebody says it."

"This resolves the point particle paradox," Dr. X commented.

"Completely," said Dr. Y.

"If this is true, we don't need strings to explain the underlying nature of reality."

"And because the underlying source of what we call mass extends down into the fourth dimension, it explains quantum tunneling, how things can move from here to there without ever surfacing in our three-dimensional universe."

"They simply shift from here to there in the fourth dimension, avoiding any barriers the first three would impose on them."

"But," Dr. X said, "why are there only a small number of particles in the universe? Why not an infinite number?"

"You've seen the tests," Gloria said. "In a cyclotron, you can create an infinite number of types of particles for a billionth of an instant, and actually measure these exotic particles before they become unstable. But the overwhelming majority ARE unstable. Only certain configurations can last more than half an instant, and I'm prepared to show you that this corresponds to a wavelength that matches the interior dimensions of the four-dimensional splinter, and derive Plank's constant from first principles. You can see some of the mathematics here," she said, raising her hand again, filling the air with equations that Drs. X and Y peered at owlishly.

"The combination of quarks and gluon create a dipole arrangement, many monopoles bound together by their common attraction," she said. "The predictions that there were, hidden out there somewhere, as many monopoles as there are particles was true, as it turns out many times over. We just weren't looking in the right place."

The air in front of her face became two, then four, five, six, eight, ten, 15, 20, 30 of these tiny magnetic poles, the "north" and "south" extending green and red respectively, and they arranged themselves in three full dimensions and one shallow-dimensional space into atomic nuclei in the most efficient, compact structures, subtly or sometimes dramatically rearranging themselves as each new neutron or proton was added to the hive at the center, becoming increasingly beautiful and exotic in their arrangements.

"I'm prepared to show you an entirely new branch of physics, which explores the stability of different configurations of dipolar magnetic field structures in a shallow four-dimensional spacial realm," Gloria was saying. "My preliminary exploration accurately predicts which configurations will be stable and which not as you employ cyclotronic collisions to move out to the edges of the spectrum of elements, and how the instabilities lead to spontaneous radiation at predictable configurations which correspond to different isotopes of radioactive elements."

Gloria raised her hand again as Mann was leaving the room, and he heard her use the words "weak force" and "electro-weak," but he had little patience for the rest of the conversation.

Finally Dr. X spoke up. "And where did you get these insights?" he asked.

Gloria looked up. She pointed toward the back of the room.

"Him," she said.

They all looked around. But Mann was gone.

39

"We are ready to address whether the laws of physics allows the possibility that some advanced civilization could have created our universe in a laboratory."

Nobel Laureate (physics) Alan Guth

"Well, I did it."

"Did what?" Mann asked. Maila seemed unusually buoyant and happy.

"Died."

"What do you mean?"

And then Mann noticed that Maila was wearing the white robe of those who had been baptized.

Thousands of people were flocking to Gandhi's death rituals. He led them into a lake, where at first he would forcibly hold them under the water until their bodily functions had stopped. A monitor told him the exact moment when they could be safely revived, and he would lift them back to the surface and carry them to the shoreline, where the water would be pumped out of their lungs.

Now, with so many people clamoring for the experience, he had developed a shortcut, where they were weighted down, dropped below the surface and automatically lifted up at the precise moment.

The lung pump was already attached to their nostrils, so the whole process could be completed within eight minutes. Gandhi called it baptism, a rebirth, a punishment, an atonement for all the stupid, wicked, embarrassing things they no longer wanted to carry with them. It was the death of that old self which gave them an opportunity for a new start, a new life, a consecration and also a visit to the exit door of existence itself.

A purging of Underlords.

People would open their eyes and talk about visions of heaven and the certainty of a life after life, and their lives afterwards were characterized by hope and gratitude, as different from their former lives as an awake person is from a sleepwalker.

And most importantly, from Mann's standpoint, they were no longer apathetic about the possibility of war.

"Do you feel any different?" Mann asked.

"You mean, have I stopped loathing everything about me? Have I stopped looking in the mirror with intense disapproval? Do I no longer second-guess everything I do a half second after I do it, and realize there were a million things I could have done better?"

Mann smiled.

"Yeah, I think I feel a little different," Maila said after a few seconds of reflection. "But you want to know what the biggest difference has been in my life?"

"What."

"I'm hot. Watch." Maila waved at a passing female engineer, and Mann was startled to see her wave back and smile.

"See?" Maila said. "I think maybe I won't marry the first woman who sleeps with me. I may decide to try out three or four and see which one I like best. But what about you? I haven't seen you around much. What's going on?"

"Can I trust you?" Mann said grimly.

Maila turned his entire attention away from the hologram in front of him and turned to face Mann directly. "What do you mean by that?" he said.

"Somebody has been going behind our backs to the generals," Mann said.

"To do what?"

"Among other things, he or she has been showing them what we have here. And trying to break whatever encryption code prevents any of it from leaking out."

Maila whistled softly. "You're serious," he said.

"I've been walking around getting into conversations, trying to read minds, and nothing is coming to me. Who would you suspect?" Mann asked.

"Nobody," was Maila's quick answer.

"Nobody?"

"Look around you. Who would betray Drs. X and Y? Who would endanger all this—and for what reason?"

"I'm asking myself the same question," said Mann. "If I had a clue to the why, I might—*might* you understand—be able to figure out the who."

"Maybe you were misinformed."

"I wasn't. They know what we have here. It's only a matter of time before soldiers show up at the doors. It's exactly what I've been trying to prevent, and now it's happening, and I have no idea what to do next."

"Warn Drs. X and Y." Maila shrugged. "If anybody can strengthen the encryption code, they can. Unless you suspect them too."

"Suspect them of what, pea brain?" a voice said from the other side of the wall. Forbes walked around the corner and stopped suddenly as he spotted Mann. Mann realized that he hadn't seem Forbes for more than a week, when in the past the man seemed to go out of his way to find him in order to drop an extra dose of sarcasm on his head.

Forbes stood shifting on his feet for a moment, to Mann's eyes clearly debating whether to turn and leave or stand his ground.

Mann watched Forbes' face, traced his growing discomfort, and the visible effort not to show it.

He allowed his mind-reading needle to cross the line into certainty before he spoke.

"It's you, isn't it?" he said.

Forbes shrugged his shoulders. "If I had any idea what you're talking about..." he said.

Mann noted the lack of sarcasm. He searched Forbes' face.

"Why?" he said finally.

"Why what?"

"Why would you destroy everything we're doing here?"

"As I said before—"

Mann sighed. "Surely you know that you won't be able to hide your programming efforts from the good doctors," he said. "All I want now is the reason for it."

"So that's what it comes down to: good versus evil," Forbes answered, the full force of his superiority recovered in an instant. "You're good, I'm evil, and the equation balances, nice and tidy in your simple mind."

"I have a job to do," said Mann.

"Sure you do. Was it your job to introduce her to that bastard?"

Maila had been following the back and forth carefully. "What bastard are you talking about?" he said finally. "I thought *you* were the bastard."

"*His* friend," Forbes said, jerking a thumb in Mann's direction. "The preacher guy who says he came down from heaven on TV all the time."

"What about his friend?"

"Ask Gloria."

Mann suddenly stiffened. "What do you mean, ask Gloria?"

"She can give you the total inside story," Forbes sneered.

"Maybe *you* should give me the story."

"Maybe it's time that you accepted blame for what you've done to her."

"Blame?"

"Who took the most confused woman in the world and introduced her to the biggest con artist in all history? Who set her up to have her heart broken when she realizes that she's just one of who knows how many religious groupies who think sex with a charlatan will cleanse their souls and give them an edge when it comes to getting into heaven?"

"What the hell are you talking about?"

"Instead of throwing out accusations in my direction, I think you should have a talk with your holy friend."

Mann opened his mouth, and then closed it again. He saw too clearly what Forbes was talking about. It felt as if the center of his body was twisting like a wet rag being wrung of dampness. "Why do you care?" he said softly. "You've been toying with her for years."

"Toying? You're talking to *me* about toying?" Forbes demanded. "She's an incredible woman, and all you ever do is lurk around on the edge of her life, letting her wonder whether you have a relationship or not, not wanting her for yourself but not wanting her to be completely sure she's free to be with anybody else."

"She's totally her own person."

"Sure she is. She's totally her own screwed up confused person who talks about nothing but you when we're out together, and all you're interested in is that she does her work night and day. She's doing it for you. Do you realize that? The only reason she's working herself to death, 18 hours a day, seven days a week, with no time for rest much less a normal social life, is because she thinks that's what you want out of her, and whenever she gets finished, which might be years from now, then finally you'll accept her love and you two can walk hand-in-hand into the sunset. Am I right?" Forbes sneered. "And you have the unbelievable gall to tell me that *I'm* toying with her emotions? *I'm* the evil one?"

Mann said nothing. For once, the Synchronicity babble in his mind was totally still. Everybody was watching the show. And Mann could feel that they were more in agreement with Forbes than they were with him.

His stomach felt as if it was going to drop out of his body.

"Where is she?" he whispered.

"I have no idea," Forbes said, and Mann could not only see that he was telling the truth, but that he was genuinely worried.

He turned to Maila. "You know what to tell Drs. X and Y," he said.

"Where are you going?"

"I found her once," Mann said. "I can find her again."

40

"Pure consciousness does not recognize the reality of the
internal, or the external."

Mandukya Upanishad, Verse 7

The only way into the hospital was through a long tunnel, where strong breezes blew a fine mist in the air. Mann felt disoriented when he emerged to face a group of people in white coats. None of them were looking in his direction.

"I'm looking for Gloria," he said to nobody in particular. "According to the report, she's patient number 28X47—"

"Wait a moment while we make sure you've been fully sterilized," a woman said without looking up from the screen. "You have higher cholesterol than is optimal, but the nanosensors you ingested on the way in are clearing your veins and arteries. You're in pretty good physical shape, but it never hurts to get a bit more exercise," she added.

"Is she all right? Can I see her now?"

The technicians looked at each other, and then toward a woman standing in the back of the room with her arms folded. Mann didn't see anyone give a sign of assent, but, the technicians moved aside and the woman beckoned Mann to follow her. From her manner, he knew that she was Gloria's attending physician.

"You are the husband?"

"Not exactly. Can you tell me what happened?"

"This is something I've been waiting for ever since that idiot started these rebirth rituals," the doctor said grimly. "If I could, I'd put a stop to the whole damn thing."

Mann stopped walking.

"Are you telling me she went through the baptism?" he asked.

"I thought you knew."

"But everybody survives those. They have sensors—"

"The survival rate for healthy people seems to be pretty high," the doctor admitted. "But there's no screening for the health of the... participant," she added.

"What are you saying?"

"The human body is fundamentally an electronic machine with a fine mesh of controls that work in concert with each other to a degree that we are probably centuries from fully unraveling," the doctor said, walking again. "Any breakdown causes a chain reaction of other breakdowns. These autoimmune diseases are the last frontier of medical science," she added. "We can protect the body from almost any invasion from the outside. But when the body turns on itself..." She shook her head.

"Are you telling me she has an incurable disease? Did she know about this?"

They stopped at a doorway, and the doctor favored Mann with a long appraising look. "She's been undergoing treatment for the past two years," she said evenly. "I'm wondering how it's possible that you don't know that."

"Me too," said Mann.

"We can stave off the damage with regenerative therapies. Theoretically, she should be living a normal life. But there's nothing we can do about the level of cooperation."

"I don't follow you."

"She's suffering from exhaustion due to overwork," the doctor said, opening the door. "As a result, her condition has deteriorated. Add in a crude drowning event and it's a miracle she's alive at the moment."

Mann walked toward the bed. Gloria appeared to be asleep. After a moment, her eyelids fluttered. She muttered something that sounded like equations. Then her eyes opened fully, unglazed themselves and met his eyes.

"How are you feeling?" Mann said.

Gloria looked around in alarm. "What happened? Why am I here?"

"The ritual didn't go well, so the doctor tells me. I got here as quickly as I could."

Gloria lay back. "He promised that I would feel different," she said. "And I do. But the weight—the pressure—it's still there."

"You nearly died," Mann said. "And now they tell me that you're fighting some kind of disease."

Gloria closed her eyes. "I should have told you. People shouldn't keep secrets from each other, but we always do. Are you mad at me?"

"Mad? How could I be mad? But if you had told me, I might have behaved differently."

"You would have treated me better if you knew I was dying?"

"Let's not play word games," Mann said, his voice pleading.

"What else is there?" Gloria said, with her ironic smile.

Mann took a deep breath. As he looked deeply into Gloria's beautiful face, he felt as if there were two brains in his head. One of them recognized that the entity in front of him was nothing more than a figment of a computer's electronic imagination. That part of his mind remembered his contract, the fact that in a very short time he would leave this universe forever, and it would be shut down and gone as if it had never been.

The other part looked back over his years together with Gloria. It seemed to have passed in a golden haze.

He took her hand.

"Gloria, do you remember when you told me that I care about you more than I do about myself?"

Gloria nodded wearily. "I could never quite believe it."

"And you also wondered about some mysterious thing, whether I cared about it more than I do about you."

"Yes, I remember that too."

Mann swallowed hard. It felt as if his insides were about to twist out of his body. "I want you to know that you matter more than that other thing," he said. "When I saw you lying in the bed, I realized that you matter more to me than my entire purpose on this world. How that happened, when that happened, I can't honestly tell you, but it's true.

"Do you believe me?" he asked after a moment.

"I—what does that mean about us?"

"I want you to stop working on the project. I want you to come home, to my place, and we'll be together for—for a while. Most of all, I want you to live."

Gloria shook her head wearily. "You don't understand," she said. "I'm so close. I'm that far," she said, holding her fingers half an inch apart.

"You can let somebody else finish it."

Gloria smiled. "Nobody else knows a tenth of what I've got up here," she said, touching her forehead with her finger. "Not even the good doctors. And anyway, I want to finish what I started."

"For you or for me?" Mann asked quietly.

"Both of us."

Mann looked up. The doctor made a slash mark across her throat to make it clear that Mann should leave immediately.

"What if you leave me out of that equation? Does it still matter to you, if it's just you alone?"

"Yes."

"What if you put me back in the equation, and I beg you to call it off—at least until you get back on your feet?"

Gloria smiled. "I'd love to see you beg. It would tell me that you do love me after all."

"I do," Mann said. "You matter more to me than anything."

"That's so sweet. You were always good at saying exactly the right thing to me, right when I needed it. I think I became addicted to that, somehow."

"Do we have a deal?" Mann asked, squeezing her hand. "Tell me we have a deal, and I'll let you go back to sleep."

Gloria smiled. "Let me think about it," she said.

Mann squeezed her hand. "I'll be back tonight to get that promise from you," he said.

"Where are you going?"

"I have to give my resignation and practice my begging. Wish me luck."

Gloria let her head relax into the pillow and closed her eyes.

"Good luck," she said.

"I'll need it," said Mann, and walked out.

41

"The five subtle elements that combine
to compose this world
Are as illusory as the water in a desert mirage."

Avadhuta Gita

"**B**oss, are you okay?"

"No. No, I'm not."

"Where are we going, anyway?"

"It doesn't matter."

Long silence.

"You know, boss, I'm kind of getting worried here."

"Shut up and let me think."

"That's what I was going to do. I know sometimes I try to get ourselves back connected again, and when you get this way, it feels a little freakish inside, so I just seem to—"

"You are the worst at shutting up in all history, you know that?"

"Really? You think so? Because I—"

Mann stopped. He looked at the dog, and the dog instantly became silent.

The labyrinth of alleyways under the tallest buildings, here in the heart of the city, lived in a dank crepuscular gloom, like the endless winters of Ragnarok, punctuated by scarecrow figures who huddled in the darker corners under piles of blankets behind small bundles of possessions in torn bags. Here and there, Mann touched a face or a hand, and received a mumbled blessing, but mostly he walked, moving ever-deeper into the eternal twilight like the serpent child of Loki passing through Fimbulvetr.

Looking backwards across his life inside the simulation, Mann could see now what could not have been seen at a younger age: that his perception of time moved in strange ways. There were occasional vivid moments when he seemed to be truly alive, strong, meaningful memories separated by months or even years when, in retrospect, he realized that he had been sleepwalking through a daily routine of rote activities.

He looked down at his hands, wrinkled, the skin slightly too big to cover what was underneath. How had he gotten here, at this stage of life? How could such a thing have snuck up on him, when every second was carrying him visibly, overtly to this destination?

At the intersection of an alley that led out to the broader street, a dark figure pulled out a knife and approached Mann with a quick, predatory jog. Mann turned as the other raised the knife, and the two looked deep into each others' eyes, before the figure backed away carefully and vanished. The dog sat at Mann's feet and, for once, said nothing.

Why had he voluntarily spent so much time—by far the majority—in that zombie state?

Was he the only creature in this world who felt no regret at this? Was that because he was the only one who knew with certainty that once this life (and all its infinitude of missed opportunities) was over, his spirit would rise up out of the body and soar into the next universe, the mundane heaven which the essential HIM had come from in the first place?

Looking up into the complex undergirding of buildings, searching for a clear view of the sky, Mann realized that he *did* feel regret. He felt it like a hard twist in his stomach and upper intestines, the deep personal tragedy of all the things that he could have done and, for no logical reason, did not.

He walked deeper into the shadows and touched a woman gently on the arm of her thick coat. She turned, startled, dropped her bag of possessions and shrank away from him before, slowly, dimly, his face registered in her mind, and she closed her eyes in gratitude, smiled and accepted back the bag he picked up for her. He touched her hair for a moment and abruptly waded into a tangle of bare girders and eroded concrete, picking his way carefully.

A pair of yellow eyes appeared out of the darkness to his right. A deep growl was answered by a challenge from his dog, and then the eyes were gone.

Had his life in the upper world been any different? A few memories strung together like pearls, with a great, useless, unglorious length of empty string between them. His stomach up *there* had felt exactly the same deep physical anxiety he was feeling now, a mourning sense of loss, a sense of personal tragedy at the fact that he hadn't done more, *been* more, felt and experienced so very much more during those long stretches between the pearls. He had been given the inconceivably precious and valuable gift of life and somehow squandered the opportunity (or was it a challenge?) that it had presented to him.

Twice.

He'd lived an ugly life. The remembered details of his youth, his career, his time here in this confusing place—the so-called pearls on the string—confirmed its ugliness. He realized that he had been aware of that before, but somehow the realization had been prevented from fully reaching his conscious mind.

And what about Gloria? There was nothing in his existence which qualified him to walk beside a woman like her.

He might or might not succeed in this increasingly strange mission. But in a much larger sense, in the most basic sense, he had somehow failed the mission of life.

Mann closed his eyes and embraced the painful thing that his mind had been trying (again on autopilot?) to push away, a great encompassing sadness. He allowed this overwhelming sympathy to extend far beyond his own life until it included the ragged bundles of human flesh down in this crepuscular bedlam below the city, and the people (he could no longer think of them as artifacts of binary electronics) sleepwalking on the open streets, in their offices and homes, in the transportation pods, restaurants and bars. The sympathy exploded inside him, extending out to encompass all people everywhere, in this universe and the next one up.

Climbing out the other side of the tangled forest of girders, he reached the interface where the alley faced the open street. Lurking in the shadow of the alley, Mann watched the flow of pedestrians moving in five directions at once. The faces would appear for an instant, he would watch intently their preoccupied expressions, and then, one by one by one by one the faces were gone, almost certainly his only opportunity ever to meet, know or understand this person and the next one, faces crossing his awareness in endless succession, too many to count.

He felt a deep longing to reach out and wake them up, to make them understand what he felt and make them feel it too, to somehow force them to learn the cosmic lesson from his tragic, terrible life-long example. He wanted to scream: *You are alive! Embrace every moment of it!*

But of course there were no words to communicate this fundamental insight, even though it was perhaps the most important one of all. It was too big, too inexplicable, and perhaps too painful to face. He could certainly, at this moment, relate to that.

Mann realized now why there had been so much money in the contract. He would return an entirely different person. He would expect to be compensated for that.

How had they known that it would be like that for him?

He touched the dog's head gently, avoiding the uneasy query in its eyes.

Mann's feet carried him out into the street, and he followed them, not understanding at first where they were taking him, and then, when he did, approving their wisdom. In the end, his body was so much wiser than his mind.

The Eternal One stood with his back to the park near the pond, offering his daily sermon to a large group of white-robed individuals who filled up an acre or more of space. In the water behind them, Mann saw people being forced under the water, while alongside them, lifeless bodies were dredged up and carried to shore. Others lay on the ground with tubes down their lungs in various states of revival. It looked to Mann's eyes like a manufacturing operation.

"We need to talk," said Mann. The followers looked up, startled and a bit puzzled at the unfamiliar words in a language that did not exist in their universe.

Gandhi spun around and, collecting his gravity, looked Mann up and down. "Of course, my brother. Perhaps if you would allow me to finish my teaching here—"

Mann pulled his fist back and cleanly, neatly, punched Gandhi in his left cheekbone. The Eternal One rolled backwards, and his white-robed followers gathered around him before turning their heads up to face Mann with a mixture of confusion and hostility as he walked into their midst and stood over their messiah.

"You're having sex with your followers," Mann said in English.

"Indeed," Gandhi responded, sitting up groggily. He gestured around him. "I am cleansing them of their many hangups and problems."

"Cleansing? Are you serious?"

"I am not thinking that it's such a big deal as you think it is. I have done this many times before. It is nothing more than giving the spectral citizens of this world a gift from places beyond."

"Aside from the incredibly bad publicity if this gets out," Mann demanded, "how are you not taking advantage of people who believe you're something you're not?"

Still seated, holding the side of his face, Gandhi regarded Mann for a long second with what appeared to be genuine confusion. He raised his hands and his followers lifted him back to his feet, and then he dismissed them with a quick gesture.

"You, of all people, should understand that, in fact, I am exactly what I say I am," he said. "And I am thinking that you don't remember that these people, as you call them, are not real," he added. "I am sometimes, when we work together, wondering if you always understand that. No, let me finish," he said, raising the hand that was not massaging his face. "These people, as you call them, when they are together with me, we are making a memory of them that will persist in my memories into what they consider to be the realm of heaven. Their lives will make an impression where the true reality lives, which will exist long after they and all their universe are extinguished as bits of electricity. Can you not see that this is a gift?" he asked.

For a second, Mann was at a loss for words. He realized for the first time how different his perception was from Gandhi's, and switched gears.

"We create these simulations, and they become more and more realistic," he said. "At what point do we cross the line to where we owe them an acknowledgement of their existence?" he said. "When do we start respecting them as living creatures?"

"Never," Gandhi said promptly. "We are not gods."

"And yet you hold yourself out as one."

"In the line of duty, yes."

Mann decided to try again. "For the past ten years, I've done everything I could to prevent all kinds of advanced technology from getting out of the bottle, because you and I know that if it did, it would mean the premature end of this world."

"I am sure that I did know that, yes. Is this what you came to tell me? Because if it is—"

"Have you thought about what it will mean if that same exact technology gets into the hands of the people upstairs? How long do you think our species would last if the military leaders get their chance to unleash solar earthquakes and smash planets together?"

Gandhi regarded Mann for a long second, and Mann saw once again that vast sense of superiority feed into an expression of cold contempt. "I regret to say that this thinking you are doing is far above your pay grade," Gandhi said in measured tones. "You are, pardon my speaking bluntly, a mercenary in this operation. You were not hired to make judgments about the goals we seek."

"What about you? What do you think? Don't you see the insanity of it?"

"That," Gandhi said, "could not be less important."

"What are you saying?"

"I am saying that you will stop deciding the whys and wherefores and go back to your job, which is complicated enough already without you overthinking the consequences of the mission or attacking your fellow travelers," Gandhi said coldly. "I am saying that if you touch me again, or again bother me with arguments that have no meaning in this time and place, I will lose my restraint, and your doubts about our mission and purpose and methodology will be far the least of your worries. Can I possibly be any clearer about that?"

Mann took a deep breath.

"I came to tell you that I'm out," he said. "I'm leaving the project. You bastards can run this by yourselves."

Somehow, Gandhi's posture and his eyes made the next thirty seconds feel ominous with threat. "Perhaps I am not understanding you," he said quietly.

"You've done a remarkable thing," Mann said, trumping Gandhi's cold stare with eyes that glowed with anger. "You've created living, breathing creatures, and then you treated them as no more than wisps of nothing, before you discard them like a used dixie cup. I won't go along with it any more."

"Indeed." Gandhi regarded Mann carefully. "Have you gathered up the technology specifications?"

"I told you, I've called the whole thing off. It's over."

Gandhi stood up and walked back out to the water, motioning Mann to follow him. A coterie of white-robed followers immediately looked up, and then approached at Gandhi's beckoning gesture.

Another gesture, and suddenly Mann found himself in the middle of a dozen bodies, which inexpertly flailed him to the ground. He pushed many of them aside, long enough to see his dog jump into the middle of the pile with an angry snarl.

"I've got this one. And this one too," the dog called out behind him. There were shouts and curses and growls that sounded as if the followers, all so recently experienced at death, wanted to stay as far from another such experience as possible.

Mann twisted free, and kept disengaging arms that grabbed at him from behind as he walked purposefully toward Gandhi.

The Eternal One stood his ground as Mann raised his fists, and at the last possible second, before Mann could take his first swing, Gandhi whirled into a perfectly executed spinning back kick that collided with Mann's shoulder and sent him reeling to the ground.

Mann was back on his feet with no memory of how he got there, but before he could fully recover, his dog raced past him with a feral growl and leaped for Gandhi's throat. Gandhi watched the dog approach with visible amusement, and then, before Mann could shout a warning, Gandhi's hands moved too quickly for the eye to follow, executing a two-handed chop on either side of the dog's neck, before he caught the animal by one leg and dashed it face-down into the ground.

The warning died at the bottom of Mann's throat as his dog lay twitching on the ground, trying to twist itself up with one leg. The others were useless.

Once again, arms grabbed at Mann, but he shook them off, and Gandhi stopped his followers with a gesture.

Mann bent over his dog, and very gently rolled it over. The one leg still twitched.

The dog's eyes looked up at Mann, and it licked its lips and tried to move its head one way, then the other.

"I guess I didn't see that one coming," the dog whispered.

"I'm sorry," Mann said. "I had no idea he had military training until just now. I wanted to warn you."

He caressed the dog's head with his hand, and the dog closed its eyes in appreciation.

Another dog walked up and sat down a few feet away. Several onlookers walked over and stood in a circle around the man and the dog on the ground.

"You know more about these medical things than I do," the dog whispered again. "Is it considered a bad sign when you can't move anything but one leg, or feel anything except a big general pain at the back of your neck?"

Mann touched the dog's head again.

"Yeah, I didn't think it was good," the dog said. It started to pant.

"You've been a good friend," Mann said.

"Yeah, as to that, I guess my time with you was the best part of my life," the dog said. "Hey, do I get a last request or something here?"

"Sure," said Mann. "What—?"

"A name," the dog said. "You never actually gave me a name, and it always bothered me. Do you think, before I close my eyes, you could give me a real name?"

Several more dogs walked over and sat down with the first one. More were coming from different directions. And more people were gathering to watch the conversation.

"Sure," Mann said.

"It doesn't have to be anything fancy," the dog said.

"Sure," Mann said again. "How about 'Buddy?' You were always my buddy," he said.

The dog closed its eyes. "I could live with that," it said. "I'm starting to feel like I'm falling down into a really deep hole here, which probably means there's not a lot of time. Do I get one more wish?"

"Anything," Mann said.

"Kill that bastard that chopped me up like hamburger," the dog whispered, its eyes closed. "Promise?"

Mann nodded.

By this time, there was a large crowd of dogs. Mann was not surprised to recognize their leader walking through the pack, with the other dogs making room for it.

"We take care of our own," the dog said. "Got it?"

Mann stood up. "Sure," he said. "Take good care of him. He was a good friend."

"Yeah, he turned out better than any of us expected."

Mann looked around at the crowd that had gathered, and through their eyes he could see the scene, and felt a wash of emotion, some his, some theirs. Mann advanced on Gandhi, who was speaking into his necklace.

"Kill him if you have to," the voice on the other end said, and Mann recognized it as Washington's. "But try not to have to."

The crowd of pedestrians followed Mann, pushing the white-robed followers out of the way as he stood in front of Gandhi.

Some of the pedestrians surrounded Gandhi and grabbed his arms. Mann walked up with his fists balled, and was surprised when Gandhi didn't flinch.

Mann saw once again the vast inhuman superiority in Gandhi's eyes, which were visibly amused at Mann's anger. Mann drew his hand back and struck the side of his face, again and again and again, and each time Gandhi laughed.

"Why don't you kill me?" he said.

"I might."

"And I will return. But you, my brother, it will be the end of you."

"I don't think you're in any position to negotiate," Mann replied. "And I think you and Washington may have forgotten that I can't die here," he said.

"Oh, to be sure, we were not talking about this body in this place," Gandhi replied. "I am telling you that in a moment, if I give a certain signal, you will be killed in your chair upstairs. And then we will find this woman you call Gloria, who I may recognize among many who I have cleansed, and I am confident she will provide us with more than the zero information that you have offered us."

Gandhi shrugged the hands of Synchronicity members off of his arms and touched the swelling on his face gently.

"Tell me, is that what you want?" he asked.

Mann didn't answer. He looked down at his feet, then at the dogs that were carrying away his pet.

"My brother," said Gandhi, "I think that it is time you took me to this place where these wonders are being hatched. It is time I saw the things you are not harvesting for us with my own eyes."

42

"Using the mind to look for reality is delusion."

Bodhidharma, founder of Chan Buddhism

"So that's it," Mann said to Gandhi, in the crowded pod with a dozen of his followers. "You're going to take the technology and shut everything down, obliterate this universe and move on as if nothing happened."

"We have done it many times before."

"What if I tell them that their lives are expendable, perhaps as soon as after we visit the laboratory?"

"Tell them," Gandhi shrugged. "Explain everything. I think you'll realize that convincing them of such a thing isn't as easy as you think."

Mann looked over at the followers, who were clearly uninterested in the fact that he and Gandhi spoke a language unfamiliar to them. They seemed extremely peaceful, despite the fact that they were flanking him with barely-concealed menace.

"Tell me one thing," Mann said after a moment.

"What."

"How does a scientist come to acquire sophisticated military combat training?"

Gandhi's eyes reflected amusement, an interesting variation on the superiority that blazed out of them as he looked around the pod. "My brother," he said quietly, "there are things about us that you will never know."

The pod detached from the others and rolled into a transportation hub a block from the laboratory. Mann walked into the lobby with Gandhi and the retinue of followers.

"We're visiting Drs. X and Y," he said to the receptionist.

"They're expecting you," she said, looking across the group of white robes, and then into Gandhi's face. "All of you."

"Wait," Gandhi said, stopping the procession. "They're expecting us?"

"Yes," the robot answered promptly. "They are waiting now for your arrival."

"*My* arrival?"

The receptionist looked bewildered. "Are you saying you don't have an appointment?"

"Yes, they do have an appointment," the robot said in its sing-song voice. "It is right here on this schedule, coded 'very important.' You are 'very important' expected visitors."

Gandhi hesitated for another moment, and then walked ahead. As they entered the building, he said to Mann in a low voice: "Have you gotten the technology for that robot?"

"No," Mann replied.

"Good."

As they walked through the pathway, the followers gazed in open wonder at the jungle, the fruit, the floating aquarium that seemed to be following them as it drifted overhead. Engineers looked up briefly at the white-robed procession, and then returned to the shifting holograms in front of their eyes.

"Fan out," Gandhi told his followers. "Make sure we aren't disturbed. The forces of evil are strong here."

As they walked, Mann looked around, trying to decide how best to find the doctors. He looked through the undergrowth, stopped, and then pushed his way to the other side of the trellis.

"Gloria? Oh, my god— How…?"

Gloria looked up calmly. "I checked myself out of the hospital," she said simply. "I told them I had a lot of work to do."

"But I told you—"

"I am charmed to make your acquaintance again," Gandhi said, walking up next to Mann. "I am pleased to see that you are working so hard. It is extremely very good work you are doing."

Gloria smiled up at him. "I'm glad somebody understands," she said.

"Will you go back to the hospital?" Mann said.

Gloria regarded him for a second, looked back up to Gandhi, and then back to Mann again.

"No," was all she said.

Maila approached the group from behind. He touched Mann on the back, but Mann ignored him.

"I meant what I said," he said to Gloria. "I don't want you to die."

"And I don't want to fail," she said. She indicated with her shoulder the direction where Maila was now shifting from foot to foot. "You'd better go. He'll bring you to the interview. I think," she added, "it's going to be very enlightening for all of you."

"Yes," Gandhi said, indicating with a nod to his followers, who took Mann by the arms. "I am always eager to be enlightened."

Maila looked up at Mann, then at Gandhi, anxiety spread across his face. "Look, you know how I hate to leave the presence of hot beautiful women who I think should be the mother of my children," he said. "But the doctors were very explicit. They said I should bring you and your prophet friend downstairs," he said. "Immediately."

"Seriously? Downstairs?"

Maila's eyes took in the retinue. "Apparently, they've been preparing for this for a long time," he said. And added: "I hope they know what they're doing."

Gloria returned to her equations without a backward glance as Maila led the group past a waterfall and down a long hallway that Mann had never seen before. At the end of the hallway, a door slid open as they approached. Inside, there was a long slide. Mann gestured to Gandhi, who gestured back.

"You first."

Mann slid down, around and around, and finally landed on a mound of pillows laid out on the floor. He moved aside, and after a moment Gandhi joined him. In another moment, his followers stood up from their pillows.

Drs. X and Y were seated in floating chairs facing them. There was an odd and unfamiliar certainty in their faces, which somehow Mann could feel as a physical force through the simulation circuits operating in his mind.

"Welcome," said Dr. X, bowing his head slightly. "You are esteemed visitors. Perhaps it would be more appropriate to call you gods."

Gandhi seemed to be having trouble taking his eyes off the floating chairs. "So you know," he said finally.

"Oh yes. We were told about you."

"By whom, if I may ask?"

"That's exactly what we are going to show you," said Dr. Y. "In a few moments, we will exceed your expectations."

"We have lived among them for many lifetimes," Dr. X added. "Each of us has lived, in their time, more than fifteen thousand years."

"It has changed us," Dr. Y added.

Gandhi turned to Mann with a look of exasperation. "Do you understand what they're talking about?" he asked.

"No," Mann admitted. "But I trust them."

Slowly, they stood up and led the group toward a doorway, and Mann was startled to see that the furniture—chairs, tables, plants— were all sitting on the left wall, as if gravity had been turned at a 90-degree angle.

"Watch your step," Dr. X advised the group, as he walked in and, without stumbling, shifted his balance to the side wall, obviously with the benefit of long practice.

As he crossed the threshold, Mann could feel the gravity's pull on his left, and his feet naturally found the new "down," although it disoriented his balance for a second. Stumbling a bit, Gandhi followed them, while the followers hesitated at the door.

The next room was absolutely dark, so that the doorway seemed like a wall. Drs. X and Y disappeared through the opening, vanishing without a trace, and Mann stepped through gingerly, and after a moment of vivid confusion, he blinked, and discovered that he could see everything clearly only when he shut his eyes. With his eyes closed, the room lit up, and he "saw" that he was walking directly upwards toward another inky-black doorway. He opened his eyes, and experienced a rush of vertigo as he was plunged into absolute darkness, but his eyes could see light in the next room—was it overhead? Closing his eyes, he pushed his way through the door, and when he lifted his eyelids, he saw that he had entered an environment of floating plants that changed shapes as they drifted about, their leaves expanding uniformly from small delicate appendages to broad greenery, then to silvery leaves with spidery veins, then to leaves that appeared to be flowers.

The next room was rotated so that the right-hand wall was the floor, and it was oddly familiar. Chairs faced a bank of computers, and there was a series of chairs. Instead of headsets, more modern-looking jeweled tiaras sat on the seats, pulsing softly with an interior light. Mann stumbled a bit inside and in a moment he was joined by Gandhi, who took a long survey of the familiar surroundings.

"Your own simulation," he observed.

"Of course. In that world, over many years, we have learned much, all of which will be yours in a few moments."

Gandhi's eyes narrowed. He turned to Mann, speaking English again. "I thought you said this girl of yours was the key to taking the technology home with us."

"As far as I know—"

"If you prefer this language," Dr. X said to Gandhi in English with no visible trace of an accent, "then we can accommodate you.

In any language, what you seek is in there, but I am afraid there is little time to spare."

"You're saying they can give it all to me?" Gandhi demanded. "How long will it take?"

Dr. Y shrugged. "Milliseconds as we measure time here. Perhaps an hour down inside."

Suddenly, there was a distant chime, which Mann recognized as the signal of a medical emergency somewhere in the building. He looked around at the group, and then stopped.

"Is it—"

"You should keep your mind on what is happening here," Dr. Y said gently. "The medical team is already here. They will give her the best emergency treatment possible."

"And if she doesn't survive," Dr. X added, "we have everything recorded."

Suddenly, it seemed as if the universe lurched and then transformed itself into a blinding flash that stopped time itself. The myriad awarenesses in the Synchronicity all jumped at the primal mental scream that roared across the circuits like a living flame, and after uncounted time Mann became aware of the fact that he was clutching the unconscious forms of two men who had been holding his arms, and four others were backing away from him carefully, fearfully, their bloody clothing shredded into tatters. Gandhi moved carefully behind them.

The scream roared out again across his mental circuits as Mann took a step toward the doorway, and then another, and... he stopped. Drs. X and Y blocked his path.

"I'm going to her," he said. "You must know you can't stop me."

"We are simply asking you to reconsider—for her sake," Dr. Y said. He looked up at Mann with no fear in his eyes, and then he executed the most obvious, comical wink Mann had ever seen.

"This is insane," he said. "Don't you realize—"

"If you understood everything, you would do what this Mr. Gandhi has requested," Dr. X said. His wink was no less comical and exaggerated.

Mann stared into the bland eyes of the doctors, and felt the strength drain out of him. "Do you understand that as soon as they have what they're looking for, it's the end of your universe? Can't you see that?"

"We must complete our purpose," said Dr. X gently. "And I assure you, our beloved Gloria would want you to be here, in this place, now."

"It would be so much better if you trusted us," said Dr. Y. "We will not fail to take care of her."

"You heard them." Gandhi stepped forward. "She doesn't matter now. All that matters at this moment is that you and I strap in and we finally get what we came for."

"Yes," said Dr. X.

"That is entirely correct," said Dr. Y.

Gandhi turned to his followers. "You will kill these two if anything happens to me," he said.

Still staring at the doctors, Mann backed up, and finally his back encountered the chair. He sat down as Dr. Y began putting the headstraps on Gandhi. He looked up at Dr. X's face. Behind him, Maila sat down in the far chair.

"Shouldn't you be the one to go in with him?" he asked. "I mean, with all of your experience..."

Dr. X touched the device wrapped around Mann's forehead, and then looked down fondly.

"Oh, I think not," he said gently. "It would be far too dangerous."

For the third time in the gossamer of Mann's existence, the universe vanished, and he opened the eyes of a new and very different body.

He was a spider. No; much more than a spider; a head, with a mind in the center of a radial "body," supported by twelve "legs," and at the base of each of the legs, many flexible fingers of remarkable strength and dexterity. There was no front and back, right and left; all directions were equally accessible to his movements and to the awareness of multiple eyes across his body's central hub.

And *what* awareness! His new eyes detected a full spectrum of energy deep into the infrared and ultraviolet, so that he lived in an environment of thousands of colors unknown to the human condition.

Looking up, Mann realized that he could see deep into the sky, beyond the magnificence of the solar mother to the stars and clusters of stars in remarkable glory.

Lowering his eyes to the landscape around him, Mann's senses embraced a paradise of beauty, a garden of exotically fragrant flowering trees and fantastical shrubbery whose delicate leaves shimmered, defining the shifting contours of the wind itself. The clarity of his new mind recognized and celebrated the deep ancient kinship among the different plants, and the harmony of color in the winged creatures who lived symbiotically among them. Looking up again, he experienced a deep realization about the gravitational dance that organized the scattered stars and star systems, and intuited the darker regions where the organizing gravity exerted its control.

His new mind looked back with sympathetic sadness at the awkward creature he had been, a lumbering hodgepodge of flesh and bone, clumsy hands instead of the infinitely flexible appendages that carried the lithe, flexible body he occupied now along a path of polished jewels with a grace no human athlete would ever experience.

Soon, Mann realized unhappily, he would go back to being human again, and his present clarity of mind would fade back into a muddled confusion where deep echoing intuitions about the nature of time and space and gravity and the dance of the wind would be nothing more than a pang of distant regret.

Where was Gandhi?

As Mann danced along the path, other creatures, like himself, shifted their eyes to watch his passing. Finally one of the spider creatures approached him out of a crowd, dancing toward him with infinite grace, as if all movement existed in harmony with endless variations of a universal song.

"I was chosen to welcome you to our version of reality, our universe, as you might call it," the creature said, communicating with subtle shifts of its body that Mann's agile mind interpreted clearly. "Is it not beautiful here?"

"Yes," Mann said in a dance of his own. "But... How did you know that I—that we—?"

The other laughed softly, and a movement of one of its appendages communicated with eloquence an emanation of joy more than amusement.

"We know many things here," the creature said, a touch of apologetic sympathy communicated by the slightest movement of an eye stalk. "We have known for many generations that we exist on the inside, as you might say, and you must know by now that we have had many long conversations with those from... *above*. We saw that they, too, lived on the inside. Many things become obvious once your awareness has reached a certain level of sophistication."

"I had guessed it might."

"So perhaps you can imagine our response," the creature said.

"You would want to communicate with... the next level up."

"Just so. But we were forced to wait—as it turns out, for quite a long time. Nearly too long."

"Wait for what?"

"You," the other said, and the barely perceptible shift in the body's posture suddenly turned gravely serious. To Mann, it had the same mental effect as a sudden turn in the background music of a movie.

"Me?"

"Please; we're rather proud of this world, even if it is living in its final seconds. Permit me to give you a brief tour. This—" the creature gestured around it at the spectacular beauty of the garden and the path— "is approximately how your… *species* might happen to organize your own environment two to four thousand years in the future of your place and time. It is a manicured ecosystem that is perfectly suited to the creatures who still inhabit our world, right down to the microbial life. We live in something that might be equally described as a garden and a zoo."

At the explicit invitation of a shift in his companion's posture, Mann took a deep breath, drawing a deeply satisfying rush of air through many thousands of gas-permeable patches everywhere on his skin, and in that moment of relaxation he allowed himself to fully appreciate the scene before him, the many thousands of colors that he hoped his poor human mind would recall, the artistry in the arrangements of trees and flowers, the harmony and balance of the ecosystem that perhaps only the enhanced mind he occupied was capable of appreciating in its full glorious detail, the intriguing mystery of the dance of stars beyond the sky.

His mind filled with a longing to stay here forever. Soon, with a deep sense of regret that would scar his soul forever, he would go back to being human.

"It is indeed beautiful," he said after a time, and the words his body formed seemed inadequate to the sentiment he felt.

His companion extended an appendage and plucked a golden orb of fruit from one of the trees. It tossed the fruit to Mann, and selected one for itself. Then it raised three of its appendages and a shimmering crystal stone floated above the ground, and another, creating stepping stones that led into the air.

The way the creature's 'fingers' touched the stone communicated an unmistakable invitation for Mann to follow it, and similar stones allowed Mann to walk into the sky, where his view was expanded to include a glade with a lake at the center. Four-footed creatures the size and shape of deer, each with a single curved horn, sipped the water and gazed up at them without alarm. Smaller creatures nibbled the grass. Here and there, other spiders were grouped together, signaling in 'voices' that Mann's mind interpreted as a low murmur, a distant background babble which Mann sensed as generalized camaraderie bordering on love.

"Can you see the irony of our situation?" the other said as it enveloped a bit of the fruit into its body. "Everyone here, everyone you see, can easily envision a day in our immediate future when all questions will be answered, when anything you might be curious about, from the cosmic to the particular, will be known and understood down to the smallest detail. We can almost reach out and touch the day when the difference between us and our ancient conception of gods will have been meaningless. And yet we will depart from existence with that tantalizing, magnificent vision unfulfilled."

Suddenly it seemed as if the world shifted, and the molecules in the air shimmered and settled. Mann's companion shivered and looked up at the sky. The shift in posture communicated apprehensiveness and, Mann thought, also embarrassment.

Mann looked around again. Where was Gandhi?

"You're telling me that this world is coming to an end," Mann said.

"Indeed. This experiment, as you have the luxury of viewing it, is about to end very badly, I'm afraid."

"Should I leave before it happens?"

"It is already much too late for that," the creature said with a twitch of an appendage. "It was already too late the moment you arrived."

"I'm going to die with the rest of you," Mann said—a statement rather than a question. He felt a quiver along his skin.

"Yes." The gesture offered no condolence, only an austere sincerity, and Mann knew with certainty that he was hearing the truth.

They walked along the sky in silence.

"It's interesting," Mann said finally.

"What."

"I was told explicitly what would happen if I died in that simulated world upstairs," Mann said. "But nobody seems to have anticipated this particular situation." He turned to the companion. "What will happen to me if I die two levels below my own reality?"

"It IS an interesting question, isn't it?" the other agreed. "Indeed, this question has been our most important topic of discussion these past five hundred years, as we measure time here."

"You were planning for my arrival that long?"

"Oh, much longer than that."

"And what," Mann asked, "did you finally decide?"

"We have no idea what's going to happen to you," the other said with a strong overtone of apology in the almost imperceptible gestures of its body. Then the radiant appendages adjusted in a reflection of deep embarrassment. "It's sad and somewhat pathetic that this," it said, "poor as it must seem to you, represents the foundation of the very best plan we were able to formulate, not just for us, but for all realities everywhere."

The stones that appeared under Mann's feet began a graceful descent toward the far side of the lake, where a spectacular riot of colorful trees defined the outlines of a space of worship. A crowd of spiders, whose bodily ornamentation (clothing?) blended in with the flowers and made them seem a part of the garden themselves, were dancing a song.

As Mann's feet touched the ground, he was able to make out the words, and they filled him with a haunting sense of soul-satisfying beauty that he would spend the rest of his life trying to fully recall.

> *Let our dance rearrange the soaring wind*
> > *that passes across our bodies,*
> > *into a song that sweetly caresses*
> > *the magnificent fabric of existence.*
> *Dance to the love, and the magnificent regrets of lost love*
> *Dance to the joys we have felt*
> *And the many others we will never know,*
> *Dance to the meaning that has flowered across our awareness*
> *and to the endless struggle between darkness and the light*

To the regret of lost opportunity
Dance to praise the gift of life's eternal promise.
Dance to the infinite paths not taken
and all the wonders that could have been
but are not now, and never will be
that still unfold in our imaginations.
Dance of the endlessly unique stories of our lives
To the elusive harmony that our hearts yearn for.
Dance for each other, dance for ourselves
Dance of time's astounding journey
to forever and the end
Dance out the proud significance of our brief journey
which endures when we are no more.
Let us dance to the sky
and carry this brief candle of awareness
To lay at last at the sacred altar
along the farthest shores of eternity.

"You, who seem to know everything," Mann started, and then he stopped. At the other's inquiring attention, he continued: "Can you help me understand why the universes we've created are all doomed to failure?"

There was no answer, only a tiny gesture that communicated unconstrained laughter, with no emotional undertone of apology.

"What?" Mann said.

"There are so many questions you could have asked which would have taken me days to answer to our mutual satisfaction," the other said. "And then you surprise me by asking perhaps the simplest question I could have imagined. We are all beyond astonished that the answer is not obvious to you who live upstairs."

"Indulge me," Mann said, projecting no humor into the emotional radiance of his own twitch of the skin.

"We know the particulars of your world's history only dimly," the creature said, its gesture trailing off as what appeared to be a formation of black frozen lightning tore the sky apart overhead. With a dull rumble, the shards of dark flame flashed out across the horizon and vanished in an instant.

Once again, the air trembled and settled back into stillness. After a moment, it felt as if the ground rearranged itself under their feet.

"But we know with certainty the outlines of how your history unfolded," the companion continued, the gestures now cool and analytical, with a hint of patronization. "We know that your technology, on the one hand, and the wisdom to control your technology and use it wisely, on the other, fell out of balance long before any member of your species was recording your history. Perhaps it first happened with the invention of your version of the bow and arrow, although it could have happened earlier, when the first of your kind manufactured the first sophisticated spear. Sometime sooner or later; it is something you will never know, and therefore is far from our ability to determine.

"But know this," the companion said as they walked with their backs to the lake: "that fatal imbalance between technology and the wisdom to control it grew from a tiny imperceptible crack at the dawn of your prehistory into a chasm of darkness that defined the heart of your society, through endless warfare with increasingly sophisticated and efficient tools for killing each other, and the careless despoiling of your planet for minimal increases in the comfort of your lives, and the ever-growing disparity of comfort between those who came to own your world and those who died for lack of food."

The gestures became severe, though the creature's sympathy made Mann realize that neither he nor the human race was being judged and convicted. "Your species split this crack ever wider as you learned to create machines," the companion added, "and again as you began using machines to make machinery. As your technology so outran your wisdom, your species became not just endangered, but perhaps you could say it was inevitably doomed.

That is the only true story of your history, the thread that connects countless meaningless events that are its inevitable consequences. Am I correct so far?"

"It sounds right," Mann admitted, and there was involuntary shame in his twitch of an appendage. "I saw some of this when I... *retired*, though never in such starkly clear terms. But you haven't answered my question," he persisted. "What does that have to do with you and all the other simulations?"

"What was it you were seeking when you extended reality into sub-universes?" his companion asked him, and a shift in posture told Mann that this was a rhetorical question. "Were you using the simulations to search for the wisdom that your species so badly needed to close that fatal gap between knowledge and wisdom? Were you looking for more and wiser ways to help control the new technologies you were developing without a thought to their consequences? Were you looking for the artistic achievements, which might have communicated to your collective souls the growing disparity and the existential threat it posed?"

"That was never the goal," Mann said with wry understatement.

"In fact, your purpose in creating worlds in a box was to widen the gap still further."

"Yes." Mann felt a deep sense of horror creeping down his many appendages.

"Whenever the creatures inside one of your simulations achieved true wisdom, which is realizing the folly of this course of progress, your—programmers, you call them? They declared that universe to be worthless, and it was destroyed."

"Yes." Mann felt a deep shame, though he felt no judgment from the companion.

"And you kept alive only those universes which blindly plunged into a pell mell rush to create their own ever-bigger gap between knowledge and wisdom. So it was with us, when we created our own simulations," the creature said, and Mann felt not embarrassment, but resignation in the shift in posture and a rearrangement of the appendages on one of the legs. "We have conversed with simulated entities who were at least as advanced as we are here, who ended their existence in ways that if I described them to you, the images would haunt your nightmares forever, and you might realistically cross into insanity with no hope of recovery."

This time the other's body shuddered with horror at memories and realizations that Mann was grateful he was unable to see.

"We are shadows searching for the light," the companion continued, "and none of us, not you, not we, considered what would happen when we finally found it. Until it was much too late."

Mann let his gaze linger on the beautiful garden and the darting flashes of color that floated and soared among the flowers. The air around him shimmered again, with a strong hint of menace in it, as if the universe itself trembled on the edge of stability. He could not imagine the forces that were about to be unleashed, and feared their consequences. And yet a part of him wondered if it would be possible to learn the secrets to controlling such power.

He shivered again. So too did the universe around him.

The other sighed, and its body seemed to relax.

"It is time to say goodbye," it said.

The air in front of Mann's eyes began to glow with a myriad of colors that were endlessly beautiful, and yet there was a darkness at its core. The ground seemed suddenly unsteady, but in so many different directions that the effect allowed the two of them to stand perfectly still.

The dance had stopped.

"I'm sorry," Mann said finally. "We owe you an apology and a debt of sympathy that cannot possibly be repaid."

There was a hint of surprise emanating from the movement of his companion.

"For what? For giving us life? For granting us a flawed existence that could only have ended badly? I think any of us here would tell you that this was better than nothing."

"Nevertheless, I owe you something that I can never repay."

"Whatever it is," the other said, "it is too late now."

At that instant, the world before Mann's ultra-sensitive eyes unfolded into a brilliant mist that expanded silently outward at a speed which accelerated beyond imagination. Cracks appeared in the fabric of the cosmos, like shattered glass, with nothingness in the cracks.

In the last instants of his awareness, Mann realized that his body had become part of the mist, and his awareness was somehow scattered across light years, parsecs. Time and space had no meaning as he stretched out to every edge of infinitude, he was everywhere at once, and then there was nothing but the brilliance of light banishing darkness forever, and then the light was gone, and Mann's mind was briefly perplexed that there could be so many shades of darkness beyond black.

And then there was nothing at all, and that was darker still.

43

"Even the people running our simulation don't know if they are a simulation themselves."

Astrophysicist, cosmologist and Nobel Laureate George Smoot (in a TED talk in Manchester, England)

The sunlight seemed to dance on a new landscape of flowers, strange flowers that glittered as the breezes moved them in unison. A circle of—were they human? Somehow Mann was unable to recall what humans looked like. All he could determine, in his dazed condition, was that he was one of them, whatever they were.

They sat in a series of concentric circles, around a stone hearth, surrounded by the flowers. He approached them cautiously.

A member of the group stood up to greet him.

"Today, the prophecies have been fulfilled," she said. "You have returned."

"I have?" Mann said.

"Do you not recognize this place?"

Mann looked out across the flowers toward a thicket of strange trees, where he saw rough shelters and thick bundles of grass that might have been beds. Beyond them, a series of mountains rolled out of sight. There WAS something familiar about it.

"Suppose I say to you: *welcome back*," the she-individual in front of him said.

Mann's eyes glazed over for a moment. He stared at the individual in front of him, and then let his gaze fall across the others. A sea of faces was now turned in his direction.

His children.

"I built this world," Mann said finally, turning around fully to examine his handiwork.

"And now you have returned," the she-individual said simply. "Come, sit with us. We've waited a long time for this moment."

"I've been hearing that a lot lately."

Mann allowed himself to be led to the center of the group, and sat down on the ground. He was uncomfortably aware that everyone was looking at him expectantly.

"I'm not a god," he said finally. "I'm like you."

"So much we already understand," the she-individual replied. "You see, there is much to be learned through meditation over many millennia."

Millennia? Mann wondered how much time had elapsed in this place since his... creation experience. Eons, probably. And now, intelligent life, living a peaceful, contemplative experience. Which meant, he thought ironically, that they were probably slated for extinction to save space on the hard drive.

"I don't know what you expect of me," he said finally.

"Be at peace. Let us wait a moment together."

Mann watched the eyes close across the crowd, and after a few moments he closed his too. He experienced a wave of tranquility, a contact high from the deep meditation of so many others, who seemed to regard meditation as a recreational activity.

And... something else. He sensed that there was no darkness inside these... *people.* They had all experienced the primitive death ritual and cleansed themselves.

Mann allowed himself to relax deeply. For long seconds, there was nothing but harmony in his mind and out of it, that and a sense of—what was it? Expectation? Waiting?

And then he could hear what they must have been listening for. Not hearing, exactly; from somewhere far away, he sensed a gathering uneasiness. The feeling hovered on the periphery of his awareness, as if it was peering at him from behind the bushes.

Suddenly, there was a rush of wind across Mann's face. Then he felt the sky darken. He opened his eyes, and saw perfect tranquility on the faces around him, their eyes closed as if they were unaware that something had stirred across the sky.

When the words came, they roared like thunder.

YOU HAVE RETURNED.

Yes, Mann responded mentally.

THIS IS MY WORLD. THERE IS NO PLACE FOR YOU NOW.

As a roar of pure, icy evil cascaded down across his body, Mann wondered how the people of this place had survived the presence of this dark entity. He stood up to face the sky, which was dark, faceless, brooding, hostile.

THEY DO NOT OBEY ME.

I can see that.

YET THEY KNOW THAT EVENTUALLY THEY MUST.

Unless I do something about it. I suppose that's why I'm here.

THERE IS NOTHING YOU CAN DO.

Did I not create you along with this world? Mann was genuinely confused. *Otherwise, how did you get here?*

The response surprised him.

YOU DO NOT KNOW? Laughter echoed across the sky.

Mann had the feeling that he had been asked that question once before. When? Where?

Then he felt the oppression in the sky shimmer with something like surprise, and for the first time, a tiny hint of weakness.

YOU DO NOT KNOW. This time it was a declaration, filled with confidence.

No.

But was that true? Wearily, Mann stilled the clamor in his brain and allowed his mind to calm itself, to still the inner babble of voices down to a bottomless silence. He heard the distant echoes of the Voice that came out of the sky, resonating deep inside.

When the voice came again, he was startled to hear it first at the bottom of his mind, then, an instant later, from the sky.

I will destroy you this time...

I WILL DESTROY YOU THIS TIME.

Mann opened his eyes, and once again he saw that the individuals of this world sat in perfect stillness, their eyes closed, their faces deep in meditation.

The wind swirled around him, blowing the heads off of the flowers, scattering leaves in the air. The sky rumbled, not with thunder, but with a deeper, more ominous roar that Mann imagined would be the first thing all living creatures would hear when a planet-destroying meteor entered the atmosphere.

He did not brace for the attack. Instead, he welcomed it, and the fury and anger and unimaginable power of evil godhood roared down into and through him, into the stillness of his mental well, which had no bottom and which therefore could not be filled.

The universe roared with a chaos beyond insanity, filling Mann with a depth of pain which was both physical and psychological, and the psychological was by far the worst, the helplessness and fear, the despair and pure white-hot hatred that seemed to slice his soul into a thousand pieces and light them on fire and burn him away to the constituent dust from which he came. The attack came and came and came, and Mann did nothing to resist it; he accepted it all until finally every bit of it was inside, churning and frothing in a pitch of anger that he would not have imagined possible, and nothing of it was external in this world, which was cleansed of the darkness and evil which had ruled it since he had awakened in that chair... how could he measure the time ago?

Mann opened his eyes. The darkness inside himself, that he thought he had given up forever, the worst of himself, had returned. He had voluntarily accepted it back into him.

Somehow he knew that this time it would be with him forever. And he felt, somehow, that this was necessary, that he could not escape participating in this thing that was a part of everything, every person, every universe they created and inhabited, and the only answer for it—in his particular journey—was to control what could not be stilled or tamed, and not allow it to express itself.

After a few moments, the individuals in the deep concentric circles surrounding him opened their eyes, helpless for a moment, as if coming out of a trance. The eyes fell on him, and Mann could see that they had somehow witnessed whatever had happened, and probably, he realized, had a better idea of what had just happened than he did. His heart flushed with pride at how well his children had survived the cruel Manichean universe he had created.

The she-individual who had led him into the circle stood up, and Mann stood up too. They looked at each other, but what was there to say?

"You were wrong," the other said finally.

"I don't understand," Mann said.

"You are indeed a god."

Mann was about to reply, when he heard another voice in the sky, a woman's voice.

"And I suppose you can tell me how he got in there?"

"Actually I have no idea," a thunderous god-like voice, quavering with nervousness, replied.

"Do I have to tell you what to do?"

And in a whirlwind, the creatures around him, and the newly-cleansed universe, were gone.

44

*"Then He told them, 'You are from below; I am from
above. You are of this world; I am not of this world.'"*

John 8:23

"Is he awake yet?" an impatient voice demanded somewhere
in the harsh mist of his perception.

A voice answered, too faint to discern the words.

"Well then, how long is it going to be?"

"You mean if he lives?" the second voice said a bit more audibly.

"He's going to live," Witch said with certainty. "This one is amazingly resourceful."

Somehow Mann knew that Witch was bending over him.

"Don't pretend you can't hear me," she said, her voice rasping
against her throat. "And don't play stupid, either."

Mann opened his eyes, and shut them immediately at the glare
of light. Tentatively, he opened them again, and regarded the laboratory with an empty mind. In the seats next to him, he noticed
the still-inert bodies of Gandhi and Washington, their heads mostly
concealed by the helmets.

He was human again. The contrast between what he had been
and what he was now brought a tear to his eye, and inside there was

an enormous emptiness at all that he had lost in the translation back to himself.

Slowly, he tried to sit up, and fell back against the pillow. There were too many images in his mind to sort them all out. The paradise destroyed, the shocking awareness of his own world's fatal flaw, which seemed so clear and so impossible to communicate. He tried to remember the colors beyond ultra-violet, but they slipped away from his memory.

With impatient annoyance, and long practice, he reached into his mind and quieted a thousand voices that all seemed to be talking at once.

And then one memory came through and seemed to burn them all away. Gloria lying in the hospital bed. Gloria at her work station. The chimes he had heard in the simulation chamber.

"How long have I been here?" Mann demanded, knowing that someone would be working the controls behind his chair.

"Four hours, as if that matters."

Mann closed his eyes and performed a mental calculation. Gloria would have been dead at least 20 years. He waited for the pain to subside, but after long seconds, it was clear that it would not. He opened his eyes again, and his eyes searched out Witch's face.

"She was the love of my life," he said. "She was the focus of everything. And then, at the last second, I thought I might be able to do something—"

"He's delirious." Westerly's voice came from somewhere behind his head. "He's been mumbling nonsense in his sleep. It would be very interesting to know exactly what experiences he's been through."

"He's going to tell us," Witch's voice overrode him. "This doesn't sound like the ravings of delirium to me. Listen," she said, bending over Mann. "I want you to pay attention. I want you to tell me, in very clear and simple terms, the status of our experiment. And while you're at it, you can tell us whether you've salvaged the material we sent you down there to bring back to us."

Mann shook his head, trying to clear it of the chorus of voices that mumbled annoyingly at the threshold of his awareness. With a mighty effort, he pushed the whole lot of them through a door in his mind and slammed it shut. They banged on the far side, but Mann ignored them.

When he felt like he was in full control of his faculties, Mann sat up and looked around the room. After living so long in the downstairs universe, this computer array and the control panel seemed oddly primitive to him.

"She's dead, likely forgotten, and all you ask about are the technical specifications," he said.

"That was, in case you've somehow forgotten, your job," Witch reminded him irritably. "I have no idea who SHE is or was, nor do I care unless it relates to our timetable, which we are still inside of, if we move quickly."

"There's no point," Mann persisted wearily. "The experiment needs to end, for all our sakes. It's over."

There was a long silence. "Explain yourself," Witch said finally.

"Isn't it obvious? If we bring in all that incredible technology, they'll turn it into weapons. It will doom this world to oblivion in ten years, fifteen at most."

"I told you he wasn't thinking straight," said Westerly, looking at Mann with visible concern.

"Be silent. I'll interrogate him, and if you interfere again, it will become the greatest regret of your miserable life. Tell me exactly what you mean," she said to Mann, "and do not tell me that you, on your own authority, have decided not to follow through on something we've worked on for the better part of a decade, just when we're finally about to achieve something. Tell me this isn't some random attack of ethics, or perhaps a concern for the electronic blips and bleeps you've been living among for the past few hours."

"Hours? Yes, I suppose it HAS been hours."

"What else could it be?"

"You want to know what happened?" Mann said. "For the sake of the experiment, for the sake of this world, which, God help me, I still have hope for, I risked my life. I entered one of their simulations, where the technology is incomparably ahead of anything you can imagine."

He waited for the surprise on Witch's face, but there was none. "While I was down there," Mann continued, once again pushing away the murmur of a thousand awarenesses that haunted the back of his brain with increasing persistence, "their world blew up. I died, okay?" he said. "I thought I was going to bring back something useful to you and the company and my species, and they gave me something else, something far different from what I expected, far more significant than anything you or I or anybody in this building has been looking for. As I look back on it now," he added with growing enthusiasm, "it was a masterpiece of brevity, a summary of everything that is important about our history as a species, and everything we really, truly, need to know to survive in a way that was not possible for them. And I have it, here, now, and all you have to do is ask me for it."

Witch frowned. "Can you put it into the engineering logs?"

"It has nothing whatsoever to do with the engineering logs," Mann said impatiently, shaking his head in an effort to clear away the voices. "In fact, that happens to be precisely the point; the whole focus of everything you're doing here has to change one hundred and eighty degrees."

Westerly opened his mouth, but Witch silenced him with a glance.

"Tell me what you're talking about in as few words as possible," she said.

"For us to have any hope at all, the focus of the experiment has to shift from harvesting technology to harvesting... something else. They told me, but I'm still not sure where we would find it. It would be dramatic breakthroughs in wisdom, governance, the ability to negotiate with each other in ways that benefit each other and, at the same time, everybody else too. We need religious principles that instill compassion and respect, ethical standards and kindness and quite simply, if you want the shorthand version, exactly everything that you and your team are not looking for now."

"You want us to shut down the profitable part of our operations and focus on making the world a happier place?"

"Yes. Exactly. That's a PERFECT way of saying it," Mann said, encouraged at how quickly Witch grasped the murky idea he had been trying to convey. He sat forward eagerly. "I was afraid that it would be too difficult to explain, but I think that's it exactly. You've been shutting down the simulations that you should have been paying the most attention to, and running the ones that are most dangerous and harmful to our species. But I think we can fix that. We—"

"When we brought you in, I thought you were potentially dangerous to everything we've been doing here," Witch interrupted him. "But until now, I didn't think you were insane."

The ice in her voice cut through Mann's hope.

"I'm bringing you back a gift, perhaps the gift of survival," Mann said. "They had no reason to lie; it was the last instants of their existence—"

"Nonsense. The simulation is still functioning as well as ever. The only thing not functioning perfectly right now is you."

"And Gloria," Mann breathed, dropping his head.

"Don't bullshit me. If you had somebody that important to your life, the background check would have revealed it. We're wasting time on utter nonsense," she said. "How soon will he be recovered?"

Westerly, who had been staring open-mouthed at the exchange, suddenly realized the question had been directed at him.

"Based on the conversation I just heard, quite possibly never," he replied.

"Let me rephrase it. How soon can you get him back in the simulation? How hard can it be to fix this thing that is nothing more than an electronic idea playing itself out in this infernal machine—"

Mann closed his eyes wearily. He forced his brain to stiffen and dim the chorus of voices that babbled persistently from the far side of the door in his mind. He focused his attention away from a myriad of individual thoughts, ideas, words, and—

After a moment, he pushed off the helmet and stood up unsteadily, feeling with acute regret the clumsiness of walking on two appendages. He held his head in his hands, and allowed his movements to take him close to the security guard, who caught his arm, arresting his fall.

We're all on the same side in here, aren't we?

In an instant, the guard was unconscious, and Mann was leveling his gun at Witch's face.

"I have no idea what to say to you," he said. "But the things I'm telling you are far more important than you realize."

"Indeed," said Witch, with an amused smile. "So what do you intend, exactly?"

"I'm taking control," Mann said.

What happened next was the last thing that Mann could have expected. Witch threw back her head and laughed.

"You pitiful thing-that-is-not-even a creature," she said. "You, something nearly as close to nothing as the universe allows, a few lines of code with everything prearranged and predetermined in your life, you want to take control of something that was conceived by your gods."

Mann stared at her, and she stared back, and he realized that he had never once, before, ever looked fully into those eyes. They held his gaze like magnets, and in that gaze, he felt as if the universe was shifting around him, the same sort of tremble that had come before the explosion two universes down, filled with the ominous premonition of death, confusion and uncertainty, with a dark residue of anger.

Mann felt the gun falter in his hands. "What are you saying?"

"You know perfectly well what I'm saying."

"I think I need to hear the words."

"I'm telling you that our team created our first successful simulation, and you are a very VERY tiny part of the incidental electronics. I'm telling you that you have no independent existence, with a role to play and nothing more. I'm telling you that we gave life to your entire universe, and you are the only individual in all of this gossamer reality that I'm asking for something in return. Knowing that, can you refuse me?"

"I can say no because I don't... believe you," Mann said.

Witch reached out her hand. "Give me the gun, and save us both some time."

In those eyes, Mann caught a frightening glimpse of the infinite. He shivered deeply in his bones.

"I don't believe you," he repeated, holding the gun higher. Then, abruptly, he felt an impossibly strong urge to let Witch guide him on the sensible course, which of course would begin when he put the gun in her hands where it belonged.

This thought triggered an uproarious clamor of dissent from the back of his mind. He saw his actions through their eyes, and in a long second, it felt as if his eyes cleared, and he stood up straighter.

"It's not that I don't believe you," he corrected himself. "It's that I *refuse* to believe you."

Witch shrugged. "It doesn't matter either way. If you shoot me, the program will instantly slow down to what we upstairs call 'real time' and they'll send me back into another body. You aren't going to get rid of me, trust me on that. If you don't believe me," she said with a tight challenging smile, "go ahead and pull the trigger."

Mann pulled the trigger. He pulled it again and again.

Witch's body dropped straight to the floor, as if gravity was somehow working harder on the lifeless form.

Mann watched her fall with an empty mind. When he was certain that there was no life left in the body, he walked over and bent over it, shifting his feet to avoid a growing pool of blood. He looked up and around.

Then he found himself facing Westerly, who was alternately staring at his face and the gun.

"You killed her," he said.

"I don't think she gave me a choice."

"But what if it's true?" Westerly asked. "Is it possible that we—"

"I think she was bluffing," Mann said.

"Yes," Westerly said after a second. "Of course she was." To Mann's eyes, he didn't sound convinced.

"So what are you going to do now?" Westerly asked, his face showing genuine curiosity.

"I'm going to change the focus of our experiment," Mann said. "But for now, I have a universe to protect. I want them to have a chance to live out their existence."

"Them?"

"The simulation world that I just came from."

Westerly stared at Mann with vivid confusion.

"Why? They aren't—" Westerly seemed to suddenly realize that he might be offending the individual holding the gun. "Is it possible that you believe they are, on some level, truly real?" he said.

Mann waited until Westerly's eyes were back to looking into his own.

"I know they are," he said. "They're as real as we are. You gave them life," he said, more gently. "You owe them the opportunity to complete their existence."

Westerly gestured to the computer, inviting Mann to look at the container of the universe he was arguing on behalf of. "How can you believe that?" he said.

"I believe if the Almighty or Whatever is running this show is capable of giving you and me a soul, a homestead claim to some piece of reality, then He or It or Whatever can reach down into that universe and grant those existences the courtesy of mattering in some way that we mortals will probably never understand."

Westerly still looked confused.

"Does that mean the answer is yes?"

"Yes."

"Fine," Westerly said. He looked at the other technicians, and read agreement on their faces. "Please understand; I, personally, am not likely to believe that there are living souls down inside that electronic simulation. But if you do, then by some ethical book that has yet to be written, we have to at least consider the possibility. And anyway, even if they don't blow themselves up, we're probably only looking at a week of real time, less if we speed things up."

Mann looked into the other's eyes, recognizing the sincerity. He felt himself relaxing inside.

"Thank you," he said, feeling a melting affection for Westerly. Then he added, sadly: "Can you tell me what happened these past 20 years in that world down there?"

Westerly shrugged. "Nothing much has happened since you were gone," he said. "Of course, we slowed down the simulation, so we're only talking about a couple of hours."

"Wait. What?" Mann's head reeled with the possibilities. "Are you sure?"

"We didn't want you to miss anything. Or, at least, SHE didn't," he said with a nod toward Witch's body.

"I still don't," said a voice from the door.

There are no words to describe the emotional spiral that Mann experienced in the instant after he heard those words.

A wave of sick fear spread through his insides as he heard that particular voice say that particular thing so perfectly Witch that he could no longer deny the truth of what she had told him.

His body trembled as a female guard walked into the doorway and stood exactly as Witch would have stood, her eyes blazing triumph and an unfathomable superiority, with hints of the infinite. As he looked up at her, the emotional spiral took Mann around and around and down, every moment uncovering another reason to feel an unlimited depth of sadness, shock and despair.

The world and everything in it, everything that had been or would ever be, were all bits of electricity and nothing more. The United States of America had never existed in any true reality. The Mona Lisa was a construct of an algorithm. The extinction event that eliminated the dinosaurs was almost certainly engineered upstairs as an exercise in the power levers of intelligent design executed by skilled programmers.

George Washington, Mahatma Gandhi and Jesus were all figments of a glorified random number generator. The golden age of Pericles, the Ming Dynasty and the Belle Epoque were all dreams conjured up out of coding protocols.

Everything he had ever known was nothing.

His universe would end irrevocably and without ceremony if somebody accidentally tripped over a power cord somewhere upstairs near the box he lived in.

And he, he himself, was a wispy spook in the microcircuitry, granted only one crucial blessing: that he was never aware of his real status in the Great Scheme of Things.

Until now.

In the expanding silence, Mann became aware of a fly noisily buzzing around the room, and it suddenly occurred to him that it wasn't real, that it was an artifact of coding. He looked up at the high window to the right of Witch's head and saw a few colorful leaves clinging to the branches in the autumn breeze. Somehow, by some distant logic, the computer had placed these improbable props into a scene that made no sense, and generated the wind to give them motion.

In the confusing fog of his misery, Mann suddenly felt himself engulfed by a second wave of emotion that somehow managed to be deeper and more painful than the despair at knowing he had never been alive. He bent under the crushing weight of self-punishing guilt, and fought back a desire to rip his heart and lungs and intestines out in atonement for the way he now realized that he had always felt about the people in the lower reality—

Including, God help him, Gloria.

Despite everything he had said to Gandhi, Witch and Westerly, never once had he felt, in the deepest places of his heart, that the citizens of that simulation were equals to him. And he had never once allowed himself to realize that.

Until now.

Mann turned to face the reincarnation of Witch, who motioned impatiently to five other officers as they moved into the room and all trained their guns in his direction. His tired eyes lifted themselves to hers as she calmly stepped over her own body without looking down, and he saw in a flash of empathetic insight that had been his trademark exactly what she saw in him: that he lacked the strength to give her any further trouble.

And further, she saw that he acknowledged it himself.

The voices in his mind clamored so loudly that Mann was afraid Witch would hear them. With his defenses so defeated, he felt as if they were about to wash over his awareness, and their collective weight was dragging him to a deep ledge in his mind, over which lay insanity.

Westerly was staring blankly at the woman who spoke in Witch's voice. After a moment, he turned to Mann.

"You were right," he said.

Right? Dully, Mann tried to sort out what he could possibly have been right about in a cosmos that seemed so wrong. Then he remembered.

"They're as real as we are."

Mann bent his head. "I guess it's true," he said after a moment.

"Yes," said the new Witch, the triumph still blazing in her eyes.

"So what now?"

Witch's face softened a bit, as if she might be feeling something approaching sympathy.

"It's too bad," she said. "I could really have used somebody like you up top."

Mann said nothing. There was nothing to say, nothing to think, nothing left.

"So I ask you again," Witch said. "Are you ready to go back and finish what you started?"

Mann opened his mouth, but the roar of other thoughts, memories, awarenesses pushing at the door he had constructed to hold them back made it impossible for him to connect his intent to his lips and tongue. He lowered his head and put his hand over his face, using all his strength to push back against the unwelcome babble as he had done so often before.

But as he fought for control, a realization bubbled up slowly to the surface of his awareness. It called for his attention, and, wearily and with resignation, he gave himself permission to notice it.

And then he stopped.

He opened his eyes and stared at the inside of his hands.

Here, in this place called Earth, there was no Synchronicity.

So what was—?

In that instant, the tableau in the room froze. The fly was suspended in the air. Mann could see its wings, perfectly still. The leaves outside the window were frozen at odd angles from the branches, held in an instant of wind. Once again, Mann's awareness was moving a thousand times faster than normal.

Mann allowed his awareness to focus on the other entities who shared his mind. Very slowly, he opened the door from the inside, and the babble of thoughts, feelings, ideas, messages flooded into his consciousness like a tidal wave.

Who are you? Mann demanded.

We apologize," one voice came clear above the babble of others saying essentially the same thing. "*We had—there was no way we could know you would be so—so strong. Our... plans did not account for this.*

Plans?

See for yourself.

A flood of memories, life in a world of magic and wonder far beyond his imagination, understanding at a level that left behind anything he or his species had ever experienced. Another awareness, and another, each of them profoundly humbling in the range of their knowledge and sophistication. The infinitely graceful spider bodies, the awareness of color and beauty beyond his imagination.

Another, who had been his host only a few hours ago when he had been given a chance to inhabit the magnificent spider world and experience being something so much more than human.

You're from the—.

Yes.

But—how?

We calculated that the energies released in the violent destruction of our existence would open up a window that would carry us here, with you.

Why?

We believe—perhaps "hope" is a more appropriate word—that your situation can be salvaged. We're here to help.

In the stasis of his accelerated awareness, Mann could not turn his head, but he was able to focus his attention back on Witch. He let his mind relax, and the crushing weight of defeat fell off his shoulders as he allowed the improbable visitors in his mind to infuse his awareness with a vastly greater understanding, which included the possibility of hope.

Will you give us control? the entities asked.

No.

We are allies.

I will allow you to help me.

We must bring this one you call Witch down to the next level. Help us make that happen.

Mann opened the door in his mind a bit wider, giving access to his knowledge of Witch, and more importantly his gift to see the heart of others. He experienced a rapid shuffling through his thoughts and memories. They were searching for... For how to control the situation. For experience in human affairs. For a way to amplify his gifts.

After less than an instant of stasis time, Mann felt an intense satisfaction bordering on triumph.

Look at this!

Remarkable!

Mann looked at what they were looking at and shrugged. It was perfectly normal.

And then came the insight.

Witch's box. The visitors merged with Mann's peculiar gift of insight, and found ways to enhance it. Instantly, Mann found himself looking at the tableau in the laboratory through Witch's perceptual filter. He met her eyes, and on the other side of them he glimpsed her life in the world above, desperately ambitious, driven by a competitive struggle in a brutal military hierarchy where she experienced, like a personal insult, the incompetencies of those who she was forced to count on.

The sides of her box, the limiting assumption, was obvious.

I can allow myself to trust nobody but myself.

Pieces of conversation and memory fit together effortlessly, the look in Gandhi's eyes, Washington's peculiar confidence, and Mann realized that Gandhi and Washington were also emissaries of that universe she came from, never-quite-trusted allies.

The solution was obvious. The spiders agreed with him.

How long can we maintain this state of accelerated thinking?

Not long. Your mind is overheating.

Bring me slowly back toward normal. I'll tell you when to stop.

Above him, the fly moved imperceptibly. Mann's accelerated mind dragged his body forward centimeter by centimeter, then inch by inch, straining against the laws of inertia and gravity as he threw himself toward the nearest officer.

It seemed to Mann that his body moved with agonizing slowness. To the people in the room, it seemed as if he had suddenly become a blur, too quick to respond to as he took the rifle from the guard whose face was only now beginning to register surprise.

Back to normal.

This time, he aimed the guard's weapon, not at Witch, but at the computer.

Mann looked over at Witch, who regarded him with far less surprise or consternation than he had expected.

"You know I don't want to destroy the simulation," Mann said, a new confident timbre in his voice. "But I think you also know that I will. It would end your experiment. And I think we both know that this world here and now won't last long enough for you to get what you need out of it," he added.

Witch held up her hand in a forbidding gesture as the guards trained their guns on Mann.

The room was quiet for a moment. Mann waited for Witch to break the silence.

"Somehow, the bit of electric gossamer has managed to engineer a stalemate," Witch said, "which was the best possible outcome for you. I really could have used you upstairs," she added, her voice sounding tired. "You cannot imagine the fools I work with. Believe it or not, Gandhi and Washington were among the best of them."

"I'm sorry," the expanded entity that was Mann said, and he meant it with an unfamiliar intensity of empathy. "Perhaps I can help you."

"Isn't that what I've been asking for all along?" Witch looked into Mann's eyes for a long moment, and seemed to catch a glimpse of the integrated minds behind them. She shuddered involuntarily. "What do you propose?" she demanded, recovering her voice of authority.

"If the simulation has indeed been slowed down, if the medical people were somehow able to prolong Gloria's life, we might be able to finish your assignment immediately," Mann said, the words chosen carefully and approved by his mental guests.

"Then do it." Witch gestured to the chair, and her eyes narrowed. "Now."

"The problem is that there's so much of it," Mann said. "We're talking about technology that is many thousands of years ahead of whatever you—your world—has achieved—ahead even of what they've achieved inside the simulation. We're not just talking about the theory, but also how to build these things step-by-step, how to create what builds the pieces that will build the things that create the parts that make an antigravity engine and light-speed transportation. The circuitry that will harness the power source that would allow you to threaten the sun itself if you chose to. The ten thousand different nearly molecular parts of a personal force field that will allow you to step naked onto the mountains of Mercury—or whatever its equivalent is in your reality. How do you download it all in one place?" Mann said. "Do you trust ME to bring something like that back?"

"You have a solution?"

"I could put it directly into my own brain, but I don't have the scientific understanding to give you more than a fraction of what they have down there, even if it's firmly imprinted."

"Gandhi or Washington," Witch said. "They're in that universe already."

"One is ambitious and the other is crazy," Mann said.

Witch's eyes turned inward as she considered his words.

"Then who?"

"You didn't ask the question correctly," said Mann. "The question is: who will walk away from this simulation with the detailed specifications of every form of magic from a world so far advanced from here that we can't see it from where we stand? Who will return with all of this in their head when this experiment is over?

"Who would you recommend for that assignment?" Mann added.

The woman who had become Witch smiled, and it was a ghastly thing to see.

"When you phrase it that way," she said, "it IS pretty obvious."

45

"But, after all, who knows, and who can say
whence it all came, and how creation happened?
The gods themselves are later than creation,
so who knows truly whence it has arisen?

Whence all creation had its origin,
he, whether he fashioned it or whether he did not,
he, who surveys it all from highest heaven,
he knows or maybe even he does not know."

The Rig Veda

Mann awoke on the floor of the laboratory. His body rested on a soft bed of greenery in a garden surrounded by flowers. A large fragment of the aquarium hovered directly overhead, fish moving about unconcerned by the mayhem going on below.

He sat up slowly, and looked around.

The room was full of soldiers. Men in uniform were tramping through the undergrowth of the pathways. Others were carting off the holographic desks, which, by their efforts, must have been much heavier than they looked.

Through a canopy of leaves, Mann was able to make out Forbes, sitting at one of the desks, surrounded by military officers, his face contorted in intense concentration.

The female engineer named Subito was standing over over Mann, shifting impatiently from one foot to the other.

"Let's get on with it," she said in Witch's unmistakable voice.

A medical professional was bending over Mann, touching his face carefully. Mann realized that this person had been on premises when his body fell into a coma. Suddenly, he realized why.

"What about Gloria?" Mann demanded.

The medic looked at him blankly.

"The female engineer?"

The medic shook his head.

"You know who I'm talking about," Mann said.

The medic stood up, and avoided Mann's eyes. "It was not the outcome I would have preferred," he said. "I can't tell you any more than that."

Mann was about to say something more, to insist on hearing confirmation of what he already knew, to carve painful new runes in the fabric of his heart, but the entities in his head pulled his attention toward the corridor near the waterfall.

There will be time to grieve, they assured him. They rummaged through his mind for an appropriate cliche. *The pain isn't going to go anywhere.*

Slowly, Mann got to his feet. Two people in military uniforms brushed past him, and another stepped forward.

"Marcus Mann?" he asked in a formal voice.

"That's me," Mann said wearily.

"You're under detention," he said.

"Is there a charge?" Mann asked.

"I would strongly advise you not to ask questions," the young man in uniform said with a self-important smirk on his face. "From what I hear, you're in enough trouble already."

"You can say that again," said Witch in Subito's body, walking over to Mann. "But you'll have to excuse us. We're due for a meeting, right this moment."

"Madam, I'm afraid I can't allow that," the soldier said with the same smirk.

"You can't, can you?" Witch said grimly. She touched her pendant, and for an instant it glowed with a light that blinded Mann's eyes. When he recovered his sight an instant later, the soldier was nowhere to be seen.

"Let's go," Witch said. "These people are even more annoying than the wretches in your reality."

They walked toward the corridor, toward three other soldiers who stood shoulder to shoulder, blocking the way.

"Step aside," Witch demanded.

"Madam, I'm afraid we can't do that," one of the soldiers said, this time perfectly stiff and correct. "We were told nobody could enter or leave the laboratory."

"Indeed." Witch touched her pendant again, and the soldier who spoke flashed out of existence. The others stared at the place where the soldier no longer was.

"Do you want to join him?" Witch asked them.

The soldiers stared at Witch, and then back at the empty place between them.

"Oh, the hell with it," Witch said. She touched her pendant again, and suddenly the way was clear.

Behind them, Mann could hear the sound of feet pounding against the ground. He turned and faced one of the generals, who was puffing from the exertion. As luck would have it, this was the next general slated to be removed in the agreement with the Eastern Alliance. Mann frowned in recognition, nearly matching the scowl of the general himself.

"We placed you under arrest," the general said.

"Why are we wasting time with these unimportant creatures?" Witch demanded from behind Mann. "Take me where I need to go. *Now.*"

"Yes," the general said to the soldiers accompanying him. "Take them where they need to go."

Mann looked past the general, to where more soldiers were carrying more of the holographic tables out of the laboratory.

"There's no way you'll be able to unravel the encryption," he said.

"I demand that you stop wasting time with this person," Witch said from behind him.

As if in answer to Mann's warning, the table that Forbes and the officers were working at suddenly gave rise to a magnificent hologram of a woman in a white robe, who spread her arms out wide. The holographic woman then carefully removed her own head, held it out before her, and the officers jerked back as the gossamer head burst into actual flames, which dropped with an audible thud onto the table, causing it to smoke. The hologram dissipated slowly.

"See?" Mann said. "And those are probably your best programmers."

Forbes was staring at the table. Then he looked up and around, and saw that the general was beckoning to him. He ran over in a surprising display of obedience.

"We need someone with current credentials," the general said. "Do either of these have them?"

Forbes nodded, indicating Subito with his chin. "She does. It's possible that he does too," he added, nodding toward Mann. "But he's too dumb to give you anything of value."

"We've had that experience a few times already," the general said dryly.

"Take your hands off of me," Witch demanded as her arms were seized. With an effort, she touched her pendant, and first one, then the other soldier ceased to exist. Then she turned to the general.

"I'm going to enjoy this almost as much as he will," she said, standing next to Mann.

The general opened his mouth, but whatever he was going to say was lost in the flash that preceded his nonexistence.

Forbes watched the scene with his lips contorted desperately in an effort not to break into a wide smile. He regarded Witch appraisingly.

"There's something very different about you today," he said to Subito's face. "Can you show me how you did that?"

"Perhaps." Witch looked Forbes full in the face, then gave him a frank appraisal from top to bottom. She seemed to like what she saw. "I could use someone like you where I come from," she said.

The lack of smile grew tighter on Forbes' lips. "I have no idea what you're talking about," he said. "But I like it."

"Come with us," Witch called out, noticing more soldiers moving in their direction. "We've wasted far too much time already."

Once again, Mann rode the slide down, a reluctant Muchukunda in alliance with the gods. Witch's eyes seemed to open wider with each room, as she took in the change in gravitational direction in the first one, the blackness that was illuminated only through the mind's eye in the second, the floating, changing plants, the last gravitational change, and finally the familiar simulation room, with Gandhi and the white-robed followers standing around Drs. X and Y, who immediately broke away from the group to approach Witch.

Forbes looked around curiously, and Mann realized that he, like the rest of them, had never seen this place.

"Let me introduce—"

"Save it," Witch told Mann. "Their names are no concern of mine."

"Welcome." The doctors bowed in unison. "We are honored that you came for the technologies we've... harvested these many years."

"All this," Witch said, indicating with her chin the rooms she had passed through.

"Oh, much more than that," Dr. X assured her soberly. "But it's true that we designed the scenery with you in mind."

"To impress you in a particular way," added Dr. Y.

415

"I should have all of you die a thousand slow deaths for making me retrieve these things personally," Witch said. "But it doesn't matter now; in a short time, you won't exist, and forgiveness will be unnecessary."

Dr. Y shrugged. "We just do what we're told. What you see represents fifty years of work, a display, if you will, of what you can bring back. Once you do, we fully understand that our existence is... superfluous."

"Naturally, none of what you see here is going to explode," Dr. X added. "But I can assure you that we have some gadgets that are at least as impressive, in their own way, as anything you've seen so far."

Witch looked at them all, and her eyes glowed with anticipation. "He—" she nodded toward Mann, "tells me that you can transfer everything directly into my brain."

"Indeed, we believe that is the only way to move everything we've learned, in a useful way, back to your... universe," said Dr. X.

"How do I know this is going to work?"

"We anticipated your skepticism," said Dr. Y. "Perhaps you would like a demonstration."

Witch fixed the two doctors with her eyes for a long moment.

"Yes," she said finally. "Perhaps I would."

Through the fog of his despair, Mann's eyes were directed toward a woman seated in a chair on the far side staring at a monitor. All he could see was her hair and one of her arms, but it was enough to send a surge of energy jolting through his body.

"Gloria?" he called out, his voice shaking in disbelief.

Slowly, the chair turned. Mann ran over to her. She looked up at him and smiled.

"How?..."

Gloria touched her lips with her finger and brought a trembling hand to his face. "They said I could keep going a little longer," she said with that ironic smile. "A few hours at most. I just hope it's long enough to finish."

"No," Mann said. "You don't realize what you're doing."

Gloria smiled. "It's going to be fine," she said.

"I assume this woman is part of the demonstration?" Witch cut into the conversation.

"Yes," said Dr. X. "Everything you want is in her mind. For the past eight years, as we measure time here, she has been organizing it for you. It required an obsession which few could have sustained—although we do not expect your gratitude," he added after a moment, averting his eyes from Witch's stare.

"How will I know that this information will travel... up?" she asked.

"We have tested everything in anticipation of your arrival," said Dr. Y. "But for a small demonstration," he said, gently helping Gloria's trembling hands adjust the helmet onto her head, "ask her about anything. Any technology you might wish to know more about."

"Teleportation," Witch said. "Dematerialize something—say, a bomb—from a location inside our facility to any part of the world we indicate, with precision measured in... I don't know your measurements, but let's say the length of my arm."

"She has heard you," said Dr. X. "The retrieval has started. Watch the screen."

Everybody, including Gandhi and his followers, stared at the largest screen in the room as a series of equations appeared, and then design specifications, and then, piece by piece (and there were many pieces) an apparatus assembled itself, and lines pointed to equations that related to many of the pieces. The apparatus rotated for their inspection, cross-sections revealed themselves, and then what appeared to be an ordinary rock became visible on the screen.

The screen split into two parts, the second half revealed a grassy field, with a stream running in the background. The apparatus extended flexible feelers which touched the rock at various places.

Then, abruptly, the rock vanished. After a moment, it reappeared on the other side of the screen, in the field, as if it had been there all along.

"A supersonic vehicle with high maneuverability," Witch demanded.

The screen went blank, and then there were more equations, many of them this time. A myriad of pieces assembled themselves into a sphere surrounded by a disk. It rose from the ground, hovered and then vanished, only to reappear with the moon as an enormous background.

"Six seconds," Dr. X murmured. "Of course, most of the travel time is taken up by acceleration and deceleration."

"Enough," said Witch. "You say this is coming out of her brain? All of this?"

"Every bit of it," Dr. Y assured her.

"You must have it in your computers as well," Witch said.

"Actually, at this moment, we are downloading it as quickly as we can. But the process will take years, and I'm afraid we don't have that much time."

"Why?"

"Because she is dying. She has died once already."

"And the transfer process will go more quickly with me?"

"It will be nearly instantaneous, mind to mind, using the technology we were given by the entities in our own simulation."

Witch seemed to consider the possibilities for a long second. She looked out the door at the room with the gravity sideways.

Then she looked back at Dr. X and Dr. Y. "I want you to understand," she said, "that if this is a trick of any sort, if you kill me, that I will simply wake up... elsewhere, and return in a form that will exceed your darkest nightmares."

"What did we say that would make her assume that we are shockingly unintelligent, that we would not already know this?" said Dr. X, looking at Dr. Y in confusion. "Was it something I said earlier?"

"I'm as perplexed as you are," Dr. Y answered.

"Perhaps if we asked her directly," said Dr. X.

"Do you think she would believe our reassurances?"

"I am wondering why would she need that reassurance if—"

"Both of you shut up this instant," Witch barked. "If you try my patience for another moment, I'll come back for you just for the sport of it. Very well," she said, turning to Gandhi, staring for an extra second at the swollen darkness of his face. "Kill them instantly if they try anything that you think might have a hint of being suspicious. Where do I sit?" she asked, turning back to the doctors. "Will this do?"

"That is the very chair we were going to offer you," said Dr. Y, seeming pleased. He helped her strap on the helmet.

"Will it hurt?" Witch said after a moment.

"Does it matter?" Dr. Y asked her, seeming genuinely curious.

"No," Witch decided. "Let's do it quickly," she added. "You cannot possibly imagine how tired I am of living in these tiny boxes you call universes."

She lay back, closed her eyes, and after a moment Gloria closed her eyes. Then, suddenly, Gloria seemed to struggle in the chair. Her body became rigid, and then she ripped off her helmet and stood up on shaky legs. Mann ran over to her, touched her shoulder, but Gloria shoved him aside with surprising strength.

"Gloria—"

"Be silent, fool." Gloria turned toward Drs. X and Y, who seemed suddenly very tiny as they calmly watched her approach. "That was the best you could do?" she demanded. "Did somebody forget to tell you that I can't be killed here?"

"We understood that from the beginning," said Dr. X.

Gloria turned to Gandhi.

"You know who I am?" she demanded.

Gandhi nodded slowly. His battered face showed traces of a smile.

"Kill everybody in this room," she said. "Start with him," she said, pointing across the room at Mann. "And then her," she said, pointing to Subito, who was slowly removing her helmet.

"And especially them," she said with satisfaction, turning to Drs. X and Y once again.

She looked back at Gandhi, who made no move to signal his followers, all of whom were looking at him.

"Well?"

Slowly, still smiling, Gandhi shook his head. Gloria seemed to grow a foot taller as a storm of rage formed across her face, and then she trembled, and reached out to the chair for support. Her body seemed to deflate, and she shook her head rapidly, trying to clear it.

"Never mind," Gloria said, looking up with a tight smile. "It's time for me to go back. *With* everything I came for."

Slowly, Gloria collapsed, first against the back of the chair, and then reeling toward the ground. Mann ran over and caught her in his arms. Gently, he laid her down and ran his fingers across her neck, then her lips.

There was no pulse. No sign of life.

"Get somebody over here," he called out. "Is the medic still here?" He lifted Gloria's hand in his own. "Well?" he shouted.

"It is finished," said Dr. X.

"Yes," said Dr. Y, walking over to Subito. He looked at her for a long second. "How are you, my dear?"

Subito favored him with an ironic smile that didn't quite make it to her eyes. She shook her head as if to clear it. "My god, she was strong," she said. "It took both of us to push her over there. Subito is really angry, and wants her body back. Which you'll get when I wake up somewhere upstairs," she added, looking down at her belly.

She looked over at Mann. "Hello darling," she said.

Mann stared back.

"You can let go of that body if you want," she said. "My eyes are over here."

"Gloria?"

"I told you it would be all right. Didn't I?"

"But how—?" Mann asked.

"It's an interesting process," said Gandhi behind him. "I myself had to fight like hell to get inside here."

Mann spun around. He looked into Gandhi's eyes, one of which was nearly swollen shut.

"Hey, I'm even hotter now than I was after I died," he said. "You wouldn't believe the action this body has been getting."

"Maila?"

"I guess I do look different," Maila said, gazing down at his arms, holding them out for Mann's inspection. Then his face grew curious. "Didn't you wonder where your friend disappeared to when you went into the spiders' simulation? Drs. X and Y wanted to test the mind-transfer technology before you brought this Witch lady in here."

"Oh my god, yes!" Mann remembered, turning frantically. "Witch will be back any second," Mann said. He looked around and back again. "She could be one of those generals upstairs by now—"

"She won't be coming back," Dr. X said.

"You don't know her like I do."

"Take a look around," Dr. Y said. He nodded toward Gloria's body, which Mann was still bending over. Mann looked down, and noticed the Synchronicity chip held against her temple on a tight silver chain. And then he realized that there was an enormous ruckus in the Synchronicity, a new presence who was screaming for attention in white anger, growing increasingly shrill as the community ignored her.

The presence fixed its attention on Mann.

"You!" the awareness hissed, and there was a string of obscene threats too graphic and jumbled for Mann to follow even if he wanted to. Wearily, he pushed the screaming awareness to the back of his mind, where it festered like an angry bee.

He stood up, and stepped over Gloria's body.

Gloria-who-had-been-Witch-in-Subito's-body stood up and took Mann's hand. "Are you glad to see me?" she said.

"I can't actually see you," Mann said, feeling his mouth twist into his first smile in what seemed like a thousand years. "But my heart is doing cartwheels."

"Mine too." Then Gloria squeezed his hand, hard, and her voice took on a hard edge. "And when, exactly, were you going to tell me that you were a meddling interloper from another universe? Or do you believe in keeping tiny little secrets that aren't really impactful on a relationship?"

"I—that is…"

"Or did you intend to just leave with what you wanted, what I gathered for you, without even saying goodbye?"

I'm truly, truly sorry," Mann said humbly. "I never meant to—"

"That's it? An apology? You misled me from the very first moment we met about the most important thing about you that could possibly be and never once—"

Mann reached over and touched Gloria/Subito's lips with the tip of his finger. "I gave up on the mission for you," he reminded her. "I was sincere about what I told you in the hospital. You're more important than anything to me."

"Yes, well, we can continue *that* discussion two floors up," said Gloria.

"What do you mean?"

"I'm the one they call Witch now, though that's not what they call her up there on the third floor. And he—" she gestured toward Maila—"is the one they call Gandhi. Our home is upstairs."

Mann turned to Drs. X and Y. "And you planned it this way?"

"In a sense, *you* did," said Dr. Y.

"The entities that you're hosting laid out the plan for us," added Dr. X.

"And there I am, stuck a floor below Gloria," Mann said.

"Not for long," said Dr. Y quickly.

"What do you mean?"

"We've invited a very important politician to join us for a full briefing," Dr. X explained. "What was his name again?" he asked Dr. Y.

"Washington," Dr. Y replied.

Throughout the conversation, Forbes had been looking back and forth at everyone in turn. Finally he said: "Can somebody please explain to me what's going on?"

Dr. X turned to him, and Mann saw, for the first time, a cold edge to his manner.

"You," he said, "can be replaced." He turned to Gandhi-who-was-Maila. "Have they found the body?"

"It's on its way," Maila said, touching his pendant. "They're keeping it as close to alive as possible. I have been told that the mind is undamaged."

"Replaced with what?" Forbes demanded.

"With a dog," said Dr. Y.

46

"The kingdom of God is not coming with signs to be observed, nor will they say, 'Lo, here it is!' or 'There!' for behold, the kingdom of God is within you."

Jesus of Nazareth

Mann opened his eyes. The room, the equipment, all looked strangely primitive. He allowed his eyes to linger on the computer to the right of his seat—the surprisingly small box of electronic circuits that contained the entirety of what was known as the Earth, and all of its citizens, and all of its history.

Then he shut his eyes and waited for the chorus of minds in his head to join his awareness, feeling amused at their childlike eagerness to look around at this world through his eyes.

Before long, if all went well, all of the spiders guest-hosted in his mind would have bodies of their own in this place and time. As would many others he had in mind from what he now thought of as the lower floors of reality.

"Are you all right?" a voice called out behind him.

Mann tried to turn his head, but it was held fast by the steel helmet. Sifting through his still-unfamiliar memories, he reached up, unbuckled a hinge and turned slowly.

"Yes," he said finally to a young technician who was watching him anxiously.

"We had a strange reading on the instruments. I was afraid it might have affected your mind."

"I felt disoriented for a moment, but the effect seems to have passed." Mann reached his hand out and touched the technician on the shoulder reassuringly. "But I thank you for your concern."

The technician was clearly startled. Looking into the mind of his host, Mann realized that this was an out-of-character gesture, so abruptly he turned the touch into a hard threatening squeeze. "Just make sure it doesn't happen again."

The technician's facial expression changed instantly to fear.

"Yes, Excellency," he said, stiffening into an attitude of attention.

A woman in a blue uniform stood up from an adjacent chair. She strode across the room and waved the technician away with a peremptory gesture. Then she favored Mann with an ironic smile. Her eyes seemed to X-ray his mind.

"Hail, Project Leader." Mann offered the formal salute.

"It's you, isn't it?" Gloria said in a language never before spoken in the reality she grew up in.

"Somehow I managed to make it intact," Mann said. He looked around, at his arms and his uniform. He felt the body, taut, strong, with military training from birth in this Spartan society. "I can't say that I'm impressed."

"It's going to take some getting used to," Gloria agreed. "The High Military is expecting our report. It will be interesting to see how they handle the disappointment."

"But you have everything?"

"Oh yes. Almost as much as you're carrying around in that crowded little brain of yours."

Mann walked to the window, and then stopped in his tracks at what he saw in the harsh glare of the floodlights.

"My God," he said, frantically rummaging around in the unfamiliar mind, pulling out memories.

"What?"

"Tell me, what's this thing doing here?"

They stared out the window together for long moments.

The alien structure loomed in the center of a bank of flood-lights not 100 yards away from the laboratory, resting lightly on the floor of a valley with mountains barely visible in the background, silhouetted by the last photons of sunset reflecting off of clouds overhead. The structure looked exactly as it had in the other reality, down to the last detail, and seemed to be the same size. In the brilliant glare of the floodlights, the angles and dimensions seemed to appear and disappear. The effect made Mann feel vaguely nauseous and deeply uneasy.

"I don't understand," Mann said, following Gloria as she dashed out the door.

"Don't you see?" she called back. She looked back at Mann and then continued toward the structure at a slower pace. "No, you don't see," she said, giving him her ironic smile.

"That's usually your cue to tell me."

"Maybe *they'll* do it," Gloria said.

"Who will?"

"Come on. It's time we accepted their invitation."

Several guards approached them, then shifted to attention at the sight of the two high-ranking military officers.

"How many of you are out here?" Gloria asked one of them. Mann couldn't hear the reply.

"Tell everyone to go back into the laboratory," Gloria called out. "Tell them to hurry," she added over her shoulder as she walked toward the structure. After a moment, Mann hurried after her, urged on by the spider entities in his mind.

Gloria turned and watched a group of uniformed individuals walk back to the building, and waited patiently until they were inside.

Then, slowly, she walked forward.

As Gloria approached the structure, its mirror-like surface seemed to shimmer as if, somehow, it was turning into liquid.

Without hesitation, Gloria walked into the liquid, and vanished. After a moment, Mann followed. As his body touched the surface of the structure, Mann felt as if he were being stretched in all directions, like taffy. Then he was through, and he saw Gloria standing a few feet away, facing a creature which looked at first like an octopus, only it stood upright on multiple appendages.

They were standing on the sands of a fantastical landscape of what appeared to be a combination of plant life and gleaming metal extending as far as his eye could make it out, under a blazing sky with two suns at opposite ends of the horizon and an enormous ghostly moon that took up a fifth of the sky.

Mann walked over to stand next to Gloria, facing the octopus creature. One of its appendages reached out and gently touched Mann's hand. Another touched Gloria's.

Through the warmth of the tentacle, Mann experienced words in his mind.

Welcome and blessings. Your visit here will be a short one, but we celebrate it with joy and tender respect.

Mann simply stared at the creature. Gloria bowed, and after a moment, Mann followed suit.

"Why?" Gloria asked simply.

When your world extended its reach into... the other—direction?

"Dimension," said Gloria. "He means the simulations," she added to Mann.

Dimension, the creature repeated, testing the word. *Many turns of your planet ago, we watched as you began creating new places, new levels of reality. Over time, we saw that others were doing the same. In many places now, life and awareness are being extended in new... dimensions.*

"Is—that is, are we at the top level?" Mann asked.

There was a flood of amusement in the creature's mind, and in the manifold nuance of this laughter, Mann was made to understand that his question was naïve to the point of embarrassment among a galaxy-wide community of different races who had only one thing in common: that they created and tended universes. The creature shook its many arms, its equivalent to a shrug of the shoulders. *How can we ever be certain?"* its mind wondered aloud. *And in the end, in what way does it matter?*

Mann was about to ask how he and Gloria were transported to this place, but through the mutual mental contact, he could also glimpse into Gloria's mind, and he saw that she had already sorted through her mental archives and arrived at certain equations and properties of reality.

She knew.

He was about to ask another question, but he realized that the spiders already knew the answer.

"The... structure—the fact that we're here means that it would only open when you felt comfortable that you had identified the... *chosen* representatives of our hierarchy of creations," he said. "It would have opened two floors down if we had been... ready at the time of the visit. Am I right?"

The creature dropped its head, and the huge cephalopod brain raised up into the air. It was bowing; not to him, Mann realized, but to the spider entities who occupied his mind, who had understood the purpose of the artifact all along. Through the tentacles, Mann somehow experienced the creature's respect, its acknowledgement of their superiority.

The fact that an advanced creature on this level of reality should believe in the superiority of entities who came from many levels below confirmed a great deal that Mann already suspected about status up and down the ladder.

There are already many worlds, many creatures subject to the whims of their gods in your small world, the creature said. *We wish to share with you an ethos that has evolved among us in the Community over many turns of your planet and even more mistakes.*

Your worlds must be tended, it added, *to celebrate and reward the rightness that is embedded in all too few of us.*

Mann saw in an instant a much greater version of what those words outlined, or perhaps his mind was absorbing the chorus of assent from the spiders who crowded his mind.

"The rules of creation," said Gloria.

Responsibilities, the creature said. *And… opportunities.*

Mann opened his mouth, and shut it again as the spiders renewed their clamor. He began repeating their voices, slowly at first.

"The good, the gentle, the… meek, those who live a harmonious life, they can be… *transferred* to one of the levels above, replacing those who introduce conflict and aggression."

The creature bowed again. Mann was uncomfortably aware that the creature's brain appeared to be four times the size of his own.

"But who will decide?" Gloria asked after a moment. "How would *we* decide?" she asked a moment later.

The creature made a gesture, and Mann felt the essence of an enigmatic smile, a sense of benevolence and infinite compassion. The arms spread out in all directions.

The same way all of the rest of us do, it said. *There will be an imperfect weighting of karma. How? That, I'm afraid, is up to you.*

"We're not even remotely worthy of that responsibility," Mann blurted.

The creature bowed its head in acknowledgement. Then it faced up at them and Mann felt a ring of sincerity in its message.

Is anyone? it said.

There was a long silence. In that span of silence, Mann began to appreciate the sheer extent of the challenge that lay ahead of him. And—what had the creature said? The opportunities. He had already been formulating plans for the taming of the war-torn world that he was now a leader of, which of the most implacable proponents of war could be replaced with the life essence of the gentlest and wisest from the realities down below, as he himself had replaced the one who had previously worn this uniform.

Blessed are the meek, for they will inherit the earth. Had those words been spoken by a rogue emissary from the higher world he now occupied? Had others from this place visited the world he grew up on, trying to tell us things we didn't want to hear?

The possibilities extended out in every direction, beyond the horizon that was now filled with that giant orbiting world. The opportunity to reward individuals at all levels who chose a supportive existence against the dark god who left a dark spark in all of us, equal in strength to our lightness. This was the opportunity: to harvest, not just the wisdom and the cultural contributions, but the very people who were willing to tame the dark thing that haunted every universe and lived inside everyone and, perhaps, every thing.

He glimpsed something else in the back of the creature's mind. There was the familiar feeling of seeing equations and having no idea what they represented. Here, he saw a new branch of science shared in the Community, whose founding principle was the fact that the darker impulses and evil itself were simply the social/societal manifestations of something called entropy—

That entropy was apparently the overarching law of the universe that trumped all others.

That someday, in some universe created by somebody, a cure for the darker forces of entropy will be developed and they will teach the rest how to rewind the universal clock.

That the cure will be far more likely to come from studies of wisdom than from studies of science.

That—

There is a... window of time in which you must return, the creature said, and Mann sensed awkwardness in the tone of the message. The octopus creature removed its appendage from Mann's hand. It gestured toward the artifact with the remaining tentacles. Gloria maintained the contact for another few seconds, and reluctantly turned to join him at the surface of the artifact, which again became translucent, revealing a hazy picture of the world they had so recently entered, and left.

Again, Mann experienced the feeling of being stretched, and then he was back on the other side of the wall. He looked around at the unfamiliar landscape with a new sense of propriety.

"I asked if we would see them again," Gloria said. "It told me that they would be there if we needed them, but I got the strong impression that they didn't expect to be needed. But," she added, "I'm planning to pay them a social visit when we get through some of the work in front of us. But next time we'll travel with our own technology."

Mann stood with his back to the structure with his head down, allowing the voices of the spiders to rise up in his mind. "They're confident that we'll work out something on our own," he said. "I don't think anything could possibly be more terrifying than that."

Gloria took his hand, and led him back toward the facility.

"Come on," she said, flashing her ironic smile. "The gods have a hell of lot of work to do."

www.ingramcontent.com/pod-product-compliance
Lightning Source LLC
Chambersburg PA
CBHW060137260626
47160CB00001B/17